# ORACLES of DELPHI

Marie Savage

Blank Slate Press | Saint Louis, MO

Published in the United States by Blank Slate Press



www.blankslatepress.com
www.kristinamakansi.com
(Kristina Makansi writing as Marie Savage)

Map of Delphi adapted from several sources including PlanetWare.com (©Baedeker), and maps obtained at the Delphi Archaeological Museum.

Book One of the Althaia of Athens Series

Library of Congress Control Number: 2014950952

ISBN: 9780989207935

*For my mother, my daughters, my sisters, my friends,*
*and all the amazing women in my life*

# Oracles of Delphi

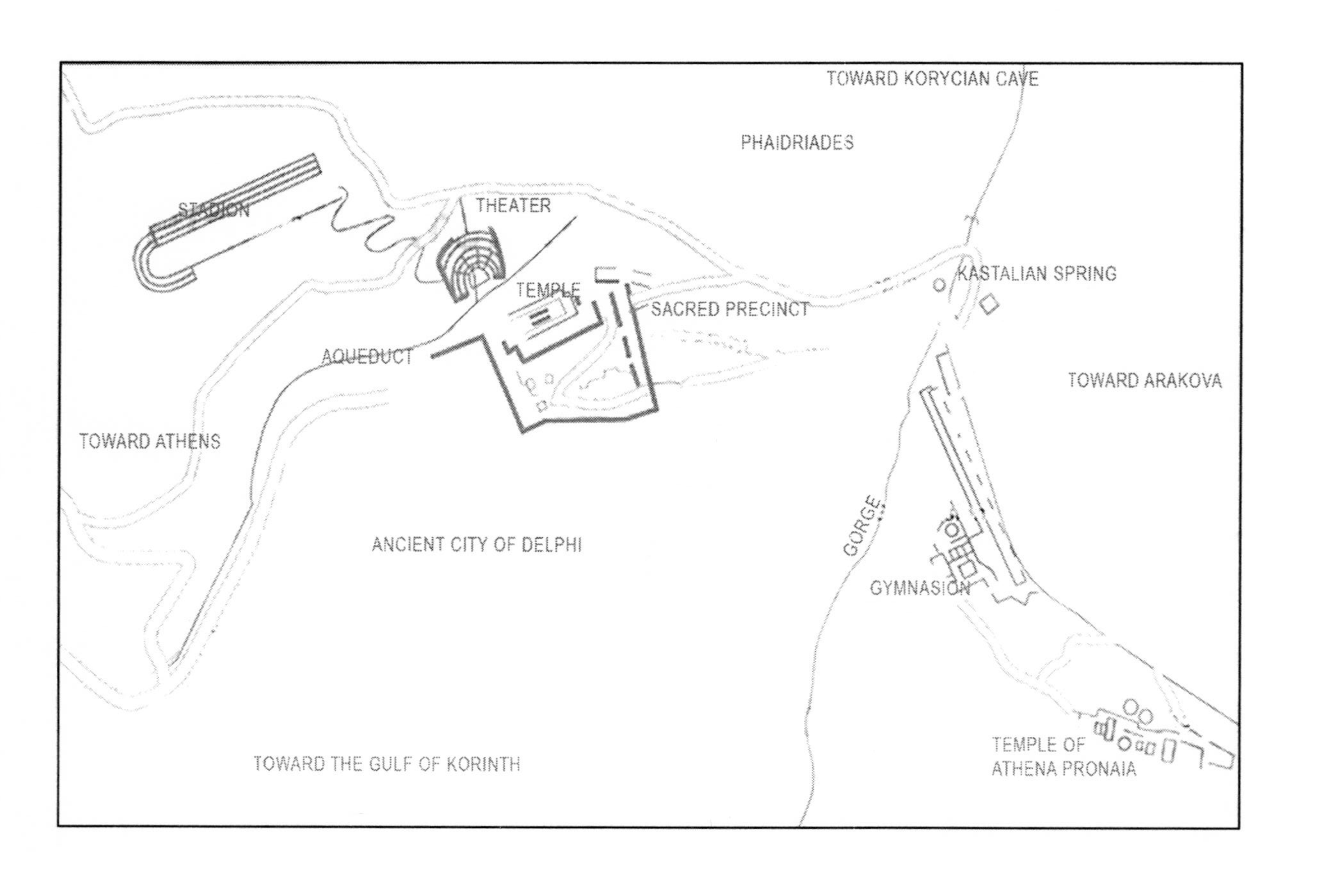
TOWARD KORYCIAN CAVE
PHAIDRIADES
STADION
THEATER
TEMPLE
SACRED PRECINCT
KASTALIAN SPRING
AQUEDUCT
TOWARD ARAKOVA
TOWARD ATHENS
GORGE
ANCIENT CITY OF DELPHI
GYMNASION
TEMPLE OF
ATHENA PRONAIA
TOWARD THE GULF OF KORINTH

# THE CAST

## FROM ATHENS

Althaia – daughter of Lysandros of Athens
Theron – Althaia's former tutor and current employee
Praxis – slave of Lysandros and Althaia
Nephthys – Althaia's slave
Lycon – Althaia's husband
Lysandros – Althaia's father, citizen of Athens, recently deceased

## IN DELPHI

Diokles – proprietor of Dolphin's Cove Inn
Heraklios – Makedonían general, Amphiktyonic League
Kalliope – attendant to Melanippe, priestess of Dodona
Menandros – playwright, director of Delphi's theater
Nikomachos (Nikos) – son of Priestess of Dodona

**The Priests**
Kleomon – priest, Temple of Apollon
Philon – senior priest, Temple of Apollon

**The Priestesses**
Phoibe – newly appointed Pythia of the Oracle of Gaia
Theodora – Priestess of Pytheion
Melanippe – priestess of Dodona
Eumelia – priestess of Argos
Sofia – recently deceased, Pythia of the Oracle of Gaia
Pythia of Apollon
Other Priestesses of Gaia (Athens, Sparta, Elis, Tegea)

**The Chorus**
Georgios – local champion training for the Pythian Games
Aphro – woman at Dolphin's Cove Inn
Baseilios – bodyguard of Philon
Palamedes – temple artisan
Rhea – mother of Phoibe
Zenon – Menandros's house slave

# TELL THE PEOPLE

Our Mother Earth has spoken.
Gaia's oracle is broken.
Apollon's hundred arrows
Silenced her sacred servant.
Now, in one or one thousand years,
His fair wrought house will fall
And a god reborn shall reign.

*Oracle of Gaia, Delphi, 340 BC*

# TELL THE KING

The fair wrought house has fallen.
No shelter has Apollon,
nor sacred laurel leaves;
The fountains are now silent;
the voice is stilled.
It is finished.

*Oracle of Apollon, Delphi, 393 AD*

*Delphi in the Region of Phokis in the Month of Mounichion in the First Year of the 110th Olympiad (340 BCE)*

# CHAPTER ONE

Nikos's heart pounded against his rib cage like a siege engine. He pressed his back into the stone wall, closed his eyes and tried to calm his breathing. He couldn't believe he'd been such a fool. "Next time I'll surrender the prize," Charis had always promised. Next time he would claim it, he always hoped. But instead….

He pulled himself to the top of the wall and lay flat. The moment of escape calmed him. The gates of the Sacred Precinct were locked, and he'd had to climb out the same way he'd climbed in. On the way out, though, he wasn't carrying a body.

He glanced to his side, toward the theater, and then down to the Temple of Apollon where he'd left Charis's body for the priests to find. Stars winked in and out as clouds drifted across the black dome blanketing the night sky. He crouched, reached for a nearby branch, and swung down to land on the ground with a soft thud.

It wasn't the first time he'd taken a life. But he'd never killed a woman, never killed anyone unarmed. Not that he'd killed Charis. Not exactly, anyway. His shoulders, red with teeth and claw marks, throbbed. And his face. He ran his tongue across his lip. At least the bleeding had stopped.

He could still smell her. Still see how she licked her lips as she loosened her braids, taste the sweetness of her breast, and feel her hot breath as she put his fingers, one by one, in her mouth, wetting them, running her tongue over them, sucking gently until his whole body trembled. When she pulled him down into the soft pile of hay and wrapped her legs around his waist, he had been ready to give her anything—even the gold tiara. His partners would never know. There were other treasures from the Sacred Precinct to sell.

Of course, none of that mattered now. None of that mattered the moment he felt her brother's blade against his throat and the trickle of blood drip across his collar bone. The moment Charis scrambled up from beneath him and laughed in his face. Brother and sister. What a pair. Charis's brother had picked up the tiara and threatened to go to Nikos's partners with proof he was double-dealing—unless he split his take fifty-fifty. And not just on the tiara. On everything. He'd still be a rich man, Charis promised, laughing.

Her brother was still laughing when Nikos' dagger pierced his heart. Didn't they know nobody bested him with a blade?

Before he could grab the tiara, Charis snatched it from her brother's grasp and backed away. "You'll pay for this," she'd hissed, tears in her eyes, her voice sharp as serpent's fangs. She held the tiara above her head, waving it like booty from a hard-fought battle. "I'll tell Heraklios. I'll tell everyone you killed him. I'll tell your mother."

She was cornered, wild-eyed, desperate. Nikos yanked his blade from her brother's chest and circled her. "It's your word against mine, and your brother's reputation as a thief and a brigand will not help your cause." She'd always been an untamed thing. That had been one of the reasons he'd wanted her, and he was used to getting what he wanted.

"Ha!" He laughed. "My mother may not love me, but she will not believe you. No one will."

"She'll believe me if I have proof. Proof you killed him, that you're the one selling the stolen goods from the temple."

"What proof will you have, Charis?" He spoke softly, trying to calm her. "Stop this nonsense. Your brother was foolish enough to hold a knife to my throat, and he paid the price. But we can come to terms." He took a step forward, his hand held out to her. "Come. We can still do business, you and I." He let a small smile flit across his lips, but kept his eyes on hers. He knew she was not to be trusted. He'd always known that, but still ... he watched her, trying to anticipate her next move. He could wait all night, but she'd be expected at the naming ceremony. She'd be missed. "Phoibe is waiting. It's time for us to come to an understanding. I'll give you—"

She jumped at him and in an instant, fingernails scraping against skin, stole his most prized possession. She yanked the silver chain from around his neck and clasped the polished orb tight in her fist. He watched, too startled to stop her, too afraid of hurting her.

"Give it back." He demanded, taking a step toward her. He held out his hand.

"No." She scrambled backward. "When your mother sees this, she'll know I'm telling the truth. She'll know you murdered my brother. Everyone will have to believe me."

"No one will believe you, Charis." He took yet another step toward her. "Do you think I will let you leave with that?" He held out his palm. "Give it to me before we're both sorry."

"You're the one who'll be sorry." Cornered, she crouched low like a cat ready to pounce.

Nikos took another step and stopped, waiting. He could easily overpower her and take the necklace back, but he didn't want to hurt her. Unlike Diokles, he didn't believe in violence unless his back was against a wall. Charis's brother had been a different story. He'd held a weapon to Nikos' throat. But Charis was different. An almost-lover, an almost-friend. But she had to know he wouldn't let her take the necklace. To her, it was just another bargaining tool, and he'd play along until he got what he wanted.

Then she screwed up her face and spat at him, turned and darted out the open door of the storage shed. He looked down at his chest where the spittle was sprayed dark across the white fabric. *She's mad*, he thought. He leapt after her, overtaking her quickly. He grabbed her shoulders and wrenched her around to face him. She fell back and he was on her, trying to pry the necklace from her clenched fist, but she kicked and bucked like an unbroken colt and then, wresting her arm free, she shoved the round silver ball and finely wrought chain into her mouth and clamped her jaw shut.

Stunned, it took him a moment to realize what she'd done. Then he grabbed her face and tried to pry her lips apart. She fought and scratched at his face, clamping her jaw shut even tighter as she struggled against him, clawing and growling like one who'd lost her senses.

She was possessed, and though he had no fear of the gods, there was something about her that scared him. Desperation flowed from her, charging the air like lightning. He could smell her fear; it wrapped around them both like a fetid fume. He sat back on his heels, but she reached for him, gurgling and gagging, eyes wide, arms whirling at him like windmills.

Then he knew. But it was too late. Too late to do anything to keep her from choking. He'd tried to hold her still, to pry open her jaw and grab hold of the chain to pull it free, but in her panic, she bit at him, clawed at him. "By the gods, Charis, stop! Don't fight me, *please*," he begged her. But she bucked beneath him, making it impossible to get a purchase on the chain. *Did she think I wanted to kill her?* Once she was still, he opened her mouth and probed her throat for the chain or the precious silver ball, but his fingers were too big, too awkward, even without her fighting him. He pulled her jaw wide and stuck his blade in, trying to catch the loop of the chain. But it was no use. Finally, he sat back and stared at her sprawled in the dirt. Hay and dust settled in her hair like a halo. He reached out and pulled her chiton down over her legs, and for the first time in more years than he could remember, he cried.

He could slice open her neck and retrieve his necklace, but he was reluctant to desecrate her body. Having grown up amongst priestesses who honored the dead and conducted burial rites with care and precision, it was a line he feared to cross. Damn her! He picked up his knife and held it poised above her neck, then slowly pressed the tip into the tender hollow at the base of her throat, the soft place his lips had lingered countless times. She's dead; what does it matter? He steadied his hand and took a deep breath. It would be a clean cut, over in a moment, and he'd have his treasure back. The necklace is mine. She has no right to take it to the grave with her. He closed his eyes and prayed. In the distance an owl hooted and he jerked back his hand. An evil omen. He shuddered, then wiped his eyes and stood. So be it. I am a man now, he told himself. The necklace had been a boy's trinket. The smooth silver ball and ornately crafted chain represented nothing more than a dream, a memory that wasn't even his. It was time to let it go.

He'd gone back into the shed and retrieved Charis's cloak, then picked her up and wrapped it around her. He didn't care about her brother—the wolves were welcome to feast on his bones—but he wouldn't leave Charis to be devoured like carrion. They had a history. They'd almost been lovers.

Now he cocked his head and listened. Not even a leaf rustled in an occasional spring breeze. Around him, Delphi slept shrouded in darkness. Under the new moon, dull patches of snow clung to nooks and crannies up and down the mountainside. The oracle wouldn't start hearing supplicants for another few weeks, and without a swarm of pilgrims, Delphi was just another remote mountain village.

In the morning, Apollon's priests would find Charis on the temple steps wrapped snug in her winter cloak. Philon and Kleomon would wait for her brother to claim her, and, after a few days, they would stop waiting and give the body to Phoibe for burial. Nikos's treasured necklace would go to the underworld with her. Maybe it was just as well.

He took a deep breath and checked to make sure the gold tiara was still tied securely to his belt. Then he ran his fingers through his hair, brushed the dust from his clothes, and headed down the path toward the Dolphin's Cove Inn.

# CHAPTER TWO

Althaia pulled the covers over her head and ignored the insistent rapping at her door.

"Are you awake?" Theron called, his voice faint through the heavy wood.

"Go away."

The rapping stopped and she heard muffled voices in the hallway.

"Althaia. Aren't you up yet?"

"I am now," she groused. She threw the covers back, swung her feet onto the cold, tile floor and stretched. A few wisps of smoke rose from the gray coals in the brazier. Nephthys, the new Egyptian handmaid Praxis had bought for her, was already up and gone.

"Can I come in?"

"No. I'm not dressed."

"Well, get dressed. Menandros is impatient to give us a tour of the theater."

She wrapped a blanket around her shoulders and opened the door. "It's too early for a tour of anything."

Theron, her childhood tutor turned mentor and confidant, scanned the room and then strode in and opened the shutters. She flinched and shaded her face as early spring sunlight assaulted her eyes.

"Nice view," he said. "Our host obviously gave you the best room in the house. Praxis and I are sharing a broom closet."

"I'm sure you both deserve it. Punishment for some heinous act you committed in the past. Or at least for waking me up so early."

Theron laughed. With sharp, gray eyes, a close-cropped head of thick graying hair, and weathered skin creased with laugh—or worry—lines, Theron looked every bit the world-weary traveler he was. He folded his arms across his broad chest and leaned against the window frame. "He's trying to bribe you. Your father's wealth—your wealth—and the hope that you'll support the theater of Delphi is making his brain soft."

"I may have inherited my father's wealth, but Menandros should know it's my dear husband he should be bribing."

"Lycon is not here."

"And we're all thankful for that," Althaia sighed. Forced to marry her cousin to keep her father's fortune within the oikos, the family unit, her husband and kyrios, controlled everything in Althaia's life: her money, her property, her body. Luckily, Lycon was more interested in spending time at the gymnasium and gambling on his lover, an Olympian hopeful pankriatist, than in paying any attention to Althaia. Whenever Althaia had grumbled about the prospect of marrying Lycon, her father teased and threatened her with marriage to one of his own brothers. A young and handsome, if disinterested, groom was definitely preferable to one thirty or forty years older than the bride. Lycon was diligent about doing his once-a-month husbandly duty in the bedroom, but the rest of the time, he behaved as if Althaia was nothing more than a piece of furniture.

"Yes, we are thankful for that."

"I had another nightmare," Althaia blurted out. She hadn't meant to say anything. They'd had so many discussions about her nightmares over the years that they now bored her.

"Ah," he said. "Do you want to talk about it?"

"No."

Theron waited.

"It was the same sort of dream I always have. Someone is in trouble and I am powerless to help them." She was quiet for a moment. "And yet, there was something different. Something felt different. And then, just before I woke, there was a man…."

"A man? What about him?"

"Nothing." She shivered. "It was nothing."

"It doesn't sound like nothing."

"Apparently I woke Nephthys up. She believes the gods are warning me."

"Warning you about what?"

"Danger. Delphi. I don't know. She thinks there is something evil here, and that I'm going to be caught up in it. But you know Egyptians—always invoking one god or another against some superstition. Remember my uncle Demetrious's cook who wouldn't get out of bed if the roosters didn't crow exactly at the crack of dawn?"

"I believe the cook ended up in the silver mines."

"With Demetrious's temper, I'm surprised the roosters didn't end up in the mines, too. But you know what I mean."

"Yes, we rational Hellenes are immune to superstition." The touch of sarcasm in his voice made Althaia wonder if he was mocking her. She glared at him.

"So back to the man in the dream."

"There's nothing more to tell. I don't remember anything else."

Theron turned back toward the window and Althaia pulled the blanket tight around her shoulders and joined him. To the east, over the rooftops, she could just catch the edge of the gymnasium and the gleaming temples and treasuries in the Sacred Precinct of Athena. To the west, the valley unfolded below her, a carpet of green cascading towad the water's edge. The city of Kirra, Delphi's port, glowed like a white pearl next to the sapphire inlet off the Gulf of Corinth.

"A charming little town for pirates," Althaia said.

"What?"

"Kirra," she pointed. "Remember all the tales of heroes, monsters, pirates, and stolen treasures that you and Papa used to tell me?"

He smiled. "You would charge around the house with a stick and try to kidnap Praxis as he was doing his chores."

"I imagined I was an Amazonian warrior, and he was a prince who had been kidnapped and sold into slavery. I found out his secret identity and wanted to ransom him for treasure. He always played along until one day I told him that the princess was in love with her captive and that he had to marry me." She grew quiet.

"I remember." Theron watched her, tried to read her mood. "It's been hard on you and Praxis, the waiting, wondering why your father wanted us here in Delphi on the anniversary of his death. But it will soon be over, and everything will make sense."

In addition to tutoring Althaia, Theron had been a long-time advisor to her father and had promised he would stay with Althaia until Lysandros' last wishes had been fulfilled.

"It's hard to believe you've been able to keep Papa's secret a whole year."

"A year?" Theron shook his head and headed for the door. "That's nothing, my dear. I've got secrets I've kept for a lifetime. Now get dressed. Praxis has already left and we're keeping Menandros waiting."

"Wait," she said. "Praxis ... I'm around him every day, but I feel I hardly know him anymore. He's changed since Papa died. He was always quiet, but now…." She trailed off.

"Perhaps Nephthys will cheer him up." Theron chuckled.

Althaia turned towards the window.

"It's hard to let go of a dream, isn't it?" Theron said.

She blushed. "Childhood dreams die hard, but for Aphrodite's sake, I'm a married woman now. Maybe Nephthys is exactly what Praxis needs."

Whenever Althaia thought of Nephthys, a vague sense of jealousy washed over her. Many, mostly men who wanted to marry her for her father's money, had called Althaia beautiful, but she didn't feel particularly beautiful when Nephthys was near. While Althaia was short, Nephthys was tall. Althaia was strong boned while Nephthys was as slim as a river reed. Althaia's skin looked as if it had been carved from alabaster while Nephthys' skin was dusky and rich, as if painted with late autumn twilight. Althaia had always prided herself on her ability to keep up with Praxis, to ride and swim as if she were a boy. She never thought of herself as ungainly or awkward, but ever since Praxis bought Nephthys, she felt like a waddling goose next to a stalking heron.

Not that Nephthys stalked. She didn't have to. Praxis stalked her—or at least watched her every move whenever he had the chance. Althaia had long ago abandoned the childish dream of marrying Praxis—wealthy Athenian maidens didn't marry slaves, no matter how much they were treated like part of the family—but that didn't mean she relished the idea of him being with someone else.

"What do you need, Althaia of Athens?" Theron asked.

Althaia turned to face her old friend. "I need to stop mourning. Start living again."

Theron turned his eyes back toward the clear blue sky out the window. "It's a fine day to start."

# CHAPTER THREE

Phoibe stood waist-deep in the icy Kastalian Spring, her himation floating around her like a red cloud. Her feet were numb, she could barely feel her legs, and she knew her skin would soon be as red as flame from the cold. Her eyes were closed, lips moving silently, automatically reciting the sacred liturgy as Melanippe of Dodona, priestess of Zeus Naios, God of the Springs, and Gaia, Mother of All, crushed the laurel and kannabis leaves and sprinkled them into the fire. The air in the grove was clear and cold, and as the pungent smoke rose from the coals, it mixed with scents of myrtle, laurel, cypress and pine, of moist earth and the first hints of spring. Phoibe breathed in deeply. *Where is Charis?*

She opened her eyes to a world as ancient as time and yet now born anew. Dawn broke and light moved through the treetops, speckling the ground with shadow. She rippled her fingers across the clear surface and watched her reflection bob and weave. How long had the sacred spring of Kastalia flowed? How many had bathed in the waters of Gaia? More than anyone could count. Maybe more than the gods could count. For endless generations, Phoibe's family had lived and farmed on the plain between Arachova and Delphi. The water, the stones, the very dirt beneath her feet, were her blood, her bones, her flesh.

But she was different from the others in her family. And she was different now from who she was that night, over twenty years ago, when she was named and chosen as an apprentice to the Pythia of the Oracle of Gaia. When she was taken from her family and given to the goddess.

She'd heard the story a thousand times. How Sofia, the old Pythia of Gaia, had dropped her into the cistern, how she had surfaced several heart-wrenching moments later, sputtering, eyes wide, fat little arms flailing against the water. After her mother, Rhea, dried, warmed and comforted her at her breast, Sofia had taken her in her arms, opened her fists and traced the lines on her plump palms. Then Sofia had closed her eyes and said:

*This child shall be called Phoibe, like the Titan of old,*
*Apollon's own grandmother.*
*She will see the Oracles of Apollon and Gaia united*
*or she will see them destroyed*
*and the Sacred Precinct claimed by yet another.*

Phoibe smiled when she thought of how the priestesses claimed the snakes tattooed on Sofia's arms had come to life, writhing across her skin as if in celebration—or fear—of the woman's words. Now Sofia had crossed the Styx. The apprenticeship was over and she, Phoibe of Arachova, was the newly named Pythia of Gaia, high priestess of the most powerful oracle of all. *But where is Charis? My friend, my confidant. My handmaid should be here with me. Where is she?*

Phoibe's people had always worshiped the Mother. Now, she would be Mother to them all. The incarnation of the goddess on earth. She would never marry as her mother and grandmother and great-grandmother before her had. She would never sit by the hearth waiting for a husband to return from war, waiting for sons to come back one by one, wounded or worse, waiting on the harvest, waiting for grandchildren. Waiting to die. She would not wait on history to overtake her. She would make history.

She looked around the glade, at the priestesses attending her, depending on her. She would not let them down. She would not be like Sofia. She would lead the people back to the Mother, away from the idolatry of gold and silver, away from the worship of war and the strength of steel, the taste of glory and death on the battlefield and back to the worship of the fruits of the Mother's womb, of sacred springs and sweet wine and warm bread and life. The new Pythia of Gaia would no longer bend to the will of the priests of Apollon, corrupt men who drugged and enslaved their own priestess, the Pythia of Apollon, and reaped the rewards of their avarice by bringing ruin upon the whole of the Sacred Precinct. As the new Pythia of Gaia, she would change everything. She could see it all. Sofia had foretold it. Melanippe had confirmed it. And now it would come to pass.

She pushed her numb feet through the water, placing them one in front of the other, climbing the stone steps until Theodora and Eumelia met her and stripped off her wet garments. The two priestesses cupped their hands as Melannippe's handmaiden, Kalliope, poured scented oil into their palms from an alabastron that had been heating on the fire. They rubbed the oil on Phoibe's shivering skin to warm her, slipped a new chiton over her head, bound it with a braided belt and wrapped a dry, finely woven woolen himation around her shoulders. Then Theodora placed the laurel wreath upon her brow, led her to the warmth of the fire and helped her sit.

Melanippe stood over Phoibe, her hand shaking with age, her eyes filmy and gray.

"Sofia is no more. She is one with the Mother. You are now Sofia. You are now every Pythia who has come before and who will ever come after. You have studied the secrets of the oracle, learned the healing lore of the land, and bathed in the sacred spring. Now you must drink." She sprinkled more of the crushed leaves into a cup, closed her eyes in prayer, and then handed the cup to Theodora. "Take this to the Mother's mouth so that Phoibe may drink of the sacred water. The water of life, the breath of life, the word of life. Mouth to mouth, the Mother to her daughter."

Theodora held the cup under the fissure where the water flowed cold and pure from the rock face and then handed it to Phoibe. And Phoibe drank. *But where was Charis?*

# CHAPTER FOUR

With his sturdy legs planted firm as tree trunks, Menandros's broad girth blocked the doorway. "We must wait but a moment. I want you to see it when the light is just so." His eyes twinkled with excitement in a ruddy face that was as round as a platter. The playwright looked like a proud father about to introduce his first-born son to the world as he swept his arm up toward the ridge of trees on the crest of the rise cradling the theater. "Soon Apollon's rays will break above those trees and Delphi's sacred theater will be bathed in the god's rapturous morning light. And just wait till you see our new altar. It is made of pure white marble and the sunlight makes it shimmer like gold."

"It must be a sight to behold." Althaia smiled. "Did you know my father always supported a playwright for the Dionysia?"

Menandros's head bobbed and his cheeks turned red. "I had heard that, yes. And I was hoping that … well …"

Theron laughed, put his arm around Menandros's fleshy shoulders and squeezed. "A poet at a loss of words. Better find your tongue, old friend, or Lysandros's daughter may lose faith in your talents."

"Well … um … I'm disappointed that your Praxis is not here for the tour as well," Menandros stammered, and turned back to Althaia. "I understand he is instrumental in managing your father's estate."

"Never fear," Althaia said. "Praxis will join us momentarily. He met an old friend for breakfast. Perhaps you know him. Palamedes. He's a temple artisan."

Menandros stopped and turned to appraise her. "By Apollon's arrows, a temple artisan? Palamedes is not just any old potter. He may be the best in all Hellas. Your painters in Athens have nothing on him." Menandros boasted as if he was personally responsible for Palamedes's abundant talents. "I own several of his pieces. Originals. Not like those copies they sell in the gift shops or hawk along the Sacred Way. But how did your slave come to know him?"

"My father arranged for them to meet on my first trip to Delphi," Althaia said. "Father paid Palamedes to write to Praxis, to help him learn to read and write in his native tongue."

"Ah, your man is a Syrian then," Menandros said, not waiting for confirmation. "He would have had a very good teacher in Palamedes. As a matter of fact, the great man has been teaching my houseboy to draw and even do a little pottery."

"My father—"

"Stop!" Menandros exclaimed. "I'm sorry to interrupt, but it's time." He stepped out of the way. "After you, my dear. You will now see for yourself that there is no theater more beautiful—or more deserving of support—in all Hellas."

Althaia cast a quick backward glance at Theron and then stepped through the arched doorway, over the threshold, and out onto the smooth paving stones of the round orchestra. It was indeed an impressive site. She squinted and shaded her eyes as she took in the sweeping rows of audience benches nestled into the cavernous hillside.

Menandros sighed in delight and turned to Theron. "I knew she would be impressed."

"By the gods!" Althaia gasped.

"Yes," Menandros said, as pleased with himself as if he'd just downed a fine kylix of wine, "the gods have indeed favored Delphi above all other sacred places."

"Shut up." Theron brushed past Menandros and caught up to Althaia as she rushed toward center of the orchestra.

"What?" Menandros, his brow furrowed in confusion, squinted into the sunlight and followed in Theron's wake. Then he saw his new thymeli, the sacred altar where libations and sacrifices were offered to Dionysos before every performance, and he staggered back as if he'd run headlong into a wall. Then he steadied himself and walked toward the altar as Althaia, clutching Theron's arm, slowly circled it.

Naked and draped upon the cold stone was the dead body of a young woman. She lay on her back, arms splayed off to each side, legs spread wide. A viper lay draped between her legs, its tail dangling toward the ground and its bashed-in head resting on a smear of blood between her breasts. Her head was tipped backward off the edge of the altar and her empty eyes stared upside down at nothing, at everything. A mass of long, tangled hair hung limp, the tips a whisper away from the paving stones. A stiff breeze picked up the woman's curls and twisted them toward Althaia like Medusa's grasping serpents.

Menandros shuddered and Theron wrapped his arm around Althaia's shoulders. She leaned into him and whispered, "Nephthys was right. There is evil in Delphi."

# CHAPTER FIVE

Standing on opposite sides of the altar, the woman's body between them, Althaia met Theron's gaze. "Other than some bruising on her arms and marks on her cheekbone, there are no signs of a struggle. Have you discovered anything?"

"No," Theron answered. "What little blood there is comes from the viper, and there are no signs of any external wound."

"Can we not turn her over? There is straw in her hair, and—"

"We dare not move her until the priests arrive. We don't want to incur their wrath before we've even met them."

Menandros, who had been pacing back and forth, stopped and stared. "What kind of man would do a thing like this?"

"As a playwright you should know mankind has made a regular practice of doing 'things like this,'" Theron said. "Murder is, unfortunately, all too common among men," Theron said.

"No, I mean who could desecrate a sacred altar like this?"

"Menandros, please," Theron looked at Althaia who had lifted the woman's hair and was bent over attempting to examine the back of her head, "a young woman is dead."

"Yes, yes, I know. It is unfortunate, terrible even, but the sacred theater and this holy altar have been defiled. Who would risk the wrath of the gods in such a brazen way?"

"Someone who does not fear them," Althaia said, looking up.

"Even men who fear the gods are capable of killing their fellow man," Theron said.

"Whoever did this might as well have killed me!" Menandros said as he set about pacing again. "Do you realize the pilgrimage season is almost upon us? When word gets out there's been a murder in the Sacred Precinct, we'll have to re-sanctify the altar. The whole theater. Possibly the whole precinct. Not since the last Sacred War have we seen death within these walls. My actors won't perform here without a purification ceremony. Theron," Menandros stopped and clutched his friend's arm. "No one will come to a theater of the dead."

"I'm certain Apollon's priests will be more than happy to put on a grand show of re-sanctifying your theater. We should be more concerned about who this woman is and how she ended up here," Theron admonished, turning as Praxis reentered the theater. Praxis had arrived just after Althaia found the body, and Theron had immediately sent him to alert the guards from the Amphiktyonik League, the association of city states with administrative authority over the holy site, and to find Philon and Kleomon, the senior priests of the Sacred Precinct and Temple of Apollon.

Praxis had been Althaia's father's slave for as long as she could remember and had always been treated more like a son than a servant. He had been groomed to serve as overseer of Lysandros's estate and bodyguard for Althaia whenever she traveled. Although she had inherited him upon her father's death, Althaia considered him a part of her family. But their relationship had changed since her father's death and she did not understand why—or what to do about it.

Now, with his broad chest heaving with exertion, he took his place back at Althaia's side. "The priests are on their way and Heraklios, the head of the Amphiktyonik League here, won't be far behind them," Praxis said. As he caught his breath, he watched Althaia examining the woman's head and gave her a dark look. "Don't tell me you are—"

"I asked her to look," Theron interrupted.

"Look for what?" Menandros said.

"For anything that might tell us how this woman died."

"Have you lost your senses, Theron? Why are you asking her—a woman?"

Menandros turned to his, hopefully, future benefactress. "No offense, my dear, but what can you possibly know about such matters?"

Praxis crossed his arms and looked down disapprovingly at her. She ignored him, dropped the dead woman's hair, and stood to face Menandros. She was used to being underestimated—not by her father or Praxis or Theron—but by everyone else, including her new husband. Theron nodded at her, as if giving her leave to speak. "Theron was my tutor, but he was not my only teacher," she said. "Ever since I was a little girl, I've been fascinated by the human body, from statues in the agora to painted people on our pottery. One winter, while we were in Egypt, he arranged for me to study with a priest of Amun-Ra, and I was allowed to observe the mummification process and taught to identify causes of death. I even participated in dissections, or what Theron calls autopsias."

Under normal circumstances, she would never have discussed her interest in human anatomy in front of anyone but Praxis and Theron, but Theron had assured her that Menandros was perfectly safe. She stifled a smile and wondered what compromising information Theron had on his old friend that he could be trusted so implicitly.

Menandros shuddered, and turned to spit to ward off the evil eye. "That is a horrifying and yet strangely fascinating idea."

"It is forbidden in Greece," Praxis added.

"Praxis does not look favorably on the idea of Althaia poking about dead bodies with sharp instruments," Theron commented.

"It is not an appropriate pastime for a respectable Athenian matron. It puts her at risk for discovery and ridicule—and punishment for impiety." Praxis looked directly at Althaia as he spoke. "But my mistress does not listen to me."

"Praxis," Althaia said with a sympathetic smile, "you are too like a lion protecting his pride. But you forget, I am not your lioness or your cub."

"More like a lowly stable boy trying to manage a stubborn ass," he grumbled under his breath.

She ignored him and turned to Theron. "Besides more straw and dirt in her hair, her head shows no sign of any obvious mortal injury. The marks on her face lead me to believe she was slapped hard, but no one dies from being slapped or there would be few respectable matrons left in Athens." She didn't look up to see how that comment had gone over, but she suspected Theron would be repressing a smile and Praxis would be sporting a scowl. Since her father's death and her unfortunate marriage to Lycon, Praxis had been like a mother hen, hovering over her constantly. Whether to protect her from Lycon, to keep her company, or to make sure she behaved like a 'respectable Athenian matron,' she didn't know. But his mood had soured and he seemed to have misplaced the sense of adventure they shared while growing up. "Without turning her over, we have little to use to extrapolate cause of death. Now, we know that bruising doesn't occur after the body's animating spirit has left the body for its journey to Hades, so we can assume she was in some sort of struggle before she died. But with no blood—"

"Menandros!"

Althaia, Praxis and Theron looked up to see two men enter the theater trailed by a host of attendants. The priests of Apollon. They wore the ornate robes and carried themselves with the air of authority typical of the priestly class. They were impressive and not just a little gaudy.

"Where is the body and who are these people?" The younger of the two men demanded.

"Philon, Kleomon, it's here, on the altar," Menandros stepped aside. "And these are my guests from Athens," he continued while the two priests walked slowly around the body, examining it from every angle.

"I want you to meet my old friend, Theron of Thessaly. You have no doubt heard of him. He has traveled the world, served kings, marched to war, studied mathematics in Persia, natural philosophy in Athens, and—"

"Tutored little girls." The younger priest smirked as he turned his back on the body to size up Theron and Althaia. "We meet at last, Theron of Thessaly. From what I hear, your reputation for observing and reading into the hearts, minds and motivations of men appears to be unparalleled. A diviner of men. Tell me, what brings you to Delphi?"

"Philon," Theron answered, "first let me say that it is my honor to meet the Priests of Apollon, even if it is at the scene of such a terrible crime. As to what brings us to Delphi, we arrived last night on a mission of a personal nature."

"Personal, hmph." The older priest, Kleomon, looked at Theron as if he carried a strange disease. "Isn't it an odd coincidence that you, of all people, arrive in Delphi on the very night this young woman turns up dead? And," he cast another disparaging glance at Althaia, "what is a woman doing here?"

Althaia and Praxis exchanged glances. *What did he mean by insinuating a connection between the timing of their trip and the murder? And what did he mean by you, of all people?* Althaia pulled her mantle down over her forehead to shield her eyes and studied the old man.

Kleomon's shoulders were slightly hunched and his belly rose grandly at his midsection like an entirely separate geological formation. The pungent smell of too much perfumed oil slathered on too few hairs caught in her nose and throat like a draught of one of Theron's medicinal cures. Althaia stifled a cough, and shot a look of disgust at Praxis. His face remained impassive, but the corner of his mouth twitched upward ever so slightly.

"She is one of my guests," Menandros said. "I was just about to give a tour of the theater when we found the body. But lucky for us, it turns out that she has studied—"

"Forgive me for interrupting, Menandros," Theron said, "but I have been remiss. Please let me introduce Althaia of Athens and her servant Praxis."

"This is no place for a—" Kleomon started.

"The daughter of Lysandros, I presume," Philon interrupted.

"Yes," Althaia replied, meeting his eyes. He was not going to intimidate her. Men more important than Philon had bounced her on their knees and brought her ribbons for her hair. She took in his handsome face with a high, broad forehead, lips that were thin with impatience and eyes that seemed weary somehow, as if he were bored with life. His hair was straight and fair, and he wore it combed back and tied tight with a leather thong. On his hand, which he held lightly at the embroidered edge of his himation, he wore an impressive gold signet ring set with the largest ruby Althaia had ever seen. Though younger, he was clearly the more senior priest. The rank of office came with privilege—and with a sense of superiority.

"Tell me, daughter of Lysandros," Philon commanded, ignoring the rest of the gathering as if they didn't exist. "What was it like to have a man like Theron as your tutor? I understand his philosophical rival also took a position as a teacher—although I believe his student was a boy, the son of a king, in fact. Is Althaia of Athens as educated and strong-willed a young woman as Alexander of Makedon is a young man? That is what my Athenian friends would have me believe."

Althaia's back stiffened. She had grown tired of hearing people whisper about Theron's supposed bad blood with Aristotle. It made her want to scream. Yes, it was true that Aristotle was brilliant, but he wasn't brave. For most of his life, he had hidden in the academy while Theron had lived and experienced the world. Althaia knew people said Theron had been a mercenary, an assassin for hire, and that his ideas were nothing more than the ravings of a half-rate philosopher with a first-rate throwing arm. But she didn't care what people said. Her father told her Theron was the most brilliant man he'd ever known, but that the world wasn't ready for his ideas. That the world was seldom ready for the truly great thinkers. Look what happened to Sokrates, he would say. A vision of Theron thrashing both Philon and Aristotle in a debate at one of her father's symposiums flashed through her mind. "I couldn't say," she answered. "I've never met Alexander. And as an Athenian, I pray I never have that privilege."

Philon chuckled and held her gaze. "A student of politics, are you? I thought your tutor and Alexander's father were old friends."

"That may well be true. After all, Theron is not Athenian. I am." Maybe Theron could forget the rhetorical devices and just skewer them both with a very sharp spear.

"Then you are indeed an independent thinker." Philon smiled. "Perhaps—"

"Stop playing games, Philon," Kleomon barked. "Heraklios will be here any moment."

"We should talk more," Philon continued. "My sources say you have lived quite an unconventional life." He dragged his eyes from Althaia, and turned to Theron. "You must bring your student to my home for dinner before you leave Delphi. Perhaps tomorrow evening?"

"As you wish," Theron answered.

"Are you finished?" Kleomon sputtered.

"Quite." Philon said.

"Then why don't you tell me what we're going to do about this." Kleomon pointed to the body. "About them."

"Who is 'them'?" Theron asked.

Kleomon glared. "Don't play ignorant with me."

"Kleomon," Philon purred. "Theron is our guest in the Sacred Precinct of

Apollon and we should treat him as such."

"I'm afraid I must disappoint you," Theron said. "I have no idea who or what you're talking about."

"Who are you trying to fool?" Kleomon blustered.

"I assure you, I have no intention of fooling anyone."

Althaia and Praxis looked at each other. Why was the old priest baiting Theron? And why was Theron taking the bait?

"Tell me, Theron of Thessaly, who would benefit most from discrediting the Sacred Precinct of Apollon?"

"Kleomon, no one profits if the Oracle of Apollon is discredited," Philon spoke up. "Even the pirates in Kirra and the bandits along the mountain roads depend on the pilgrims coming to Delphi for their livelihood."

"You both know who would benefit. There can be no doubt—especially since the murder took place on the very night of their naming ceremony."

Naming ceremony? Althaia wondered what in the world the old man was going on about.

"If you are implying—" Theron began.

"I'm not implying anything. I don't have to. It is perfectly clear that this is a human sacrifice and it is perfectly clear that those women, those priestesses, they're the ones behind it."

"Human sacrifice? That's ridiculous," Althaia muttered before she could catch herself.

"Ridiculous?" Kleomon spun toward her. "What do you know about this? Or are you one of them, too? Is that why you're in Delphi? To join them?"

"Them who?" Althaia spoke without thinking.

"Your tutor must have schooled you in their ways, taught you all their secrets."

"I don't know what you're talking about," Althaia retorted. "Besides, a priest of Apollon should be able to tell this is no sacrifice. Where is the blood offering? How can it be a sacrifice when no blood is spilled?" She felt Theron's eyes on her. He always warned her to watch her mouth.

The priest's face purpled as he advanced on Althaia. "Who are you to instruct me about sacrifices to the gods?"

With his blue eyes glaring, Praxis stepped in front of Althaia and faced the old man down.

Philon grasped his counterpart's arm. "Kleomon," he said in a voice as soothing as warm honey. "This conversation is doing us no good. Heraklios will track down the woman's kin and his soldiers will find the killer and force him to pay the blood price for her murder. It is our task to make sure she gets a proper burial, to re-sanctify the sacred altar of Dionysos, and purify the theater that the body has defiled. As priests we must do our duty and let Heraklios do his."

"Do not tell me how to do my duty." Kleomon wrenched away, and turned on Theron. "Is that why you're here with your acolyte? To do your duty, Theron of Pytheion?" Kleomon turned to Philon, "Do you honestly believe it is a coincidence that the son of a known priestess of Gaia turns up in Delphi the very night of this terrible murder?"

"Kleomon!" Menandros, who had been watching the interaction with a mixture of confusion and alarm, gasped. He puffed out his ample chest as if his sheer bulk would defend Theron from Kleomon's accusation. "Surely you are not insinuating that my friend—"

With a bemused look on his face, Theron taunted the old priest. "Do not hold your tongue on my account." Althaia and Praxis watched Theron. They knew to pay attention when his voice took on that calm, confident quality. It meant a challenge.

"Oh, Kleomon," Philon sighed as if tired of the whole subject—whatever the subject was. Althaia couldn't follow the conversation. She had no idea what was going on.

"All right, I'll say it, since no one else will. It's worshippers of Gaia and her drakon, the serpent Apollon defeated. They're the ones who killed this girl. They're the ones who descend on this place every winter. Celebrating the Dionysia." Kleomon waved his arms wildly toward the cliffs behind the theater. "Hiding in the hills, in the caves. The goddess goes by a thousand names. Ge, Gaia, Cybele, mountain mother, mistress of animals, it doesn't matter. She and wine-drunk Dionysos lead fools and idiots into frenzied orgies, wearing fawnskin or dancing naked—even here! Above our own sacred precinct—they come here, like winged harpies to Parnassus, thyrsus bearers, dripping honey, smearing their blood, wearing the earth all over their naked bodies. Women young and old taunting young boys and grown men with their nakedness...."

"Stop now, Kleomon, before you say something you will regret," Philon growled, no longer bored.

Kleomon took another step toward Althaia. Praxis stood immobile in front of her, his body as taut as Odysseus's bowstring.

"And the men!" The old priest continued, spittle flying, his face mottled and red. "Drunk on wine and mead. Oh, we put up with the Dance of the Fiery Stars at the rising of the Pleiades, but then they go too far. Grown men dance naked like satyrs among the maenads. The Olympians be damned, these people worship the earth, they rut like animals, right here. I tell you they will tear the flesh off human bone and not even remember it in the morning. That's the sacrilege. That's the crime. Find the priestesses of Gaia and you'll find the ones responsible for this murder. And I'm sure that you," he poked his fleshy finger at Theron, "know exactly where to find them."

# CHAPTER SIX

"Theron?" Heraklios' voice boomed as he swept into the theater like a wave crashing against the shore. Tall and thick as a trireme's mast, he was dressed in calf-high leather boots and a soldier's short chitoniskos and matching cloak. He wore a thick beard and a floppy, fawn-skin, Makedonían-style hat on top of a tightly curled mass of graying hair, and was, as opposed to Philon and Kleomon, obviously glad to see Theron.

"By the gods, man," he slapped Menandros on the back so hard the playwright fell into Praxis, "why didn't you tell me your Athenian guests included Theron of Thessaly?"

"Heraklios," Theron smiled and stepped forward. "I didn't know if you would remember."

"Of course I remember," Heraklios gripped Theron's arm with both hands. "Saved Philip's life. Who could forget that? Now, tell me what we have here." He strode up to the altar, walked around it once, and then turned and eyed Althaia.

"We were just going to move the body so we can prepare her for burial," Philon said. "Kleomon and I will—"

"You must be Lysandros' daughter." Heraklios ignored Philon and looked Althaia up and down more thoroughly than he did the dead woman. He turned back to Theron. "Philip said you'd taken a different sort of position. She's a beauty. A student or something more?"

Althaia blushed, Praxis bristled, and Theron just laughed in that way he had of putting everyone at ease. "I am her humble employee, nothing more."

"Well, daughter of Lysandros, I am Heraklios, cousin to King Philip II of Makedon, by way of his first wife Audata, daughter of Bardyllis, King of Illyria, who is my own uncle. Your old tutor has quite a reputation in Pella. I'm sure he's told you all sorts of tales of court intrigue and attempted murder."

"No, actually he's—" Althaia started.

"If it weren't for Theron, who knows whose flabby ass would be warming the throne of Makedon. And, as Philon and Kleomon well know," Heraklios continued without even taking a breath, "without Philip's aid in ending the last Sacred War, Apollon's Precinct would still be at the mercy of those thieving Phokians and everyone who aided their cause." He cast a pompous glance toward Kleomon who rolled his eyes in answer. "So, in a way, we all have Theron here to thank for us winning that damnable war. Don't we?"

"Well, I—" Althaia began and glanced at Theron who just smiled and watched Heraklios's performance, which was not, apparently, anywhere near over.

"Now, I'm not sure if you know how it works here," he said, eyeing Althaia, "but as a general in Philip's service, my appointment as Makedon's representative to the Amphiktyonic League puts me in charge of maintaining and protecting the sacred lands of Apollon, including the Sacred Precinct's temples and treasuries and the people who journey here to see them and to seek guidance from the Oracle of Apollon, so—"

Philon adjusted his himation. "As high priest of Apollon—"

"So," Heraklios repeated, knowing full well that the only way to deal with Philon and Kleomon was to put them in their places early and often, "to honor Theron and his service to Philip, I will treat your safety as my personal responsibility while you are here. I know finding this body must have been very upsetting for a young woman such as yourself, being Athenian and all." Heraklios had nothing against Athenians in particular, he just thought they were soft. In fact, he prayed daily that the Atheian soldiers he would one day face on the battlefield would disappear as quickly as an Athenian matron once the whores arrived at her husband's symposia. Maybe Athens would even capitulate, he thought. Either way, it would be nice to have a friendly face in Athens when it was all over. A young, wealthy and very beautiful face. "Be assured that I will see to it that you are in no danger from whoever committed this horrible crime."

Heraklios turned and signaled to one of his men, and a group of soldiers marched into the theater. It was a pity he always had to make such a show of force, but Philon didn't seem to understand who was really in charge unless you paraded a whole phalanx of soldiers under his nose. "My men will remove the body, seek to identify her and search for next of kin to claim her."

Philon's fingers gripped at the embroidered edge of his cloak. A muscle along his jaw line twitched. "My personal guards have been instructed to—"

"Your personal guards will follow orders from my men."

"Kleomon and I are perfectly capable of handling the body. Just now we were preparing to remove it to the storeroom for safekeeping. If no one claims her, we will make sure she receives a proper burial."

"But who is—" Menandros started.

Heraklios exhaled expansively, cutting the playwright off. "Philon, you're welcome to keep the body in the storeroom until it is claimed, but my sentries will be posted outside to guard it and I will, of course, oversee the investigation into her death. By the way, anyone know who she is?"

Heraklios stared at the two priests, but neither said a word. "Well, once word gets out someone will claim her. If not, then you two can do your duty and handle the pyre and burial."

"For a thousand years we have done our duty." Philon's voice was tight.

"And for a thousand years, the Amphiktyonic League has provided protection so you priests can perform your duties. If anyone or anything interferes with the administration of the Sacred Precinct or Sacred Lands," Heraklios said, "the League will take all steps necessary to eliminate that threat."

"Of course, the League has responsibility in times of grave threat," Philon agreed with ice in his voice. "But, the murder of a single young woman doesn't rise to that level."

Heraklios was tired of Philon's interference in his work. He didn't trust either priest and knew for a fact they were both as corrupt as, well, as he was. But getting first choice of the best whores and the best wine at the Dolphin's Cove was a far cry from what he suspected Philon and Kleomon were up to.

Presumptious, pompous priests! He had to bite his tongue to stop himself from spitting to ward off the evil eye. "I wasn't talking about the girl," he growled.

For a moment, it seemed as if Zeus had turned Philon to stone. He didn't move a muscle, didn't take a breath. Then the moment passed and he appeared relaxed, in control. "Since you seem to have this investigation well in hand, we humble priests will leave you to it. I will send one of my guards up to oversee removal of the body. Please keep us informed of your investigation's progress."

Kleomon opened his mouth to speak, but Philon gripped his arm and guided the glowering priest toward the door of the theater.

Heraklios called out, "You two sure you have no idea who this girl is?"

Before disappearing through the doorway, Philon turned. "The investigation is in your capable hands now, Heraklios."

Heraklios watched them go, then turned to Theron and snorted. "Priests and bureaucrats—I don't know which is worse. Now, you ready to undertake the task of bringing this young woman's murderer to justice?"

"Me? I thank you for your confidence," Theron said, "but—"

The general leaned in. "To be frank, I'm shorthanded at the moment and could use your help. I've got a new group of psiloi in and they're too busy exercising their cocks to train with their spears." He walked around the altar. "Looks to me like someone's sending someone a message, and I think you're just the man to figure out who's who and what's what."

"As I told Philon and Kleomon," Theron protested, "we've come to Delphi on a mission of a personal nature—to fulfill Althaia's father's final wishes."

Heraklios threw back his head and laughed. "By Zeus's beard, man, I'd wager a year's pay that old Lysandros will still be dead after the murderer is found."

Theron opened his mouth, but Heraklios clutched his elbow and guided him toward the body on the altar.

"Now," Heraklios pressed, "why don't you give me your expert assessment of the situation."

Theron looked up questioningly at Althaia and she shrugged in answer. She glanced at Praxis and as their eyes met, she knew it was a foregone conclusion. They both knew that when Theron was presented with a problem to solve, nothing could stand in his way. And it couldn't hurt to wait a few more days to find the answers to their own mystery. Besides, Althaia thought, she could certainly use a little excitement. Her life had changed dramatically after losing the protection of her indulgent father. Athenian society suddenly expected her to grow up and act like a respectable matron even though her husband couldn't care less whether she came or went—as long as her money was within his easy reach. Praxis had slowly changed from best friend and childhood confidant to distant bodyguard, and Theron was busier than ever working with Praxis to manage her father's vast estate. A little adventure could be good for the soul.

"I don't have an expert assessment—at least not yet," Theron answered. "I do think whoever did this wants us to think it was a sacrifice. Why else strip her naked and leave the body on the altar of Dionysos? It's clear that old Kleomon is taking the bait—or he is providing the bait."

"Surely, you don't think he's involved," Menandros exclaimed.

"He seemed awfully eager to point the finger at the priestesses of Gaia—or anyone associated with them," Theron replied. "And the priests have unfettered access to the Sacred Precinct. He, or someone he knows, could have left the body here."

"Is it true? What he said about you?" Menandros asked. "I've known you a long time and it seems odd that such a skeptic and admirer of atomists like Leucippus and Democritus could be the son of a priestess."

"None of us can escape our history, my friend, but at least we have some say about our destiny," Theron replied.

"The Fates might argue with you on that point." Heraklios laughed. "But one thing is for sure, we all have family members we'd rather not claim. As for the priestesses, I know there are a few folks scattered here and there who still practice the old ways. I say let them. You're not going to find me saying anything bad about any god or goddess—I'd just as soon have them all on my side. But, as far as I know, Apollon long ago replaced the old beliefs here in Delphi," Heraklios said.

"That may be true," Althaia spoke up. "But, that is not what the murderer wants us to believe."

"The cult lives on in Delphi," Theron whispered. "Of that, I am certain."

# Chapter Seven

Georgios raced up the hillside, his leather sandals barely touching the rock-strewn path. I should not have left her, he thought. Even though he had never heard such a brutal cry pass Phoibe's lips, he knew it was her voice. And he knew something was terribly wrong. He pushed past her retinue of protesting handmaidens and burst through the door to find her on the floor, wailing, tearing at her clothes and hair. Theodora of Pytheion, one of the other priestesses, was trying to comfort her, but Phoibe was inconsolable, thrashing at her like a wild thing.

"I'm here," he said as he dropped to the floor beside her, wrapping his arms around her thin frame, drawing her tight against his chest. Theodora knelt beside him. "It's Charis." Her voice was tired. "Dead. Murdered. That's why she wasn't at the naming ceremony."

Georgios nodded, but didn't really understand. Charis dead? Murdered? Perhaps the gods really did answer prayers. Half a dozen names flew through his mind, names of people who could very well have had a hand in ushering Phoibe's handmaiden across the river Acheron and into the Underworld, people who would not grieve Charis's passing. He would be one of them. As much as he loved Phoibe, he had no love for her best friend, her closest attendant. How many times had he warned Phoibe about Charis? Delphi was rife with rumors about her, but Phoibe would listen to none of them. And so he had learned to keep his mouth shut. Now Charis was dead. Who had finally rid the world of her manipulating and scheming? He had to grit his teeth to keep a grim smile from taking shape on his lips. Finally Phoibe would be free of Charis's influence. Finally her mind would clear and she would return to herself. He held Phoibe even closer. "I'm here," he whispered again and again until her eyes found his face.

He was tired of keeping his distance, of playing by Gaia's—or Charis's—rules. Over the last several months, Phoibe had tried to keep up appearances, tried to be strong. But he could see the signs. The sickness. He was afraid it would kill her just as it had killed Sofia, the Pythia of Gaia before Phoibe. Charis had brushed away his worries and said she was taking care of Phoibe herself. That she had been trained in the healing arts, but Georgios knew Phoibe was getting worse. Before the naming ceremony, he had even approached the other priestesses as they arrived in Delphi. Melanippe of Dodona wouldn't even see him, but several of the others at least listened. Theodora had asked him to describe Phoibe's symptoms, scratching them onto a wax tablet as he spoke. He'd had to clasp his hands in his lap to keep them still, and more than once had to blink back tears. As a pankriatist, he had been pummeled many times in the gymnasium and had always clambered to his feet and gone back for more. He never stopped fighting, and the fact that he was a favorite for the next Olympic games was a testament more to his determination than to his skill. But the thought of losing Phoibe was like a lance through the heart, and he wondered how, if the worst happened, he could ever get on his feet again.

Phoibe pulled away. Her eyes were rimmed red and her face was blotchy and streaked.

"Her body was found this morning at the theater." She clutched at Georgios's cloak.

"How do you know this already? It is morning still."

"One of our spies from the temple sent word. I told you something was wrong when she didn't come to the naming ceremony last night," Phoibe sobbed. "She was to stand with me. To hold the sacred barley bowl and pour the libations."

He studied her face, but said nothing. What was there to say?

"I depended on her," Phoibe said, finally calming her tears. "Who will stand beside me now? Since the first day I came to Delphi, she was there for me. You know how lonely I was. How much I wanted to go home. I tried to be brave, but I wasn't. I was scared. Scared of Sofia. Scared of the visions. But whenever I cried at night, Charis would crawl under the covers with me. When I had a bad vision, when I couldn't talk for hours after, she would appear with a piece of gastrin dripping with honey or a loaf of bread still warm from the oven. Like a conjurer, she always found a way to bring me exactly what I needed, exactly what I wanted. She loved me and without her, I would not be the Pythia today."

Her words stripped him bare, flaying the flesh from his bones as he realized Charis's love had meant more to Phoibe than his own. He wanted to cry out that he had been there for her, too. That they had been there for each other, the orphan boy with a talent for fighting and the promising young priestess with the gift of sight. They had stolen away together as often as possible and she had told him about learning how to be a priestess and he had told her about learning to throw a man twice his size to the ground. They had shared their secrets, and as they got older, they shared their bodies and pledged that they would never leave each other. He thought they meant everything to each other, but now....

He knew Phoibe was the culmination of all her family's hopes. Since time began, her ancestors had worshiped Gaia above all. They made their sacrifices at the Korycian Cave. They supported the priestesses with offerings of meat, bread, oil and what little silver they could spare. And they stayed as far away as possible from the corrupt practices of the priests at the Temple of Apollon. He understood and respected what she was, what she would become. And he knew that there was a part of her that belonged to the goddess, a part he could never have. He could accept that. But he couldn't accept sharing her with Charis. Charis had been there from the beginning, too. Always trying to undermine him. Always manipulating Phoibe. He shook himself as if waking from a dream. He did not to need to be jealous of Charis. Not anymore.

"Who would want to kill her?" he asked.

"Philon and Kleomon," Phoibe whispered hoarsely. "They killed her as a warning to me."

"You can't mean that," he said and shot a glance up at Theodora.

"Of course I mean it! Who else could it be? They know the prophecy.

I'll never understand why, but Sofia told Philon. Now she's dead, and Philon knows he can't control me as he did her."

"He didn't control her, Phoibe," Theodora spoke up.

"What do you know about it?" Phoibe wiped her eyes and scrambled to her feet. "You weren't here all those years. Sofia was a stupid, gullible woman. Charis saw them together. More than once. And more than friends." Phoibe shuddered.

"She had no right to spy on them," Georgios said, trying to keep the bitterness out of his voice. He pushed himself up, towering over Phoibe.

"She had every right. She was my handmaiden! She knew it was my destiny to become Pythia of Gaia so it was her duty to protect me and protect the oracle—even from Gaia's own misguided priestess." Phoibe choked back a sob. "Philon and Kleomon know and fear the prophecy. Year after year, we go on. Even as their power is waning, even as fewer and fewer travel to Delphi to seek the Oracle of Apollon's guidance, our followers remain true. They resort to drugging their pathetic Pythia while we seek and find new sacred chasms for Gaia's pneuma. Apollon's voice grows faint. His power dims. And if the god's power dims, the priests' power dims."

Georgios drew in a breath and chose his words carefully. "Phoibe, the Oracle of Gaia is no threat to the famous Oracle of Apollon. Prophecy or no. If the priest's power is waning, it is not because of you. There must be another explanation."

Phoibe spun around. "There is no other explanation! Charis was stripped naked, murdered and left like a sacrificial offering. She may even have been raped. And there was a snake … Oh, Gaia! I am told there was a dead snake laid out on her belly from between her legs to her breasts. What else are we to think?"

Georgios kept his voice even. "It doesn't make sense. What would Philon and Kleomon have to gain from murdering Charis? She was nothing to them."

"Don't you see? This has nothing to do with Charis. She is—she was—simply a piece in a game of power. Two oracles claiming one sacred ground. Like any game, it cannot go on forever. There must be a winner."

"Murder is no game." he whispered. Even with Charis gone, he could hear Phoibe speaking her words.

Phoibe continued as if she hadn't heard him. "They will end it or I will end it. In Gaia's name, I swear. That was the prophecy, was it not? That I would see the two oracles joined or I would see them destroyed?"

"You would destroy the sacred Oracle of Gaia to revenge Charis?" Theodora challenged.

"Of course not! The Oracle of Gaia can never be destroyed. Sofia did not understand the prophecy. She chose not to understand it because she was blind. Her friendship with Philon—even with Apollon's Pythia—prevented her from seeing the truth. She chose to believe we could all go on claiming the same sacred ground forever. But Charis understood. She believed in me. She believed I will reclaim the Sacred Precinct that was stolen from us. That Gaia's Oracle will be reborn, stronger and more powerful than ever before. For his crimes against the goddess, we will send Apollon far beyond the Vale of Tempe and this time he will not return."

"You don't know what you're saying. Apollon's Oracle is strong; the priests are among the most powerful men in all Hellas. We are weak; our numbers are few," Theodora protested. Her heart was heavy with worry and doubt. Could Phoibe replace Sofia? Would she be able to withstand the pressures from within and without—from the gift of sight and the manipulations of those who would have her be nothing more than a political pawn?

"You cannot take them on and win," Georgios added, thankful Theodora had the courage to speak up, to challenge Phoibe. He hoped that even if Phoibe wouldn't listen to him, she would listen to Theodora. She needed another priestess to guide her. Someone other than Charis, someone other than that damned witch from Dodona.

"I know perfectly well what I am saying. This is what I was born for. This is why I was chosen."

"It's the priestess of Dodona," Theodora said, her voice measured, cautious. "She and Charis have filled your head with these ideas."

"As the eldest priestess of the Oracle of Zeus and Gaia in Dodona, Melanippe has long wielded great power in the lives of men. Even Alexander of Makedon sought her wise counsel."

"She was wise in her youth, but there are many who believe the years have turned her thoughts as rancid as the summer sun turns uncured meat," Theodora said. "You must tread carefully around her. Her influence over your thoughts troubles me."

"You should be more troubled by the fact that Charis is dead. If the priests are not responsible for her death, tell me who is, Theodora? You profess to know my thoughts; perhaps you know the killer's thoughts, too."

"Phoibe—" Georgios started.

"I know you would caution me to hold my tongue," Phoibe said as she pulled away from Georgios and swayed unsteadily on her feet. "But I am the Pythia of Gaia, and I will not be talked down to by other priestesses, no matter how many years they wear on their brow."

Georgios stood and took her hand in his even as she tried to pull away. "It is because you *are* the Pythia of Gaia that, more than ever before, you must take care to act with caution and wisdom. To accuse the priests of Apollon of murder is not a thing to be done lightly and certainly not a thing to be done on the counsel of an old woman whose mind is bent by more than years."

Phoibe pulled her hand away and twisted the gold ring on her finger. "This ring," she said finally, "is a symbol of my position." She slid it from her finger and pressed it into Georgios' s palm. It was but a glittering trifle against the wide landscape of his roughened skin. He said nothing, and she picked it up again and held it up for Theodora to see, as if the older priestess had never seen the ancient ring before.

"Two intertwined serpents. The symbol of Gaia's guardian, the drakon Apollon slew with a hundred arrows, and me, her Pythia."

Phoibe slipped it back on and then dangled her fingers toward the ground. The ring slipped off and landed noiselessly on the furred rug at their feet.

"It's too big," she said with a stifled sob. "Sometimes I feel this is all too big for me, but Charis believed in me. Melanippe believes in me." She drew in a deep breath. "I don't know what to do without Charis," Phoibe said softly. She looked as if her daimon, her life spirit and creative energy, had abandoned her. As if she were an empty vessel too faded and cracked for use.

Theodora bent, picked the ring up and slipped it back on Phoibe's finger. "You are Pythia of Gaia. You were chosen as a child, and now you have been named by the goddess herself. She will show you what to do."

Phoibe looked up at the older woman. "Today I achieved everything I had always dreamed about and yet what do I have? My best friend is dead. I have no husband. No children."

"You have me," Georgios's voice cracked as he spoke. Was there nothing he could do to ease her pain or share her burden? Nothing to convince her that he was what she needed more than handmaidens or priestesses—or even goddesses?

Phoibe reached out and ran her fingers down Georgios's cheek. "You love me, but you do not love Gaia."

"I will not abandon you." His voice was hot with determination and passion—and sadness. He knew she could not control the trembling of her limbs or the wayward paths her mind wandered down. How many nights had it been since she had slept undisturbed? She barely ate and when she did, she could not keep her food down. He would never abandon her, but he prayed to every god he knew that she would abandon the goddess. And yet he knew she would rather die than make such a choice.

"You do not want this life," she said. "You fear it. Sometimes I think you fear me. My visions are coming now even without Gaia's sacred pneuma. I hear her voice in my head and see things I do not understand even when I do not seek it. The visions are getting stronger and I am getting weaker."

"The gift of sight was always strong in your father's family," Theodora spoke up, "and now it will finally be used to honor Gaia. I know the visions can be frightening, but you must not let them overtake your senses. That is why you must seek guidance from all of us gathered here for your naming ceremony. Take counsel from each priestess before you decide on a course of action."

"What you mean is that I should not listen to Melanippe of Dodona."

"What I mean is that a wise person does not take counsel from only one counselor."

Phoibe searched the face of the older woman and then looked around the room at her other handmaidens. "Tomorrow we will meet midday at the sacred Korycian Cave. It will be within the womb of the goddess and the birthplace of her drakon that together we will find the strength to counter our adversaries."

Theodora smiled. "This is a good first step. Let Georgios attend you, and I will tell the others." Theodora's handmaid stepped forward, cloak in hand.

"Wait," Phoibe said. "According to our informer in the Sacred Precinct, there is a man, recently arrived from Athens, who will help us. According to Kleomon, the man is the son of a priestess of Gaia. If that is true, he will gladly do my bidding and exact blood payment for Charis's death."

"From whence does he hail?" Theodora asked. "We must know his mother as there are so few priestesses left."

"Apparently he is an old man. He could be the son of a priestess who long since joined the Mother."

"Old to you or old to me?" Theodora asked with a smile.

"I know only this: he hails from Thessaly, and he arrived yesterday from Athens in the company of a woman and several attendants. He is staying with Menandros the playwright, and he has the reputation of being a man who will, for the right price, administer justice with a sip of soup or the tip of a spear. Once I confirm that he is indeed one of us, I will send him a message to join us tomorrow. He will, surely, be eager to help us, and I am prepared to reward him handsomely for the deed. In the meantime," Phoibe said, reaching out to Georgios again, "you must travel to Charis's village to find her brother. He is all the family she had left."

"Send someone else, Phoibe," he protested. "I dare not leave you now." He could not leave, not when she looked as fragile as a withered leaf in the wind. Not when her visions came upon her like thieves, leaving her bereft of hope and bruised in both body and soul. If he left, who would look after her? Who would keep Melanippe of Dodona away from her?

"I can do without you for a few days," Phoibe said. "You are the only messenger I can truly trust."

Theodora reached out to reassure Georgios who looked as if Phoibe had slapped him full across the face. "She will be well protected while you are gone," Theodora said. "We will make sure of it."

# CHAPTER EIGHT

The door slammed shut. Startled, Kleomon turned to see Philon lunge toward him like an enraged hoplite breaking ranks for the kill. Philon pushed the older man up against the wall, and Kleomon kicked and flailed until he realized it was futile. He went limp and Philon loosened his grip for a moment—just long enough for Kleomon to narrow his rheumy eyes and spit in Philon's face. Philon twisted the front of the old man's chiton in a wad and pushed it up into his throat.

"Who do you think you are?" Philon's knee pinioned Kleomon's groin and he pressed the old man's arms against his sides. Though smaller and lighter than the heavily built Kleomon, Philon was younger and in better shape than any casual observer would suspect.

"Get off me! I can't breathe," the old man gasped.

"You tell me what you're playing at accusing Theron like that."

"Let go of me," Kleomon whispered, eyes bulging.

"I let go and you tell me what you are up to. I think that's a fair deal," Philon taunted as the old man struggled to break free.

"C-c-can't breathe," Kleomon sputtered.

"Give me your word," Philon demanded. He pushed his fist into Kleomon's throat.

"I said—"

"Your word," Philon snarled.

Kleomon nodded and blinked then slumped to the floor as Philon let go. Breathing hard, Kleomon sat against the wall, chiton twisted beneath him, bare legs splayed out on the cold tile floor like dead fish displayed in the marketplace. Philon dipped a jeweled goblet into a krater of wine, and reclined on a sumptuously pillowed couch across the room. He looked around, as if surveying his surroundings for the first time, taking in Kleomon's choice of decorations for his private quarters in the temple.

Kleomon knew from the look on Philon's face that the man was biding his time, making him wait, attempting to wield his superior status over him like a blunt club. Philon was insufferable. He'd been in Kleomon's private quarters in the temple complex hundreds of times and every single time Philon acted as if there was a bad smell in the air, as if he might at any moment choke on his own bile. Let him choke.

The walls were painted in brilliant yellows and blues, with murals of satyrs chasing maenads and virile youth while sporting phalluses so thick and long it was laughable. That was the point. That was the fun. But there was nothing fun about Philon. Kleomon waited. He followed Philon's eyes as the younger, but more senior priest let his gaze track around the room, taking in every piece of furniture and pottery, every detail as if it were some new and repulsive revelation.

"So, my esteemed friend," Philon began, "Why did you kill her?"

Kleomon pulled himself to his feet, dusted himself off and poured a rhyton of wine into a goblet. He pulled a chair next to the table and sat down. "I didn't kill her."

"Honestly, I don't understand why those poor women bother you so. They are no threat to us." His voice was sing-song, mocking.

"Phoibe will not be as easily controlled as the old Pythia of Gaia, your old—what do we call her?"

"I'm not so sure of that." Philon twirled the stem of his glass between his fingers and watched the honey-colored wine swirl in the goblet. "And you can call her what you like. I care not, and as she is dead and buried I'd wager she cares not as well."

"Unlike your friend, Phoibe will not be so easily cowed. She's a firebrand."

"A firebrand can be doused."

"Good luck with that. Georgios, that giant, guards her like a newborn babe. The way he dotes on her … what a waste.…"

"Careful or you'll start drooling."

"Shut up. At least I appreciate beauty when I see it." Kleomon's voice was ragged.

"Did you kill the girl, Kleomon? Or was it one of those thuggish boys that follow you around? Your own little flock of admirers. You're like Sokrates without the philosophy. Tell me, if you're convicted of murder will you be so eager to drink your hemlock?"

"By the gods, you don't really think I killed her?"

Philon sighed deeply. "No. I don't think you have it in you."

"Maybe it was one of your own bodyguards, Philon. Maybe you don't keep as tight a leash on your men as you think you do."

Philon closed his eyes and leaned his head back against the wall. He was quiet for a moment, as if considering the possibility. "No. No, I don't think it was one of my men."

"Then who did it?"

"I don't know."

"What about Theron? Don't you think it's a little strange—him turning up in Delphi at the same time as those priestesses?"

"Perhaps it was just a coincidence."

"You don't believe that for a moment," Kleomon retorted.

"Stranger things have happened in this world."

"The strangest thing is that someone got the best of her. Charis was devoted to Phoibe, but aside from that, I don't think she had a human bone in her body. More like Pseudologos, the very embodiment of lies. You couldn't trust a word she said."

"She was no innocent, that is one thing on which we can both agree," Philon said. "But why accuse the priestesses, Kleomon? They would never kill one of their own followers. And why, by all the gods on Olympos, would you ever accuse Theron?"

"Perhaps I got carried away," Kleomon admitted. "But it was your Sofia that prophesied trouble for us. It is that damnable prophecy that has filled Phoibe's head with the idea that it is her destiny to reclaim our sacred site here for the earth-worshippers. Now that Phoibe is the Pythia of Gaia, who knows to what lengths she would go in order to discredit The Oracle of

Apollon. Is murder such a stretch?"

"She might want to murder you or me," Philon chuckled, "but Phoibe would never sacrifice Charis. Every time I laid eyes on the girl, she was either with Georgios or Charis. Besides, if you really believe the Oracle of Apollon can be destroyed by a lone girl who, even now, is falling victim to the power of her visions, then you are well past the time of retirement."

"Wait—what do you mean 'even now falling victim to her visions?'"

"According to my sources, Phoibe's visions are becoming, shall we say, debilitating. Sofia said the power of prophecy runs strong in Phoibe's bloodlines. That in some generations it borders on madness."

Kleomon studied Philon. He knew Phoibe's gift of sight was strong. She was rumored to be like the great priestesses of old. But, Kleomon wondered, were these recent visions the result of a gift from the gods, a madness of some sort—or, more likely, poison?

"You're a fool, Philon," he blurted.

"Is that so?"

"You think I'm a stupid old man, but you're the one who doesn't understand the threats we face. You think you can just snap your fingers and they will disappear, that things will go on the way they were before. But they won't. We are threatened by more than Phoibe and her aging band of deluded priestesses. We're threatened by all those sophisticated philosophers of yours who worship reason over the gods."

"What a paranoid little fellow you've turned out to be."

"I'm not paranoid. You're blind."

"Yes, I can see it now. Aristotle storming the Sacred Precinct with old Isocrates, Speusippus and Xenocrates close behind him! Is that the real reason you're so afraid of Theron? Because he worships reason above all else?"

"I'm not afraid of Theron. Armies do not always come bearing weapons of steel."

"Believe me, I am well aware of that. And I am well aware of the fact that as times change, as new ideas emerge and people's faith in the gods ebb, it is essential that we control the oracles. Whether in Delphi or Dodona, it is up to us to manipulate the messages in order to perpetuate our power. After all, what need will the people have for priests if the gods no longer speak through them?"

"So you agree with me."

"Of course, but that is not the point. The point is that we have the upper hand and you lack subtlety. Implicating the priestesses is one thing. Accusing Theron is quite another. And threatening to strike his precious Althaia was a supreme miscalculation."

"He is one of them. His mother was a priestess. Doesn't it make sense that he still has loyalties to the cult, to the Pythia?"

"The last thing Theron has loyalty to is any priestess of Gaia. His interests lay not in gods or goddesses, heavenly spheres, prime movers or ultimate causes. He's interested in the causality of here and now and, most likely, in exactly where you were last night when a certain girl appeared dead in the Sacred Precinct."

"I said I don't know anything about the girl!"

"You don't have to justify yourself to me. It's Theron you have to worry about. Let me give you a little background on your new friend."

"I don't need a lecture from you. I've heard the rumors."

"So you know about Theron's history?"

"I have my spies," Kleomon growled as he stared into his wine.

"Apparently, your spies have let you down, so let me put your rumors in context. Maybe that will help you grasp the foolishness of your outburst. King Philip and Theron met when they were boys. But it was when Philip was held in Thebes that they became fast friends. I have never heard how it was that Theron of Thessaly turned up on his own in Thebes, but that is of no consequence to my story.

"As you might guess, becoming king is a difficult business. People all around you may decide at any moment they could do the job better. That's when Philip turned to Theron. Rather than the kind of philosopher who contemplated the nature of the heavens, he has always been interested in more immediate questions. Questions such as who would gain if the king were to suddenly have an accident with a rogue horse, a spicy bowl of soup, or, perhaps, an errant spear to the groin.

"Of course, we all know how that turned out. After Philip felt he had matters well in hand, Theron did a bit of traveling and disappeared for a while. Then suddenly he is in Athens in the very lucrative employ of Lysandros who, as you may know, had more money than Apollon himself."

Kleomon shifted in his seat.

"Rich as Croesus. And the daughter you spat at today inherited everything."

Kleomon examined the jewels on his goblet. He didn't want to hear one more word from Philon, but figured he might as well listen now as be dogged by Philon for days.

"Yes, it is true that Lysandros came from a long line of distinguished archons and strategos, but doesn't it sound odd that a man who had worked for a king would suddenly decide to hire on with a mere merchant? And as a tutor to a ten-year old girl?"

"So? Maybe he prefers nubile little girls to pretty young boys."

Philon threw his head back and laughed until his eyes were bleary with tears. "Ah, Kleomon, you are entertaining if nothing else. Must everything for you revolve around sexual pleasure?"

"Money and sex, Philon. They're the only two things you can count on. Even you take your pleasure where you can."

"Do you honestly think a man such as Lysandros would bring a rangy traveler like Theron into his household and allow him to bed his only child?"

Kleomon shrugged. "Who knows what men do when no one else is looking? Besides, why else would a beautiful young woman like her take an older man like Theron as her confidant if he were not also her lover?"

"Perhaps because she grew up in a household full of men. Perhaps because he was her tutor. Perhaps because he's the only man who treats her like she has a brain in her head. Who knows? For Zeus's sake, I can't believe I'm sitting here discussing Theron's sexual proclivities with you."

"At least it's an entertaining subject."

"By the gods, I don't know why I bother even trying to reason with you."

"And I don't know why I bother to listen."

"Because life is precarious for those who incur Theron's wrath."

"So the rumors are true. That he was Lysandros's paid assassin?"

"Perhaps, perhaps not. But he will not hesitate to kill when necessary. And neither he nor that silent Syrian slave they call Praxis will hesitate to eliminate anyone that threatens their precious Althaia."

"That Praxis is a marvelous specimen. I wouldn't mind finding out what his proclivities are."

Philon stood, drained his goblet and set it firmly on the table in front of Kleomon. "Listen to me, Kleomon. Theron has his sights trained on you. You invited it with your outburst. I want to make certain I'm not in his peripheral vision. The last thing either one of us needs is for a man like him to start asking questions. And, by the gods, I fear we may both pay a high price if he discovers something he does not like."

Kleomon listened to the door shut behind him and then dipped his goblet in the krater and filled it with wine. His hand shook and the golden liquid dripped over his fingers. He put the cup to his lips and drained it in one gulp.

# CHAPTER NINE

Praxis piled more coals on the brazier as Althaia pulled off her boots, tucked a woolen throw around her shoulders and curled up on the couch in Menandros's andron. He saw her shiver and watched as she stared into the fire, deep in thought. He had been a favored slave in her household since she was five years old and knew her as well—better, even—than if she'd been his own sister. And he knew that her chill had nothing to do with the weather or with the body on the altar. Years earlier, he had been appalled when he'd learned that Theron had arranged for Althaia to study the mummification process with that damnable Egyptian priest, but as a result of her time with Inaros she'd seen—and touched and probed—plenty of dead, naked bodies. No, it wasn't the weather or the body that was on her mind. It was Kleomon.

"You can't let that fat old priest get to you."

Althaia shuddered and drew the throw closer around her shoulders. She looked up at him and smiled.

"You know me too well."

"He's likely mad. No sane man would imply Theron had anything to do with the murder."

"I know, I know. The mere idea is ridiculous. But what if the rest of what he said was true? What if the young woman's death was some sort of sacrifice?"

"You said it yourself. Sacrifices require blood and there was no blood."

"Then how did she die?"

"I don't—" Praxis started.

"Did you notice the slight bluish tint to her skin, around her mouth and eyes?" Althaia interrupted, thinking out loud. "What was it Inaros taught me about strangulation? Suffocation?" Praxis sat back on his heels and listened. "And there were bruises on her face, but people don't die from bruises, do they?" She looked up.

"No," Praxis said.

"Of course not. And why would the killer strip her body and place her just so on the altar? What was the message he wanted to send? Did he force himself on her? Did he violate her before—?" Althaia stopped and shook her head vigorously. "No, I didn't see any blood or bruising on her thighs. If only I'd had more time…" she trailed off.

Praxis stood quickly and ran his fingers through his unruly hair as Nephthys appeared with a platter of dried fruits, a loaf of steaming brown bread and a jug of warmed wine. "Master Theron asked that I bring you refreshments, and Menandros's larder is well stocked."

Nephthys placed the platter on a long low table next to the brazier. Althaia absently plucked a fig from the platter and stuck it in her mouth as she turned her attention back to the flickering embers. Nephthys poured a cup of wine and set it on the table in front of her mistress, then poured another, cupped it in her hands, and presented it to Praxis like a priestess offering libations to a god. He placed his hands over hers and brought the cup to his lips, never taking his eyes from Nephthys' face. She looked up at him and desire—more than desire, longing and tenderness, too—splintered his heart.

"Ahem," Theron cleared his throat as he entered the room. Nephthys started, pulled away and sloshed wine over the rim of the cup as Praxis glared at the source of the intrusion. But he came back to himself. Now was not the time for Nephthys.

She poured another glass and started to hand it to Theron when Menandros's houseboy, Zenon, stuck his head in the room.

"Master Theron? There's a man here to see you. He says he carries an urgent message."

"So soon," Theron muttered. He glanced at Althaia and caught Praxis's eyes. There was a touch of sadness in Theron's gaze that Praxis recognized. It was a look that, he suspected, was too often in his own eyes. The look one has when you've been staring too long out the window at nothing, at everything. At the past. Thinking how strange it is that no matter how hard you try to leave one life behind to start another, the first always haunts you. Always finds you.

"Soon? What do you mean? Who is it?" Althaia asked.

"He says his name is Nikomachos of Dodona," Zenon piped up, "and that the message is confidential—for Master Theron's eyes only."

Theron took a deep breath and exhaled slowly. "Send him in."

"You don't seem surprised," Praxis observed. "Yet, I'm guessing this is no old friend coming to call."

"I've never met him, but I know who he is and I think I know who sent him."

"Hail, Theron of Thessaly," Nikomachos said as he crossed the threshold into the andron. The man quickly took in the room and all its contents, including, Praxis noted, a moment too long spent on Althaia. He reached out to clasp Theron's outstretched hand. "The message I carry is intended for your eyes only."

"Nikomachos of Dodona. You are Melanippe's son."

"I have that privilege." His eyes swept over the room again and again lingerered on Althaia. "But the nature of the message I carry—"

"Don't worry," Theron interrupted. "The time for keeping secrets from friends is over."

"Then you know who—"

"Yes. I'm just surprised it came so quickly."

"She is here, in Delphi. Our informant in the Sacred Precinct overhead Philon's guards describe a man from Thessaly, the son of a priestess, traveling with a woman from Athens," his eyes flicked toward Althaia, "and staying with the playwright. She suspected it might be you, and asked me to speak with you. Please know that, to the extent possible, she has followed your career over the years. I grew up hearing stories about you."

"As I have followed hers," Theron said, smiling a wistful smile the likes of which Praxis had never seen before. Praxis and Theron had regaled each other with stories of conquests in battle and in bed during their long years traveling together in the service of Althaia's father. Theron had always been a great storyteller, but there were places and parts of his past he had never shared. Now Praxis was beginning to suspect that his past, or at least a piece of it, was in Delphi.

Suddenly Praxis was keenly aware that Althaia could not keep her eyes from Nikomachos. It was Praxis's job—his life's work—to keep Althaia out of trouble. That had never been an easy task—trouble seemed to find Althaia as easily as mystery and intrigue found Theron. He could feel in his bones that there was nothing good about the way she was looking at this man. As she stood to join Theron, Praxis followed her gaze, trying to see what she was seeing. Nikomachos was not quite as tall as either he or Theron, but he was certainly as well-built. It would be a difficult fight if it came to that. The man's hair was the color of burnished bronze and his face was dominated by startling green eyes, full lips, and a strong jaw line that was clean-shaven in the style the young Alexander of Makedon was making fashionable everywhere but Athens. There wasn't anything particular about him that he didn't like, other than the way he glanced at Althaia and the way she held his gaze, but Praxis decided he didn't want this Nikomachos of Dodona spending too much time near his matron.

Nikomachos held out a scroll bound by a green ribbon and a wax seal. Theron stared at it, but did not reach out to take it.

"Let me introduce my employer, Althaia of Athens, and my friend, Praxis of Syria," he said, as if delaying the moment he had to grasp the scroll in his hand.

"I am glad to make the acquaintance of your friends." Nikomachos acknowledged Althaia with a nod as Praxis drew himself up in height and took a step closer. As if he knew he'd been caught looking once too often at the woman, Nikomachos squared his shoulders and returned his full attention to Theron. He thrust the scroll toward Theron again, and finally Theron took it, turning it over to examine the wax seal.

"Is it true you discovered the body?" Nikomachos asked. "That it was … that she was … naked … in the theater? On the altar?"

Praxis saw a shadow pass over Nikomachos's face. The dead woman and this man were friends, or maybe more than friends. He'd put good money on that wager. Another reason to keep Althaia as far away from him as possible.

"Althaia saw the body first,"Theron said.

Nikomachos's eyes widened and he looked at Althaia with obvious interest.

"You found her in the theater?"

"Yes," she said. "Stretched out like a lover, as if she were offering herself to the god."

*Like a lover?* Zeus's balls, this is not good. Praxis had to stop himself from grabbing her shoulders and shaking her until she remembered she was a prominent matron of Athens with a reputation to consider. She never did care much for the rules of propriety, but his life depended on her following them. If she were caught in an adulterous relationship, Lycon would blame him for the scandal and shame it would bring upon the family. It could mean disgrace—or worse. Lycon was already none too happy with the freedom Althaia gave him and would be more than eager to sell him to the highest bidder the first chance he got.

Nikomachos's brow knotted and the muscles along his jaw twitched.

"You knew her." Althaia's voice was soft and low.

"I did," Nikomachos whispered. He stared at the tiled mosaic on the floor as if he could not meet Althaia's eyes.

*At least he is taking care,* Praxis thought.

"Who was she?"Theron asked, breaking the strange spell. Is he oblivious to Althaia's behavior? Praxis wondered. There must be something powerfully interesting in that scroll, he thought. Then again, Theron didn't care much for rules and took delight in flouting the bounds of propriety. Too often, Theron turned a blind eye or even encouraged Althaia's wild behavior instead of helping rein it in.

"Her name was Charis," Nikomachos said, his voice ragged. "Over the years, my mother traveled often to Delphi, and when she could not come herself, I came in her stead. Charis was a loyal and beloved attendant to Phoibe, and I saw her often when I was visiting. It is a great shock for Phoibe." He looked up at Theron.

Who is Phoibe? Praxis felt he was missing some crucial piece of the conversation.

"A murder is a shock to everyone but the murderer," Theron observed, his finger still rubbing the wax seal.

"Naked … in the theater," Nikomachos repeated. "Unbelievable." He cleared his throat. Theron still had not broken the seal. "Should I leave you to read your message in private? She asked me to stay in case you wanted to send a reply."

Praxis studied Theron. *Who is this mysterious woman?*

"Stay," Theron said. In a sudden flourish, he untied the ribbon and broke the seal. He unrolled the scroll and stared at the careful script, his lips moving as he read silently. Althaia, Praxis, Nephthys, and Nikomachos watched in silence. After a moment, he let it roll back up in his hand and turned to Nikomachos.

"Nikos, is it?"

"It is what my friends call me."

"Well, Nikos, tell her I will be there."

Nikos turned to leave, but not before he cast one more glance back toward Althaia. Praxis scowled as Althaia met the man's gaze openly, boldly.

"Let me show you out," Praxis said, stepping up to escort Nikos. He'd kick him through the door and bolt it behind him if he thought that would help keep the two away from each other until they returned to Athens. But given the way Nikos and Althaia looked at each other, he doubted his job would be that easy.

# CHAPTER TEN

"If it's suspense you're going for, you've achieved your goal," Althaia said. "What is all this about?" She sat across the table from Theron, her throw wrapped snugly around her shoulders. The scroll lay between them. Praxis dragged a chair toward the table and joined them.

Theron replied with a sigh and a sad, knowing smile. The kind of smile reserved for occasions when there is nothing left to do but smile as you surrender to the fates.

"Well, well. This is a first. I've never seen you at a loss for words," Praxis said.

"My friend," Theron began, "in all our years, all our adventures together, we've seldom spoken of our childhoods. But it seems that painful memories can only remain buried for so long. Yesterday, of course, determines who we are today, and as much as we might like to leave the past behind, it always dogs our heels, snapping and yelping even as we try to outrun it. We served Lysandros of Athens and now we serve his daughter. Me, willingly. You, well, life is not always just. But when I broke the seal on this scroll, my past became my present. And by the nature of our relationships, how we are all tied together in our unconventional little family, it became your present as well. Now, I'd like to savor this last moment of freedom before the dog finally catches up and clamps down hard."

"Whatever is in the scroll, Theron, you will always have my love and friendship." Althaia searched her tutor's face, placed her hand over his and gave it a reassuring squeeze.

"Oh, it's not that bad. Just … complicated. Especially in light of this morning. The girl."

"Perhaps old Kleomon isn't quite as addled as we thought," Praxis mused.

"Perhaps, indeed." Theron took a deep breath and handed the scroll to Althaia. "Read it. Aloud."

She cleared her throat and began:

"Brother —"

She looked up, astonished.

"Go on." Theron leaned back in his chair and closed his eyes.

> "Brother - How many years have passed since last we sneaked into the hills to swim in our favorite stream and share a lunch of bread and honey? Too many. I will never forget the last time I saw your face. You did not come for Mother's funeral and so I did not expect to see you at Father's. And yet as I looked across his pyre, through the flames and smoke of the offering, I found your eyes. My eyes. We are as one. We did not speak that day and you, like the flames, were as quickly gone as if you were an apparition. Perhaps, I thought, I had conjured you out of my dreams. It had been so long.
>
> Your reputation, whether deserved or not, has brought you to the attention of the newly anointed Pythia of Gaia. She does not yet know your name, but I suspected, as did Melanippe, that the man from Thessaly at the theater this morning was none other than my own Theron. A few simple inquiries confirmed my suspicions and led me to you.
>
> Brother, suspicion and ambition gnaw at the heart of Gaia's young Pythia and she hopes to enlist your aid in seeking swift retribution for the girl who, as you may have guessed, was one of our own. We are divided and I fear everything is at stake. You will soon receive a message begging your attendance at a gathering tomorrow midmorning at the Korycian Cave.
>
> I will be there and I hope to see you at last. Please send word if you will come. You can trust Nikos.
>
> - Thea"

"Not addled at all," Praxis said.

"Wait, I don't understand," Althaia said. "You have a sister?"

"Theodora," Theron said, his voice barely audible. He opened his eyes and stared into the fire. "My twin."

"A twin sister! Why did you never tell me you had a sister? A twin? All these years, you never said a word."

"I wanted to tell you many times, believe me. But I hadn't spoken about her for so long that sometimes she didn't even seem real anymore. As if I had cobbled together the story of a family from bits and pieces of other people's lives."

"But why? Why did you never talk about it?"

"Why does anyone keep secrets?"

"To hide from ourselves," Praxis said. "But it seldom works."

"And I am getting old...."

"You're not old," Althaia grumbled. She hated this talk of memories. She had her own memories to overcome. Memories that kept her awake at night or that swept her into nightmares from which she could barely wake. Memories that both Theron and Praxis knew about. And for all the times she had shared her darkest fears with Theron, or asked about his childhood, or pressed Praxis to tell her how he came to be a slave, for all the times she had been as transparent as the Aegean Sea on a brilliant summer's day, these two men, the only family she had left, had kept the secrets of their pasts to themselves. How much of yourself can you give to another without getting anything in return? Was she nothing more to them than an employer and a master? The betrayal burned and she looked away to hide the flame in her cheeks.

"Not ancient, perhaps," Theron went on, "but older, and since my father's funeral, I have not seen my sister's face. Now, with all this ...."

Praxis studied his old friend. "Why have you avoided her all these years? And what has this to do with the girl at the theater?"

"Kleomon was right. My mother was a priestess of Gaia. When she died, my sister took her place."

Althaia pushed her anger aside and steadied her voice. "Of course all Hellenes worship the mother goddess, but I didn't know there were still priestesses dedicated to her cult here in Delphi. Do not the priests of Apollon run the Sacred Precinct?"

"Besides the Pythia, there are only eight priestesses left who are dedicated to Gaia, and few people visit the sacred places anymore. There were never any temples, just groves or caves. That's why Delphi is so important. The Korycian Cave and the Spring of Ge are the most sacred places for the cult. Except for the exact position of the oracle, of course."

"Did you know she would be here?" Althaia asked, her voice hollow, fearful of what his answer might be. "Is that why you were anxious to come to Delphi?"

Had he wanted to come because he hoped to be reunited with his sister—his twin sister? After all these years, would he go to his sister, become a part of her life, leave Athens behind? Her hurt and frustration drained away, leaving her empty, lonely. What would she do if she lost Theron or Praxis? She would be alone. Alone in a houseful of slaves with a husband who hardly acknowledged she existed, in a city that refused to recognize that an educated woman merited even the most basic rights of citizenship, amidst a controlling group of domineering uncles, meddling aunts, and mindless cousins who thought a busy day was worrying about which ribbons to wear in their hair, telling cook what to buy at the market, and weaving a new blanket for the next baby on the way. No, she could not lose Theron or Praxis.

"I was anxious to come to Delphi because it was your father's last wishes. But, yes, I had my suspicions that Thea would be here, too. I try to keep track, to know where she is, how she is. So when I heard the priestesses would be gathering here, I knew she would be among them."

"You never answered my question," Praxis said. "Why did you avoid her? How long has it been since you last spoke?"

Theron paused, his voice tight when he finally spoke. "Almost thirty years."

Thirty years? Althaia stayed her hand. She wanted to reach out to him, to reassure herself that he was still her own Theron as much as she wanted to comfort him and encourage him to go on.

"I did not go to our mother's funeral. As her message said, I saw her last at our father's funeral, but I didn't speak. As children, my sister and I were taught to worship Gaia blindly, without question, without thought, and to follow my mother's every command completely. My father, a soldier and a farmer, was a good man, but he left us to my mother's care. My sister had little choice but to follow in our mother's footsteps, ultimately taking her place as priestess. My footsteps, as you well know, led me in a different direction. When I left, I was … well, I was an innocent. When I returned, when I saw my twin over the funeral pyre, I could not bring myself to speak. I was no longer that innocent boy and I wondered if I even had a right to reclaim my place in the family."

"Thirty years … you would have been about fifteen. What made you leave home so young and why have you never returned?" Althaia couldn't resist the question.

He drew in his breath. "That story is best left for another day."

"But—"

"More important, at least for now," Praxis interrupted, "is why Kleomon would think either you or the priestesses of Gaia would have anything to do with the girl's murder."

"I don't know. No one familiar with the cult's traditions would suspect such a thing. They would never sacrifice one of their own."

"You said Delphi is sacred to the cult of Gaia," Althaia said. "But today at the theater, it sounded like the priests of Apollon are not on good terms with the priestesses of Gaia."

"They're not. And the tension between them may explain why Kleomon was anxious to point the finger at Gaia's followers when he most likely knew better."

"Why don't they get along?" Althaia asked. "Priests and priestesses worship side by side at temples all over Hellas."

"The fact that Delphi is sacred to both cults is precisely why there is such animosity, and the reason many are no longer aware the Oracle of Gaia still exists. While Apollon's influence has grown, Gaia's has faded. Gaia's followers now amount to no more than a few isolated clans scattered here and there. In fact, today most of the priestesses serve more than Gaia. Nikomachos's mother, the priestess of Dodona, for instance, serves Zeus and Gaia. The priestess of Argos: Hera and Gaia. My own sister: Demeter and Gaia. But the enclave here in Delphi refuses to acknowledge Apollon's rights because they are so tied to the sacred land here where Gaia's oracle was stolen by Apollon."

"Yes," Althaia said, "every child knows the story of how Apollon slew Gaia's protector, her sacred drakon, and took control of the site. But that was a long time ago, back when the gods walked the earth."

"To Gaia's followers in Delphi, it could have been yesterday. They live in a state of fear, constantly blaming Apollon's priests for their fading influence. There are some among them who believe Apollon and his priests are plotting against them to this day. Because of this, the Pythia of Gaia will only meet and prophesy for those who are true believers in the founding myth of Gaia."

"As usual, paranoia, seclusion and fear breed hatred," Praxis muttered.

"Exactly. Kleomon is probably suspicious of the priestesses precisely because they are suspicious of him." He picked up the scroll again and read aloud:

"Suspicion and ambition gnaw at the heart of Gaia's young Pythia and she hopes to enlist your aid in seeking swift retribution for the girl who, as you may have guessed, was one of our own. We are divided and I fear everything is at stake."

"I still don't understand why there is such a rivalry or competition between the priests and priestesses," Althaia said. "If Delphi is sacred to both Apollon and Gaia, so be it. Delphi is also home to a Sacred Precinct of Athena. One cannot honor one god above all others or honor one to the exclusion of the others. Even the gods are not so selfish as to demand such singular devotion, and if the gods themselves do not demand it, then how can a priests or priestess dare demand it in their names?"

"I can think of two reasons," Praxis said. "Power and money."

"For many, those are the only two reasons for getting up in the morning," Theron said.

"I'm not naïve," Althaia protested.

"I'm not suggesting that. But remember Delphi is no ordinary sacred place. It is the omphalos, the navel of the universe, with a power that both the priests and the priestesses want to wield. Before the fissure in the mountainside through which the sacred pneuma issues forth was claimed by Apollon, anyone could come and experience the guidance of the goddess for themselves. The Pythia of Gaia, a priestess who has the gift of sight, simply helped seekers interpret their visions. But once Apollon claimed the oracle for himself, he appointed priests to build a temple over the fissure, and, from that point on, anyone who sought wisdom or guidance had to go through Apollon's priests and the voice of the Oracle of Apollon, the Pythia. And they had to pay. This enraged Gaia as her oracle had always been open to the sky, the air and the wind. But most of all, Gaia was enraged because no man has the right to charge a fee to anyone seeking the wisdom of Mother Earth. Even today, the Oracle of Gaia demands no payment."

"Even today?" Althaia asked. "How is it that the so-called Pythia of Gaia gains access to the fissure beneath Apollon's temple?"

"She doesn't. Gaia was so enraged at Apollon, she asked her consort, Poseidon, to cause an earthquake. When the earth shifted, the site of the oracle shifted, too. They believe each time there is an earthquake in Delphi, it is Poseidon punishing Apollon for some additional slight toward Gaia. And each time the earth shakes, the site of the true oracle moves. The sacred fumes issue from the earth in a new place. Gaia's followers seek this place and their Pythia sets up shop, so to speak, at this new location."

"An itinerant oracle," Praxis suggested.

"Well, I hadn't thought of it like that, but yes. To followers of Gaia, the Oracle of Apollon, locked away in the bowels of a stone temple, is a sacrilege, and Apollon's Pythia just a poor, misguided woman who is generally drugged into submission, and the priests are money-grubbing pretenders manipulating the rich, powerful and gullible from behind the temple curtain. The true oracle, the Oracle of Gaia, is still open to anyone who seeks wisdom. It is somewhere," Theron waived his arm, "up there on the mountainside. Only Gaia's true followers know where."

"This is all so strange," Althaia said.

"The priestesses' meeting. You told Nikomachos of Dodona you would go," Praxis said.

At the mention of Nikomachos's name, Althaia felt the blood rise in her cheeks. The image of him standing in the room just moments earlier came back unbidden and she found herself comparing Nikomachos to Praxis and Theron.

She could picture the three of them standing there, sizing each other up. While Praxis was the slave, any stranger might think he was master of the house. He was tall, broad shouldered, and carried himself with an easy confidence. His dark complexion and full head of dirty blond curls contrasted sharply with intelligent blue eyes. His beauty was pure, statuesque, as though one of Praxilites' acclaimed figures had sprung to life. Her father always teased that he had named Praxis after the sculptor. Theron, at about forty-five, was fifteen years older than Praxis and he wore every year as if in both testimony and defiance of his age. He was lean and leathery and his well-muscled body looked as if it had been chiseled from ancient bedrock. When he was serious, his face was as hard as stone, but when he was lighthearted; it lit up like a child's and Althaia loved him the more for it. Nikomachos of Dodona, in contrast, was younger than Praxis, closer to Althaia's own age. Though just as powerfully built, he was not as tall as either of the other two men. Where Praxis was as refined as polished marble and Theron as weathered as ancient stone, Nikos was as fluid as quicksilver. She thought of how the cats in the stable yard back home stalked their prey and then pounced in a lightning flash.

But there was something more in his face, a hint of sadness, or maybe more like the wistfulness she sometimes saw in Praxis. She had wanted to comfort him when she realized the dead woman had been a friend, but yet just being near him had made Althaia's pulse quicken. It dawned on her that he, in the few moments she'd been in his presence, had awakened deeper feelings than Lycon had in their thirteen months of marriage. Of course she had always known Lycon's interests lay elsewhere. Where did Nikomachos's interests lie?

Theron's voice brought her back to herself. "Heraklios seeks my help in resolving the murder and, according to Thea's note, the Pythia of Gaia will soon request my help as well. Therefore, I think I must—or rather, we must go. I want you both with me. Three sets of eyes and ears are better than one, although I fear the priestesses will not welcome strangers."

"Especially since we were not invited," Althaia said. She wondered if Nikomachos would accompany his mother to the priestesses' meeting.

"Nevertheless, I am inviting you. And, Althaia, I think we must press them to allow you to examine the body."

Althaia studied Theron for a moment, and the vision of the girl's body floated before her eyes. "You'll ask, but you don't believe they'll allow it," she said.

"There may be some among them who will understand the purpose of an autopsia, and not fear it as a violation."

Althaia knew one thing was certain: now that Heraklios had pressed Theron into his service, the murderer would be quickly discovered and held accountable. And, the prospect of Theron asking for her assistance, asking her to use the skills she learned in Egypt, was thrilling—if a little frightening. It had been over five years since that summer in Naukratis and, besides using them on a few dead cats, a couple of birds and fish, and one or two still-born pigs from the farm, she hadn't touched her autopsia instruments since then.

"Perhaps my skills will finally be put to good use."

# CHAPTER ELEVEN

Nephthys watched Althaia open the olivewood case and set out her instruments one by one. Two scalpels, one with a long bronze handle and one with a short one. Two hooks, one sharp, one blunt. A bone drill and forceps. Spring scissors and a scoop Hippokrates called a spoon of Diokles. Nephthys had seen such tools before. Egyptian priests used them during the mummification process, but they always looked like instruments of torture to her. What a strange woman, she thought. Why would Althaia, a beautiful, rich Hellene, want to learn the secrets of the body? In Egypt, such knowledge was the province of priests and physicians. What good would it do Althaia? As an Athenian woman, she would have no opportunity to use it. And who would have taken the risk to teach her?

"Here," Althaia handed Nephthys one of the scalpels and a piece of linen. "Never use a filthy instrument on a body made in the likeness of the gods. That's what my teacher said. He was from Naukratis, you know."

"An Egyptian?"

"A priest of Amun-Ra."

"How did you come to know this man?"

"Theron. We spent a season in Egypt. The winter of my sixteenth birthday. Papa rented a house for the winter. Papa, Theron, and Praxis spent most of the time meeting and negotiating with merchants, but Theron also made sure I kept up my studies. One evening when the house was full of guests, he came to my room with this box. For years I had begged him for an opportunity to learn more about anatomy, and although Theron encouraged it, there were few opportunities for me to try anything new. I was tired of dissecting dead cats and still-born pigs. I wanted more. I can't explain why it fascinates me." She breathed on the blade and wiped it with her cloth. "Anyway, just as the wine started flowing and the performers started arriving, Theron made his excuses and slipped out. Then we rode out to the home of Inaros, the priest.

"I had no idea what to expect. We rode past the edge of the city toward a ramshackle series of connected huts all leaning precariously over the Nile as if the hot breath of the Sahara was blowing them into the river. I think they floated during the annual floods. I'm not sure; but I'd never seen anything like them before."

"Probably made of reeds."

Althaia nodded. "Anyway, once we arrived, Theron led me into a small, squat building glowing with what seemed to be hundreds of dripping, flickering, smoking oil lamps. I could hardly breathe." Althaia stared into the distance, remembering. "There was a naked body, a man, pale, ghostly, like a shade from Hades. He was laid out on a narrow table. Later I learned Inaros had long been suspected of digging up the recently dead, those who couldn't afford mummification, for midnight dissections."

Nephthys shuddered.

"At first, we stood quietly against the wall watching. Inaros's eyes flickered over us, acknowledging our presence, but he said nothing. He was preoccupied with some sort of ritual, lighting incense, casting out the evil eye, praying to the cadaver's relatives and asking for their forgiveness. I'll never forget his face, so gaunt. He had surprisingly alert eyes, though. Bulging from sunken sockets, they peered into the smoky room as if they could see through the pretense of this world and into the reality of the next. He had sharp cheekbones that jutted out like little mountain peaks," she chuckled. "Such a strange man. I've seen cadavers that looked healthier. His shoulders permanently arched forward as if designed for tending the bodies laid out on his dissection table. He seemed to be among the waking dead, as if he had already been mummified without being informed and was going about his business until he simply fell into the nearest open grave."

"I know old men like that. It's the remorseless Egyptian sun that does it. The older they get, the more they seem to shrivel in on themselves." Nephthys thought of her husband, thirty years her senior, whose body had already begun yielding skin and bone to the sun. She thought of his hands, as brown and weathered as old leather, and how they had touched her skin and claimed her body as his own.

"Inaros finally completed his ritual. He stepped to the table and motioned to me. I moved closer. I didn't want to miss anything. He took a gleaming blade in hand, bent over the body, and sliced open the man's abdomen in one stroke. Then I threw up."

"What did he do?"

"He smiled."

"That's all?"

"That's all. He never even spoke to me that first night. But over the course of the next two months, I spent much of my free time bent over his dissection table. I don't know what Papa would have done if he'd known about Inaros. Killed him? Fired Theron? Had us both flogged? I have no idea. I do know he would not have been pleased."

"And now you hope to use what you learned to try to discover how this girl died?"

Althaia smiled. She realized it felt good to talk to someone her own age. It felt good to talk to a woman. "I've spent my whole life in the company of three men: my father, Praxis, and Theron. They told me I could do anything. Ride, hunt, swim, study. Anything. But they were wrong. I think at the end, when I had to marry my cousin Lycon, right before my father died, he realized the one thing he had raised me for was disappointment. In reality, my life is completely proscribed by the rules of citizenship, of property, of propriety. In Athens, a woman has no rights. Even a woman from a family like mine. But this knowledge I have, these skills I learned from Inaros, no one can take them away from me."

The room was quiet. Althaia glanced over at Nephthys. Was there even the slightest possibility that Nephthys was warming up to her? That they could become friends? Of course, Nephthys had to sit there and listen to her ramble on and on. She was a slave. She had no choice. But Althaia couldn't help that. She hadn't made Nephthys a slave. That was just the way it was. "So, the answer to your question is yes. I hope to use what I know to reveal the secrets of Charis's last moments. Perhaps, Nephthys, you could help me."

Nephthys could feel Althaia looking at her expectantly. She kept her eyes lowered, focused on her fingers as she buffed the steel blade of the scalpel. Did her mistress expect her to jump for joy because she was being asked to help her? What did she want from her, anyway? So Althaia was raised with high expectations and now lived with disappointment. So what? Althaia had never once asked how she was raised or what disappointments she had experienced. Althaia never asked who she was or where she came from or who she might long for. She had never asked if she were scared or sad. Or lonely. She never asked anything.

After a moment, Althaia continued. "Two days ago Charis was as alive and vibrant as we are now. Her body responded to touch, to hot and cold, to fear and desire just as our own bodies still do. Now she is dead, and we may have the opportunity to give her a chance to speak one last time, to reveal the secrets of her last moments. The moment when all her mortal dreams and possibilities died. She deserves that. She deserves to know somebody cares about who she was before."

"Everyone deserves that," Nephthys whispered.

"What?"

"Nothing."

# CHAPTER TWELVE

A stiff breeze whipped through the pass and Althaia's hand flew up to keep her traveling hat snug on her head. She pulled at the ribbon and re-knotted it under her chin. It was six stadia from Delphi to the Korycian Cave and though they'd been walking since daybreak, they still had at least an hour to go because of the steep terrain and rocky, narrow path. They'd reach the cave by mid-morning and, if the gathering didn't last too long, they'd be able to eat the lunch Nephthys had packed before heading back down to Delphi and the dreaded dinner with Philon.

The official invitation to call at Philon's residence had arrived the night before. She didn't want to go, but as Theron said, you can't say no to the high priest of Delphi. She knew talk would eventually turn to politics and possible war between Makedon and Athens. She also knew that because her family's roots could be traced back to the very foundations of her city, she could not be trusted to say anything that would be considered appropriate for the dinner table. She wondered what her father would have thought of her dining with Philon, and the pain of his loss splintered her heart once again. She bit her lip, determined to stop the tears before they had a chance to get started. Her father gone, her husband's interests focused elsewhere, the sudden discovery of Theron's long-lost sister, and Praxis.... She wondered again why her father had stipulated that she and Praxis travel to Delphi before his last wishes could be revealed, but she knew better than to pester Theron with any more questions. He'd made it clear that all would be revealed in good time. It was better to focus on the murder and the priestesses—and the fact that one of them was Theron's twin.

"Why won't you tell me the priestesses?" Althaia asked.

"As for my sister, I told you now is not the time for that story," Theron answered. "And I can tell you little of the others because I have only met one of them and that was many years ago."

"When the Pythia's messenger came last night, what exactly did he say?"

"He asked—no, demanded—that I fulfill my duty to Gaia."

"So the Pythia knows you are Theodora's brother."

"That information could not long remain secret."

"Tell me something, anything, about your sister. What is she like? Why were you were separated?"

"You are nothing if not persistent, but I cannot tell you what she is like. I myself do not know. I have not spoken to her since I was a boy."

"Why did you never tell me? You and Praxis are the only family I have, but now, suddenly, you have a sister." Althaia bit her lip again. "She is your real family and now that you are to be reunited…."

Without breaking his stride, Theron reached out and pulled Althaia to him. His arm, as weathered and strong as a ship's rigging, clasped her to his side even as he walked on without saying a word.

"Theron—" Althaia began.

"My dear, it was a lifetime ago." He squeezed her shoulder, and they walked in silence for a few moments before Althaia could trust her voice.

"If you won't tell me anything about your sister, tell me why you turned away from Gaia. Especially since your mother was a priestess."

"Not just from Gaia."

"What do you mean?"

"Have we not spoken of this before?"

"You always speak in riddles and questions, master teacher. Come, tell me straight. For once, do not make this a lesson or dialectic."

Theron drew in a deep breathe and squinted up into the deepening blue sky. "Then no more inquisition, master student. Are we agreed?"

"Agreed, no more questions—for now," Althaia said.

"Hmph." Theron's mouth twisted in a skeptical frown. "Alright. After I left home, I began traveling, asking questions, and listening to wise men and women from around the Middle Sea and beyond. I could recite Hesiod and Homer and I knew the history of the gods. Mother made sure of it. The more I traveled, the more I began to see through the veil that separates us from the world around us. Again and again, the wise told tales of days long past when gods and giants walked the earth, of winged creatures with many heads and even more tails, of magical spells and ritual sacrifices that could guarantee a fair voyage, a victory on the battlefield, or a lover's devoted embrace. And yet, in each town or village or great city where the wise preached and kings and peasants alike paid for their advice and made their appropriate sacrifices, voyagers were still lost at sea, victors were still vanquished on the battlefield, and lovers were still betrayed." He stole a glance at Althaia before beginning again.

"I began to realize that the veil is one we ourselves have woven to help us sleep at night, to convince ourselves that we can, through supplication and right worship, gain the favor of the gods and therefore protect us from the unknown, from what we fear. So I tore the veil aside and now I look at the world as it is. Yes, it is still a mystery. No, I do not have the answers. Why the sun rises in the east and sets in the west making our shadows stalk us through the day like enemy spies, why the tides roll in and out, splashing and spilling up on the shore as if Titans were sloshing their wine cups to and fro, or why a soft breeze that tantalizes and teases the skin one minute can, in a few short hours, turn into a violent wind that drives ships to the bottom of the sea and sailors to their watery graves—all these are mysteries to me. But, I have come to understand that Gaia, Hera, and Demeter, or Mut, Hathor, and Isis, Ishtar, Cybele and all the other goddesses we worship exist because we have invented them. If I acknowledge the pretense behind the worship of the mother goddess—or of any god—then must I not doubt the power of the others as well?"

"No wonder you speak in riddles. Many might think your impiety a danger to civic order. Like Sokrates."

Theron threw his head back and laughed. "I have been compared unfavorably to snakes and scorpions, but I am quite sure no one will compare me to Sokrates, my dear."

"Be serious! Even you cannot doubt Apollon and the Oracle of Delphi."

He remained silent.

"What about Croesus? With his test, he proved the Delphic Oracle has power beyond all others. If the Pythia couldn't see, how else would she know that a king as far away as Lydia would be making tortoise and lamb stew at that precise moment?"

"So the legend goes," Theron said. "But what about her prediction that Croesus would destroy a mighty empire if he attacked Persia? Did she get it wrong or did Croesus get it wrong?"

"A mighty empire did fall!" Althaia answered.

"Indeed," Theron chuckled. "Although I doubt Croesus was comforted by the verity of the Pythia's prediction when it was his empire that fell and not his enemies'."

"That doesn't make the prediction any less true," Althaia countered. "Apollon is one of the most revered gods in the world!"

"In the whole world? Really, my girl, I thought I had taught you better. We do not even know the extent of the whole world let alone what people in distant places believe. It's my observation that the gods people worship reflect the lands in which they live, the dangers they face, or the desires they share as a people. As Zenonphon said:

*'The Ethiopes say that their gods are flat-nosed and black,*
*While the Thracians say that theirs have blue eyes and red hair.*
*Yet if cattle or horses or lions had hands and could draw,*
*And could sculpt like men, then the horses would draw their gods*
*Like horses, and cattle like cattle; and each they would shape*
*Bodies of gods in the likeness, each kind, of their own.'"*

"We are not Ethiopes or Thracians. We are Hellenes," Althaia protested.

"That is not the point and you know it. I have trained you in the use of logic, so use it. How likely is it that seers can speak on behalf of the gods based on the examination and interpretation of cow livers, bird entrails, the arrangement of clouds, or the tossing of stones? Or because they are overcome by vapors issuing from deep within the earth?"

Althaia sucked in a breath. "You know, despite the popularity of his fables, the Delphinians convicted Aesop for impiety toward the gods. They tossed him to his death from a cliff very much like the one beneath our feet now."

"I am well aware of the dangerous path I tread," he laughed and clasped

Althaia to his side again. "That's why, while in Delphi, I stay well away from the edge."

As they continued up the mountain, the path wound through thick groves of olive trees and tracked above the wide expanse of the plain stretching out toward Arachova below them. Most of the time, the trail was wide enough for Althaia to walk beside Theron, but in a few places it was perilously close to the cliff's edge and too narrow for anything but single-file. They fell into an easy rhythm, Althaia trying to pry information from Theron and Theron studiously avoiding her most probing questions even as they both kept their heads down to watch their footing. Trailing behind them, Nephthys and Praxis walked alongside a donkey carrying blankets, bladders of wine, and a basket of food for lunch. An awkward silence, like an unwanted chaperone riding atop the donkey, hovered between the two slaves.

Then a startled yelp rang out. Althaia and Theron turned to see the animal shy away from something—a bee sting? a shadow?—and knock Nephthys sideways. Her arms spun like chariot wheels as she lost her footing on the loose rock scattered on the steep, winding path. Praxis's arm shot out across the animal's back, but his fingers caught only empty air as Nephthys skidded backward and then fell, tumbling toward the edge. Praxis dropped to his backside and scrambled in her wake as Nephthys's fingers dug into the ground and clawed at loose stones and roots. But nothing stopped her momentum. Then she grabbed at the burned stump of an old olive tree, and, like a prisoner struggling to break free from his bonds, the stump strained at the ground. Althaia thought all was lost, but the age-old bond of root and soil remained strong. The stump held. Praxis inched up behind Nephthys, braced his foot against the blackened wood, clasped her arm and pulled her back against him.

On the path above, Althaia started down toward them. But Theron clutched her arm. "Wait."

"But—"

"Praxis has her," he said softly. She stopped and watched the two figures below. She was ashamed to admit it, but as Praxis drew Nephthys into his arms, her relief gave way to the selfish thought that Theron was right. Praxis did have Nephthys. And Nephthys had Praxis. And Theron had a twin sister. And she had no one.

# CHAPTER THIRTEEN

Theodora and Phoibe stood on the windswept ledge before the mouth of the cave watching as Theron and Althaia made their way up the rocky path toward them.

"Why did I have to learn from Melanippe that this man is your brother?" Phoibe asked through gritted teeth.

"I was not certain myself—at first," Theodora said. She had known Phoibe since the girl was a baby and had first been named and chosen as an attendant to Sofia, the former Pythia. Although she only saw her once a year, she knew Phoibe had been a sweet, but fearful child who had grown into a determined, confident, and headstrong young woman.

"I should not be forced to rely on one priestess to inform on another."

"I should have been the one to tell you," Theodora acknowledged. Age had never mattered when it came to selecting the Pythia of Gaia. The only thing that mattered was The Sight. And Phoibe most definitely had that. Her visions were legendary—at least among the priestesses still left. But the Pythia was simply one of equals in their sisterhood, and Theodora did not appreciate a woman more than half her age speaking to her with such an air of disdain and superiority. It was unbecoming of a servant of the goddess.

"Who is the woman accompanying him?" Phoibe demanded.

"I don't know," Theodora admitted. "Perhaps she is a slave." Theodora knew so little about her brother. For months after he left, she did not even know whether he still lived. When her father finally brought word of him, she was overwhelmed with relief—and anger. For years, she struggled through periods when she hated her twin for abandoning her to their mother and periods when she wanted nothing more than to touch his face and look into his familiar eyes. Now that he was walking toward her, she did not know what to feel or what she should say. Or what he would say to her.

* * * *

After her traumatic morning at the site of the Oracle of Gaia, Phoibe was still unsteady. Her stomach unsettled—even more than it had been of late. She was feverish, and her thoughts were scattered; she felt dangerously unhinged. She had arrived at the cave early enough to see the other priestesses come one by one, and was now anxious to retreat into its shadowed recesses. To hide from Apollon's rays. And yet here she was waiting in the full sun for Theron of Thessaly, a man whose reputation as a mercenary who had worked for both Makedonians and Athenians contributed to her unease.

She shaded her eyes and studied Theron and the woman with him as they approached. The similarity between Theron and his sister was unmistakable—the same tall frame, angular face, and deep-set eyes. Again, it angered her that their kinship was revealed not by Theodora, but by Melanippe. As for the woman with Theron, she was no slave, of that Phoibe was certain. According to Theodora, Theron had for several years been employed by an Athenian merchant as a tutor for his only child, a daughter. But surely this woman was not his student. A wealthy Athenian would never be allowed to travel with an unmarried man who was not her relative, and, even if she was, she would be pampered and perfumed, carried everywhere in a closed litter. Whoever this was, walking so easily in the company of a man, she was no respectable woman. She must be a hetaera! What kind of man would bring a high-priced prostitute to their holy gathering? It was unthinkable. But there she was. The wide, pretty face set off by arched, well-tended brows. The expensive beaded headband. The garnet necklace and matching earrings dangling from the woman's lobes. It was obvious. She had to be Theron's whore.

Phoibe had sought the man's help, but now that he approached, she was seized by a desire to turn and run. A gnawing dread took root in her belly, and she cringed as its grasping tentacles clawed at her spine. No matter what connections Theron had to Gaia, Phoibe knew with certainty he was not a man who would easily bend to her will. The Sight clouded her eyes and she swayed slightly before Theodora reached out to her. Phoibe pulled away, took a deep breath and forced herself to stand tall. She was unwilling to let the older priestess know how vulnerable she felt.

She was the Pythia and no man or woman would intimidate her. She would conquer her fears. She would not let them overwhelm and blind her. Not like the last time she panicked, when the torch went out in the cave's inner chamber and she could not find Georgios though her arms flailed wildly and he stood but a few cubits away. Georgios was the only one—he and Charis—who knew she feared the dark, feared the cave, feared the visions.

But even as her visions became more frightening, more frequent, more vivid, and more fiercely insistent, Phoibe fed on them and they nourished her desire and ambition like mother's milk nourishes the newborn babe. Just that morning, before daybreak, she had sought Gaia's voice and now the vision she experienced haunted her.

* * * *

At dawn that morning, she had carried a blanket, a small tripod for her offering, a pouch of smoldering coals, and two bladders, one filled with wine, the other with oil. She spread the blanket on the ground beside the sacred crevice and smoothed it out carefully. Shivering, she took off her boots, stripped and bathed in the spring melt water rushing down from Mt. Parnassus. She paid no attention to the cold even as her teeth chattered uncontrollably and her pale skin turned blue. This was her ritual. She was becoming the oracle.

She squeezed the water out of her thick hair and twisted it into a heavy braid that hung past the small of her back, past the dimples Georgios loved to outline with his tongue. She wrapped her winter cloak around her shoulders and dipped the bowl of her tripod in the freezing water. She closed her eyes and drank deeply. The water etched a frigid path down her throat to the center of her being. She closed her eyes and gave thanks for its cleansing purity. The spirit of Gaia was within her. It was beginning.

She poured the glowing coals from her pouch and arranged them carefully atop the cold pile of ash and old coals. She placed the small tripod and bowl above them. Droplets of water spit and sizzled as they fell onto the hot embers. She plucked a few dried laurel and kannabis leaves from her purse, rubbed them between her palms and sprinkled them into the bowl.

All was silent around her, save the distant tap-tap-tap of a woodpecker and the music of the stream behind her. She paused in prayer and then poured the libations into the ground. Wisps of smoke began to rise from the offering bowl. She leaned over it and breathed deeply. Her pulse slowed and her inner eye began to wake as her heart opened to the goddess's voice. Phoibe bowed over the narrow fissure, closed her eyes and drew her cloak up over her head to block out the morning sun and concentrate the vapors and the offering smoke.

She breathed in deeply again and again and soon the stones and trees—the very ground beneath her—began to whisper the names of all the Pythias who came before her. Her own name drifted by on the breeze, softly at first and then louder and more insistent as the wind grew stronger. She felt the words form in her mind: Pythia. Pythia. I am the Pythia. The Python. The mouthpiece and guardian of Gaia."

A harsh wind whistled around her. It pushed her back and forth like a fly caught in a spider's web buffeted by a gale. The ages of the world rushed through her, and surf pounded in her ears as Poseidon rose from the depths and battered the shorelines of Hellas with wave upon wave of bright foam. The colors of creation crashed against the wide valleys and soared skyward to dance wildly behind her lids, drawing nearer and then chasing away, one after the other moving forward and back, in and out of memory.

Then all was still and she saw herself emerge from the fissure and slither across the ground, her belly against the cool earth. The earth moved within her, as though she were the Mother Goddess incarnate, her womb full of titans, gods and heroes wrestling with their destinies. Then, her stomach lurched. There is danger approaching, Gaia hummed in warning. Phoibe felt the vibrations ripple across her skin, as if she were a lyre string yearning, aching, for the musician's fingers.

The humming grew louder and louder until her body throbbed with the rhythm of it. She feared her ears would burst, that skin could no longer contain her. That she would fracture the frail envelope that separated her soul from the world. She threw back her head and her cloak fell to the ground as the morning sun streaked across the sky to embrace her. Like a lover's fingers, the golden rays ran along her neck, down between her breasts and then lower. His presence loomed over her as the sun god blinded her with the brilliant heat of his desire. Of her desire. Her body flushed as he caressed her and she arched back to meet him in his need. She could see his outline and trace his form on her flesh with her own fingers. Like a nameless fear in the dark, he consumed her body and soul and she welcomed him. Despite herself, she welcomed Apollon.

She shuddered with release and knew her face was wet with tears. She closed her eyes tight and rocked back and forth as if Grandmother Earth held her to her breast, arms swaddling her to protect and comfort her. She swayed with the rhythm of Gaia's voice as it flooded her body. It was a familiar tune, Gaia's lullaby, but the words were not right.

My time has passed. It is over. You are the last. The words were whispered with love but they hung in the air like a curse. They were full of death and sorrow and suddenly all Phoibe could see were Charis's eyes staring into hers. They were not frightened or pleading. They were not reassuring. They were simply dead.

She opened her eyes. He stood before her as if he were flesh and blood. And then he was gone. Just like his father. As Zeus had laid claim to Leda, Apollon now laid claim to Phoibe. Disguised as the rays of morning sun, Apollon had violated the sacred bond with Gaia and had taken Phoibe as his lover. And she had surrendered to him. Willingly.

There was no question—Phoibe now knew the Oracle's very existence was in danger. In her vision, she had seen it, felt it. She knew it was by Apollon's hand that Charis had died. And it would be by his hand that Gaia herself would be vanquished. Once and for all. And his instrument of destruction would be Phoibe herself. She had seen it. She did not understand it. And she would fight it. But she would lose. She knew that now.

# CHAPTER FOURTEEN

Theron felt his sister's presence before he saw her. He took a deep breath, rounded the last corner, and looked up toward where he knew the mouth of the cave was hidden. Forty-five years old or not, travel-worn and battle-hardened or not, the memories of their last days together threatened to sweep his feet from under him like a riptide. In the distance, Theodora stood in the bright morning sun but all he could see was his sixteen-year-old twin framed against the moonlight as he turned his back one last time and rode away from everything he had ever known or loved.

As he drew near, he reached into his belt and pulled out a sprig of olive. He was seldom at a loss for words, but when he finally spoke, his voice was rough, barely a whisper.

"Thea." He held out his hand to his sister. "For you."

Theodora's face tightened, and her eyes shone with tears. "Like the ones we used to award each other."

"With great ceremony," Theron smiled. "Winning an Olympic event is no laughing matter."

"Especially if getting caught avoiding our chores meant another whipping." Theodora pressed it to her breast and then stuck it in her embroidered headband. The sheen on the leaves highlighted her dark hair where age had begun to paint it silver. She took her brother's hand and raised it to her lips.

"Thank you. For this," she touched the sprig again, "and for coming. I wasn't certain you would."

"It was time."

Theron took his sister's measure. Even after all these years, the similarities were clear, especially in their build, in the angles and shadows of their faces, and in their eyes. But the passage of time had been kinder to Thea than to him. She was tall and thin like he was, but where age had hardened him, it had softened her, rounded the edges.

He turned and motioned to Althaia. "This is—"

"As a son of Gaia, you are expected and welcome," the young woman beside Thea interrupted. Theron noted that, whoever she was, she certainly did not seem welcoming. "Now, if your touching reunion is over, follow me," she demanded. "The others are waiting." She turned on her heel and started back toward the cave. Then she stopped and her eyes flickered over Althaia. "Your friend will wait outside with the rest of the servants."

"I would have her accompany me," Theron said. "She is to me as a second set of eyes and ears. At my age, I find her assistance invaluable."

"But she was not invited to this gathering; you were," the woman said, a stubborn edge in her voice.

Theron noted that even though his sister held her tongue, she couldn't possibly look more uncomfortable, and he guessed that the impertinent young woman with the welcoming attitude was none other than the newly named Pythia herself.

"Then I will wait outside with the servants as well," Theron replied. He took off his hat and hoisted the pack over his shoulders as though he intended to settle in right where he stood. "Sister, would you please be so kind as to inform the Pythia that I have come when called. I will await an audience with her at her earliest convenience." He looked around and nodded toward a an old twisted and gnarled tree on the wide ledge below the cave's mouth. "She can find me down there, in the shade."

"Theron, I will wait—" Althaia started.

"No, no," Theron put his hand up to silence her. "I did not ask you to trudge all the way up here from Delphi to have you loiter on the mountainside alone. You will accompany me inside, or I will accompany you outside." He smiled and turned to Thea. "After your gathering, perhaps you will join us for lunch."

Her cheeks flushed blood red, but the young woman kept her voice even as she turned to Thea. "You are responsible for them both." She strode away and ducked into the cave.

"And that was our new Pythia," Theodora said quietly. "Phoibe of Arachova. She is of a different sort than my dear friend Sofia, and I thought it best that I not interrupt so you could see for yourself. It was her handmaiden who was murdered, and she thirsts for vengeance. After she learned that a mercenary with ties to Gaia was in Delphi, she sent for you with the expectation that you will see to it that her thirst is quenched."

"I did not answer her summons with that aim. I seek only to uncover the truth."

"She will be sorely disappointed," Thea said. "Come, let's not keep her waiting."

"First let me introduce Althaia of Athens, my friend and employer," Theron said as he followed his sister toward the mouth of the cave. "Who else is here?"

Theodora acknowledged Althaia with a nod and then said, "We are all here—all the priestesses of Gaia left in Hellas. We hail from Dodona, Athens, Sparta, Elis, Corinth, Tegea, Argos, and me, of course, from Thessaly. Please remove your boots." Theodora waited. "The ground upon which we walk is sacred and must not be polluted with the soles of one's shoes," she said to Althaia. "You must feel the earth beneath your feet. Here, nothing separates the mother from the child."

# CHAPTER FIFTEEN

Althaia untied and slipped off her boots, waited for Theron to do the same. Then she followed him into the dim of the cave, blinking as her eyes adjusted. She had entered another realm. Tiny dust motes hung in the shafts of sunlight. She breathed in deeply. The air smelled of moist earth and ancient stone.

The cavern was huge, the vault of the walls and ceiling arching over her like the dome of the moonless night. A few steps in from the mouth, the ground fell away in a grand sweep until it flattened out to a large level area. There, settled in a circle around a small fire, the priestesses waited. Beyond them, the floor climbed up again toward the back of the cave where a shiny, moss-covered tumble of rocks shimmered in the firelight with an eerie green glow. Where the ceiling and wall met, another opening led to what she guessed was the cave's inner chamber. Black as the abyss, surrounded with stalactites and stalagmites, it gaped like a monstrous, ravenous mouth. No way Althaia was going near there.

How long had people worshiped here, she wondered. Figures and designs scratched into the walls looked like nothing she had ever seen. They were crude, primitive, but oddly beautiful. Old. She had been in awe of the pyramids of Giza and the ancient Egyptian temples in Thebes, but this was different. This was the womb of Mother Earth, a place to commune with the goddess. It was full of power. She could almost see the maenads dancing and singing around cloven-hoofed Pan while he played his pipes and beckoned them to slake his most animalistic desires. The hair on her arms stood up at the thought.

"We must be careful as it can be slippery," Theodora smiled as she pointed to the steep slope. "Otherwise, we might all end up sliding down this hill and landing in a pile of priestesses. And that would not be very dignified."

So Theodora and Theron shared more than looks. They shared a sense of humor. Althaia smiled back into the dark before she stepped gingerly down the carpeted slope.

Once they reached the bottom, Theron lowered himself to the ground next to his sister and Althaia sat beside him. The priestesses and their attendants, girls dressed in simple white chitons, sat on thick carpets and pillows spread upon the cave floor. Althaia was thankful Theodora's "nothing separates the mother from the child" rule didn't include the damp earthen floor and her own backside.

When they had all settled in, Phoibe leaned forward and poured a libation of oil onto the fire. Sparks flew and flames danced, orange tendrils stretching toward the ceiling. When the fire had settled again, she began.

"When the gods walked the earth, Gaia suffered a grievous injustice. Apollon came from the east and claimed the power of the sacred pneuma of Delphi as his own. Today we also suffer. And we mourn. But we will not mourn for long, for soon our tears of sorrow will be replaced by the joy of vengeance. We will have justice from the priests of Apollon for Charis's death."

"You speak of justice, but what proofs of the priests' s guilt do you offer us?" Althaia was startled when Theodora interrupted Phoibe's speech. Although Phoibe's hands rested easily in her lap, Althaia could see that her body tensed, as taut and stretched as a sail straining against a raging storm.

"We all know the vapors in the adyton beneath the temple are weak and inconstant—they come and go as they will and yield little of their ancient power. If the vapors continue to diminish, the power invested in the priests of Apollon will fade, too. How long can they get away with drugging the Pythia of Apollon just so supplicants can hear incoherent babbling from behind the curtain?" Phoibe paused and looked darkly into the flames.

"She speaks the truth." Althaia turned toward the voice. On the other side of the fire pit, she could see the filmy opacity of old eyes staring into the glowing embers. "I have seen it," the old woman said.

"We know the Sacred Wars have taken their toll," Phoibe went on. "Some have hailed Philip II of Makedon as savior of Delphi. He seeks to force my fellow Phokians to restore the treasures used during the last Sacred War, and is repairing the temple. This endears him to many, but in truth he seeks only to placate his allies while he prepares his armies to conquer Athens, to conquer all Greece, and then to challenge Persia. He cares nothing for Delphi. He cares only for empire."

"Philip is only the latest in a long line of men who seek to control our destiny," the old woman added.

"Yes," Phoibe continued, "and Philon and Kleomon must know Philip will only support Delphi as long as Delphi supports Phillip—or serves his purposes. The priests are besieged on all sides, so they must consolidate their power and reassert their control of the Sacred Precinct and all the wealth it represents. The easiest way to do that is to eliminate the people's goddess once and for all and claim sole sovereignty over the Sacred Precinct for Apollon."

"But we will not let them take what is ours by right," the old woman chimed in, like the refrain in a chorus.

"I aim to reinstate the Oracle of Gaia in the Sacred Precinct, to reclaim our place at the Spring of Ge. To claim Apollon's temple as our own."

"That is a grand speech, Phoibe," Theodora spoke again. "Full of political intrigue and danger. But, as I have asked you before, if the cleft below the temple no longer retains the power of the gods, why do you seek to reclaim it?"

"Two gods cannot lay claim to the same sacred ground. There cannot be two oracles in Delphi."

"There have always been two oracles in Delphi. And what about the prophecy? One oracle falls, the other falls with it."

The old woman spoke up again. "Theodora, what would your mother say? I begin to wonder if you even hold to our most basic beliefs. Perhaps the reunion with your impious brother has affected your faith."

Theodora leaned forward. "Melanippe"—Melanippe! Althaia peered through the flames at the priestess she presumed was Nikos's mother—"I hold to the same beliefs my mother and my mother before her held to. That you now question me is testament to your desire to influence Phoibe, not my impiety."

"Quiet!" Phoibe looked at each of the priestesses in turn and then settled on Theodora. "I have the gift of sight. You do not. I am the Pythia. You are not. I have seen the danger facing us. I have seen this crime. I know who killed Charis, and I know who seeks to eliminate Gaia's cult once and for all. I swear on Gaia's eternal name, the most sacred oath in all Greece, if Philon and Kleomon seek to destroy the Oracle of Gaia to protect the Oracle of Apollon, they will find a worthy opponent in me. Even if I pay the ultimate price, the fraud, deceit, and corruption of Apollon and his priests will be exposed once and for all. I swear it!"

Phoibe's words hung in the air as ominously as the craggy stalactites looming above them. No Greek swore an oath in Gaia's name lightly.

"Beyond a history lesson and a political dialectic, you have yet to offer a single proof." Althaia jumped as Theron' smooth voice sliced through the tension. "I must tell you that the priests have asserted that you killed Charis yourselves. A sort of a Dionysian sacrifice. Kleomon even went so far as to suggest I might have done it for you."

"Kleomon," Melanippe spat his name, "would like nothing more than to extinguish our faith once and for all. He is a man of little imagination and even littler intelligence."

"Ignorance alone does not make one a murderer," Theron replied. "Having seen the body, I would wager this murderer was quite intelligent. Hardly a mark on her."

"Then Philon's your man," Melanippe croaked. Althaia saw the old priestess's attendant lean toward her and then hesitate, as if she wanted to shush the old woman but was afraid of getting bitten.

"Philon has every reason to fear me, to fear us," Phoibe cut in. "He has been skimming money from the pilgrim's offerings for years. Our resurgence and the failing power of the Oracle of Apollon threaten not only his power, but his wealth as well."

"But why would Philon not kill you, the new Pythia? If he was so afraid of you, why kill a mere attendant?" Theron pressed.

"Charis was no mere attendant! She was my ... my closest confidant and advisor." Phoibe took a breath and tried to regain her composure. "Philon is a learned man who can read and write in a dozen tongues and yet has spent the better part of his life composing obtuse verse for young and old seeking guidance for their love lives, or asking whether or not they should buy this horse or that, or purchase this estate or that, or take this woman or that to bed. It is only when a tyrant or king seeks the oracle that Philon believes his true worth is known. To the powerful, he is at once a wise advisor and a manipulative schemer. His verse, like the Gordion knot, cannot be cut through or unraveled by mere mortals. He has a stunning mind, a silken tongue, and a shrunken heart, and his deceit of the protectors of Delphi, the Amphiktyonic League, is testament to all three."

"And that proves what?"

Phoibe could not believe Theodora's brother, son and sister of priestesses, was speaking to her in such a way. "It proves he has everything to gain from eliminating the threat we pose!"

In one movement, Theron stood and towered over the group of women. "Honored Pythia. You have characterized the priests of Apollon as nothing more than craven, ignorant, greedy, and power hungry men. Yesterday morning at the theater, what Kleomon had to say about you was equally flattering. Your opinions of each other do not matter, and for all I know—or care—you both may be right. Distaste and distrust, however, do not necessarily a murderer make. If you know who killed her, and if you want my help in pursuing her killer, then you must give me more convincing evidence than what you have presented thus far. And you must think. Could there be no other motive? No other guilty party?"

"None," Phoibe said flatly. "It was the priests. I knew Charis like no other. There can be no other reason."

"You may have known Charis, but I know men. I assure you there could be many other reasons."

"Are not the priests of Apollon men?" Melanippe screeched, her voice sawing into the cool damp air like a dull blade as her filmy eyes sought Theron in the firelight. "The minds of men are easily corrupted, their hearts easily seduced. Priests are no different from soldiers or politicians or, even, philosophers." Althaia could almost hear the old woman's spittle pop and sizzle as it hit the glowing coals.

"Indeed," Theron said, his voice cool and composed. "Which is why it is premature to rule out as suspects soldiers, politicians, or even philosophers. Perhaps Kleomon was right as well. Perhaps I killed the young woman."

Water dripped deep within the cave, and a cloaked figure—a bodyguard?—shifted in the shadows. Althaia could barely sit still. Theron looked around the circle at the priestesses, several of whom put their heads together and whispered while their young attendants kept their wide eyes focused on him as if he were a shade from Hades sent to snatch them across the River Styx without so much as a coin for safe passage.

"How will you really know who killed Charis unless you seek to discover the truth instead of simply declaring that you already know it? There is a way, Pythia, to discover the truth. Or at least attempt to."

"And pray what is that, wise son of Gaia?"

"It's a procedure I call an autopsia."

"To see for oneself? What are you talking about?"

"An autopsia. Yes, it means, literally, to see for oneself, to examine, and if necessary even dissect, a body with the intent to see with our own eyes how the person died. My employer and friend Althaia has been trained in the procedure." As if their heads were controlled by a master puppeteer, everyone turned at once to look at Althaia. Everyone but Phoibe, who could not bring herself to look at Theron's companion. "If you give her permission to perform an examination of Charis's body, there is a chance she can find something that will help us determine how your attendant died. If we know how she died, we may be able to determine who killed her. And why."

"Out of the question. I've never heard of such a thing." Phoibe's low growl emanated from deep in her chest.

"It is a sacrilege! That's what it is!" Melanippe hissed. She tried to rise and turned to glare at her attendant. "Kalliope!" she barked, and the girl, with a barely concealed look of contempt on her face, jumped to her feet and helped the old woman stand. Melanippe hobbled around the circle toward Theron. As she drew near, Althaia smelled the stale sickly-sweet odor of old age, moist skin, and rotting teeth. She crinkled her nose and tried not to inhale. "We will never allow anyone to paw over her body as if it were nothing more than a philosopher's plaything! You should be ashamed of yourself. You were a disgrace as a boy and you are a disgrace now."

"Melanippe, you forget you are speaking to my brother!" Theodora's voice was harsh.

"I know exactly to whom I am speaking, Theodora."

Althaia wanted to defend Theron but knew that he could take care of himself. In fact, he seemed to be the only one in the cave not ready to ignite like a well-oiled pyre.

"It is up to you, Pythia," he said. "Do you want my help or not? Do you seek the truth or not?"

"I already know the truth," Phoibe said.

"Then you must already know that Heraklios has engaged my services to help find the girl's killer. I came today only to honor my sister, and to discover what you know about the girl's death. If I am to seek the truth, I will follow whatever path takes me there."

Phoibe had finally had enough. "Fine words for a man with your reputation!" she spat. "You and your rich whore."

*Theron's whore?* Althaia's tongue stuck in her throat. So that's why Phoibe wouldn't look at her.

"If you are as ill-informed about Charis's death as you are about my relationship with my employer, then you will be more hindrance than help in seeking to find your attendant's killer. Further, if you seek to impede my pursuit of the truth, I will be forced to consider what you may have to gain by obstructing my inquiry. Perhaps you seek to hide the truth about her death because you are protecting someone. Or maybe you see the opportunity to advance your own political ends."

"How dare you suggest I would have anything to gain! That the Pythia of Gaia would seek to benefit from such a crime. From the death of my handmaid and my closest friend!" Her voice was rough, as if dragging the words from her throat had rubbed it raw.

Althaia had no idea what proofs she might find if she were able to examine Charis. Maybe none at all. But the august and imposing priestesses had none either. As much as she could imagine Kleomon as the killer, she knew no jury in all Hellas would render a guilty verdict—especially when women were usually not even allowed to testify.

She turned to Phoibe, leaned forward and spoke through clenched teeth. "You say you know who killed your attendant. You say you've seen it. So tell us. How was she killed? Where did it happen? When? If you know, tell Theron, and he and Heraklios will bring her killer to justice. If not, do not hinder our efforts to find out."

The growl that rumbled from Phoibe's chest roiled upward like steam from a boiling pot. She struggled to her feet and loomed over Althaia, her hand raised as if ready to strike. Althaia couldn't take her eyes off her. Phoibe's face was contorted in rage. She trembled as if Poseidon himself possessed her limbs. "None of you are willing to recognize what Apollon and his priests are up to. Charis's death is just the tip of the arrow. Right now they are sowing the seeds of our destruction. Using every instrument in their power. Yes! Every instrument. Even—"

She broke off suddenly, looking around as if she just discovered where she was. Every priestess and every attendant watched her, waiting, expecting something. She turned, tripped over her skirts, regained her balance and scrambled up the slippery rocks toward the monster's gaping maw. Althaia watched and wondered how anyone could go into the inner chamber of the cave alone, without a torch. She must be mad. Althaia shuddered and watched with fascination as Phoibe slipped and fell to her knees, then crawled her way up to the jagged lip and disappeared into the black.

# CHAPTER SIXTEEN

Praxis was waiting when Althaia and Theron, followed by several priestesses, emerged from the cave, squinting into the bright sunshine. On the wide grassy ledge below the cave, the slaves and guards looked up with interest. Nephthys was among them, setting out bread, cheese, wine and dried fish for lunch. Except for favoring her left leg, she appeared to have recovered from her nearly disastrous tumble.

He didn't think he would ever forget that moment, the moment when he thought he had lost her before he'd ever had a chance to really have her, before he could tell her how he felt, tell her all the things he'd been thinking since he first saw her up on the slaver's auction block. When he'd seen her grab that blackened tree stump, he'd prayed to every god he'd ever heard of to make it hold. His prayers were answered, and he'd pulled her back, away from the edge. "I've got you," he'd whispered. But she'd said nothing. "Nephthys, look at me. I've got you." Still she did not turn. He wrapped one arm around her waist, pried her fingers from the ancient wood, and pulled her to him. Every muscle in her body was rigid. He'd scooted backward again and again, slowly moving back toward the path, toward safety. As he scooted, he kicked at the ground, sending loose stones disappearing over the edge, into the blue. "You're safe," he whispered in her ear. "I've got you." Finally, far enough from the edge to breathe easily, he stopped and held her snug against him. Her muscles slowly loosened, like snow pack melting on a warm spring day.

He'd put his hands on her shoulders and turned her to face him. She began to tremble, and then her shoulders shook and he recognized the months of fear, anger, dread, self-pity, and loneliness spilling out in a torrent of tears. Nephthys was never meant to be a slave. He didn't know how she'd come to be in Piraeus, but she'd not been born to servitude, that much was certain. She leaned into him, and buried her face in his neck. He held her against his chest and rocked her back and forth. A stone the size of a fist and as sharp as a Makedonían sarissa stabbed at his backside. But he didn't care. He squinted out at the blue void beyond the cliff's edge where a lone raptor circled in a cloudless sky. Her tears ran down his neck and tickled as they formed little rivulets on his chest. He stroked her back and whispered, "I'm here. I'm here. I'm here," until it sounded like a lullaby, a love song. Finally, her sobs quieted. She took a deep breath and her body settled into his as if it were a long lost key finally at home in its lock.

After a moment, she pushed away from him. She wiped her face with her cloak, smearing tears, snot, and dirt across her cheeks. He took the hem of his cloak, wetted it in his mouth, and wiped her face. As though he was Hippokrates himself, he probed her shoulder and looked her over for cuts and bruises.

"You're going to be sore," he'd told her. "You almost pulled your shoulder out of its bone socket. Good thing you were wearing a heavy cloak. Otherwise, you'd be really scraped up. As it is," he traced the edge of a long scratch on her slender brown leg, "you look like a wild boar got hold of you. But you will live."

She nodded and kept her eyes fixed on his face.

"Can you walk?" he asked, as he helped her to her feet.

"I think so." She took a few tentative steps and glanced fearfully back toward the edge of the cliff.

"I tell you what, let's get you away from here." He bent, swept her into his arms, and strode back up the path to where Theron and Althaia stood waiting. Nephthys wrapped her arms around his neck and rested her still tear-stained face against his chest as if he'd carried her that way a thousand times. As he climbed, he became acutely aware of the rise and fall of her breasts against his. He held her closer and felt her arms tighten around his shoulders in response. And now every time he looked at her, thought of her, the emotion of that moment filled him so full he wondered if he would choke on it. She had very nearly gone over the cliff, and he couldn't remember when he'd ever been happier.

"Praxis, join us," Theron said, bringing him back to the moment with a start. "This is my sister, Theodora." Praxis did not have to look too closely to see the resemblance. "And this," Theodora said, "is Eumelia, priestess of Argos." Praxis acknowledged the two women, but Theodora was already on to business.

"Recently," Theodora said, "we have discovered our counsel is not welcome in Delphi. Melanippe and Charis and their desire to wield power through Phoibe have taken precedence over the guidance of all the other priestesses. Even though the others grumble, we are the only two who dared to challenge them. Phoibe says the priests of Apollon murdered Charis and in her rage and sorrow, she wants revenge. But we, Eumelia and I, are not so sure. If this autopsia you spoke of can help us avert a disaster, an irreparable rift between Apollon and Gaia, then we would know more of it."

Praxis tensed as Althaia began. In his heart, he had hoped none of the priestesses would support Theron's idea that Althaia examine the body. It was selfish of him, but the risks outweighed the rewards. No one deserved to be treated as the dead woman had been treated, but if Althaia was discovered handling the dead....

"As Theron said, while in Egypt I studied with a priest who was an expert in mummification. He also studied human anatomy to satisfy his own curiosity. As a healer and philosopher, he believed that through careful, systematic observation he could identify how someone had died. After an examination, which he conducted during the mummification process, he would speak to the relatives to confirm whether or not his findings were correct. During my time with him, I learned how to identify the four humors, the major organs, and the source of blood and bile. I also learned how to identify certain tell-tale signs of age and disease that can be read only by the trained eye. By reading these signs, it is almost as if the dead can speak to the living, as if they can reveal the secrets of their last moments."

"If you perform such an examination, do you think Charis will speak to you?" Theodora asked.

"If the gods will it, yes."

"As women, we are limited in what we can do to right this wrong. But yet we must see that justice is done and that a greater injustice is averted," Theodora said.

"We can go to the Amphiktyonik League and ask that Heraklios find Charis's killer and bring him to justice, but we are not family," Eumelia added. "We have no standing in the courts of Delphi and we cannot expect Heraklios to protect Phoibe after we are gone. He cares little for our concerns or fears."

"On the contrary," Althaia said. "Remember, Heraklios has already retained Theron's services to help him find Charis's killer. Even if he puts his own political position above all, he surely knows that he will not long keep that position if there is an unresolved murder in the Sacred Precinct."

"If you are to conduct this examination, you must act tonight," Theodora said. "Phoibe sent her consort Georgios to Charis's village to notify her brother. Both her parents are dead and she had no other living family. We expect Georgios to return with the brother sometime tomorrow. At that point, they will take custody of the body and bring it here for her funeral rites."

"Will Heraklios allow the examination?" Eumelia asked.

"Because most believe the whole idea of such an examination is a sacrilege, I believe it is better if we keep our plans to ourselves," Theron answered.

His sister studied him a moment. "Very well. So how do you propose to arrange it on such short notice?" she said.

Praxis suddenly felt Theron's eyes—and everyone else's—turn toward him. Typical, he thought. He knew exactly what was coming. *I will be dragged into this scheme whether I will it or not,* he thought.

Theron turned toward his sister. "Praxis and I have a history of, shall we say, embarking on adventures together. We will find a way."

"However you accomplish it," Theodora said, clasping her brother's hand in hers, "send word to me of your findings. I am staying with Melanippe at a farmhouse just north of the Delphi-Krissa road. We will determine what action to take after we hear from you. For now, we must return to the Pythia." She kissed her brother's weathered cheek and took Althaia's face in her hands. "Our hopes rest on you, Althaia of Athens. I pray Gaia is with you and that the voice of Charis reveals her secrets to you." With that, she and

Eumelia slipped back into the cave.

Althaia looked at Theron and then Praxis. "I don't know how you'll pull this off, but I have no doubt the two of you will see that this examination happens." She took Praxis's hand in hers. "And I feel sure the gods will protect me and guide my hand. We will discover the truth."

Praxis sighed, squeezed her hand, and shook his head. "I feel sure it is my lot to protect you no matter what the gods do or say and that this 'adventure' is dangerous, misguided, and … god's balls, we better start planning. We don't have much time."

# CHAPTER SEVENTEEN

Nephthys pushed Menandros's front door open with her hip. Carrying the blanket, lunch basket, and empty wine flask, she hesitated in the hallway and listened to the voices coming from the andron. Her hope for a leisurely lunch sitting on a blanket next to Praxis had been dashed as soon as Althaia and Theron emerged from the cave. She could not stop thinking about how his arms felt around her after he pulled her back from the edge of the cliff. There had been such an ease and familiarity after that—until Althaia and Theron joined them. Before, she had been the center of Praxis's attention. But once they appeared, she disappeared, forgotten. They had hurriedly gulped down their food while Praxis listened intently as they told of their encounter with the priestesses. She had watched in silence as the three leaned in toward each other, talking in hushed tones, planning how to get Althaia into the storehouse where the priests were keeping the body.

And now she could hear them in the andron with Menandros. They talked over one another, interrupted, argued. They sounded like a family. Where was her family? Where were her brothers? Her sisters? Her knees threatened to buckle beneath her, and she leaned against the wall. "No! I cannot think of them," she whispered. But it was too late.

The images flooded back. Images of the day she had finished her tasks at the Temple of Amun-Ra, the day she had escaped her husband's unwelcome attentions and joined her friends in a race down to the river. They laughed while they ran, pushing and jostling to see who could dive in first. The sun was directly overhead and the High Priest rested in his cool, shaded chambers in the temple. Most likely neither he, nor her husband, an adept to the High Priest, heard them scream when the slavers sprang from their watching places in the reeds and caught them, right there on the banks of the Nile in front of the most sacred monuments in Egypt. That was the last time she touched her foot to the land of the Pharaohs, the land where her parents surely wept for their stolen daughter. Had her husband wept for her? Perhaps, perhaps not. As she listened to voices from the andron, she wondered where her friends were. Bought? Sold? Dead?

The voices got louder and Nephthys flattened herself against the wall. Praxis hurried from the room and headed toward the front door with his traveling cloak swirling behind him. He didn't turn around, didn't notice her. Maybe dead was preferable to invisible.

# CHAPTER EIGHTEEN

"Palamedes has been a temple slave most of his life, and he knows every inch of the Sacred Precinct. If anyone can get you in and out without being seen, it will be him," Menandros said as he waved at a slave to refill their wine cups. Althaia was comfortably ensconced on a couch and Theron leaned against the wall looking as if, like a Spartan, he was ready to leap into action at the sound of an aulos. Menandros adjusted the pillows behind him, settled back on his couch and propped up his feet. Although custom dictated that respectable women were not allowed into the andron of a house, Menandros prided himself on breaking staid old rules and welcomed Althaia into his. Besides, because he was not married, he had no use for a gynaikon and so didn't have a room equipped for female guests. And he knew Theron would have invited Althaia into the andron anyway—and probably already had—so he might as well make her comfortable.

"I won't be satisfied until our plans are firm," Theron said. "As loathe as I am to dine with Philon this evening, the distraction it provides us will be useful."

"How so? I've suffered through more of Philon's symposia than I care to remember—many of which I don't remember—and none of them were particularly useful," Menandros said.

"From what you've told me," Theron said, "Philon believes himself the intellectual equal of any philosopher in Hellas, and I do not doubt he has spies and informants in every city who help him stay abreast of ideas and intrigues. The information he accumulates surely helps him in his position as an interpreter for the Oracle of Apollon, and during the pilgrimage season, he must have ample opportunity to spar with tyrants, kings, princes, and other important men—and women—over the news of the day. But during the cold winter months, how does he satisfy his need to demonstrate his superiority of mind? Wrestling with Kleomon?

Menandros barked a laugh and nearly spilled his wine. "By the gods, Theron, you've ruined me for life. I'll never get the vision of fat old Kleomon and wily Philon naked, oiled up, and circling each other in the gymnasium. That's a wrestling match I would pay to not see."

"I may not sleep for weeks," Althaia added.

"You certainly will not sleep tonight, I fear," Theron said. "I say our time spent with Philon will be useful because it will provide a distraction from the body in the temple storeroom. A murder in the Sacred Precinct is no trifling matter, and Philon must be concerned about the consequences and about any uproar in the community from having the precinct so defiled."

"He better be," Menandros interrupted. "My theater must be purified and re-sanctified immediately."

"The sooner things return to normal the better. There are always some who look for opportunities to cause trouble, and an open rift between the priests of Apollon and the priestesses of Gaia may provide just such an opportunity. Our job tonight is to keep Philon's mind off of Charis."

"He didn't seem all that interested in her in the first place," Althaia interjected. The way Philon, Kleomon, and even Heraklios, dismissed the girl's body as if she were a mere nuisance angered and disappointed her. Who should mourn the taking of a life if not the priests and enforcers of the law?

"True," Theron said. "He must be concerned about the possible fall out, and it is obvious you—the educated daughter of a wealthy man—intrigue him. So tonight you must distract him. Impress him. Charm him. We don't want him sending any servants over to check on the body in the middle of the night."

"Charm him how?" She cocked an eyebrow at Theron. "I am no hetaira practiced in the arts of entertaining drunken men. It sounds like you want me to pluck the lyre while standing on my head."

"I'm asking you to use your wits, my dear." His voice was edged with exasperation, but he offered her a please-forgive-me smile. "If you have any left," he added under his breath and then ducked as Althaia whipped a pillow at his head.

"I wish Praxis would return soon." She sighed. "I would feel much better about the evening if I knew our plan before we left for Philon's."

"Of course." Menandros reached over and patted her hand like she was a little girl. "If Praxis doesn't return before you leave, I'll send my houseboy to Philon's with a message as soon as he gets back."

"What sort of message will allow us to abandon our host in the middle of a meal?" Althaia asked.

"Don't you worry about that. I'll think of something that is sure to work. I'm a playwright after all! In the meantime, you tell Philon to get my theater re-sanctified."

Althaia shuddered. "I don't think people tell Philon to do anything. He seems the sort to give commands, not take them."

"Philon is more bark than bite." Menandros appeared to dismiss the entire idea of Philon with a wave of his hand. "I need my theater back. We had just started rehearsing my new play."

"A new play? What is it about?" she asked.

"Oh, no," Theron said with an exaggerated groan and pushed himself away from the wall. He sat down, reclining his long frame on an empty couch. "Make sure you're comfortable, Althaia. We're going to be here for a while."

"Don't pay any attention to him," Menandros said with a laugh. "Theron is a frustrated poet himself and is tormented with jealousy."

"Tormented. Yes, I keep forgetting," Theron said.

"Keep quiet, old man. I have a beautiful woman asking about my work." Menandros turned to Althaia. "Your tutor and I have lived very different lives, but we have similar goals. Every time he thinks he has stumbled on an answer to one of life's vexing questions, he finds himself tripping over yet another problem, yet another unanswered question which bores into his mind like an awl into wood, leaving holes in his logic and gaps in his understanding. In other words, my dear, it seems the more he learns—whether about this old world or the people who populate it—the littler he knows." Menandros stopped to take a long drink.

"Go on, old friend, I am anxious to learn the inner workings of my mind."

"I'm sure you are, but I'm getting to my point, so be quiet." Menandros turned his attention back to Althaia. "We are, unfortunately, kindred brethren in this respect. Every answer seems to spontaneously generate a new question, and answering those questions is like embarking on a journey. We think we know our destination—let's say we want to climb to the top of a mountain. We can survey the path from a distance and even guess how long it might take. But we cannot know what we will encounter along the way. And then, once we arrive at the top, once we achieve our goal, what will we see but a whole new vista, a whole new landscape to explore. *A whole new question.* For Theron, answering those questions has been a life-long journey. He has traveled farther than I can even comprehend. But for me, a playwright, answering those questions requires putting words on the page. In the past, I concentrated on tragedy, on the anguish that arises from never having your questions answered. But these days, I'm concentrating on comedies because they are more tragic than tragedies."

"More tragic than tragedy?" Althaia asked, brows knitted in confusion. "How can that be?"

"Reflecting the human condition and making the audience laugh at themselves in the process is much more difficult than writing a tragedy. Life itself is tragic. To write a tragedy is simply to be a copyist. There is no true creativity involved. Oh, I've cried and drunk my way through many a tragedy." He was quiet for a moment, staring off into the distance. "With tragedy there is pain, to be sure. Deep pain. Timeless pain. But comedy is something else entirely. Indeed, the act of writing a true comedy is a tragic endeavor for the playwright. He struggles with each line. He pours his deepest insights onto the page. He crafts them and molds them and tortures them into witticisms that must make the audience laugh—lest he be laughed at. He invests the essence of his very being in the turn of a phrase, in the timing of each poisoned dart. And all the time, he is stripping himself bare, naked, flagellating himself before the eyes of everyone he has loved—or wanted to love. With each word, his soul dies a little more. Sooner or later, he wastes away until there is nothing left...."

Menandros' trailed off into an anguished whisper. He dabbed his eyes with his sleeve and Althaia, deeply moved to see a man so affected by the toll of his work, reached out to comfort him.

Theron laughed and raised his cup in a toast. "Bravo! That is tragic indeed, Menandros. You're going to have to write many a comedy before you waste away to nothing."

"Thank you for reminding me why I like you much better when you live far away."

"Lest you've forgotten, Althaia," Theron said, "Menandros was an accomplished actor before he picked up his pen and unrolled his first scroll."

"You are a spoilsport. Can you not allow me the enjoyment of the comforting touch of a beautiful woman—even if for but a brief moment?"

"Enjoy, my friend. And while we wait for Praxis, go ahead and tell her about your play. I need a nap anyway." Theron laughed as the playwright cleared his throat and threw his arms wide, ready to deliver a soliloquy.

# Chapter Nineteen

"Sir, I am sorry to interrupt."

"What is it, Basileios?"

"A messenger has come from the playwright's. Your guests are to return immediately."

Althaia jumped up so quickly Philon was taken aback.

It was still early in the evening, but to Theron time seemed to be slipping away. He'd had to shoot Althaia several dark glances to warn her to stop fidgeting. As Philon interrogated them both, they grew increasingly anxious that there had been no message from Menandros, no news from Praxis. And there seemed to be no escape from Philon who, while maintaining a façade of genteel hospitality, treated them both with condescension and barely concealed arrogance.

"Return? Whatever for? We've barely begun our repast," Philon said, waving at a servant to refill his glass of wine.

"It seems your guests' handmaid has taken ill," Basileios said.

"What an unfortunate turn of events." Philon looked up at Althaia. "You do not seem surprised."

Althaia held his gaze. "I fear she was overly tired from our travels and has not recovered," She looked to Theron for help, and he rose to stand at her side. "She is new to my service, but I have grown quite fond of her," she continued.

"I see," Philon said. "In that case, Basileios, fetch the physician and take him to the playwright's house." He waved the guard away and turned back to Althaia and Theron. "Sit, please. There's no question of us cutting our evening short. Basileios will see to it that my own personal physician examines her. She will receive the finest care Delphi has to offer," he said with a self-satisfied smile.

Althaia sank back to her couch with a forced smile painted across her lips, but Theron remained standing. "We thank you, of course, but I'm sure the handmaid would be more comfortable being treated by someone she knows."

"Your concern for this poor girl does you justice, but her comfort will be better ensured by seeing to it that she is healed. My physician has read every treatise written by Hippokrates of Kos. I'm sure even you, in all your travels, cannot boast that accomplishment."

No, Theron thought, I have not read every damn thing Hippokrates wrote down, and I am no physician, but then again we have no patient. And I've actually been to Kos and toured Hippokrates' Asklepieion and my patience is running thin. "She speaks little Greek, I'm afraid," Theron said. "She's Egyptian."

"Ah!" Philon clapped. "All the better. Sit now and drink up. My physician speaks Egyptian like a native."

* * * *

As slaves brought out the next course, a thick lentil stew with spiced lamb served with warm brown bread, Philon pressed Theron on his travels and Althaia on her political views. Theron tried to keep himself calm by studying their host, watching how he interacted with his servants, and trying to gain a measure of the man who was one of the most powerful priests in all Greece. But eventually, he could think of nothing else but getting Althaia out of Philon's dining room and into the temple storeroom.

"I have been truly delighted by your conversation, Althaia of Athens," Philon said at last. "I can now report back to my friends in your fair city that you are indeed as educated and self-possessed a young woman as I am ever likely to meet. Your father, and your tutor," he raised a glass to Theron, "clearly spared nothing in your education."

"I thank you for the compliment," Althaia said as her knee jittered up and down.

"But the evening cannot end, before—"

"Sir, I am sorry to interrupt again." Basileios stood in the doorway.

"What news? Have you returned with the physician? Has he treated the slave?" Philon asked.

"He has concluded the examination and is concocting a medicinal draught for her now."

"Excellent. That will be all."

Basileios didn't move from the doorway.

"What?" Philon demanded.

"The playwright is complaining of a bad case of the unwalkable disease and insists Theron return to look at his toe."

"His toe?"

"His toe, sir. He is sitting there in his andron with his foot up on a cushion moaning and groaning about his toe."

"Isn't the physician still there?"

"Yes, sir."

"Then by the gods, man, have him look at the playwright's toe."

"But Menandros wants him." Basileios cast a disdainful look at Theron.

Theron and Althaia stood, but Philon motioned them to sit back down.

"I daresay the playwright's toe will not fall off before our dinner is concluded."

"His humors must be out of equilibrium again," Theron offered. "I've treated his gout before, and I know it can be quite painful." He wanted to wring Philon's and Menandros's necks. He and Althaia needed to escape, but they couldn't raise Philon's suspicions and this excuse was ridiculous. If they left because of Menandros's damnable toe, Philon would surely suspect something odd was going on.

"Painful or not, no one dies of the gout. Now sit down and let us at least finish our meal."

* * * *

Even as Theron and Althaia parried Philon's queries about his travels and her education, Theron searched for ways to extract themselves from the grip of the priest's wearying hospitality. Though the whole evening had lasted no more than three hours, time seemed to pass as slow as Aesopos's tortoise on the race course, while ideas for new excuses to take their leave flitted through his mind like the fleet-footed hare. The conversation finally turned from politics and petty gossip to philosophy and Theron tried his best to answer quickly without betraying his frustration and eagerness to be done with the whole wretched evening.

Where do you stand on his theory of universals? Are you with Plato or Aristotle? What do you think about causation and the idea of a prime mover? Do you agree with Democritus, Plato, or Aristotle on the nature of matter and the elements? Are you a follower of Pythagoras and do you know why he is afraid of beans? Do you believe the earth is round and that the face of it changes dramatically over time? That the sun is larger than the earth and far enough away to shine even on the Milky Way? What do you think of Protagoras's belief that man is the measure of all things? Philon's questions went on and on until Theron felt he might truly strangle the man. He is playing with us, Theron thought. We are nothing more than entertaining diversions on an otherwise tedious evening. Finally, just as he feared they would grow old in Philon's company, the priest suddenly stood and motioned for servants to clear the tables.

"I'm afraid our delightful evening must come to a close," he said. "I have obligations to attend to, and I'm certain you are eager to check on your handmaid and make sure Menandros's toe is still attached to his foot."

The torture was over.

# CHAPTER TWENTY

Althaia held the kylix to her nose, sniffed, and made a face. She handed it to Theron who smelled it and then took a sip.

"What is it?" Nephthys asked.

"Most likely crushed iris and rose mixed with vinegar," he said.

"The physician mixed it up and made a poultice for my head. I moaned a bit and then pretended I had fallen asleep." Theron handed the drinking cup back. "It smells sickly sweet," Nephthys said.

"Perhaps we should make Menandros drink the rest," Theron said, casting a dark look at the playwright.

"It all turned out well enough," Menandros said, a trifle defensively.

"Well enough? Is that what you call it?" Theron laughed. "The one thing you accomplished is that Philon believes you are an idiot."

"Oh, that's nothing new," Menandros declared. "He thinks everyone is an idiot. Now shut up and let's hear the news from Praxis." Menandros unlatched a wax tablet and took out a sharpened stylus.

Praxis looked up from where he reclined, finishing his late dinner. "Everyone's talking about it. News of a murder in the Sacred Precinct is spreading across Phokis like a gale, and apparently Philon now fears the news will incite a mob." He tore off a piece of bread from a long loaf, smashed it in a bowl of shimmering olive oil, mushed it into a soft lump of goat cheese and stuffed it in his mouth.

"A mob? Why?" Althaia asked.

"Tensions between the priests and the priestesses, I gather. And because locals are upset the body is being kept so near the temple. The body is polluting all Delphi, some are saying."

"I presume Heraklios posted guards outside the storehouse?" Theron asked.

"He did and they remain at their posts although there is nothing to guard."

"Nothing to guard?" Althaia said. "I don't understand."

"The body is no longer in the storehouse. Philon had it moved and neglected to inform Heraklios. Palamedes only found out because he ran into a couple of Philon's bodyguards deep inside the temple complex. Down where the slave quarters are. Suspicious, he poked around after the guards left. Once he found the girl's body, he went back to his quarters where he had a little visit from Basileios, Philon's personal bodyguard." Praxis tore off another piece of bread.

"We met Basileios this evening at Philon's," Theron said.

Praxis nodded as he took a long drink of water.

"Get on with it, man," Menandros cried, tapping his stylus against his wax tablet. "This is better than any play I could write."

"I'm sorry. I haven't eaten since up at the cave," Praxis said through another mouthful of bread and cheese. "Basileios urged Palamedes to keep quiet about the girl's body. He said Philon fears that Kleomon's gang of 'rabble rousers' will make trouble. According to Palamedes, Kleomon fancies himself some sort of Sokrates with a group of young men as his acolytes, and since the old priest despises the followers of Gaia, Philon suspects that the young men will break in and try to desecrate the body—just for entertainment—or to impress Kleomon with their bravery."

"I know Kleomon's group," Mendandros said. "They're a bunch of rich, privileged sycophants who would rather fawn over the old man than do an honest day's work, but they don't seem violent. They gather at the inn right up the road. The Dolphin's Cove. It's owned by a man named Diokles. Now there's an interesting character."

Nephthys refilled Praxis's glass and he drained it. "That's where Nikos, Theron's messenger, is staying. In fact, he should be here in just a moment.

He was right behind me."

"The priestess's son? Coming here?" Althaia heard herself ask as her heart flip-flopped at the sound of Nikos's name. The idea of a mob outside the storehouse was unnerving, but seeing Nikos again....

Before Praxis had answered, the door swung open and Zenon announced Nikomachos of Dodona. Althaia barely had a chance to adjust her headband before the man was standing just a few feet from her.

"Ah, here he is," Praxis said. "Zenon, bring another chair."

"No need," Nikos said. "I can only stay a moment."

"Do you know our host, Menandros the playwright?" Theron asked.

"Not formally." He greeted Menandros, who sized him up as if determining what role to cast him in.

"I ran into Nikos on my way back from the Sacred Precinct," Praxis continued. "We were able to strike a deal of sorts."

"How so?" Theron turned to Nikos.

"I understand that Thea and Eumelia sanctioned the examination you proposed. If they are in favor of the idea, then I would like to help you make it happen."

"What about your mother?" Althaia asked.

A shadow flickered across Nikos's brow. "I understand she was less than welcoming at the Korycian Cave, but I wouldn't concern yourself. If Thea thinks what you're doing is a good idea, then I will do my part to help you."

Althaia couldn't sit still while Nikos stood so calmly before her, looking down at her with his bright green eyes. She got up and poked at the fire so she could look across at him, see the full length of him.

"So what is this deal?" Theron asked.

"Praxis explained that you are in need of a diversion so you can get into the storehouse. I believe Diokles and I will be able to give you one. It will not take much to get a few men riled up and ready to confront the priests over the desecration of the Sacred Precinct. Some of the townspeople are clamoring for blood anyway."

"Diokles?" Althaia asked. "He's the one who owns that inn. Is he a man to be trusted?"

"The Dolphin's Cove. I've known him most of my life and when I'm in Delphi, I always stay at The Cove."

"So," Theron said, "while you create a diversion, we will be able to get Althaia into the storehouse."

"Exactly," Nikos said.

"And what do you get in return?" Theron asked.

"I will be the conduit for taking what you learn from the autopsia to Thea and, yes, to my mother. My mother will want—will expect—to know what you find. I will pass your findings to her. It is part of the role I play for her."

Theron considered Nikos for a moment. "Does Thea know about this?"

"Not about the diversion, but it was she who told me about the examination."

"Well then, go make your plans with Diokles. Send a messenger when you are setting out and we will send word back to you when it is all over."

Nikos's eyes rested on Althaia. "May the goddess watch over you." He turned to Theron and Praxis. "I will take your leave then." And without another word, he disappeared into the corridor.

The room was silent a moment until Theron was sure he heard the front door shut behind Nikos. He got up, went to the door and checked the corridor. He turned to Praxis. "You made a deal with Nikos to provide a diversion so we can get Althaia into the storehouse. And yet you told us the body is no longer in the storehouse."

"Ah, you are right, my friend," Praxis wiped the back of his hand across his lips and answered with a sly smile. "It is not in the storehouse. It is in the temple. Where no one would ever think to look for it."

"In the temple!" Menandros squirmed in his seat and clapped like a child presented with a new toy.

"Are you saying that the body is in—" Theron started.

"—the *adyton*," Praxis finished.

"The inner sanctum!" Menandros exclaimed, nearly jumping up and down in his chair. "Ooh, even I couldn't have thought of that."

Althaia was stunned. Surely, they did not still hope to perform an examination on the body if it rested in the inner sanctum of the Temple of Apollon. How would they even get in there? Entry by anyone but the Pythia and the priests was forbidden.

Theron met Praxis's eyes. "You did not tell Nikos the body had been moved."

"I did not see the need to share that information," Praxis said. "He believes we will be entering the storehouse from a passage inside the temple complex. He does not need to know Althaia will instead be descending into the adyton."

"Is Palamedes willing to help us even though the body was moved to the adyton?" Theron asked.

"The plan we put together was his idea."

Althaia's heart pounded. "By the gods, Praxis, I can't go in there by myself!"

"Of course not," he turned to face Nephthys, who stood quietly in a corner. "Nephthys is going in with you."

"But, wait!" Through the throbbing noise in her ears, Althaia heard her own voice as if it echoed from a great distance. "Isn't it a sacrilege—a dead body in the adyton, where the god speaks through the Pythia?"

"That's exactly what Palamedes asked Basileios. The guard said Philon performed rituals on the room itself—to de-sanctify it while the body is in there. Just in case Apollon takes offense that the place is being used as a morgue. When the body is removed, he'll go back in and re-sanctify it. Since the Pythia hasn't started prophesying yet this season, no one ever goes in there. It's the safest place."

"That Philon is a delightfully clever man," Menandros said.

"Should we inform Heraklios that the body has been moved?" Theron asked.

"Will he be an ally or an impediment to our plans?" Praxis asked. "You are the one intent on having Althaia examine the body. I have devised a plan. It is up to you to decide whether to let the general in on it or not."

"Perhaps we will be better served if no one outside this room knows of the full extent of our activities."

Althaia said nothing. She felt like a child trying hard to work out three plus eight and finally deciding she lacked the requisite fingers to solve the equation. It seemed, as far as she could tell, that she was going to be expected to enter the Temple of Apollon, descend to the adyton, and perform an autopsia examination on an associate of the Oracle of Gaia in the very room where the Pythia of Apollon sat on her tripod and drank from the sacred spring of Kassotis, where she chewed her laurel leaves and breathed in the sacred vapors that issued from the earth beneath her feet, the very room where she becomes the mouthpiece of the gods, revealing the word of Zeus and Apollon for kings, princes, tyrants, and pilgrims from throughout Greece, where the omphalos, the naval stone of the earth, sat and where Dionysos himself was buried. It was sacrilege. It was madness. It was brilliant.

# CHAPTER TWENTY-ONE

Diokles stepped outside and peered up into the darkness. The stars were so thick it looked like one of his cooks had spilled a bag of salt across the night sky. Kleomon's boys, along with a crowd of regular troublemakers Diokles kept on the payroll, gathered in front of his doorway. So far, things were going as well as could be expected for a rapidly deteriorating situation. It wasn't quite time to get the mob moving. It was a small consolation for the mess Nikos had gotten them in, but perhaps there was still an opportunity to make an extra drachma or two for the night before they had to go create this damnable distraction.

"Boys, come on in out of the night air. It's not quite time for the show."

"You better make this worth my while," one voice called out. "I couldn't care less if they had Hera herself on a slab in the temple storeroom. I've got better things to do than aggravate Heraklios."

"Pollux's prick, man? What about aggravating Philon? Nothing's better than that!" Another man said to a chorus of laughter.

"I'll tell you what's better than that," Diokles said. "Chilled wine, warm women, and the opportunity to aggravate Philon. Plus, I've got fish stew, fresh bread, and a blazing fire. And our old friend from Dodona is here. He says he'll buy a round for everybody."

"But isn't his mother one of *them*?" a voice whispered.

"Who cares as long as he's buying?" another man said. "Besides, I've known Nikos all my life." He tossed a silver obol high and reached up and plucked it out of the air, holding it up for his friend to see. "The only goddess he worships is on the backside of an Athenian owl—and he's got plenty of those to keep us in wine all night long."

"I think he worships the backside of Diokles's woman, too," another said.

"I heard that!" Diokles laughed. "You're buying your own wine, my friend. For the rest of you, Nikomachos's generosity may not last all night. Better come on in now, and after we all get something to eat and drink, we can march down there and show Philon what we think about him keeping that girl's body in the temple storehouse."

"By Zeus' beard, Diokles, you'll never change!" Someone laughed as they filed through the front door. "You'll be prying the silver from our fingertips when it's time for our burial rites!"

"I wouldn't mind a good cup of wine or two before we go, though."

"Or a steaming bowl of stew."

"Or a steamy turn with that new red-headed Illyrian!"

"That's the spirit!" Diokles said. "Come on in. We'll give ol' Philon something to think about after we sate our appetites."

# CHAPTER TWENTY-TWO

Althaia pulled her cloak around her shoulders and again patted the instrument case bound to her waist. She heard the shouts of the mob coming from farther up the hill and prayed that Nikos could keep the guards occupied. The air had turned cold and it felt like snow. Goat's bells tinkled somewhere down the hillside as they crept along the deserted street. She could barely breathe. She concentrated on Praxis's broad shoulders and padded in his wake as Nephthys followed close behind.

Before they had left the house, she had caught Praxis watching her. He'd reached up and tugged at his right earlobe—their private signal that an adventure was about to commence. It was a signal they had not used in years—not since Theron caught on to the fact that Praxis was helping her escape her lessons. She remembered the last time the signal had worked. It was during the summer and they were staying in the country. Theron was leading her through a particularly difficult mathematics lesson. Praxis had delivered a pitcher of water and shortly thereafter, she had excused herself to use the bathroom only to run down to the stables where Praxis waited with two horses bridled and ready to run. They galloped through the vineyard and down to the sea, swam the afternoon away, and returned sunburned and exhausted only to find Theron waiting in the stables. She went to bed without dinner and Praxis spent the night scrubbing tack and shoveling shit.

She had met Praxis's gaze and smiled. All the years they had shared together blurred into a single image: Her father's deathbed. Praxis's tears. The two of them holding her father's hands as he breathed his last. Lysandros had loved Praxis as dearly as he loved her. It suddenly hit her. Why her father had never taken that final step, why he had never granted Praxis his freedom. Manumission was a simple matter. Masters freed their favored slaves every day. Over the years, she had lectured her father. You know as well as I do, she would argue, a man like Praxis should be bound to no one, owned by no one. Praxis is my concern, her father would reply. But at that moment she knew. Her father never took that step for the same reason she had not taken it once she became Praxis's master. Her knees buckled and she'd grabbed the back of a chair. Praxis was still a slave because she could not bear to free him, because she could not bear to lose him. She'd stared into his Aegean blue eyes and returned their childhood signal. She had his loyalty and his friendship, but she did not deserve it.

Now she pushed those thoughts aside and made herself think of the task ahead. There was nothing she could do about Praxis now anyway. A dog barked in the distance followed by the screeching yowl of a cat and she felt the hair stand up on the back of her neck. After a while, the massive stone walls of the Sacred Precinct loomed before them and a figure stepped out from the shadows.

Palamedes. A wordless greeting. The potter looked Althaia and Nephthys over and then turned to lead them down a steep hill on what, in some long-forgotten time, might have been a path along the wall. Brambles tugged at her chiton and cloak. Branches scraped against her face and caught in her hair. She stepped sideways, hands braced against the stone to keep from slipping. The ground fell away below them, sloping down until it flattened out at the path that led from town to the lower side gate. Without warning, Palamedes stopped and she bumped hard into his back. He knelt and pushed the tangled branches of a rambling clump of overgrown bushes out of the way to reveal a small opening in the stone wall. A stone, perfectly fitted to the hole, had been pushed out of the way.

Palamedes dropped to his knees and disappeared through the opening. Althaia turned to Praxis. He took her hand, squeezed it and motioned her on. She unclasped her cloak and handed it to him. She hiked up the hem of her chiton, tucked it into her belt, lowered herself to the ground, and crawled into the black. It was as if she'd gone blind. She put her hand before her face and wiggled her fingers. Nothing. She could hear Palamedes scuffling ahead of her and Nephthys scuffling behind. Rats, she thought. We're like unwanted rats scurrying along unseen corridors. By the gods, she shivered, I hope we're the only rats in here!

# CHAPTER TWENTY-THREE

"Approach no further!" A guard warned the crowd as a man on a lively dappled grey stallion rode forward. Heraklios. If Nikos hadn't been so nervous about the whole affair, he would have laughed out loud, but as it was all he could muster was a grim smile. He had to admit that Heraklios had style, though. And he was obviously prepared. He must have had his own informers at The Cove.

The general was dressed as if he'd come from a meeting with the king. No one needed to ask whether or not he was Makedonían—but if they did, they'd likely be treated to a lengthy genealogical discourse on how he and Philip were practically blood brothers. As if Heraklios's own personage wasn't impressive enough, he was flanked by a line of six fully armed Makedonían hoplites. Nikos knew that for Heraklios there was more than a dead girl at stake. The general had to put on a good show and discourage the mob; otherwise he'd appear weak. Growing up among the priestesses of Dodona, Nikos had had plenty of experience with the Argead dynasty, and he knew Heraklios couldn't risk some spoiled Delphinian politician complaining to Philip that the Sacred Precinct was not being administered properly. If there was one thing King Phillip did not tolerate, it was weakness.

"The ground upon which you tread is sacred," Heraklios declared. "Put away your torches and come back tomorrow in the light of day."

"This ground is no more sacred than my pigsty," a voice rang out from the gathering.

"It's a blasted storehouse! We're not treading on temple grounds," another voiced yelled.

Built just outside the walls of the Sacred Precinct, the long, low wooden building Heraklios guarded so extravagantly was used to warehouse food and supplies for those who served Apollon. Connected to the precinct by an underground tunnel, the storehouse enabled goods to be delivered to and from the temple without clattering, clanking carts disturbing visitors along the Sacred Way.

"We're glad to go, Heraklios, as soon as you give us the girl," Diokles said. He and Nikos stood in the front ranks of the crowd.

"Wherever the gods are served, the ground is sacred," Heraklios's voice boomed.

"Come now, what are you protecting? The Pythia's stock of sacred chickpeas?" The crowd laughed and cheered Diokles on. "It is to please Apollon that we seek the girl's body. If Apollon's priests give refuge to the remains of such a heretic, I, for one, fear for our future!" The crowd yelled in agreement.

Nikos listened as Diokles and Heraklios traded barbs until the wide wooden doors swung open and the mournful strains of a lyre plucked to perfection poured out from within. Heraklios' soldiers parted as two hooded temple attendants stepped forward. With upraised arms they held filigreed lamps whose eerie shadows glowed and glittered on the polished helmets, breastplates and greaves of the hoplites. Behind them stood Philon.

The senior priest of the Temple of Apollon was in full regalia. A sparkling, jewel-studded gold diadem fashioned in the shape of a laurel wreath crowned Philon's brow. Around his shoulders, he wore a flowing robe dyed deep crimson and woven through with silver threads that shimmered in the lamplight. In his right hand, he carried Apollon's bow, adorned with serpents entwined around olivewood limbs, and on his outstretched left arm, the sharp talons of the god's sacred black crow clutched an oxhide gauntlet. The crow, black as pitch with eyes blacker still, stared menacingly at the crowd. Seldom were these treasures displayed to any but the most powerful men of Hellas—or those with the heaviest purses. There was a low murmuring among the men as they stumbled over themselves in a rush to back away. Only two men remained unmoved—Diokles at the front of the crowd and Nikos at his side. Along with Heraklios, Philon was certainly intent on putting on a show Delphinians would talk about for weeks.

"Philon, did you dress up just for us? If we had known this was to be a formal occasion, we would have all worn our best cloaks and boots."

"No matter what you are wearing, you will not gain entry to either the storehouse or the temple."

"We don't need to go in as long as you bring the girl out. Right, boys?" Diokles turned to the men behind him, who were again gathering their courage.

"Do you have so little faith in Apollon? Do you not think the god can take care of his own affairs?"

"We are just simple, humble sons of Delphi who seek to ensure that the sacred sanctuary remains unspoiled."

"I see before me more than just the sons of Delphi. Nikomachos of Dodona, what connection can you have with the poor deceased girl inside our storehouse?"

"Have you forgotten that my mother serves as priestess of Zeus as well as Gaia? Any violation of Apollon's sacred ground is naturally of concern to a priestess of the Lord of Olympos and father of Apollon. I merely represent her wishes to ensure that all due respect is paid to the gods."

"Family is an interesting thing. It is clear you are your mother's son. It is a pity I cannot compare you to your father as well."

Diokles gripped Nikos's arm. "My friend's parentage is of no consequence to the issue at hand. We want assurances that Apollon's Sacred Precinct remains unblemished. Are you the priest to give us those assurances or should we seek Kleomon? As the elder of Apollon's priests, perhaps he can bring his wisdom to bear on the situation."

Philon snorted, then caught himself. "Unblemished? So that's what you Phokians call stripping the Sacred Precinct clean of its treasures to pay your mercenaries."

Diokles sighed elaborately. "The good men before you played no part in that sad chapter of our history. Besides, from the looks of you, Apollon remains richly blessed. I don't think I've ever seen a bow so handsome."

"Enjoy the view now, because you'll not be so privileged again," Philon growled.

"You should not keep such treasures hidden. It makes Apollon seem, well, stingy. As loyal servants, we deserve to enjoy the god's riches as much as some potentate from afar."

"If you seek to serve Apollon, he might find it more pleasing if you sought entry through his front door instead of trying to bully your way in through his back."

"We do seek to serve Apollon—by ridding him of the pollution that is the girl's body." Diokles answered.

"The body will stay where it is. And you will go home."

"You seem to know just what is going to happen next. Are you the new Pythia?" Laughing and goading Diokles, the men in the crowd inched closer to Philon.

"Philon the Pythia! That's rich!" one laughed.

"He wishes," called another.

"Ah, no," Philon answered calmly. "Unfortunately, I am not so privileged as to commune directly with the god. Nor do I claim to know more than what I am able to ensure will come to pass. But, I do know your very presence here represents the opposite of those qualities Apollon seeks in his followers. Reason. Order. Harmony. It is not for you, Diokles, proprietor of the Dolphin's Cove Inn, proprietor of prostitutes and pillagers, to take the matters of Apollon into your own hands. Indeed, I warn you that my patience is wearing thin and I pledge that the first man who breeches the property of Apollon without my permission will be struck dead before his foot treads beyond the threshold." At that, Heraklios's hoplites stepped toward the crowd and drew their swords. The crow buffeted the air with its wings and cawed loudly.

"Prostitutes and pillagers!" Diokles scoffed as he and Nikos held their ground. "Philon, you've offended me and insulted your neighbors. My friends here are simple folk. Our only concern is to see justice done. As for me, the girl means nothing, just as I'm sure she means nothing to you. So why don't you let the boys have her? They just want to light a pyre under her and be done with it."

"Whether I have any personal interest in the girl's fate or not is irrelevant. As a priest of Apollon, indeed as an honorable man, I would never hand over the young woman's body for a mob to tear limb from limb or burn on a pyre without any regard to her family's rights or wishes."

"Ah, yes, Philon the honorable," Diokles laughed and turned to the crowd behind him. "We're all honorable men here tonight. Right?"

"As honorable as Philon and Kleomon, that's for sure!" a voice from the crowd yelled and the whole group burst into laughter.

"Maybe Philon will let us have ten percent of the girl," another called out.

Philon remained silent, but his eyes narrowed and his lips tightened at the thought of once again being so closely associated with the imbecilic, lecherous old man he had been forced to deal with everyday. He deserved his measly five percent off the top of the temple's take —it was five and not ten as Kleomon told everyone—just for putting up with that man for so many years.

"Tonight, Philon the honorable," Diokles said, "you have the upper hand—or at least more hands with swords. But, the residents of Delphi must insist that this sacrilege not go unpunished."

"Indeed, it will not. The time of judgment and place of purification, however, will be determined by the legal and religious authorities, not by the mob. I advise you to take your friends and return home where hopefully your wives and lovers will be more forgiving of your absence than Apollon is of your presence."

"All right, Philon. We tried our best, boys." Diokles turned to the crowd behind him. "Now let's go warm ourselves before the fire at The Cove. The first round is on the house!" The men cheered and slapped each other on the back as if their chariot team had taken first place at the hippodrome. Diokles slung his arm across Nikos's wide shoulders.

"What do you think? We gave them enough time to get in and out of the storehouse, but hopefully not enough time for a thorough examination of the body. I hope this will put an end to it," Diokles said.

"I don't know," Nikos said. "Something tells me there was more to Praxis's and Theron's plan than a simple diversion. I wonder what they're really up to."

"I don't care what they're up to. As long as they don't find anything. Hopefully, this will all be over tomorrow and we can get back to business."

# Chapter Twenty-Four

Praxis listened to the voices of the mob fade. He sat completely still, the hood of his cloak pulled over his forehead, his presence hidden by the overgrown brush. His job was to watch and wait.

And listen.

And worry. How could he have gotten so carried away with this ludicrous scheme? It didn't matter that it was his ludicrous scheme. Now that he was alone in the dark, now that Althaia and Nephthys were scuttling blindly toward the subterranean levels of the Temple of Apollon, he wanted to throttle something. Someone. Theron, preferably.

He fought the need to shift on the cold hard ground beneath him. He swore at the rough stone at his back. He imagined Althaia and Nephthys crawling on all fours in the dark and could barely stop himself from crawling in after them, pulling them both back to safety. Althaia was the closest thing to family he had, the closest thing to love he had known—or remembered. Of course he loved her father. It was Lysandros who had saved him from certain death on the battlefield, who had nursed him back to health, educated him and raised him as the son he never had. But it was Althaia who, from the innocence of childhood until he saw her disappear into the tunnel, had loved and accepted him as a brother and as a man—not as a mere slave. And Nephthys … he didn't know what to think about Nephthys. From the moment he saw her on the auction block at Piraeus, he knew he had to have her. Not to own and possess her, but, rather, to protect and shield her. But even more than that. To know her—and to have her know him.

He peered out through the brambles and took a deep breath to calm himself. It's all Theron's fault, he thought. He was the reason they always got mixed up in messes like this. Praxis smiled in spite of himself. Damn that Thessalian son of a bitch!

* * * *

At first, the passageway was a narrow tunnel with just enough room for the shoulders of a man. Thankfully, after crawling just a few steps, the tunnel widened and Althaia's heart slowed its violent knocking against her ribs. The tunnel was no longer small enough to induce total panic, but neither was it large enough to sit in without keeping her head bowed. She reached out to either side and discovered it was wide enough to crawl two abreast if needed. Several times she felt cool air and a deepening black off to one side or the other as the tunnel branched off in different directions. The dirt floor was cold and packed hard and smooth, although once in a while a stray pebble pierced her palm or knee.

To stay calm in the confined space, she counted her "kneesteps" and found that she crawled seventeen steps along a relatively flat plane and then four or five more at a slight incline. In the distance, there was a soft light. As they approached, the passage got taller and Althaia and Nephthys were able to walk upright although Palamedes still had to hunch his shoulders. But even as the light seemed just steps away, the passage narrowed so that they had to slide sideways, back against the wall, until they emerged from a tall, slender opening into an ample, but simply furnished room.

Silently, Palamedes bowed, hands clasped together. Althaia gathered that they had entered his chamber. On a large table stood a lamp, its wick burning low. Scattered about were several open scrolls, writing pens, and ink pots. Along the short wall was a sleeping pallet piled with blankets and, in the corner, a stool, several buckets, and a potter's wheel sat together. Lined up against the long wall were delicate bowls and vases and small amphorae painted with scenes from the countryside, images of the Pythia, and dedications to Apollon. Althaia picked up a painted kylix and turned it over in her hands. So lifelike. So delicate. A white bowl on a black base. Apollon sat on a lion-paw stool plucking his kithara. His sacred crow watched from a bare branch, head cocked slightly as if listening to the music. It was a masterpiece.

Palamedes handed a wax writing tablet to Althaia and held up the lamp so she could read it. *When you leave, move the shelves to close the tunnel entrance.* Althaia looked up as Palamedes indicated a large case with several shelves on which sat a large number of pots in various stages of completion. The case partially blocked the opening, but Althaia could not see how to move it with the pots still on it. She looked back at the tablet. *Move the rug to the opposite side of the case, enter the tunnel, and slide the case back over the opening.* Confused, she watched as Palamedes demonstrated. He lifted the rug to reveal two deep trenches in the stone floor filled with iron balls. He rolled the shelf back and forth over the balls and showed them where a handle had been fitted into the back of the shelves. As he moved the shelf to block the tunnel opening, the rug flopped into place, hiding the exposed trenches. He scratched again at his tablet. *No one will ever know you were here.*

Althaia and Nephthys smiled at the ingenious secret passage. They indicated their understanding and readjusted their chitons. Palamedes motioned for them to take off their boots. He laid them carefully back inside the dark of the tunnel. He picked up the tablet again, wiped his thumb across the pliant wax, held it up to the lamp and wrote a new message: *Like Theseus, you must follow the thread. But, do not linger. For no one knows the waxing and waning power of the sacred vapors. I will not be here when you return.*

As every child knew, Theseus of Athens followed the twists and turns of the Cretan Minotaur's labyrinth by following the string that Ariadne used to mark his path. Now, Palamedes counted on the same trick to guide Althaia and Nephthys to the adyton where Charis's body waited. He reached down to the floor and picked up a string that snaked under the doorway. The other end was tied to the table leg. He motioned for both of them to take the string in hand. Satisfied they were ready, he drew down the wick and opened the door to the dark corridor. Before they took one step forward, Althaia panicked, and reached back frantically, groping for Nephthys' hand. At that moment, Nephthys reached out for Althaia. They found each other in the dark and stepped into the corridor.

# CHAPTER TWENTY-FIVE

"Nikomachos," a young boy stuck his head through the door to Diokles's office. "I have a message for you."

Nikos looked at Diokles. "That was quick." He took the scroll and then closed the door behind the boy. He rolled the hemp tie off, broke the wax seal, glanced at the writing and tossed the scroll at Diokles. "I'm to meet them at daybreak. At Menandros's."

Diokles picked up it up and scanned the message. "Not now? Why daybreak?"

"How should I know?"

"Hmmm." Diokles was silent for a moment. He leaned back in his chair and peered at Nikos. "So, what do you suppose they are doing between now and then?"

"Sleeping? By the gods, I don't know. We gave them the diversion they asked for."

"So, explain this to me again, this autopsia examination."

"They examine the body for clues that will help them determine the cause of death. If they find something, it may lead them to the killer," Nikos's fingers played absently at his throat.

"Is there something for them to find?"

Nikos ignored the question. "We didn't give them enough time to find anything. And if they didn't find something tonight, they won't have another chance. They think Charis's brother will arrive to claim her tomorrow."

"Think? Didn't Georgios go to retrieve him?"

"Phoibe sent him yesterday, but—"

"Maybe Theron and Praxis didn't trust you with their all their plans, after all."

Nikos held Diokles's gaze. "They trust me because of my relationship with Thea."

"Theron and Thea had not seen each other in years, and if Theron so valued his sister, he would have sent for you immediately after this autopsia was concluded. He knows the priestesses are awaiting word, so why keep them waiting? I suspect they do not trust you enough."

"I think Althaia trusts me, too."

"Zeus's beard, Nikos. You just met her. Have you even exchanged two words with her?"

"Of course I've spoken to her." He felt the heat rise in his face. Just thinking of the dark-haired Athenian made him flush with desire. From the first moment he stepped into Menandros's andron with Thea's note, he hadn't been able to get her out of his mind. His body stirred as he remembered how she looked up at him with those deep brown eyes and long lashes. Bold. Unafraid. He thought of her in the cave earlier that morning when she challenged Phoibe. He had wanted to step out of the shadows and take her in his arms right then. In front of everyone—even his mother. And when she turned and sought him out, he could feel the heat in her eyes. She might not have been sure it was him, but she sensed it. Of that, he was certain. He had known many women, but this one was different. Exciting. And yet somehow familiar, like there already existed a silent understanding between them. Something about her drew him in as if she were a lodestone and he an iron filing. Just thinking about the power she held over him sent shockwaves through his system—and blood to his cheeks.

"By Aphrodite, I do believe Nikomachos of Dodona just blushed. With you, it's always a woman, but I've never seen one make you blush."

"She's worth it."

"Don't get me wrong. I heartily approve. Lysandros was one of richest merchants in all Attika."

"That's not what I meant. You may not believe it, but I'm not always thinking about silver and gold."

"I'm well aware of what else you think about. Every time you turn up in Delphi, my bed turns up empty."

"I can't help it if your whores prefer me."

"Pray tell me. What else keeps your mind occupied?"

"This woman, Althaia. She's rich to be sure. And beautiful. But there's something else about her. There's an inner strength that radiates from her. Like Thea. Thea answers to no man, she lives on their own terms, choses her own lovers, and yet she performs her duties with care and deliberation. I sense Althaia is like that. A woman who knows her own mind."

Diokles threw back his head, laughing so hard he nearly toppled his chair. "Oh, Nikos, you fool, how is it that Aphrodite and Eros so easily lay claim to your heart? You spent five minutes in this woman's presence and now you know the deepest contours of her character? If it weren't for the trouble it gets us in, your ignorance would be endlessly entertaining. It is a puzzle for the philosophers that you, a man who has little trouble keeping women in your bed, know so little about the creatures."

"You think owning a stable full of pornai makes you an expert?"

"And you think growing up in the midst of a bunch of priestesses who hear voices in the rustling of oak leaves and see visions in smoke rising up from the bedrock makes you one?"

"Maybe not, but—"

"Nikos, you play games with women, but you never latch on to one because you don't understand what they need or what they want. You never stick. They may flock to your bed because you flatter them and buy them expensive trinkets, but ultimately you end up alone. I, on the other hand, always have a companion and the only time I go to bed alone is if you're in town. The women here know they'll have plenty to eat and always have a roof over their heads. They know they'll be protected and that I'll stick a broom in their hand and give them a job to do if they get too old to keep the customers happy upstairs. The difference between you and me is that the women here at The Cove know they can count on me."

"I've seen you charm a woman until she's bent over and begging for it and I've seen you flog a woman till her back bleeds. The only thing the women of The Cove can count on is that they have no other choices in life, that working as a whore for Diokles beats begging in the street."

"That's life, my friend. I didn't write the rules, I just try to bend them to my ends."

"You say I'm not dependable, Diokles, but most of my life you've been urging me to leave Dodona, to leave the one person who does count on me."

"There's a difference between someone depending on you and someone using you like a slave."

"I will not have this conversation again."

The two men stared at each other over the desk. The fire in the brazier crackled. Muffled footsteps and indistinct voices passed in the hallway. Finally, Diokles sighed and leaned forward.

"All I'm saying is that you should be careful. We don't know what Theron is up to, and no matter how taken you are with Lysandros's daughter, you don't know her. You don't know if you can trust her, let alone if she trusts you. We've got ourselves in a mess because of your willingness to be taken in by a woman. Granted, Charis was more a hound from Hades than a woman, but still....You must tread carefully. You can't let your cock get you into any more trouble. Next time, I may not be able—or willing—to help get you out of it."

Nikos looked Diokles in the eye. It wasn't the first time he'd wanted to plow his fist into his partner's face, and he'd wager it wouldn't be the last.

Diokles sensed he'd pushed the conversation too far. He watched the muscles of Nikos's jaw clench and unclench. "I'm just pointing out the obvious," he said quietly.

"I don't want to hear this again," Nikos muttered through gritted teeth.

"Your problem is you're obsessed with women. My problem is I always have to manage your messes."

"It was an accident. I didn't kill her."

"It is of little matter, Nikos. I'm not just talking about Charis and you know it. Besides, she had it coming. I wouldn't have put up with it for as long as you did. I only hope you were man enough to finally taste her treasures before she tried to cheat you out of ours."

The memory of Charis leading him into the old shed, promising, finally, to give him what he'd been dreaming of—if only he'd be a bit more generous with the tiara—washed over Nikos. Diokles need never know, she said as her fingers traced the musculature of his arm. It will be our secret, she murmured as she unpinned his cloak. We will be a team, you and I, she whispered, her hot breath tickling his ear. She had played him for a fool for months. It's not that he loved her. Gods, no. It was that he couldn't have her. The need for her would have been over as soon as it began if only she had kept her promises. Each time they met, she took him right to the edge and then left him there. Each time she'd brush up against him, shake her hair loose, let her chiton slip to expose the swell of her breast. He remembered that night and how he could have taken what she promised … but he didn't.

"Ah," Diokles sighed. "Don't tell me you didn't—"

"Shut up."

"Come, my friend. You tried reasoning. You tried kindness. You even almost persuaded me to give her a bigger cut on the stolen goods we got from that rat of a brother of hers. But none of that was enough. She wanted more. You always say a little kindness works? A compliment or two? Where has that gotten you? By the gods, I've never heard such drivel. Kindness and compliments got us in this mess. Kindness and compliments embolden women, they breed an avaricious need for more and more until you are on your knees asking forgiveness just for being a man. Meanwhile, the object of your desire smiles as she squeezes your balls and schools you on the proper way to run your business."

"Always the voice of experience, Diokles."

"That's right. I run a very profitable business and I know how to take care of troublesome women—and men."

"Your way is not very pretty."

"It may not be pretty, but it is effective. And final."

"Nothing's final," Nikos said. At least not yet, he thought. Someone would find the remains of Charis's brother under that stack of hay in the shed. And someone had picked up Charis's body from the temple steps and moved her to the altar in the theater. That same person had stripped her naked, a violation he couldn't have committed even though had the chance. *But who had moved her? And why?* Had they seen him leave the body? If so, why hadn't he heard from them? Why hadn't he been accused? Exposed? Blackmailed? Could it have been Kleomon? If so, did the man sitting across the desk from him know about it? It had been Diokles's and Kleomon's business from the beginning. They had started selling temple treasures to overseas collectors before the last Sacred War was even over. He was the latecomer. Was Kleomon trying to cut him out?

As he looked across the table at his oldest friend, it hit him. He wanted out. He wanted out of everything. He had only joined the venture to make enough money to leave Dodona and get away from his mother once and for all. Now, he wanted to start over. Away from Diokles, away from priestesses and prophecies, and most especially, away from the guilt. By the gods, he had just as good as killed an unarmed woman and with each hour that passed since he left Charis on the temple steps, that reality ate a little deeper into his gut. Burrowed a little further into his brain. What would Thea say if she knew? How could I have let it go this far? But he knew he couldn't leave now. There were too many questions and none of this nightmare would be over, would be final, until he found the answers. And now there was another consideration: Althaia of Athens.

"Face it, Nikos, your method for dealing with women is flawed." Diokles paused and then said, "and, as hard as you try, it will never make your mother love you."

Nikos exploded. His chair clattered backward across the floor as he slammed his fists on the table and leaned over Diokles. "How many times do I have to tell you? I will not have this conversation."

Diokles looked up at him calmly. "We've been friends since we were boys, Nikos, and every time I see you it gets worse. In fact, it's pathetic. The more you cater to that old harpy, the worse she treats you. Sometimes I think I ought to arrange a tragic accident as a gift for you."

"A gift? Diokles, what kind of man are you?"

"Since you're not man enough to take your freedom for yourself, maybe you need a friend to give it to you."

"By the gods, sometimes I wonder if I even know you."

"Come now, if she were my mother...."

"She is *not* your mother. And I am not another Orestes and Melanippe of Dodona is not another Clytemnestra!"

"Orestes only did what needed to be done."

"I will not murder my own mother—whether for revenge or for convenience."

"Remember, Orestes was acquitted."

# CHAPTER TWENTY-SIX

As her fingers slid along the string, Althaia wondered about Nikos. He must think the examination in the storehouse complete—when in fact it hadn't yet begun. And he must have had no idea where it was really taking place. He probably thought she was back at Menandros's, not walking blindly through the deep corridors of the temple complex with nothing more than a piece of string to guide her. That is, if he thought about her at all. Maybe she had read too much into his gaze, thought too much about the way his eyes caught hers. Maybe she should stop thinking about those green eyes and broad shoulders, about how her fingers might feel in his thick curls. After all, no matter what she thought about Nikomachos of Dodona, she was married to Lycon. And that was that.

She began counting her footsteps again. They made their way along a straight but slightly inclined corridor. After twenty-three steps, they began to veer to the right. Seven more steps and there was a knot in the string and a sudden turn right followed by fifteen more steps. Sliding her fingers along the string, she suddenly came across a great, thick knot. She stopped and stuck her foot forward, feeling with her toes that just ahead there were steps hewn into the stone floor. One, two, three, four, five, she counted as they ascended slowly and then came to another thick knot. The floor was flat and smooth and they shuffled forward a few steps until she felt the third thick knot. This time, she could sense something was different. She took a deep breath and noticed the distinct fragrance of myrrh in the air. She put her hand out before her face and pushed forward into the black emptiness until she felt it. A thick wall of fabric hung before them. She squeezed Nephthys's hand, pushed the fabric aside and there before them, in the flickering lamplight, was the adyton of the Temple of Apollon with Charis's body, deformed in its death pose and sheathed in a pale linen shroud, stretched out on a long table.

Nephthys stepped through the curtain and stood beside Althaia. Their hands, still clasped, followed the string until they saw the end tied to the table leg. They let it drop and looked about the room. Large lamps, already lit, sat on pedestals in the four corners of the room. Sitting next to the lamps were incense burners from which thin wisps of smoke rose to fill the room with the clean, faintly bitter scent of myrrh used to mask the smell of death.

On the opposite side of the room, another wall of thick fabric hung from a series of hooks fastened in the frame of a wooden doorway. The supplicants must stay on the other side as they descend from the temple, Althaia remembered. Althaia imagined the Pythia sitting upon the tripod over the fissure and listening as her father posed his question from the other side of the fabric. That had been the summer after her mother died. What had her father asked? And what had the Pythia answered?

The room had a low painted ceiling with a single slender column supporting it. It was smaller than she had imagined. The floor was bare rock scarred only by the jagged crevice that opened to the womb of the world below and a narrow, shallow trough through which poured the sacred waters of the Spring of Kassotis. Now, however, the trough was dry.

Nephthys tugged at Althaia's sleeve and pointed at the trough. In the middle of the far wall, where the floor and the wall met, waters from the spring normally flowed through a drain and into the small channel from which the Pythia could drink. There, peeking out from just above the plane of the floor, two eyes gleamed at them in the darkness and a little hand poked out and waved. Zenon. Just as Theron and Praxis had planned. They both smiled, but dared not acknowledge the boy any further. He was sitting in the damp drain with a rope tied around his waist, positioned out of sight and ready to alert the others in case they were discovered or overcome by the sacred vapors.

Althaia turned her attention back to the adyton. Just beyond the table and straddling the crevice was a block of stone. The three legs of the tripod were fitted securely into three holes drilled into the stone. The Pythia would sit atop the tripod and breathe in the sacred vapors, preparing to deliver Apollon's messages. The tripod itself was tall and simply decorated. The pockmarks of the hammered bronze reflected the flickering lamplight, and she could well imagine Herakles and Apollon fighting over it. In front of the tripod, also resting on the stone block, sat the famous omphalos, the navel stone of the earth. It was from a hole at the top of the omphalos that the sacred pneuma of Apollon issued. The Pythia would lean over and breathe in the vapors and fall into her trance. It was only then, when she became the nexus between god and man, that she could give the supplicants what they came for.

She took in the gold, silver, and bronze treasures—an ornamental kithara carved in ebony, inlaid with ivory and mother of pearl and strung with golden filaments, the eagles of Zeus, and a small figure of Apollon as a boy standing over the simple bronze garland of grape leaves marking the grave of his dark-natured brother, Dionysos. Born of Zeus and Semele, killed by his enemies, resurrected and taken into the heavens by Zeus himself. Light and dark, day and night, reason and abandon; the two brothers represented the opposite natures of the human spirit. Althaia whispered a prayer to both.

Nephthys slipped the tablet from the linen wrap around her waist, and Althaia removed her box from the binding around hers and laid it carefully on the floor under the table. Together they rolled Charis's body sideways and pulled the shroud away until only one layer remained between her body and the table. As they removed the shroud, Althaia noted the abrasions, scrapes, and dirt on her shoulders, back, and buttocks.

Finally, she lay naked before them, and Althaia thought of Inaros and his respect for the souls of the dead. Instinctively, she placed her fingertips on Charis's cold lips and whispered part of the prayer from the Egyptian Book of the Dead that Inaros taught her. Startled, she heard Nephthys join the recitation:

*May my mouth be opened by Ptah; may the cords,*
*the cords belonging to my mouth, be untied by the god of my city.*
*May Thoth come, provided with words of power, to untie the cords,*
*the cords of Set which guard my mouth.*

*Atum is driven back; he has cast away they who guard it.*
*May my mouth be unfastened, may my mouth be opened by Shu,*
*with that piece of iron of heaven with which he opened the mouths of the gods.*

Althaia looked inquiringly at Nephthys. Of course she knew Nephthys was Egyptian, and knew that she could read and write, but that didn't explain how she could recite random passages from the Book of the Dead.

"My husband was a priest of Amun-Ra in the Sacred Precinct of Karnak in Thebes on the banks of the life-giving Nile," Nephthys whispered. "I was a temple wife and chantress."

Althaia's eyes widened. The wife of a priest! A chantress from the famous temple at Thebes? How could it be that a woman like that could become a slave? Althaia read a flash of bitterness in Nephthys's eyes as if to say, "What, did you not guess I was an educated woman? Did you not wonder who I was and from whence I came? Did you not think I could be worthy of being your companion?"

But perhaps Althaia read those things in her own heart, for Nephthys had already reached down to Althaia's box and handed the probe to her.

"Let us see if Ptah will open Charis's mouth and tell us who sent her to the afterlife before her time," Nephthys whispered.

Althaia walked around the body as she had done at the theater. She kept her mind focused, listening intently, willing Charis to speak to her, to reveal her last moments. Althaia was sure the answers they sought were within reach, hidden somewhere within the mortal envelope that had been Charis.

Nephthys stood across the table as Althaia pointed out the bruising on Charis's cheeks and shoulders. Someone had hit or slapped her. A man with hands large and strong enough to grip her shoulders and clasp his fingers around her arms had left mottled bruises on her fair skin. She tipped the body sideways and noted the blackened skin where the blood had pooled on her backside. She leaned over and pointed to fine abrasions on the skin of her buttocks. Althaia moved down to examine the inner thighs. If Charis had been raped, blood or bruising on her pubis or legs might still be visible. But Althaia saw no sign of forced assault.

She examined the girl's hands, and looked carefully at her fingers. She motioned for Nephthys to hand her a probe and then ran it under the girl's finger nails. She held the probe up to the lamplight for Nephthys to see.

Dried skin, flecks of blood. Charis had fought for her life.

She continued around the body and ran her fingers through Charis's hair, along her scalp to feel for any hidden cuts, bumps or abrasions. Her fingers loosened more straw and dirt ground into her hair, but discovered no evidence of any deadly blow. Charis's neck was distended and her shoulders still arched back as they had been when she was found draped across the altar. Her head was cocked backward, face colorless, and her skin puffed and pulled tight on her cheekbones. Because her head had been upside down and hanging off the edge of the altar as the death stiffness set in, her mouth was frozen into a bizarre smile. Althaia laid the probe on the table and tested her jaw.

The clench was problematic, still stiff and difficult to move. Althaia could tell the body was in the process of accepting its death. Usually, that began with the face, the eyelids, lips, and jaw. Inaros said the timing of tissue relaxation depended upon the deceased's willingness to leave this world and join the next. And it also depended upon the deceased's age and the temperature in which the body was stored. Charis was young, and the weather was still cool in the day and could get quite cold at night. So, stiffness may have set in early, but in the warmth of the storehouse and adyton, the body may have begun to relax more quickly. According to Inaros's timetable, Charis had not yet been dead three full days. However, Althaia reminded herself, they did not actually know when Charis had died—only when she had been discovered. She had been found nearly two days prior, but had she died much earlier than that?

Althaia stuck the probe in Charis's mouth and worked it up between her teeth. Using it as a lever, she pulled the jaw down while Nephthys held the head still. Once the jaw was open, she motioned for Nephthys to bring a lamp over and hold it above the table. Her fingers swept and probed the interior of the mouth. Althaia remembered in the theater that, although her skin had a slight blue tint, it was not as blue as she thought a choking victim would be. While Inaros had talked about choking, Althaia had never actually seen someone who had died that way. She just imagined the body would be blue enough for it to be obvious. But, maybe, Charis had died earlier than they thought and was moved to the theater later. Maybe the blue tint fades quickly once the death pallor sets in. There was so much Althaia still didn't know.

Then, she felt something odd. She pulled out her fingers and wiped them clean. She then opened the jaw as wide as she could and tried to peer into the girl's throat. Even with the lamplight, it was too dark. She put her fingers back down into the throat and probed as far back as she could get them until she felt it again. There was definitely something different down there. It was slick and she couldn't get her fingers around it.

Althaia tried the probe and then the hook, wiggling them around, trying to catch whatever was lodged to drag it up into the mouth. All she did was push whatever it was farther down into the trachea. She pulled the instruments out and wiped them on her cloak. She pressed against the base of the throat. Perhaps there was something she could feel with her fingers. She couldn't be sure, though there did seem to be something she could push back and forth. There was only one thing to do.

Althaia motioned for Nephthys to hand her the scalpel. Physicians in Egypt had long performed tracheotomies, although Hippokrates spoke against them for fear of damaging the carotid artery and killing the patient. That's why she was interested in dissections—not operations. She didn't want to be responsible for the life or death of anyone under her scalpel. Neither the physician nor the midwife at her mother's bedside had been able to do anything to save her mother or her baby brother. Althaia didn't want to have to stand by and watch her patients die knowing she could do nothing. That's why it was so important to discover how the body worked, how it was constructed, how organs were connected. Like now, if Charis died choking on something, no one would have known simply by staring at the body and lamenting the girl's untimely death. No, you have to go in there and find out what happened.

"It's the only way," she whispered as she pressed the scalpel into the skin and pushed down into the trachea.

Nephthys reached out and laid her hand on Althaia's. She sniffed the air. "The air is changing," Nephthys whispered.

Althaia looked over at the drain; the two eyes were still there, watching silently. She breathed in deeply. The scent of the myrrh was shifting, mixing with something else. She looked down at the fissure in the bare stone floor but saw nothing different. She sniffed again. Overwhelming the clean, fresh scent of myrrh was the sickly sweet smell of overripe fruit mixed with the faint scent of rotted eggs. She knew at once it was Apollon's sacred vapors beginning to waft through the room. Nephthys took the tablet—she hadn't written anything anyway—and latched it closed and began to wave it in front of their faces like a fan. Nephthys didn't have to say a word; Althaia knew she had to be quick.

With one hand, Althaia opened the slit wider and with the other, she felt into the tracheal tube. Just below the cut, she could feel something like a small stone. She picked up her scalpel again, extended the slit and used the probe to open the trachea even wider. There, lodged at the base of Charis' throat, was a small slippery ball of dull silver attached to fragments of a looped chain.

Althaia pulled them from the girl's throat, wiped them hastily on her chiton and held it up to the lamplight. The ball was a bit larger than the pieces used in a game of draughts—it would have fit snugly in a small child's palm—and she could clearly see where the links in the chain had been pulled apart.

Nephthys touched the ball with her fingertip and it swung back and forth on the broken chain. They looked at each other knowing they had discovered the object that killed Charis. Tears sprung into Althaia's eyes. She tried to put the pieces together, to reconstruct the moment of death, but was too overcome by emotion to think straight. She, and she alone, had the skills to discover how Charis died. She and she alone held the clue to the killer's identity. She wanted to dance, to sing, to shout her discovery to the world.

She headed for the kithara, but Nephthys stood in her way. Althaia swerved and then stopped. She closed her eyes and raised her face, and inhaled deeply. For some reason, Nephthys was frantically fanning the writing tablet in front of her face. Althaia pushed past her only to have the slave shove the tablet in her belt, grab Althaia's face with one hand, clamp the other hand over her mouth and lead her through the fabric curtain and into the black of the corridor. Nephthys, cheeks strangely bloated, stood in front of her, nose to nose, breathing in and out extravagantly. Althaia focused on Nephthys' s face and nodded. She understood, then, that she had fallen under the influence of Apollon's sacred vapors.

Althaia filled her lungs with the cool, earthy air from the hallway and began breathing in and out in a synchronous rhythm with Nephthys. She knew she must clear her head, finish and get out, but she couldn't stop staring at Nephthys' s bulging eyes and brown cheeks puffing in and out like some demented Egyptian blowfish bearing down on her from the depths of the sea. She snorted loudly and then clamped her hand over her mouth to suppress the wave of giggles that threatened to sweep both her and the blowfish away. Nephthys pinched Althaia's cheek hard and clinched her face tight in her hand. Althaia nodded and tried to concentrate all her mental faculties on getting both her and the blowfish out of there.

After a moment, they both took deep breaths and pushed back through the thick curtain into the adyton. Althaia placed the silver ball and chain in her box along with her scalpel and probe and slipped it back into the binding around her waist as Nephthys tightened the tablet in hers. Then she pressed closed the slit of Charis's throat while Nephthys held the shroud ready to rewrap the body. They looked around the room one last time and signaled to Zenon that they were done. But the drain was now black, empty.

Quickly, Althaia and Nephthys rewrapped the body, and stepped back out into the corridor. They pulled the string taut and worked their way along it in the dark hallway. Althaia wondered what Theron and Praxis would say when she showed them the silver ball. Then she stopped. She felt something—a breeze moved across her face making the hairs on her arms and back of her neck stand on end. Nephthys gripped her tight. She had felt it, too. They waited, not daring to move, not daring to breathe. But there was nothing more. They stepped forward, in unison, and hurried toward Palamedes's door. When they felt the string dive down toward the floor, they slipped into Palamedes's room and shut the door behind them.

The lamp was nearly out as they followed the string down to the table leg. Althaia untied it and left it in a little tangled pile on the table. If someone entered his room, no one would know they had been as clever as Theseus and Ariadne in the Minotaur's labyrinth. Nephthys placed the rug on the other side of the case, just as Palamedes instructed, and they slipped back into the tunnel, found their boots, and pulled the sliding case across the opening. They clasped one hand together and they each held one hand outstretched above their heads to keep from knocking themselves out as the roof got lower and lower. In the pitch black they started down the tunnel toward Praxis.

* * * *

On the far side of the Sacred Precinct, sitting near an open drain, Theron had one hand clapped hard across Zenon's mouth and another cupped to his own. He whistled three times—three short calls of the Alpine Swift—and then waited for a reply. Soon, two short calls broke the silence followed by a longer trill. Zenon breathed heavily through his nose and rubbed his scraped knees and his wounded bottom. Moments earlier he had emerged from the drainage tunnel, eyes wild as he tried to pantomime Nephthys and Althaia fanning and swooning in the adyton. When Theron did not jump up to mount a rescue, Zenon turned and started back toward the temple. Theron jerked the rope sharply and sat the boy down hard on the ground.

"We wait," Theron whispered.

"We can't wait!"

"Did you see them swoon? Did you see them fall?"

"No."

"Was there anyone else there? Did someone enter the adyton?

"No, but—"

"Did you see Nephthys fanning the vapors from Althaia's face?"

"Yes."

"So, they could have reentered the room—after you left."

"Yes, but—"

"We wait. Just a moment more."

The world was silent. Then, the faint sound of trickling then rushing water filled the air as the Kassotis Spring began flowing through the elaborate drainage system again. Palamedes had waited for Theron's call indicating Zenon was out of the tunnel and had then unblocked the sacred stream.

* * * *

Praxis heard the soft shuffle of hands and knees coming toward him in the tunnel. He cupped his hands around his mouth and hooted. It was the call to signal Theron that Althaia and Nephthys were out.

"Quiet," Praxis mouthed as he reached into the tunnel and helped Althaia up and out of the way of the opening. Then he knelt and helped

Nephthys to her feet.

"Praxis—"

He put his finger to her lips. "Quiet," he mouthed again. He pushed the stone back in front of the opening where it fit seamlessly into the face of the foundation. Then he motioned for them to follow him through the brambles and they set out to trace their path back to Menandros's. No one said a word as they moved through empty village streets in the stillness of the night. As they approached Menandros's street, a dog darted from the shadows and ran in front of them. Nephthys jumped, Praxis drew his blade, and Althaia clamped her hand over her mouth to keep herself from crying out. He shot both of them a dark glare and hurried them forward.

Menandros met them at the door and led them into the andron where couches loaded with fleecy blankets waited. Althaia and Nephthys wrapped blankets around their shoulders and curled up near the well-tended brazier glowing hot with orange and red coals blinking against the evening shadows. Praxis paced back and forth from the living room to the front gate. Menandros found his cook asleep in a kitchen corner and woke her with a gentle nudge. Soon cups of warmed wine were passed out, but still no one said a word—not even Menandros. It wasn't until Theron and Zenon closed and latched the front door behind them that they relaxed and all began talking at once.

# CHAPTER TWENTY-SEVEN

Theron grabbed a cup of wine, drained it in one gulp, and looked at Althaia, who sported a wide smile.

"Tell us," he said.

She set the box down on the couch, opened the lid, and held up the silver ball, dangling it from its chain. It gleamed in the lamplight like a miniature moon. "I believe she choked to death on this. I—we," Althaia looked at Nephthys, "found it lodged in her trachea."

"Well, this is disappointing." Menandros's stylus lay slack in his hand as if he'd forgotten how to use it. "There's no mystery, no intrigue, no drama in an accident." He slouched back on his cushions.

"Don't get discouraged. We can discount any scenarios just yet," Theron replied. He took the ball and examined it in the lamplight. "Looks like part of a necklace."

"That's what I think," Althaia said. "The links where it is broken have been pulled apart like it was ripped from the wearer's neck."

"I've got it!" Menandros sat forward with a flourish. "A suicide. Her lover gave her the bauble in a pledge of his undying love. They met at night, in secret, to consummate their union and after he had taken her, after he had used her, he spurned her. Threw her away like a dirty rag. She knew she was ruined, and in her grief she ripped his gift from her own neck and swallowed it. 'I'll show him!' she thought as she gagged. 'I'll dine on the cold, bitter remnants of our love.' And then she breathed her last." Menandros looked around the room. "Now, that would be something, wouldn't it?"

"Yes, that would be something," Theron said. "Something highly unlikely." He handed the trinket on to Praxis. "What else did you find? There has to be more. If it was just an accident, someone would have reported her death to Heraklios or the authorities in Delphi."

"There is more," Althaia said. "At the theater, we saw the marks on her face and the bruises on her shoulders and arms. In the adyton, we were able to identify chafing on her buttocks and dried skin and blood under her fingernails. I thought perhaps she was taken against her will—raped—but there was no indication that the murderer, or that whoever was with her when she breathed her last, sunk that low. There was a struggle, but the ultimate cause of her death was that ball lodged in her throat."

"It is an unusual piece. I've never seen another like it." Praxis handed the necklace on to Nephthys. "None of it makes sense." He turned to Althaia. "At the theater, we also noticed hay in her hair."

"Yes, and in the adyton, I looked again. Hay and dirt."

Theron took the necklace from Nephthys and held it up to the light again. "There's no stable in the Sacred Precinct, so she must have been moved. Before or after she died is the question."

"Why would someone want an accidental death to look like a ritual sacrifice?" Althaia asked. "What would they have to gain by it? And how did they get away with it? Isn't the Sacred Precinct guarded at night? Especially since the last Sacred War."

Theron laughed. "I'm sure it is, but tensions between the native Phokians and the Amphiktyonik League have simmered down and, in my experience, if there is no imminent threat, a man standing guard in the middle of the night is just as likely to be sleeping at his post as he would be if he were snug in his bed."

"But still, how does one get away with carting a body around in the middle of the night without being seen? Maybe Charis was having an affair with a temple slave—or one of the priests! Maybe she was Philon's lover!"

"It isn't out of the realm of possibility, but I don't see Phoibe's handmaid, an acolyte of the Pythia of Gaia, being Philon's lover. It does make sense that whoever was with her enjoys unfettered access to the Sacred Precinct.

A temple slave or even a guard. We should get a list of everyone who would have been in the precinct that night. Heraklios will have a list of the guards, and Philon should have a list of all the temple staff."

"It's a place to start," Praxis agreed. "But no matter who killed her or who was with her when she accidentally choked to death, why would they go to the trouble of making a spectacle of her death?"

Menandros stood and rubbed his hands together. "We are going round and round in circles." He began to pace in a circle around the brazier. "We must approach the problem like a playwright. In the theater, there is a purpose for every prop. We must think of her attacker as the writer, scripting this play. First let us suppose this was no accident. Perhaps the man with whom she struggled—and I'm presuming it was a man although I've met more than a few women who I'm sure were perfectly capable of such an act—let's presume the man intentionally jammed that little orb down her throat, clamped her mouth shut, and watched her die. As a playwright, I find this makes little sense. Where is the drama in such a murder? While it may be devious and the murderer may have all the characteristics of an evil madman, he alone would be privy to his genius. He would never expect the body to be examined and no one would ever discover the murder weapon. I find that scenario unsatisfying because someone who kills in such a creative way must surely be someone who would crave acknowledgment for his accomplishment." He turned to his audience and waited.

"Go on, master playwright," Theron obliged him.

"Now let us suppose this was an accident, that this man did not intend to kill her. First there is a scuffle." Menandros placed his hands around his neck, pantomiming choking. "But, no, wait. Let's step back a moment." He began pacing again. "Maybe it is not a scuffle. Maybe it is a bit of rough foreplay. You said there was chafing on her backside, but no sign, er, um, of uh, penetration." He glanced at Zenon who sat on the floor near the doorway. "There is no accounting for people's sexual appetites, my boy. What if, in the midst of this, uh, strenuous activity, he gets a bit too rough—or maybe she gets a bit too rough. She bites his neck and instead gets the necklace. She chokes. He doesn't know what is going on. One minute he's having a good time and the next his partner is turning blue. And then she is dead. What does he do? If he is her lover, he would go for help. But if he is someone who is not supposed to be her lover, he must not go for help. Instead, he must dispose of the body in a way that will not incriminate him."

"But why go to all the trouble of laying her out just so on the altar in your theater? Maybe the question is who would be interested in incriminating you," Theron asked.

"Me?" Menandros looked horrified. "I don't have any enemies!"

"Then why the altar of Dionysos and not the altar of Chios or anywhere else in the Sacred Precinct or, for that matter, in Delphi itself?"

"By the gods, I don't know!" Menandros flopped back in his chair.

Praxis stood up. "I say we all sleep on this since we're right back where we started."

"Not quite. Now we know how Charis died," Althaia said.

"And we know that the last person to see Charis alive would never expect that the body would be examined and the trinket retrieved. He—or she—must surely believe that the secrets of Charis's last moments would go to the grave with her," Theron added.

"It's a good thing he's never met Althaia," Praxis said, his lips curling in a half smile. "Perhaps poking and probing around dead bodies is a useful endeavor after all."

# CHAPTER TWENTY-EIGHT

Althaia lay in bed staring at the ceiling. She was covered in sweat, and the blankets she had kicked off during her nightmare were piled in a tangled mound on the floor. At least Nephthys was already up and gone. She wouldn't be able to interrogate Althaia again or demand that she go running to some Sibyl in the marketplace for dream interpretation. Especially since this dream was different. Very different. For one thing, the shadowed figure from the cave was in it and for another, there was a body, not dead, but nearly so. And there was one more thing different about this dream; she remembered it perfectly.

She closed her eyes. She was in the Korycian Cave. The fire was lit, but no one was there but the hooded figure. He stepped from the shadow and held his hand out to her. And she took it. Then he was leading her up toward the gaping black of the inner chamber and she was going—willingly. Her heart pounded, but it wasn't fear that drove her. It was desire. Then she wasn't in the cave anymore. A body was lying on the ground, broken, awkward in its death throes. But it wasn't Charis. It had no face, but it was moaning, trying to say something. She realized it was telling a story, explaining something, but it wasn't talking to her. It was talking to the man from the cave. And then all she could hear was pounding again. This time it wasn't her heartbeat. It was the pounding of hooves, and then the flash of light like the glint of a blade. She turned to look behind her—and then she woke.

She sighed and sat up. "Maybe Nephthys is right. If a Sibyl can help me make sense of this one," she mumbled, "it may well be worth a few drachma." She forced herself to get up and push open the shutters. It was past daybreak! Why had Theron let her sleep so long? She quickly attended to her toilet, dragged a comb through her unruly hair and threw on her clothes. She hurried downstairs and barged into the andron. It was empty. Where was everybody? Why didn't Nephthys wake me? Then she heard voices. She followed them down the hall toward the back of the house. She threw open the doors to the kitchen and ran right into Nikos, spilling his glass of water down the front of his chitoniska. Theron and Praxis were right behind him.

"Good morning." The corner of his mouth tugged up in a smile.

Flustered and embarrassed, she realized her hair was still a mess and she wasn't wearing shoes. Had she remembered to chew mint leaves before she left her room?

She turned to Theron and Praxis. "Why did you not wake me?" she demanded.

"Nephthys said you slept fitfully last night so we thought it best to allow you to rest this morning. Nikos had just arrived when the cook pulled the bread from the oven, and we couldn't resist." Theron broke off a piece of bread from a still-warm loaf and handed it to her. She took it and stood there like she didn't know what to do with it.

"Menandros already left for the theater," Praxis said. "Zenon, Palamedes, and I are going to meet him there. I promised to help him move some props and work with some of the new gears and gadgets he has assembled for his stagecraft."

He pulled off chunk of bread, dipped it in a bowl of honey, and stuffed it in his mouth. He picked up his cloak and wrapped it around his shoulders, and in one elegant flourish he disappeared down the hallway and out the front door.

"Come," Theron said, "let us take advantage of the comforts of Menandros's hospitality and sit by the brazier." In the andron, Althaia perched on the edge of a chair, poked at the fire and watched Nikos out of the corner of her eye. He settled in a chair opposite her and leaned forward. Had she dared, she could have stretched out her fingers and touched him. Sappho's lines flooded her memory:

*When I see you, for a moment,*
*My voice goes,*
*My tongue freezes. Fire,*
*Delicate fire, in the flesh.*
*Blind, stunned, the sound*
*Of thunder, in my ears.*
*Shivering with sweat, cold*
*Tremors over the skin,*
*I turn the color of dead grass,*
*And I'm an inch from dying.*

"Now, what news can I deliver to the priestesses of Gaia?" His voice was low, as if the question was for Althaia's ears only.

Althaia locked her eyes on his. "I found a—"

She jumped as Theron clapped his hands and stood in a flourish. "I forgot Menandros has fresh goat's milk for us. Nephthys! Nephthys!" Nephthys hurried in as if the house were aflame. "Please see to it that we have a pitcher of milk and three cups. And warm it, please. That's the way I like it best."

Nephthys, confused, hastily returned to the kitchen and Theron returned to his chair by the fire. "Now, where were we? Ah, yes. We're still trying to understand what Althaia discovered," Theron said. "The practice of the autopsia examination is complicated, and we did not have much time."

Althaia saw the muscles in Nikos's jaw clench. He surely knew she had started to tell him something Theron did not want him to know. "I must have something to tell Thea, to tell my mother," he protested.

He is eager for news, she thought. And not just for the priestesses. Perhaps his interest in the girl was deeper than he let on. The muscles in her own jaw clenched as she fought to keep her mouth shut. I must watch myself. I do not know this man. She reminded herself that no matter how much she felt drawn to him, she must not say more than Theron felt appropriate. She had, after all, agreed to keep the findings secret for now.

"Yes," Theron agreed, "but it is important to set our findings in context so we can make sense of them. You said you often saw Charis on your visits to Delphi."

"We were often in the same company, yes."

"Nikos, we are all adults here, so I will speak frankly," Theron said. "I wonder if you knew whether or not she had a lover, perhaps someone who would not want the relationship to become known."

Nikos's face went ashen. He ran his tongue over his lip and fought the instinct to reach up and touch the scratches on his shoulders where Charis had clawed at him in her death throes. His voice was low, but steady. "What do you mean? Was she ... violated?"

Althaia's heart skipped a beat, and she prayed his look of alarm was simply the face of a man who cared for a friend, not a man who mourned a lover. "Her shoulders and arms were bruised, but I did not find evidence of a violation," she said, her voice quiet. "I did find skin and dried blood under her fingernails. Whoever was with her still bears her marks on his skin."

"We have reason to believe Charis's death occurred in the heat of a struggle," Theron added. "The question is what kind of struggle. Was it an attempted robbery? A lover's quarrel? Or something else entirely? Determining what happened in her last moments will help us discover the motive for leaving her body in the theater. Based on Althaia's examination, we believe she died somewhere else and was moved. We also believe her death was an accident. Of course we cannot be certain, but it is possible this is no longer a murder investigation, but rather an investigation into the desecration of the body and the sacred altar of Dionysos."

Nikos's heart clutched in his chest as if grasping at the possibility—the hope—that this investigation would be dismissed and Charis's death would soon be behind him. He sat forward. "If she was not murdered, how did she die? Of natural causes?"

"We are not prepared to detail our proofs at this time, and I did not say her death was natural. Only that it may not have been purposeful." Theron stood. "As for the priestesses, tell them we are still working to find the man responsible for desecrating her body and the sacred altar. For now, that must be enough."

"There is nothing more I can tell them?" Nikos stood, realizing the meeting was over.

"Nothing at pres—" Theron started.

"Tell them Phoibe is wrong," Althaia interrupted as she stood to face him. "The power of Apollon is undiminished, and the vapors of the oracle still emanate from the sacred fissure."

Nikos whirled to look down at Althaia. "You were in the adyton?"

From Theron's glare, Althaia knew he thought she'd said too much. He'd most likely want to throttle her as soon as Nikos left. But she knew what she was doing. Once Nikos delivered this news to the priestesses, Phoibe would surely know their cult was no threat to Apollon's great Oracle of Delphi, and perhaps the enmity between the two cults would diminish. "Apparently Philon had advance knowledge of your diversion, of the mob you organized to give us time to to get into the storehouse, and he saw fit to move the body for safekeeping. What safer place is there than the adyton?"

"But … how?" Nikos looked to Theron for answers. "How did you know? How did you get in there?"

"Ah, 'we' did not get in there," Theron said. "The examination was conducted by Althaia and her handmaid. They went in alone."

"Alone? But was it not guarded? Was it not reckless to send two women on such a mission? How could you make her do such a thing?"

Theron smiled and put his arm around Althaia's shoulders. "As you can see, she returned perfectly sound. And, always remember one thing, Nikomachos of Dodona, no man makes Althaia of Athens do what she does not wish to do herself."

"But still…."

"But still," Althaia placed her hand on Nikomachos's arm. "I went willingly into the dark and returned the richer for it." Nikos looked down at her, his gaze a branding iron on her soul. His face flushed, and her desire awoke as every logical thought flew from her mind. *I would go into the dark again, if it was with you….*

# CHAPTER TWENT-NINE

Nikos leaned forward, urging his horse into a canter. What happened back there? Not a murder investigation? The relief that had flooded through him when Theron said those words almost brought tears to his eyes. For a brief moment, he wanted to confess everything, but the truth was that Charis had died because of him, he had killed her brother, and he was trafficking in stolen treasures from the Sacred Precinct. Charis might not have died by his own hand, but he was no innocent. But how did they know? His horse slowed to round a narrow bend in the road, but he dug his heels in and pressed on as stones skittered under his mount's hooves. What kind of woman would examine a dead body? Would sneak into the sacred adyton? What kind of woman was Althaia of Athens?

At least he now knew Theron would be asking the same questions he had been asking himself: who placed Charis on the altar in the theater? Who moved her body and why? Nikos could think of only one man who would have had both motive and opportunity—Kleomon.

"Damn him!" Nikos swore, and his horse's ears flickered flat at the sound of his voice. With unfettered access to the Sacred Precinct, Kleomon could have seen him leave Charis on the temple steps. He would have realized it was an opportunity too good to pass up—eliminate Nikos, keep his share from the sale of the stolen temple treasures, and cause problems for the priestesses. All he would have had to do was move the body away from his temple and up to the altar of Dionysos, a favorite god of the women who also worshipped Gaia. Once the body was discovered, he could accuse the priestesses of practicing some ancient and long-forgotten sacrificial rite and get Heraklios looking in their direction—which also happened to be Nikos's direction. Take care of two problems in one swoop. The only thing Nikos had ever been good for was the contacts he'd made while traveling with or on behalf of his mother. But those contacts were already made. Kleomon and Diokles didn't need him anymore, and Kleomon, who hadn't been in favor of him getting involved in the first place, had made that clear on more than one occasion.

There was only one problem with this theory. Kleomon was not as stupid as he appeared—if he had known it had been Nikos who left the body on the temple steps, he would have already used that information against him. He was not the type of man to waste time with silly games. If he'd known, he would have had Heraklios tracking him down before morning's first light. So why hadn't he?

* * * *

"Can you do nothing right?" Melanippe's fingers, gnarled and knobby with arthritis, shook as she grasped her walking stick and tried to stand. Her handmaid, Kalliope, always at her side, jumped to help.

"Mother—" Nikos started.

"You did not stop the cursed examination. You did not discover what supposed proofs they found regarding Charis's murderer. In fact, you now say it was likely not a murder at all when it is obvious to everyone that her death cannot be explained any other way! You carry a torch and lead a band of misfits to the storehouse without even knowing Charis's body had been moved to the adyton. Once again, you disappoint me."

"Melanippe," Theodora soothed. "How could he know what the gods have hidden from us? He has discovered a great deal."

"He discovered nothing useful. He brought us no information that can help bring Charis's murderers to justice."

"But, what if it is as Nikos says? What if it was not murder at all?"

"Theodora, where is your respect for the Pythia? For Phoibe? She has seen that Apollon's priests are responsible for Charis's death and desecration. Why do you find it so hard to believe her?"

Theodora glanced at Kalliope, whose face was pale and tight with frustration. Theodora wasn't fond of Kalliope, but the gods only knew how the girl had put up with Melanippe these last few years. The old woman's illness had warped not only her body, but her mind—and she had always been quick to anger and even quicker to judge. Now she saw plots and threats in every shadow and around every corner.

"I do not discount what Phoibe saw in her vision," Theodora replied evenly. "But neither do I believe we should discount what Nikos learned from his visit with Theron."

Melanippe leaned on her walking stick and struggled toward the front door of their host's farmhouse. She wrestled with the heavy bolt and Kalliope once again leapt to her side. The girl, her face like a mask, void of all emotion, lifted the bolt and opened the door. Melanippe stood, back bent with years and framed against an increasingly angry sky. It was not even noon, but already the lamps were lit. The wind was picking up and a light mist threatened to turn into sleet. "Always the diplomat, Theodora. Perhaps if you had a son of your own, you would not be so inclined to favor mine."

Nikos stood and towered over his mother. "I will suffer on your behalf, but I will not permit you to lash out at Thea for no cause."

"No cause?" Melanippe laughed. "Listen to you both defending each other. Always it is the two of you together, always my son runs to another woman for comfort, always to Theodora when your knee is scraped or your precious feelings are hurt. And when she was not around? When she returned home to tend to her own duties, you wrote to her of my cruelty or turned to the women from the village and relied on the tradesmen and hunters to feed and nurture you. Yes, I admit it. I read your silly letters always complaining that I did not love you, always wishing you could have gone 'home' with her. So what allegiance do I owe you? You are nothing but a bastard son."

"Melanippe!" Theodora jumped to her feet and Kalliope looked as if she could strike the old woman where she stood. Nikos held his hand up to the two women and advanced on his mother.

"What you say is nothing new. You have spent the better part of my life telling me I am nothing but a burden. Theodora's friendship has always been a refuge when you turned away, when you set me aside even when I sought nothing more but to serve you. It is I who have no allegiance to you. And from this day forward I will serve you no more. We, Melanippe and Nikomachos of Dodona, are mother and son no longer." He gathered his cloak around him and stormed out the door past her. His horse reared as he yanked its head around, leapt on its back, and rode off into the gathering darkness at a gallop.

"Finally," Melanippe said. She leaned heavily on her walking staff—the same staff Nikos had so patiently carved for her years before. Her thumb rubbed absently over the head of the ruby-eyed serpent carved into it, and she stared after him. "Finally, he is a man."

# CHAPTER THIRTY

Sweating and breathing heavily beneath the blanket, Althaia opened her eyes to find Theron sitting in a chair watching her. "How long have you been there?"

"Long enough." In truth, he hadn't been there more than a few moments.

Althaia reddened, her face flush with embarrassment.

She looked around. Thank the gods no one else was in the room. She had fallen asleep on the couch in the andron, and was now groggy, with no conception of time. She readjusted her chiton, pulled the blanket around her, and sat up. "I was dreaming."

"Another nightmare or a dream of a different sort?"

Oh gods, could he know? Had she talked in her sleep? Had she touched herself? Had she cried out? What had he seen? Or heard? She brushed the hair out of her eyes and tried to read his face.

"It's all right," he said, his voice tender, soft, like when she was younger, when she confided her fears about the monsters and shades that had stalked her dreams since the day her mother died. She'd described the dreams to him a thousand times and each time he said they wouldn't stop until she stopped tormenting herself. Women died in childbirth all the time. Infant sons were mourned every day. She had been just a little girl who wanted her mother when she pushed past Praxis to burst in on the physician as he sliced open her mother's belly and pulled the stillborn baby out feet first. Theron insisted she could not blame herself for screaming and crying so hard that her father had to drag her from the room even as her mother's life-blood blossomed crimson on the pale sheet below her.

It didn't matter what Theron told her because the old mantis had told her otherwise. The blind soothsayer sat at the city gate near Keramikos, at the edge of the ancient cemetery where Althaia's ancestors were buried.

"Stay away from that old woman," her father had warned. "She's lost her senses. She sits at the city gates with the sole purpose of relieving passersby of an obol or two for her wine and bread. She deserves pity, not payment."

"Besides," Praxis teased, "If she is such an expert in divination, she should divine where to take a bath. She stinks of urine and incense."

No matter what her father said, Althaia was fascinated by the old woman. The day the mantis finally spoke to her, her mother and brother had not been dead a year. Althaia had sped down the road ahead of Praxis and as she swept through the city gates, the old crone called her name.

"Althaia of Athens."

Althaia skidded to a stop.

"How is it you live though the heir of Lysandros has been ferried across the Styx?"

Althaia took a step toward the old woman. The mantis sniffed the air and laughed softly.

"Pretty flowers and fragrant offerings will not appease the gods," the woman continued. "Such gifts will never change the fact that fathers want sons, not daughters."

The fistful of crocuses clenched in Althaia's hand fell to the dusty paving stones.

"You must atone for your father's loss. You must satisfy the gods by bringing me—"

Althaia never heard the old woman finish. She fainted dead away and did not wake until Praxis had carried her well away from the city gates. Then she clung to his neck and cried until he laid her on the couch in her father's study. She opened her eyes to the dark fury on her father's face and soaked Praxis's cloak wet with tears after Lysandros stormed out of the house. Her father's anger merely confirmed the mantis's words. Althaia lived while the son of Lysandros was no more. At seven years old, she did not realize her father loved her more than many men loved their sons, that he feared only for her safety. All she knew was that the blind woman had known who she was, and that the gods wanted something from her. After that day, her father forbade her from visiting the cemetery without him, and the next time they passed near the city gates, the old woman was nowhere to be seen.

Fourteen years later, Althaia's dreams still haunted her. A dreaded marriage to her cousin Lycon finally gave her father a male heir, but she knew the old mantis was right. The gods wanted something more. They wanted atonement. Maybe using her skills to find Charis's killer would finally satisfy them. Maybe helping someone in need would get rid of the nightmares once and for all.

But this dream was not a nightmare. This dream was something altogether different. Her heart still thudded in her chest.

"There is a man," she said and then looked away.

Without a word, Theron got up and opened the shutters. Cold, damp air washed across his face and spilled into the room. Heavy clouds squatted above the mountain tops and sprawled across the valley. "It is stifling in here. A bit of fresh air will make you feel better."

"Looks like a storm," she said.

He closed one of the shutters but left the other one cracked open. "I received a message from Heraklios. He wants me to meet him at his office, but I didn't want to leave until you were awake."

"I'll get my cloak." Althaia pushed the blanket off and tried to stand. She wobbled on her feet and sat back down.

He turned to face her. "I'm taking Praxis."

"But I'm the one who examined Charis," she protested.

"Philon and Kleomon will be there. They don't know you examined the body, and I plan to keep it that way. At least until we know more about the trinket you found."

He was right. Even if she didn't want to admit it, the prospect of facing Philon and Kleomon was not one she relished. "So, what time is it?"

"Midafternoon." Theron sat down again. He reached out and took Althaia's hands in his. "Dreams are funny things," he said. "Sometimes they show us aspects of ourselves the waking eye is not able or does not want to see. Sometimes they are like a theater in which the mind stages elaborate tragedies. From these we can gain insights about our innermost fears and desires. And sometimes they are just dreams. Sometimes, they mean nothing."

"But how is one to tell the difference?"

"Time? Distance? I don't know," he admitted. "Sometimes you never know."

"He seemed so real," she whispered. "The man in the dream, I mean. Flesh and blood. I could feel … it was … I mean … it was as if…." Her voice caught in her throat. "As if he was here with me, touching me."

"But he is not. As long as Praxis and I breathe, we will make sure you are safe."

"I know that," Althaia said. "That is not what scares me."

"What then?"

"I don't want to be kept safe. Not from him."

# CHAPTER THIRTY-ONE

Heraklios' office was large and generously appointed with a wide window that offered a view of the Temple. There was an impressive wooden desk, thick rugs to cover the stone floor, several braziers to keep away the chill, large torch stands to keep the room lit even in the darkest night, and two ornate high-backed chairs that Philon and Kleomon now occupied. Praxis and Theron stood in the middle of the room watching while Heraklios harangued the two priests from the comfort of a well-worn soldier's three-legged camp stool.

"How many times must I repeat myself?" Heraklios sounded as if he were dead tired of the refrain. "You get to run your temple your way, and as long as you don't cause me trouble, I look the other way. But I am in charge of everything else. And that means when someone shows up to claim a body found in the theater—not in the temple—you send a messenger for me. You do not just hand the body over."

Theron exchanged a glance with Praxis and said, "Philon, you said it was the girl's mother who claimed the body. Was there not a male relative with her? A brother?" Theron recalled his sister's words: Phoibe sent her consort Georgios to Charis's village to notify her brother. Both her parents are dead and she had no other living family.

"No. Only Georgios, Phoibe's consort."

"This Georgios, is he the same one that trains over at the gymnasium?

The pankratiast?" Heraklios asked.

"The same," Kleomon said. "And it proves the priestesses are involved. They want their sacrificial offering back. Phoibe wouldn't send her lover to get the body otherwise. Ignorant peasant. The man practically accused me of murder to my face," the old priest huffed.

"Just two weeks ago he was a brilliant champion when you bet on him to win his last competition." Utter contempt flashed across Philon's face as he spoke, and Theron wondered why the relationship between the two men was so poisonous.

"Just two weeks ago, we hadn't had a murder in the—" Kleomon said.

"This is troubling," Theron said, interrupting the priests' squabbling. "What about her brother?"

"What about him?" Philon asked.

"I expected him to claim the body."

"It is a man's job, but perhaps he was away from home and couldn't come. Why? What are you thinking?" Heraklios asked.

"That whoever claimed the body, it was certainly not anyone in her family."

"Why do you say that?" Kleomon said. "The mother was with Georgios."

"Her mother is dead. The girl's brother is her only surviving family."

"Impossible! How do you know this? Georgios would not dare lie to the priests of Apollon."

"Describe the woman," Theron commanded.

"There is little to describe," Philon answered. "She kept her face covered as if in mourning and her cloak was pulled up over her hair."

"Did she speak?" Theron asked.

"Not a word," Kleomon said, as he turned toward Philon. "It was you who wanted to be rid of the body. It was your decision to let them have it, and now it appears you have handed it over to Phoibe, and who knows what twisted rites those women will perform over it."

Philon's jaw clenched, his face flushed slightly, and his voice was low and even. "Kleomon, my friend, your general contempt for the female sex has clouded your thinking. We too honor the mother goddess and broadcasting your distaste for whatever rites the priestesses choose to perform in her name can only bring dishonor on us, on the Sacred Precinct, and on Apollon. I suggest you keep your opinions to yourself from now on."

Heraklios sighed and shook his head. "So there you have it, Theron. The body is gone. Claimed by someone posing as her mother—most likely one of Phoibe's followers. She probably let Georgios do all the talking so her voice would not be recognized. But unless we want to go retrieve it, cart it back here, and hold it here until her brother appears, there's nothing more to be done. If her brother does appear and seeks official help bringing her murderer to justice, we will do what we can to help him. But until that time, the matter is closed."

"Now, we must concentrate on re-sanctifying the theater," Philon said.

"On that, at least, we agree," Kleomon said. "The sooner we rid the Sacred Precinct of the stench of death, the better."

"How soon can you be prepared to conduct the ceremony?" Herklios asked.

"In three days time, we honor the death and resurrection of Dionysos," Philon answered, ignoring Kleomon's icy glare. "It is a favorite rite of Kleomon's as you can tell. We will be prepared to rededicate the theater at the same time."

"Excellent," Heraklios clapped his hands and stood. "That should make ol' Menandros happy. But are you certain you can be ready by then?"

"Of course." Philon waved his hand as if to dismiss Heraklios's concerns.

"We'll have the traditional music, plays, competitions? The people of Delphi will expect a show."

"Because of the short time frame, it will be a more subdued affair, but we'll give the playwright a ceremony that will satisfy his actors—and the public," Philon said as he stood to leave. He draped his cloak around him and looked down at Kleomon. The older priest, a grimace on his face, pushed himself up out of his chair as if every bone in his body ached.

"That's all we can ask for," Heraklios said as he opened the door wide. "Good day, gentlemen. In three days time, this murder will be nothing more than a bad memory, and we shall all be enjoying the pleasures of a celebration. Let us pray we can put this whole matter behind us."

Philon swept through the door imperiously as Kleomon waddled behind, and Theron and Praxis exchanged glances. "If prayer alone kept trouble at bay, the world would be a different place," Theron muttered.

"Words of wisdom from the famed philosopher," Heraklios said with a laugh, and slapped Theron on the back. "How long are you in Dephi?" he asked, and without waiting for an answer, said, "Before you head back to Athens, we must drink to old times and the king's health. Philip would not forgive me if I did not entertain you like one of the family."

Theron started to reply, but one of Heraklios's aides, a young soldier with an honest face and an efficient manner, hurried down the long corridor and said, "Sir, there's a man out in the portico. He insists on seeing you."

"What does he want?" Heraklios asked.

"There's been an accident. An old woman found in a ravine."

Heraklios turned to Theron and Praxis. "It's inevitable. Every season we find a few old men or women—even a youngster now and again—who slip on an icy path and end up at the bottom of a ravine. The locals come to us because they know I'll dispatch a soldier or two to drag the body out. A nasty business, but it's part of the job." He turned back to his aide. "Can't you take care of him?"

"He insists on seeing you."

Heraklios sighed. "Okay, take me to him."

Theron and Praxis followed Heraklios and his aide out to the portico where a weather-beaten peasant and a young boy waited. Outside, the sky was dark and heavy, and a thick mist seemed to hover in the air like a swarm. In the distance, the hooded figures of Philon and Kleomon trudged back toward the Sacred Precinct, their cloaks heavy in the damp.

"Tell the general what you found," the aide commanded.

The little boy looked up at the man, who nodded in encouragement, and said, "My brother and I were tending our sheep along the edge of the ravine behind our shepherd's hut when I first saw her."

"Who did you see?" Heraklios asked.

"The old lady. She's got a gold cloak and it stood out against the rocks. She was in the ravine. I think she fell from the outcrop above the creek. I left my brother with the flock and climbed down to see if she was still alive."

"And?"

The boy lowered his head. "She opened her eyes and she tried to speak, but I couldn't hear her. Her voice was too weak, but I tried to help her sit up. And then ... there wasn't anything I could do, so I went to find my father."

The boy looked up at his father, then back at Heraklios.

Heraklios squatted down before the boy. "Did you know her? Had you ever seen her before?"

"No. She was old. Older than my grandmother. But she looked rich, fancy."

"Rich, how?"

"Her cloak was fine spun, embroidered with shimmery threads like I never saw before, and she had lots of jewelry. Gold, and big stones."

"Gold, you say," Heraklios stood, his knees creaking and glanced at Theron before he turned to the boy's father, "Did you go down into the ravine?"

"I was already on my way to town when the boy caught up with me. We thought it best to come straight here instead of going back. My other son is still there, watching over the body to make sure no one comes along to disturb it—or rob it."

"Can you show my men exactly where you found her?" Heraklios asked the boy.

"The ravine runs down below our shepherd's hut. South of Delphi, off the road to Krissa."

He looked down at the boy, and clasped a strong hand on his bony shoulder. "You did a brave thing, young man, going down into that ravine by yourself. I'm sure your father is proud, and the old woman's family will be grateful. Who knows? There may even be a reward." He took his aide aside and said, just within Theron's hearing, "Take these two out to the stable and requisition a cart. Find my sister's son and have him take a couple of men to get the body. Tell him I want them back here as soon as possible. I've got a bad feeling about this."

As the aide ushered the man and his son toward the stable, Heraklios turned back to Theron and Praxis. "What is the world coming to? What kind of family would let an old woman wander around unescorted on a day like this?"

The news of a rich old woman at the bottom of a ravine set off alarm bells, but Theron couldn't say exactly why. He didn't ignore his intuition lightly, but there was no reason to suspect the old woman had anything to do with Charis.

"I guess your men don't need any help," Praxis said. Must be hearing the same alarm bells, Theron thought.

"My men?" Heraklios raised an eyebrow. "They need lots of help. But I think they can handle pulling an old lady out of a ditch." He eyed both Praxis and Theron. "Why? You two looking for a new mystery now there is nothing more to be done about Charis?"

Theron smiled. "I don't believe we've heard the last from Charis."

"Ha! I just hope to Zeus I don't ever hear from that Georgios. I'd prostrate myself before a Persian prince just to make sure I didn't get on his bad side. You ever hear of him?"

"Not before today. Is he any good?"

"He's a favorite for a laurel wreath in the next Pythian Games. Maybe even at Olympia. If you've got time, you should watch him train before you leave. One thing's for sure, though, we won't hear from the girl. The dead do not speak to the living, my friend."

"Maybe that's because the living don't take the time to listen," Theron said.

"This old lady may have a story to tell," Heraklios muttered.

"What do you mean?" Praxis asked.

"Oh, nothing." Heraklios said. "You had lunch yet?"

"No," Theron answered, watching Heraklios carefully. "We were going to stop at the Dolphin's Cove to get something on our way back to Menandros's. Want to join us?"

Heraklios snickered. "The Cove, huh? I'd better pass."

"It has quite a reputation apparently," Praxis said.

"Diokles and I have a healthy respect for each other. My men are regulars, but it's best for me not to patronize the place personally."

"Rumor has it the two of you had a confrontation at the temple storehouse last night," Praxis said.

"We all have to keep up appearances. Especially Diokles. A man of the people and all that. He's a wily one. Got his fingers in most every purse around here. But we keep an eye on him, and make sure he doesn't cause too much trouble. Besides, every town needs a place for the men to vent, get away from their wives and lovers, taste a few foreign delicacies, if you know what I mean. As long as Diokles doesn't get out of line, we leave him alone."

"And if he does?" Theron asked.

"Why would he?"

"I don't know," Theron said. "Do you think he could shed some light on who might have killed Charis? Every town boasts a man who knows what's what. Seems like we might be able to learn something from him."

"I tell you that investigation is over. But you'll like Diokles. No matter what he gets himself into, he always manages to come out on the right side of the law—and with a few more drachmas in his purse. If you stop in, try the lamb stew. It's the best I've ever had, and make sure he gives you the best wine in the house. Tell him I said to charge it to my nephew's account."

# CHAPTER THIRTY-TWO

The main room of The Cove was large and welcoming, although the light was dim and lamps were needed to brighten the rainy day. A long bar ran against one side of the room and people bustled in the kitchen beyond it. A young girl swept the floor and another dusted the staircase. Theron and Praxis settled in at a table near the fireplace and ordered wine, cheese, and bread from a lovely young boy who couldn't keep his eyes off Praxis.

"Is Diokles around?" Theron asked the boy.

"He's down in Kirra."

"He picked a wet day to travel."

"He went down first thing this morning, before the weather turned. Is there anything I can tempt either of you with?" The boy leaned provocatively over the table.

"Is he coming back? We'd like to meet him."

"I don't know. Probably. He seldom stays long."

"Seems like the mountain paths would be pretty dangerous on a day like today," Praxis said.

"Not for Diokles. He could travel those paths with his eyes shut." The boy brushed up against Praxis. "Even though he's not here, he would want me to make you as comfortable as possible. Are you sure there's nothing else I can get for you?"

"There is nothing else we desire at present," Praxis added. He fished a coin out of his purse and sent him on his way.

"I don't know why you pay them for batting their eyes at you," Theron said, watching the boy disappear into the back room.

"Sometimes it's the only way to get rid of them. Besides, a boy's got to make a living. And remember," Praxis said softly, "if it wasn't for Lysandros, that could have been me."

Praxis tried not to wonder where he might have ended up if it weren't for Lysandros. But sometimes he couldn't help it. All in all, his life had turned out well. There was little to complain about and sometimes it was easy to forget that, while he'd been born a free man, he'd spent most of his life a slave. But lately, he'd had trouble putting it out of his mind.

He had hoped, dreamed, prayed that Lysandros would free him upon his death, but that hadn't happened. And so he'd gone back to ignoring the little voice in his head that yearned to be his own man. That had worked for a while, but it all changed the morning he saw Nephthys on the auction block in Piraeus. He was walking by on the way to one of their dockside warehouses when he happened to notice her standing on the platform, men milling around, picking up her skirts, running their hands up and down her legs, feeling her hair, opening her mouth to examine her teeth. He'd stopped and stared, and then she slowly raised her face and met his gaze. He had seen thousands of slaves unloaded and sold in the market, and he'd bought more than a few for Lysandros, but at that moment a lightning bolt splintered his chest and settled as a smoldering coil in his gut. He recognized the look in her eyes, felt the fear and the sadness, the helplessness, and knew he had to save her.

He still hadn't had the courage to ask how she came to be on the auction block; all he knew was that she could read and write in Egyptian, Greek, and Phoenician and that she obviously had not been born into slavery. He didn't need to ask what had happened on the slaver's boat—he could see it in the way she stared off into the distance, in the way she wrapped her arms around herself. He no longer wanted to save her, protect her. He wanted to love her completely—love her as only a free man could.

After a few moments, Theron broke the silence. "I wonder what the priestesses said when Nikos delivered his news about the autopsia this morning."

"I was just thinking of that," Praxis lied and forced his thoughts back to the events of the last few days.

"I'd have thought we'd heard from him—or from Thea—by now. Perhaps Nikos is still with them. I can't imagine his mother being satisfied with his news."

Praxis nodded. "There's probably a message waiting at Menandros's."

"I told Zenon to find us at Heraklios's if a message came...." He trailed off and they drank in silence, leaving the plate of food untouched. Praxis stared into the fire and Theron watched the doorway as if he were expecting an unwelcome visitor to barge through at any moment.

Something's wrong. Praxis could feel it, but he couldn't put his finger on what was nagging at him. Lysandros's last wishes, Charis's murder, Theron's sister, the way Althaia and Nikos looked at each other, Nephthys, the old lady in the ravine—he turned it all over in his mind, examining everything from this way and that, just as the flames danced this way and that, licking the walls of the blackened fireplace. The day closed in about them and they sat, hunched over their mugs of wine as if a heavy blanket of dread hung over their heads.

"Dammit," he said abruptly, slamming his cup on the table.

"We should have gone with Heraklios's men," Theron said. "You're thinking about the old woman in the ravine."

"Another body, another woman, so soon after Charis. We should have at least checked to make certain they were unrelated, especially with all the priestesses of Gaia in Delphi for the Pythia's naming ceremony."

"That was my first reaction, too, but as Heraklios said, falls are not uncommon. And Nephthys was very nearly a victim of the steep pathways herself. Besides, the boy found the body down toward Krissa where the roads are—" Theron stood suddenly, sending the chair toppling backward. "Thea. That's what's been preying on my mind." He gripped the table. "She said she was staying with a 'family whose farmhouse sits north of the Delphi-Krissa road.'"

Praxis stood and grabbed his cloak, following Theron who was already striding toward the door.

"How could I have been so stupid?" Theron muttered as he threw open the door only to find Zenon running toward them.

"Master Theron!" Zenon called out.

*Please*, Theron thought, *do not let it be Thea.*

"A message came to the house," Zenon started, but Theron and Praxis were already running down the street, and it was all Zenon could do to keep up with them.

# CHAPTER THIRTY-THREE

Nephthys and Menandros watched as Althaia paced back and forth, biting her lip and rolling the scroll between her fingertips. Finally, Theron, with Praxis and Zenon behind him, barged into the room and Althaia rushed to meet them.

"A boy brought it and then left again right away," she said, handing him the scroll. "He wouldn't give his name. All he said was that it was urgent."

Theron stood near a lamp, ripped the twine, and unfurled the scroll. It was written in a rushed hand and the ink was smudged from being rolled too soon, but there was no mistaking the message. He let out an audible sigh, cleared his throat, and began:

*Melanippe is missing. Nikos came to us this morning, told us little, and left after he and his mother argued. Shortly after, a messenger came and Melanippe went out. At first she insisted on going alone, but her handmaid would not hear of it. Several hours later, Kalliope returned alone—wet and bleeding. She says Melanippe would not tell her where they were going, but that they were quickly set upon by roadside bandits. The priestess is not well. Her sight is poor and we fear the worst. Nikos does not know about his mother. Find him and bring him to us. Take the road toward Athens and at the turnoff for Krissa, go north instead. There is a path leading up toward the ridge. You will see a grove of plane trees around a spring. The house is there. We will be waiting.*

*-Thea*

“There’s still time to catch up to Heraklios’s men.” Praxis said. “They hadn’t started out yet when we left him and we were not long at the Cove.”

“Get the horses ready,” Theron said.

Praxis started out the door and then stopped and turned to Nephthys, “Get a bladder of oil and two torches and meet me in the stable. It will be full dark by the time we get to the ravine.”

“Wait, why are you looking for Heraklios’s men?” Althaia asked.

“A young shepherd found an old woman’s body in a ravine south of Delphi, near the road to Krissa,” Theron answered. “Praxis and I were still at Heraklios’s office when the boy and his father came in to report it, and the boy is leading a couple of soldiers to the body now. They were pulling a cart, so we can probably overtake them. If we catch up to them, we may be able to identify the body.”

“Nikos’s mother,” she whispered and grasped Theron’s arm. “I’m going,” she said. “If I go with Praxis, you can find Nikos.”

“All right,” Theron said, “but hurry, and dress warmly, the weather will only get worse as night falls.” Theron handed the scroll to Menandros. “You and Nephthys keep the note in case Nikos returns here. Give it to him, but make sure you tell him nothing more. There is hope yet we may be wrong in our suspicions. Send him on to the farmhouse.”

“You can count on me,” Menandros said.

Althaia ran to her room, grabbed her gloves and heavy traveling cloak, then followed Theron out into the street. Before he turned back toward Delphi to search for Nikos, he took her hand. “If it is the priestess of Dodona, you and Praxis must convince Heraklios’s men to take the body to the house where my sister is staying. We don’t want news of her death to get out until we’re sure how she died, and this time, I want to make sure you can examine the body without having to crawl through the bowels of a temple. Tell them it is Heraklios’s instructions, if need be. I’ll take care of any repercussions later. I will meet you at the farmhouse as soon as I can. You remember the directions?”

“At the turnoff for Krissa, go north on a path up toward the ridge. There’s a spring and a grove of plane trees,” she repeated. “I am sure Heraklios’s men will know it.”

“Be careful. Slippery roads are dangerous enough, but Praxis and I fear more than a slick path is to blame for the old woman's fall."

"But we cannot know until we get there," Althaia said.

"And maybe not even then. But our soldier's bones tell us something more dangerous than bad weather is loose in Delphi."

# CHAPTER THIRTY-FOUR

As the nearly invisible sun sank lower behind them, a deepening gloom crept across the sky. Clouds heavy with the promise of still more rain pressed down into the mountain passes where drizzle gave way to thick fog. *Death is in the air,* Althaia thought with a shudder. The road was muddy with patches of ice covering rain-filled ruts, and though they were anxious to overtake Heraklios's men, they dared not urge their horses into a canter or even a fast trot, so slick was the path.

She kept her eyes ahead, but every once in a while stole a glance sideways and was comforted when Praxis returned her glance with a reassuring smile. More than once, she thanked the gods her father had found Praxis and brought him home to Athens. Had they answered her prayers for a perfect brother, the gods could not have done better than the man riding next to her. He had been her friend, confidant, and protector, and her childish infatuation had deepened into something that she could not even name. Someday she would have to face the prospect of manumission. She owed him that. If any man deserved his freedom, it was Praxis.

"What are you thinking?" he asked.

Her cheeks flushed and she was glad for the gray mist. "I'm thinking about us. About how you've always looked after me and how I probably don't tell you enough how much I depend on you."

He was silent, and she didn't know whether she should give voice to her thoughts or not. They rode on for a while and finally she said, "I used to imagine you were as strong as Herakles. I'd make up all sorts of horrible tasks for you to undertake before you could come back home and claim me for your bride." She laughed softly. "Little girls…."

"I would have gladly undertaken those tasks, but I would never have been allowed to claim my prize. That's not the world we live in."

"I know that now. They were foolish daydreams."

Praxis sighed and said nothing.

* * * *

The path grew wider as Althaia and Praxis approached where the road to Athens intersected the road to Krissa and on down to the port town of Kirra. It wasn't long before they overtook Heraklios's men. A slender, well-scrubbed young lieutenant led the group, followed by an older, heavy-set soldier with half of his ear missing and a thick, jagged scar running down the side of his neck. Another soldier, barely more than a boy, with eager eyes, long, stringy curls, and pockmarked skin drove a donkey pulling a small cart in which the shepherd and his son sat. The group had already turned south toward Krissa and had just left the road to cut across the field toward the small shepherd's hut in the distance.

Praxis made the appropriate introductions, invoked Heraklios's name and insisted he and Althaia had instructions to help identify the body. After a heated discussion, and over the angry objections of the old soldier—"Half-an-ear," Althaia named him—the lieutenant decided to allow them to ride along. Few, male or female, were immune to Praxis's powers of persuasion.

The lieutenant rode beside the wagon, getting directions from the boy, while Half-an-ear brought up the rear. As they rode, Althaia felt the man's eyes boring into her back. It made her skin crawl. It was only a little farther, she told herself, and she must keep her mind on the task ahead.

"There's my brother," the boy said excitedly. "And the body is down there," he pointed toward the bottom of the small cliff. "She's right below that overhang. See? At the bottom of the ravine."

"I think I see where you mean," the lieutenant said. He turned to the boy's father. "You should take your boys home now. Rest assured, we will let you know if there is any reward."

"Thank you." The boy jumped out of the wagon and ran over to his brother. "There might even be a reward! We could be rich!"

Althaia smiled in the darkness as the boy began helping his brother gather the flock and, with their father beside them, guide them toward home.

"Here!" The lieutenant called to the skinny, pockmarked soldier. "Get these torches lit. And you," he turned to Half-an-ear, "take that blanket in the back of the wagon. You can carry the body back up. Let's go."

Praxis lit a torch for himself and another for Althaia. "The lieutenant insists you stay up here with the horses," he said. She shot him a *that's ridiculous* look and he sighed. "Be patient, Althaia."

"I will not be patient, Praxis. You must convince him. Seeing the body where it fell can give us important clues. I'm going with you," she insisted as she dismounted.

Praxis sighed. "Okay, but remember, if it is the priestess, we need to convince the lieutenant to take the body to Thea, and that means we do not want him angry at you and unwilling to cooperate." He tied their horses to the back of the cart, lit both torches, and handed one to her. "Come. I'll make the case again, but do not challenge the lieutenant. If he relents, fine. If not, you must stay up here and trust me to do my best to report what we find back to you. We can always return tomorrow in the daylight and you can poke around in the rocks as much as you want."

"But—"

"Before you start arguing with me, let's talk to the lieutenant."

They made it to the edge of the ravine when the lieutenant, who was figuring out the best way to climb down the muddy slope into the deep rock-filled ditch, turned around, took one look at Althaia, and said, "No."

"But—" she started.

"This is no place for a woman, and I'm certainly not going to be responsible for your safety down there in the dark," he waved his torch and flames danced and sputtered in the damp air. "One slip and I'd have two bodies to deal with."

"But I may be able to identify her."

"You can identify her when we bring the body back up. You're staying up here, and that's final." He glared at her and turned to Praxis. "Tell her to stay or I won't let you go down, either."

"I'll stay," Althaia relented. "But I'm staying right here so I can watch what you're doing."

The lieutenant ignored her and began climbing down into the ravine with Praxis behind him.

Althaia then raised her torch and surveyed the landscape around her. Bells tinkled in the distance. The flock the boys and their father were shepherding home? She studied the outcropping looming above the far side of the ravine. Tufts of brush clung to otherwise exposed rock where the relentless march of time had sent crumbling earth and stone into the ancient stream bed below. The road to Krissa was up there, back a ways from the edge. But close enough for a traveler to see her torch. She hoped there were no bandits working the mountain paths tonight.

It wasn't long before she heard grunting and swearing. The two soldiers scrambled back up the slope with the body wrapped in a woolen blanket and slung over The Skinny One's shoulder. Half-an-ear had obviously pulled rank.

"Is Praxis coming up soon?" Althaia asked as she climbed out of the wagon. The evening was closing in around her and she was suddenly uneasy about being in the company of the two soldiers.

"Your friend is scouring the rocks for something," The Skinny One said as he flopped the body down in the bed of the wagon. "And the lieutenant is helping him."

"Blood and brains. That's all they're gonna find down there." Half-an-ear said. He reached out and unceremoniously unfurled the blanket, rolling the old woman over and up against the side of the wagon. "Head's bashed in pretty good. Don't look like a fall did that," he said as he rolled her over so she lay face up.

Althaia bent down and touched the battered face of Melanippe, priestess of Dodona. She ran her fingertip along the thin, blue lips that had once uttered the words that connected men to the gods and said her own silent prayer for the woman's soul. News of her death would spread quickly among the priests and priestesses throughout Greece and into Epirus, Illyria, Makedon and even Egypt. Dodona, along with Siwa in the Egyptian desert, was the oldest and most mysterious of all the oracles. Anything other than an accidental death would be devastating news for those who served the gods.

Althaia prayed Melanippe met her death peacefully, a slip of the foot on the slick path or a wrong turn in the fog and mist. Although her only meeting with the priestess had been a disaster, she did not wish her ill. She was, after all, Nikos's mother. She pictured his green eyes and a jolt shot through her chest.

She wedged the end of her torch in the corner of the wagon and looked at the priestess. Her straggly gray hair was wet and matted with rain and blood and the side of her face had been crushed and lacerated by the jagged rocks. Althaia gently rolled her head to one side and found that the back of her skull had been crushed as well and was still sticky with blood. Althaia wiped her fingers on the blanket and looked back across the ravine to the outcrop above it; was it high enough for the fall to have done such damage? It was surely no more than a twenty-five or thirty foot drop. But, the priestess was ill and frail. Her bones, weakened by age, may have been more easily broken from such a fall. Althaia pulled back her bloodied cloak and looked at her bare arms. There were scratches but no significant bruises. Melanippe must have been dead before she landed in the ravine. Half-an-ear was probably right. The fall didn't cause her death. One thing was certain; she was not the victim of a robbery. Althaia ran her fingers over the thick gold necklace Melanippe wore and looked closely at the gnarled fingers still adorned by rings set with the precious stones befitting a priestess of Zeus.

She carefully covered Melanippe's face and tucked the blanket back around her body. She turned to face Half-an-ear, who stood much too close to her, arms crossed, staring. "I know this woman," she said. "We have instructions to take her body to her nearest kin."

"You related?"

"No. She is not from here, but we know where her people are staying."

"If you're not a relative, she goes back to Delphi."

"What is your name?" Althaia asked, sharply. Maybe it was time for her to pull rank. "Heraklios would be interested to know you're being uncooperative."

"My name don't matter. I asked if you was family, you said no. So she goes back to Delphi. Standard procedure."

Maybe a more measured approach would work better, she thought.

"We expect you to accompany us, to escort the body up to where she's been staying. It's not far. We'll find her son—in fact, someone is looking for him right now."

"When you find him, send him to Delphi. His momma will be waiting."

"You don't understand," Althaia started.

"I understand perfectly," Half-an-ear grinned and Althaia's stomach flip-flopped. "I saw the way you looked at that necklace, those rings. I'm sure they're worth a fortune. Looks to me like you didn't have time to steal her jewels before your lover bashed her head in. Don't take too much hard thinking to figure he's down there trying to hide whatever we might find by light of day."

"What? That's ridiculous," Althaia sputtered, unable to comprehend what the man had just said.

"How else you two come to be out here?" Half-an-ear retorted.

"What are you saying? We didn't kill her! You have no idea who you're dealing with, who this woman is," Althaia stood her ground.

"I could give a gryphon's prick who she is. Our orders were to retrieve the body and take it back to Delphi. Then you two show up and claim you have news of a missing person. You claim Heraklios knows you. You claim he sent you to join us, to identify the body. But you have no proof. You can't ride in here and pull the wool over my eyes like that damn fool, pretty-boy lieutenant down their swooning over your lover. If Heraklios sent you, you would've had written orders. But you don't." He sneered and licked his lips.

"How dare you talk to me like that? He is not my lover, we most certainly did not kill her and we are not after her jewels."

"I'm willing to believe any story you want...." Half-an-ear took a step toward her.

"It's not up to you. It's up to the lieutenant." Althaia was not going to let this ignorant, filthy man intimidate her.

"You see the lieutenant here?"

She turned to The Skinny One standing over by the edge of the ravine. "Call the lieutenant back up here," she demanded.

"Hoo boy! That's a bold one for you," Half-an-ear laughed and slapped his thigh. "A woman giving orders to a Makedonían soldier. Can't wait to tell that one back at barracks tonight."

"I'll get him myself," she said and started toward the ravine. Half-an-ear blocked her way and took another step closer.

"You make a sound, and you'll be sorrier than you can imagine."

Althaia stepped backward. She could feel the flat board of the wagon's side wall against her back.

"Truth is you're lying," he said. He chuckled and glanced over his shoulder toward The Skinny One who looked down into the ravine and then nodded. "But I'm willing to believe any story you want to spin—for a favor," he rasped and pulled his chiton up to his waist with one hand and grabbed himself with the other.

"Stay away from me," Althaia growled, willing herself to hold his stare.

"No." He advanced on her, stroking himself with slow, deliberate movements. "You make a noise and we just say we caught you trying to take them baubles right off the old lady's fingers." He laughed, a low, guttural laugh that made the bile rise in Althaia's throat and her knees buckle beneath her. "Then when your lover comes running up here, we say we think he's coming to attack us. My friend over there's not very smart, but he knows how to stick a dagger in a man's belly. We Makedoníans don't much like folks who murder defenseless old ladies. And seeing how he's a slave—that's right, I saw his brand, may be faded, but it's still there—loverboy'll be punished but good."

Althaia thought of the first time she fell off a horse. It was the pretty little mare Praxis gentled for her. She remembered lying on the ground, all the breath knocked out of her. She couldn't speak, couldn't move. Now, it was the same. But this was a man, not a mare, and she was too terrified to open her mouth, too terrified to call Praxis for help. Too terrified Praxis would die if she did.

She struggled to find her voice. "We didn't kill her, ask Heraklios."

"But you give me what I want—" he whispered, then planted his mouth on hers, pushing his hot tongue through her clenched teeth. Her knees gave way, but the pressure of his body held her up against the wagon, even as the torch she'd wedged in the corner toppled to the ground. He pulled back and looked into her eyes. Smiling hungrily, he cupped her breast in his hand and squeezed hard. "—and I let you take a trinket or two off the old lady and let your friend live. You keep your mouth shut. I keep my mouth shut. We all go home happy."

"Please don't do this," she begged, struggling to make her mind work, to sort out what was happening. The ground seemed to spin out from under her when Half-an-ear grunted, pushed her cloak aside, and thrust his hand between her legs nearly lifting her off the ground. His breath smelled of bad teeth, sour wine and day-old onions, and she willed herself not to faint. But he was right. She was lying. There were no written orders. Heraklios had no idea they were there. And she would do anything to make sure Praxis did not meet a dagger in the dark as he climbed up out of the ravine.

He pressed against her and pushed her chiton up to her waist. I must not scream, she told herself, and maybe Praxis will live. I will not scream. I will not ... The blood pounded in her ears like galloping hoof beats as Half-an-ear's mouth clamped down on hers. She squeezed her eyes shut and steeled herself for what she knew was coming next. And she began to pray. Please. Please. She prayed for Praxis to hurry up from the ravine to protect her, and she prayed for him to stay down in the ravine so she could protect him. She prayed that every rumor she had ever heard about Theron was true and that he would carve Half-an-ear up and feed him to the wolves, raw, and that he would know how to purge the man's seed from her body before it took root. She prayed that the skinny, pockmarked soldier laughing in the distance would never see the sunrise. And she prayed that her father would forgive her for not keeping a knife in her boot like he always told her to.

She heard a gasp and felt the weight of Half-an-ear's body fall slack against her. Had she fainted? Was it over already? She slid down to the ground and he rolled off her. There were hoof beats, footsteps, voices. Someone was yelling. She opened her eyes. Half-an-ear lay beside her, face down, with a still-quivering dagger sticking out from between his shoulder blades. Near the edge of the ravine, someone leapt from a horse and tackled The Skinny One as he tried to run. She could see the glint of steel against that bastard's scrawny neck and, at that moment, wanted nothing more than to see that glint disappear.

And then she saw him. Nikos. Jumping down from his horse and running toward her, his cloak trailing behind like a wave. He knelt beside her and held out his hand. And it hit her. *Nikos had been the hooded man in the cave.* The crumpled body was his mother, trying to explain, trying to tell him something. The pounding hoof beats, the glint of the blade. It was all Nikos. Just like in the dream.

"It's you," she whispered as he gathered her in his arms. Then, as the emotion of the moment and the knowledge she was safe washed over her, she wondered: Does he know? Does he know it's his mother in the wagon?

*And where is Praxis?*

# CHAPTER THIRTY-FIVE

Since he and Praxis had just been at The Cove, Theron skipped it and made the rounds of the other inns and taverns in town. Even though no one had seen him all day, most people Theron asked either knew Nikos personally or knew him by reputation. And it was Nikos's reputation that, by the end of his search, had Theron determined to keep Nikos as far away from Althaia as possible. Theron didn't begrudge any man the right to spend his money on pleasures of the flesh, but the rumors were rife that Nikos didn't have to spend his money, that more than one innocent maid, or even bored matron, had fallen for his supposed charms. He'd known too many men who made a hobby of seducing and abandoning lovely young maidens and matrons alike. For some soldiers, mercenaries for hire like he had been, a beautiful face, beckoning arms, and warm legs wrapped around your waist were the only thing that kept a man sane. Some kept camp wives. Some looked for a new home port wherever they pitched their tent. For men like that, they just needed a safe place where they didn't have to think about killing—or being killed.

But some men didn't look for comfort or companionship, they looked for release. Physical, emotional, it didn't matter. They'd take a woman and break her just like they'd break a horse. Only difference was, they'd keep the horse and walk away from the woman.

A man like that was the last thing Althaia needed. A life of loneliness as Lycon's wife would be better than being one more in a long line of used goods. The more he thought about Nikos and the way he looked at Althaia—and the way she looked back—the more he worried about the dream she'd had that afternoon when he'd walked in and overheard more than he'd ever admit, the more he was thankful they weren't going to be in Delphi long. Once they were back in Athens, whatever Althaia thought she felt for Nikos wouldn't matter.

* * * *

Eventually Theron made his way back to The Cove, took an empty table, ordered some wine, and sat back to watch and wait. If Nikos didn't show up soon, he would return to Menandros's and then head up to the farmhouse. It was full dark now and he hoped that if it was Melanippe in the ravine, Praxis and Althaia would already be escorting the body up to the farmhouse. Or perhaps it wasn't Melanippe after all. No, the priestess was dead. He knew it in his gut, and he knew it wasn't an accident.

He took a long draught from his cup and looked around the room. Heraklios's opinion of the food and wine must be shared by more than a few of Delphi's residents. The place was full. He wondered about the men and women of Delphi—those who lived off the land and those who lived off the Sacred Precinct. According to the ancient myths, both men and gods had fought battles over the sacred mountainside and the vast, fertile plain that lay in its shadow. So much bloodshed, so many lives lost, for what? Power? Money? What was one more dead girl, one more priestess? Even if he could find the killer, or killers, what would it change in the long run? Life would continue as it always had with pilgrims traveling days and sometimes weeks from across Hellas to pay for the privilege of asking a single question of a woman they would never set eyes on. Another priestess who gives her life over to the gods. Just like my mother, he thought. Just like Nikos's mother.

He finished his wine and made his way over to the long table separating the main room from the kitchen. Five or six men were lined up along its length sharing wine, bread and a pungent hot fish soup. A young woman with flashing, charcoal-lined eyes, henna-dyed hair, and ample, inviting breasts stood behind the table mixing water into a large krater of wine and laughing at the men who seemed to be taking bets on who would bed her first that evening.

"You're wasting your time tonight, gentlemen. I'm spoken for," she said.

"Diokles will never know," one of the men said with a conspiratorial look. "None of us will tell," he whispered loud enough for all to hear.

"It's not Diokles she's waiting for," another said.

"Yes, the man with all the pretty silver owls!" The whole group laughed.

"His silver owls are very lovely, aren't they," she laughed. "Almost as lovely as he is!"

"I'd just like to know where he gets them all," another said. "Escorting mama here and there doesn't seem to be a very profitable livelihood if you ask me."

"If you really want to know where he gets it, you could ask Diokles—or even old Kleomon. But if you prefer to keep your anatomy intact, it's wiser to keep your questions to yourself."

"Excuse me," Theron interrupted the banter. "I wonder if you could help me. I'm looking for someone who is supposed to be staying here—Nikomachos of Dodona."

The group erupted in laughter. "You've come to the right place, stranger. This little lady is aching to find him, too!"

"If you've come to pay a debt, you might find him in later," another voice joined in. "If you've come to collect a debt, well, you'll have better luck waiting for Zeus to show up and buy a round of drinks for the house!"

"Are you expecting him tonight?" Theron asked.

"Are you a friend?" the young woman asked.

"Are you here to pay up or get paid is what she wants to know," prodded the man sitting nearest Theron.

"Neither. I have news I am sure he will want to hear."

"Then maybe you can tell me," the woman said. "I will pass the message along when I see him."

"What is your name?" Theron asked.

"Aphro."

He raised an eyebrow.

"My mother was one of the sacred servants of the Temple of Aphrodite in Corinth. She said I was the most beautiful baby she had ever seen. A child destined for love." She batted her lashes, and tilted her head seductively to one side. "She was afraid to name me Aphrodite. Afraid the goddess might get jealous and strike me—or more likely, her—dead. So I am simply Aphro."

"Well, Aphro, do you have any idea where I might find Nikos? I have urgent news for him."

"He may walk in at any moment. Or he may not turn up for another six months. But, in point of fact, I've been expecting them back all day."

"Them?"

"He went down to Kirra to meet Diokles."

"When he returns, tell him Theron has gone to pay his respects to his sister and that it is imperative he join him as soon as possible."

"I take it you are Theron."

"I am. The message is urgent, Aphro. It cannot wait. Even for love."

The playfulness fell from her face and Aphro looked at Theron with genuine concern. "I'll make sure he gets it."

* * * *

Nephthys had been pacing for so long her legs were tired. The note from Theodora was sweaty in her hand. She looked down at Zenon, snoring softly by the brazier. Had she ever slept so soundly? If so, she couldn't remember. She sat and watched the boy sleep. *How did you end up a slave?* she wondered. In what distant land were you born? Are you better off here with a kind master and a warm house with plenty of food? *Fate is a funny thing, she thought.* In Egypt I was a free woman with wealthy parents and a respected husband. But my husband did not love me, did not ask me what I wanted, what I thought, or how I felt. He bedded me and I felt nothing. Each month he waited to see if his seed would grow. Each month, nothing. Each month, a beating. Here, I am a slave. Yet Praxis and Theron ask me what I think and have not whipped or beat me yet. And every time Praxis reaches out his hand and touches mine, my heart feels as though it has been pierced through with a burning spear. And perhaps Althaia—my mistress—is even growing to respect me. *Maybe it was my fate to come to Greece.*

The door swung open and Theron strode into the room. "No word?"

"Nothing," she jumped up, startled, even as Zenon slept soundly.

"Where is Menandros?"

"Retired to his study."

"Come, I must speak to you both."

She followed Theron to Menandros's private rooms where they found him at a large table with sheaves of papyrus and sheets of parchment spread before him. He was so engrossed in his work that he didn't look up until Theron spoke. Then he jumped as if a snake had crawled up his leg.

"By the gods, Theron, knock next time!"

"There is no time for niceties at present."

"See all this?" Menandros spread his arms out across the desk. "I'm not exactly sure how I am going to fit it together—it will be a completely new kind of play!—but, I am determined to make it work."

"I'll congratulate you when you wear the laurel wreath, but in the meantime, you must pay attention. As far as I know, Nikomachos is not aware his mother is missing. I left word at The Cove for him to go to the farmhouse, and I am going there now, but I want Nephthys to stay with you. It's dark and cold and I can travel better alone. Besides, there is still a chance I will meet Praxis and Althaia on their way back—if they found that the old woman was not the priestess. Otherwise they will already be at the farmhouse. I will return in the morning or will send word first thing. I want you to keep the dogs in the yard and the gates locked.

"Oh, Theron, you should have been a dramatist. We are in no danger here."

"I'm sure you're right, but the girl was found in your theater, I was charged with investigating her death, and it is known that our party is staying in your house. And if something were to happen to Nephthys," he caught her gaze and smiled, "Praxis would not be a happy man."

"I'll lock up tight and keep the dogs outside," Menandros said. "But, you worry too much, my friend,"

"Perhaps. But if something were to happen to you, well, I would miss making your life miserable."

# CHAPTER THIRTY-SIX

Nikos held Althaia's trembling body in his arms, stroked her hair, and whispered *It's alright, it's alright* over and over again. He brushed the hem of her chiton back into place over her legs, and turned her face away from the loathsome soldier who lay face down on the ground behind him. What in Zeus's name was she doing out in the middle of nowhere on a night like this? Where was Theron? Where was Praxis? *Why was she with these soldiers?*

He glanced over at Diokles standing at the edge of the ravine. His blade was pressed into the throat of the skinny soldier as he yelled down at the men in the ravine. This was Diokles's territory, and he wanted an explanation. Now. He and his partners in Kirra controlled the bandits operating between Delphi and the port. They viewed the whole enterprise as a sort of toll, a tax to keep the roads relatively safe. The point was to help travelers lighten their loads just a bit, but not enough to frighten pilgrims from traveling to Delphi. That would benefit no one. Murder and rape were absolutely forbidden, and Diokles was known for handing over to the authorities the names and addresses of anyone who was too rough or who didn't share a cut of the takings. After all, they had to pass on a share to Heraklios, too. So when they were returning from their business at the coast—from selling the gold tiara Charis's brother had stolen—and saw the torches in the ravine and the activity clustered around the cart, Diokles wanted to know exactly what was going on. As they rode toward the figures around the cart, Nikos had been stunned to recognize Althaia, and, at that point, instinct took over.

Now he held Althaia in his arms and wanted nothing more than to keep her there, to bury his face in her hair, to wash away any memory of what had just happened to her. Then he heard voices and turned to see Praxis and another man scramble up from the ravine. As Praxis ran toward them, Nikos could hear the other man sputtering as Diokles demanded an explanation. Then Praxis was there. He dropped to his knees and Althaia fell into his arms.

Nikos stood and stepped away as Althaia clung to Praxis.

"Did he…?" Praxis whispered. He looked up and Nikos shook his head.

Her voice caught in her throat. "He said—"

"Shh. I never should have left you up here alone."

Althaia's voice was just a whisper, and Nikos tried not to listen, but as he moved away he caught her words.

"He said we were thieves, that we'd murdered her for her jewels."

Nikos saw the blood drain from Praxis's face. "Why didn't you call out for me? Why didn't you scream?"

"I couldn't. I had to let him…." Althaia stammered. "He said they'd kill you if I screamed … because … because you're just a slave and he'd say you tried to run.'"

Praxis's voice was ragged, thick with rage. "I am pledged to protect you, Althaia. Not the other way around."

She was quiet for a moment, and then she wiped her eyes and pushed herself away from Praxis. "No," she said. "We protect each other. That's what family does."

Nikos gripped the hilt of his sword till his fingers turned white and clenched the muscles in his jaw so hard his teeth hurt. *We protect each other. That's what family does.* So this is what a true family is like. Even though this man is a slave, his mistress treats him better than my own mother treats me. No, he told himself, after this morning, I have no mother. I have no family.

* * * *

"Nikos," Diokles said. "I'm sorry."

The lieutenant held the skinny soldier at a respectful, and safe, distance while Althaia unwrapped the blanket from around Melanippe of Dodona's body. Nikos sucked in his breath, but stood as still as a graven image.

"How long has she been dead?" he asked without looking up. He should feel something. Anything. Sorrow? Anger? Hatred? Disgust? But there was nothing. Or nothing he wanted to admit to. He could feel Diokles watching him.

"There is really no way to know for certain," Althaia replied. "The death rigor has begun to set in, so several hours at least."

Several hours? Nikos fought to make sense of everything. He looked up at his friend standing across the cart. So, it wasn't you, Nikos thought. As often as Diokles had talked about giving Melanippe of Dodona a little nudge into the afterlife, Nikos didn't really believe his best friend would have actually killed her. Or had her killed. Besides, they both knew her illness was getting the best of her, that she wasn't long for this world, anyway. And there were plenty of other people who would be happy see his mother on the far side of the Styx.

He had to think. He reached out and took his mother's hand in his. Cold. Just like it had been his whole life. Actually, that wasn't right. He was her bodyguard and errand boy, not her nursemaid, and the truth was he couldn't remember the last time he touched her. He looked at the rings on her fingers. The signet rings of a priestess. All except one. He tugged at the plain silver band, twisted it over her swollen knuckle, and placed it on his little finger. *This one is mine.*

He examined her face. Her neck. It must be back in Dodona, he thought. She didn't wear her necklace anymore. Had refused to wear it since the day he started wearing his. And now his was gone. The necklace was the only thing he had ever owned that belonged to his father, besides the ring he now wore. The day his father walked into the Sacred Grove in Dodona, he was wearing a plain silver band on one finger and a torc with three silver balls—one for each orb in the sky, the sun, the moon and the earth—around his neck. He was red-headed and broad shouldered and he spoke but a little Greek. He told the priestesses he was a Brythonik Kelt from the Stone Circle at the center of the world. He'd been traveling for two years and was seeking wisdom. Melanippe did not know where Brythonik was, but she told him the center of the world was in Delphi, that Zeus himself had let loose two eagles and they had crossed over the exact spot now marked with the omphalos stone. And she told him all he needed to do to find wisdom was to stay right there and ask her. Zeus's Sacred Oak would tell him whatever he needed to know. He doubted that could be true, but decided to stay for a while to find out.

He stayed long enough to get Melanippe with child and see his son born. Then he slipped his ring off and placed it on her finger. And he took two of the silver balls from his torc, threaded them on silver chains and gave them to her. One for his lover. One for his son. To remember him by. Then he walked back out of the grove and never returned.

At least that's the story he heard from Thea, and she'd heard it from her mother. The great priestess of Dodona never mentioned it. Not once. He didn't even know if it was true, although every time he caught his reflection in a pool of water and saw the reddish hair and green eyes staring back at him, he knew there was at least a fragment of truth to the story.

Now he would never hear the truth from his mother's lips. It didn't matter. He was finally free of her and he had someone to thank for doing what he could never have done himself. But if Diokles didn't kill her, who did? Kleomon? Philon? Any of the other jealous priests or priestesses across Hellas who wondered how a rheumy, demented old woman could still wield such power and respect?

Althaia watched the emotion play out across Nikos's face and her heart caught in her throat. It was all she could do to stand apart from him, to not take him in her arms, press his head against her breast and comfort him as he had comforted her.

"Several hours," he mumbled. "I left her at midday."

"The message from Thea said—" Praxis started.

"What message?"

"Thea sent a note to Theron. She didn't know where you were. She said your mother received a message and that after that she and her handmaid left the farmhouse. The handmaid returned several hours later. But she was alone."

"Theron is looking for you in Delphi and will meet us at the farmhouse where your mother was staying," Althaia added.

Praxis gripped Nikos's arm, "Know that we will do everything in our power to help you find your mother's killer." Praxis hadn't liked the naked hunger in Nikos's eyes when he looked at Althaia, but he had saved Althaia's honor—and likely his own life. There was a debt to be paid.

Nikos met Praxis's eyes. "Thank you."

Diokles spoke up. "The lieutenant has agreed to escort you up to where your mother was staying. If you want me to, I'll accompany you."

"No," Nikos said. "Go home. Aphro will be waiting, and there's nothing you can do."

"Send word if you need anything." Diokles jumped up to mount his horse, and then looked down at his friend. "I wish it didn't have to happen like this," he whispered. "Truly."

Nikos felt the pinpricks behind his eyes. He nodded at his friend and turned away.

* * * *

After Diokles rode off toward Delphi, Nikos mounted and led the way toward the farmhouse with Althaia at his side while Praxis followed behind the wagon driven by the Lieutenant. In the back of the wagon, the young soldier, hands and feet bound, rode next to the two bodies—the priestess wrapped in her cloak and covered by the blanket and the other soldier staring, sightless, up at the night sky.

Althaia and Nikos rode in silence. The cold fog penetrated everything—cloaks, chitons, skin, bones, but Nikos paid no attention to it. Instead, he struggled to ignore the faint mixture of jasmine and fresh-pressed olive oil clinging to Althaia's hair, tried to stop imagining what would have happened had they not been returning from Kirra, and did his best to catalogue the many people who may have wanted to see Melanippe of Dodona crumpled in a heap at the bottom of a ravine. He gripped the reins in his fist and swore softly. He was failing miserably at all three.

"Nikos," Althaia rasped, then cleared her throat and tried again. "I don't know what to say, how to thank you for … for you know … and for saving Praxis's life."

The catch in her voice as she said his name nearly unmanned him. Two days earlier, he hadn't even known she existed. Now he felt as if he'd been kicked by a rogue stallion. He didn't want her to matter. But the mere sound of her voice drew him to her as if there were invisible ropes binding them together. He'd never felt anything like it before and wasn't sure he wanted to feel it now. Now was not a good time.

He was afraid to turn to face her, unsure of his voice. "You're safe," he finally managed.

"I'm so sorry about your mother," she whispered and reached out to him, her fingers brushing lightly against the hair on his arm, sending a shudder into his very core. "My father died last year, so I know how you must feel."

*I doubt it,* he thought. He looked down at the long, tapered fingers, moving on his skin with the rhythm of the horses beneath them. "You, being here … it's good," he murmured. He held his breath and placed a hand over hers, felt her hand turn over and her fingers curl into his. They rode like that, side by side in silence, and by the time they saw the lights of the farmhouse in the distance, he was almost able to breathe again.

# CHAPTER THIRTY-SEVEN

Althaia saw the house ahead, set back from the path amidst a grove of plane trees that loomed like charcoal smears against the bleak night sky. Smoke rose from an unseen chimney inviting the group inside with the promise of a crackling fire and warm wine. But as cold as she was, she was not eager to go in and face any more strangers. Too much had happened.

Nikos dismounted and walked away from her without a word. He had withdrawn into his own thoughts as soon as Theron had caught up with them. After Praxis filled Theron in on everything that had happened and Althaia had assured him she was not hurt, Theron pledged to repay the debt Althaia's family owed Nikos for protecting her honor, and he thanked him for his role in saving Praxis and swore he would help see Melanippe's killer brought to justice.

But Althaia sensed something had changed. When they first met, Theron had welcomed Nikos as an old friend because of his relationship with Thea, but now he now seemed wary, distant. What had happened? She slipped off her horse and watched Nikos go to the back of the wagon, scoop his mother's frail body into his arms and walk purposefully toward the front door.

Diffuse light poured into the yard as the door swung open to reveal Thea at the threshold. She pushed the door wide and stepped aside as Nikos carried his mother's body into the house. The main room was small and full of people. A group of children who sat in front of a stone fireplace grew wide-eyed and clamped their hands over their ears as several women began to wail in mourning. A couple of the attendants Althaia recognized from the Korycian Cave stood somber-faced against the wall. Two boys shuffled in carrying a long table. They set it in the center of the room and waited as Nikos placed the body upon it. Althaia, Theron, Praxis, and the lieutenant stood against the wall by the door watching, waiting. The scraggly-haired soldier sat tied to the wagon out in the cold.

Thea pulled back the blanket to reveal the woman's battered face. She gently turned Melanippe's head side to side to examine her bloodied skull. Without a word, she replaced the blanket and turned to the lieutenant. "I come from a long line of soldiers, farmers, and priestesses. I have seen death in all its forms—when disease creeps into the house at night and steals children away, when accidents take the young and vibrant before their time, when war cuts deep, slicing limbs and piercing flesh, and when old age whispers softly and leads loved ones across the river to the underworld. I know a violent death when I see one. Go now and tell Heraklios that Melanippe, priestess of Zeus and Gaia of Dodona, has been murdered."

"Madam," the lieutenant began, but Thea had turned her back on him as the room erupted in a cacophony of keening. No one could hear another word he said. Althaia thought her head would explode at the noise, but the lieutenant looked relieved. He glanced at Praxis, shrugged, and backed out the door as fast as he could.

Stuck inside the room with the ululating women, Althaia fought the urge to stick her fingers in her ears. She glanced at Theron, who appeared unfazed, and at Praxis, who looked stricken and was edging toward the door. She wanted nothing more than to escape with him, and yet, Nikos was here and she felt, somehow, that her place was here, too.

Thea held up a hand and the racket subsided. "Kalliope." She motioned to the attendant Althaia remembered sitting behind Melanippe at the cave. The girl couldn't have been more than fifteen. She stepped forward and stood across Melanippe's body from Nikos. She was about Althaia's height, but was very thin and her pale face was pinched into a severe expression, like an attempted frown with a hint of anticipation lurking just beneath. Her chestnut hair was pulled back in a bun so tight it gave Althaia a headache. The girl could have been pretty, Althaia thought, in a delicate, ethereal sort of way, had she not seemed so intense, so driven, so miserable. And had she not been looking up at Nikos with such unconcealed hunger.

"You have studied and traveled by Melanippe's side for over five years," Thea said. "On this trip, especially, she wished for you to travel with her to Delphi so you would meet the new Pythia of Gaia and be prepared for that day when you would replace her as priestess of Zeus and Gaia at Dodona. Unfortunately, that day has come sooner than we thought. You were at her side until the very end and even protected her with your very body." Kalliope touched a scratch on her sallow cheek as Thea spoke. "And, yes, you bear the scars of that honor."

Thea paused and looked down at the fallen priestess before continuing. "Kalliope of Patra, you will, of course, be sanctified when you return to Dodona, but for now, we recognize you as Melanippe's successor and a priestess in your own right. Tomorrow I will present you to the others when we meet at the Korycian Cave." Thea turned to address everyone in the room. "The Pythia of Gaia is still in mourning and is feeling unwell. She is anxious to celebrate the funeral rites for her friend and she sent word this afternoon that although Georgios has been unable to find Charis's brother, he and Phoibe's mother claimed Charis's mortal remains in the Sacred Precinct earlier today. We can wait no longer to perform the burial rites." Thea turned back to Nikos and laid a familiar, comforting hand on his shoulder. "With your permission, we will build a pyre outside the sacred cave and celebrate the passing of these two servants of the goddess together. Afterward, you and Kalliope can escort your mother's bones back to Dodona for burial."

* * * *

Nikos ignored Kalliope and took Thea's hand, touching his lips to her palm and clutching it to his heart. This woman, now, was the closest thing he had to family. She had visited Dodona every summer since he could barely crawl. She had been more mother, sister, and friend to him than any of the other priestesses at Dodona. Maybe it was because she, too, had been lonely. Maybe he had simply been a stand-in for the little brother who died and the twin who left. It didn't matter. Thea would not abandon him—surely. Even if she knew about the stolen treasures he, Diokles, and Kleomon sold to collectors across the Middle Sea and beyond, even if she knew about Charis, and about her brother's still undiscovered body probably now half eaten by wild animals.

He never meant to hurt anyone. No, that's not true. He had wanted to hurt her, the woman lying dead on the table before him. Despite all her fame, despite all those who respected her just because she wore the mantle of a priestess, just because she served Zeus and Gaia, despite all those who came from the four corners of the world to seek her wisdom, he, Nikos the son, knew she was a fraud. A cold, spiteful, lying, pathetic fraud who hadn't heard the voice of the gods in years, since his father abandoned her. As a boy, he had hidden in dark corners when she had cried out in vain, begging the gods to speak to her. And then he had followed her into the daylight as she proclaimed to all what the gods had revealed. He had loved her for her determination, for her unwillingness to admit defeat, and he had hated her for her pride, for assuming she knew the wishes of the gods even though they had long been silent.

For years he had wanted to escape the long tentacles of her influence, to be free of the recrimination and disappointment. But she had chained him to her like an intemperate dog. Every time he threatened to leave, she accused him of impiety, of abandoning the gods and their great priestess. She said she'd tell the authorities what she knew about his business with Diokles, or she would cry and say she was sorry she hadn't been a better mother, that he couldn't leave because he was all she had left. That lovely sentiment sometimes lasted as long as a whole day, and he fell for it every time. He knew each time his mother looked at him, she saw his father. She saw the Kelt, the one man she had ever loved, the one man who had shown her no more respect than a common whore. He had paid for her favors with silver trinkets and left a son who was his mirror image. Melanippe never forgave the father and spent the rest of her life punishing the son.

He looked up when Kalliope cleared her throat. "Thea, priestess of Pytheion, it will be my honor," she said. She raised her face and looked at Nikos with such calculation it made his blood run cold. Then she reached across Melanippe's body to press her palm against Nikos's chest. "Nikomachos, son of Melanippe, from this day forward, I will honor your mother with you. Together, as one, we will keep her memory alive."

Nikos jerked away as if Kalliope held scorpions in her hand. "Do what you need to do, Thea," he choked. He couldn't stand to have that fawning, grasping thing touch him, and he couldn't pretend he'd honor his mother and travel back to Dodona with her lackey. It was too much to ask any man. Ever since Kalliope had arrived in Dodona, she'd been a black shadow on their threshold. Catering to his mother's every whim and agreeing with every word she said until even the other priests and priestesses could hardly stand to be in the same room with them. And it had never been enough for her to sink her claws into Melanippe. It had been clear from the way Kalliope mooned at him and followed him around when his mother wasn't looking that she had plans for him, too. And now that she was taking his mother's place, would she expect him to attend to her as he attended his mother?

"I'll be at The Cove," he said as he turned his back on Kalliope and his mother's body and strode to the door. Without so much as a glance at Althaia, he yanked it open and stormed into the dark alone.

# CHAPTER THIRTY-EIGHT

Thea cleared the room as soon as Nikos stormed out. "Kalliope and I must prepare the body," she said. She met her brother's gaze. "Althaia may stay and observe, but you and your friend—"

"Praxis."

"You two must wait outside. You may shelter in the barn out back. Althaia will come for you when we're finished."

After the door closed behind them, Kalliope wasted no time taking charge. She pulled away the blanket and untied the cloak until Melanippe lay clothed in just her winter-weight chiton and worn leather boots. Kalliope's face was fixed, determined.

"Before we begin the rites," the new priestess of Dodona said, "there is something I must do." She shoved the old woman's woolen chiton and her undergarment, a sheath of finespun linen, up to her waist exposing thin, flabby legs attached to wide hips and a bloated belly. Thea struggled to keep her face expressionless, but saw Althaia fall back a step and her eyes widen in horror at the callous and disrespectful action. Kalliope tugged at a leather thong tied around the old woman's waist and pulled a small purse from between Melanippe's legs. Her fingers stroked the soft leather before she loosened the drawstring, held it to the lamp and peered inside. The hint of a smile played at her lips. She looked up.

"Melanippe always wore this small purse around her waist. In it, she kept her most treasured personal possessions. Tokens of her long life dear to her alone." She unknotted the thong and unceremoniously pulled it free. "She instructed me, upon her death, to take it and keep it as my own. As her successor, and as the woman she hoped would one day be her daughter." Her eyes flicked up toward Althaia. "It is not an official gift, but a personal one."

"Kalliope, I do not doubt the sincerity of Melanippe's wishes, but should not her personal possessions pass to her son?" Thea said.

"You know, better than most, that relations between the priestess and her son were strained. Often it was only my close, my intimate, relationship with each of them that kept them bound together."

Intimate! Thea had seen how Nikos stiffened and jerked his hand away when Kalliope touched him. She knew well how he felt about Kalliope. "But still—"

"She wanted me to have these trinkets," Kalliope interrupted as she looked once more into the purse.

"Nikos has the right to know what is in there. Perhaps there are things that belong to him. Melanippe's ring, for instance. Her silver band, is it in there?" Thea asked. "It is not on her hand, and it should definitely pass to him. That and whatever other gifts his father gave to her."

"She was wearing a plain silver band when we found her," Althaia spoke up. "Nikos took it from her finger at the ravine."

"Good," Thea said. "Kalliope, I must insist you see to it Nikos gets the mementos his father left. They must go to him."

"Believe me, Theodora," Kalliope said with a strange smile, "I will show Nikos what is in the purse and we will come to terms over the contents."

It was no longer 'honored priestess of Pytheion,' Theodora noted. And there was that edge to Kalliope's voice. Thea had heard it before, and she didn't like it. Truth be told, she did not trust Kalliope and never had. Thea had been visiting Dodona when the girl first arrived from Patra as an apprentice. She had seen pride and ambition before, but Kalliope topped those with a grand sense of entitlement. Not yet eleven, she acted like the Sacred Oak had been bequeathed to her and her alone. She latched onto Melanippe immediately, barely acknowledging the other priestesses. It became apparent, at least to Thea, that Kalliope studied Melanippe, knew her history, knew her weaknesses, and played them pitch perfect. How a child from Patra knew so much about a nearly fifty-year-old priestess from Dodona was a mystery. Now, Melanippe was dead and Kalliope clearly had her sights on Nikos. Thea scolded herself, *this is not my business*. Melanippe was right. He is not my son, and it has been many years since he needed me to shield him.

Kalliope closed the purse and cinched it tight. She tied it with the thong and then hiked up her chiton and secured the leather tie around her waist just as Melanippe had worn it. The sight of Kalliope's pale, bony legs and narrow, boyish hips was startling. There was hardly anything to the girl, and yet, Thea had to admit she unnerved her. Her cold resolve was intimidating and not a little frightening, and Thea turned her eyes away from Kalliope's nakedness and back to Melanippe's body. Whatever she felt about the Kalliope or Melanippe, it was her duty to perform the ritual washing and preparation of the body. She knew Althaia would be standing beside her, watching carefully, trying to see if there were any clues to how Melanippe died. But Thea didn't need Althaia to tell her how the priestess died. She believed she already knew. The question was not how, but who.

* * * *

Althaia watched quietly as Theodora's attendant entered the room followed by several younger girls. They carried a basin of water, olive oil, an incense burner, spring scissors, and several cotton cloths. They were followed by the matron of the house, a strong, broad shouldered woman with a gentle face. Folded neatly over her arm was a plain white linen chiton, a braided hemp belt and a sheer white burial shroud. She handed it reverentially to Theodora.

"I wove this myself, for my own shroud. Melanippe often honored our home with her presence on her visits to Delphi, and I would like to give her this one last gift. I would be glad if you would use my shroud for the priestess."

"Your generosity is overwhelming," Thea said. "I pray the goddess gives you many more years in which to live abundantly and that your daughters help you weave a shroud even more lovely than this one."

The matron bent, kissed Melanippe's bloodied forehead, backed away, and then turned and followed the attendants out.

Theodora used the scissors to cut Melanippe's bloody chiton and undergarment open down the front and to cut it off her arms while Kalliope worked to remove her boots. The death rigor had set in and they both worked with care around the stiff limbs until they peeled the last vestiges of mortal drapery from the body.

Then, as if on an invisible cue, Theodora and Kalliope began to sing. Their voices were as soft as the snow that had begun falling outside, dusting Delphi and the shoulders of Mt. Parnassus in a white mantle of mourning. Theodora lit the incense while Kalliope dipped the cloths into the basin. She handed one to Theodora and together they began to wash the body. Their hands were gentle, loving, as they wiped away the cares of this world and prepared the body for an eternity of purity in the next.

Mesmerized by the ritual, Althaia wondered if this was how her aunts had prepared her mother's body for burial. She hoped so. It was one thing for families to pay professional mourners for the funeral procession, but this, this final act of respect, was the true testament of love. The tenderness of the priestesses's touch—even Kalliope's—was comforting, reassuring, and Althaia realized she was weeping. She wiped the tears away and fought to concentrate on the task at hand.

Melanippe's skin, though mottled with age, was translucent, like light from a new moon. Blue and green veins traced their way beneath it like tiny tributaries of a distant river. A sparse patch of grey wiry hair was all that remained to mark her womanhood. Althaia could see none of the bruises that would have come from a twenty-five or thirty foot fall into a creek-bed filled with rocks. If she had been killed earlier, then wrapped in her heavy himation and rolled over the ledge into the ravine, it would explain why the fall had not caused more damage to her legs or torso.

Theodora gently rolled the body onto its side and Althaia craned her neck so she could see Melanippe's back. Again, nothing other than the normal marks of a long life. Other than the damage done to the skull and side of the face, there was no obvious evidence of any other injury that could have caused her death. It was clear to Althaia that Melanippe had been beaten with a blunt weapon and had been dead well before she landed at the bottom of the ravine.

Something caught Althaia's eye. Something brown. A twig or fragment of wood was stuck in the snarled strands of hair matted to the back of the battered skull. It fell to the floor when Theodora worked her oiled fingers through the hair. Althaia bent to pick it up but Kalliope's fingers closed over it before she could reach it. Their eyes met. Kalliope's lips tightened across her teeth in something that resembled a smile, or a snarl, and a chill ran up Althaia' s spine.

Then the ritual washing was over and it was time to wrap Melanippe in her final garment. "Althaia, please remove the blanket and cloak," Theodora asked while she and Kalliope gently rolled the body. Althaia pulled the old garments off the table and then handed the white chiton to Theodora. They slipped it over Melanippe's head and cinched it loosely around her waist with the hemp belt. "The shroud, please," Theodora said. The priestesses once again rolled the body so Althaia could unfold the shroud and spread it on the table. Whether for spending money in the afterlife or to pay Charon for passage across the Acheron, every corpse needed a coin placed in or on the mouth. Theodora now produced a shiny new obol with Zeus Dodona and his wreath of oak-leaves on one side and the obelisk of Apollon Ambrakia on the other. She placed it between Melanippe's lips, said a silent prayer, and began to wrap the shroud around the body.

Her observations complete, Althaia picked up the blanket and folded it carefully, then did the same for the bloodied remnants of the chiton and undergarment. She picked up Melanippe's cloak and shook it slightly to straighten it and make it easier to fold. That's when she found them. Two fragments of wood, one nothing more than a long, jagged splinter, but the other was something far more interesting—the broken head of a finely carved serpent with two tiny ruby eyes staring up at her.

* * * *

Althaia shook the snow from her cloak as she stepped into the barn where Theron was pacing and Praxis was sitting silently staring at the floor.

"Well?" Theron asked.

"As I suspected, I believe she was struck on the head with a blunt object. Multiple times. I think she was hit both from behind and from the side and that she bled profusely from both locations. The shoulders and back of her chiton and linen undergarment were soaked with blood. There were no lacerations, as such, anywhere else. Legs, arms, chest or the rest of the torso. Just the normal signs of age. And there was no significant bruising on the body. Nothing that would indicate she fell and hit the rocks while her body was animated and the blood was still coursing in her veins."

"We need to talk to Kalliope," Theron said. "According to Thea's message, she went out with Melanippe and returned bleeding."

"Kalliope—" Althaia started, but didn't know how to continue. She couldn't trust her feelings about the new priestess now that she knew Kalliope had designs on Nikos. But why should I care? She chided herself. I'm a married woman!

"Kalliope what?" Theron said.

"She ... I don't know ... she behaved very strangely after you left."

"How so?"

"It's hard to describe. At first she was abrupt, callous even. She yanked Melanippe's clothes up and laid claim to a small purse full of trinkets the priestess wore around her waist. She said Melanippe had bequeathed the contents to her, but Thea challenged her saying Nikos should at least see what was in the bag. They seemed to be talking about items from Nikos's father. But then, Kalliope said of course she would see to it that she and Nikos 'came to terms about the contents. There was something very calculating about her manner. But then, during the ritual cleansing, her manner changed. She was respectful, tender even. The process was quite lovely." Althaia's eyes filled with tears, but she held them at bay. "I'm glad Thea allowed me to witness it."

"Are you sure you're alright?" Theron asked.

"She would have been fine had I listened to her and not the lieutenant, had I kept her by my side instead of leaving her alone with those bastards at the ravine," Praxis growled.

Althaia dropped to the hard, dusty floor beside Praxis, whose face was twisted in a dark glower, and took his hand in hers. Some say the gods are harsh masters, she thought. Others say men. But as Theron always insisted when they talked about her dreams, about her need to forgive herself for her childish actions on the day her mother and brother died, she realized the harshest master of all was the self. She knew Praxis blamed himself for not protecting her, and she was determined he know that she did not hold him responsible.

From inside the house, the cries of lamentation suddenly shattered the night. The ritual washing complete, the priestesses must have opened the doors to the rest of the attendants and the farmer's household. She imagined the women pulling at their hair, ripping their gowns and bursting their lungs to out-mourn each other. The murder of the eldest priestess of Dodona was no small thing, and Althaia could not help but think that what had been her father's idea of a trip to mark the anniversary of his death had turned into one marked by murder. But she would not have it turned into one that marked a breach in her relationship with Praxis.

She looked up at the man she considered confidant, friend, brother, and said, "You must not blame yourself, Praxis. Look at me." She took his chin in her hand and turned his face toward hers. "See? I am whole. I am uninjured either in body or soul." She held Praxis's hand to her cheek. "I am unhurt. Truly."

Praxis took a deep breath and then nodded slightly. "So, what do you think is in the little purse?"

Althaia smiled and looked up at Theron. "That is a very good question. One to which I have no answer." She stood and reached into the fold of her chiton and pulled out the broken fragment of wood with the serpent's head and ruby eyes. "I do know this was not in the purse, and I also know that, had I not clasped my fingers around it first, Kalliope would have snatched it away."

"Where did you find this?" Theron asked.

"It fell out as I was folding Melanippe's cloak," Althaia said, handing it to Theron. "That and another fragment of splintered wood that, unfortunately, Kalliope reached before I did."

"That must be a piece of the murder weapon," Praxis said.

"I believe you're right," Theron agreed as Althaia beamed at both of them.

"This is no ordinary splinter. This was broken off of something precious. The question is what," she said. "After the mourning ritual quiets in the house, we should take your sister aside and see if she recognizes this."

"First Charis and now Melanippe…." Theron said.

"Are you thinking now Charis's death might not have been an accident?" Praxis asked.

"Whether her death was an accident or not, the presentation of her body was designed to send a message. And we still have no idea what that message was or for whom it was meant. And if it was meant for Phoibe, as she claims, is her life in danger, too?"

# CHAPTER THIRTY-NINE

"You're forgiven."

"I didn't say I was sorry." Nikos opened one eye and looked up at Diokles standing in the doorway. He had passed out in his clothes the night before and was still in bed, flat on his back, and was in no mood for company.

"No matter. I forgive you anyway." Diokles pulled in a stool from the hallway and plopped down in it. He tipped it back, leaned against the wall, and looked around the room. Since Nikos often stayed at The Cove for weeks at a time, he always kept the same room. He traveled light and kept his room spare but neat and always decorated with a few favorite pieces of painted pottery or gold or silver ornaments waiting to be sold down at the port in Kirra or delivered to buyers on Nikos's next trip abroad. Now kindling, or what had been his table and chair, was lying scattered across the floor among pieces of shattered pottery. The room looked like the site of a tavern brawl. "You had Aphro pretty worried. She thought the Furies had taken you."

"Maybe they had."

"A woman doesn't like to be interrupted by a madman while she is getting fucked."

"Oh, so now you're the considerate gentleman."

"I'm clearly not the murderous son of a bitch you thought I was last night."

"All right. I was wrong to suspect you."

"No, not wrong to suspect me. Just wrong. You know there've been plenty of times I wished your mother a swift trip to the underworld. And there've been plenty of times I was tempted to escort her to the gates of Hades myself, but I told you at the ravine I didn't do it."

"You said you were sorry it had to happen this way."

"And I am. Do you honestly think I would have chosen a blow to the head instead of nice sip of poisoned wine? I'm not a barbarian."

"By the gods, Diokles, as much as I could hardly bear the woman, she was still my mother. And seeing her like that…." Nikos swung his legs over the side of the bed and sat up. He ran his fingers through his hair, and hung his head in his hands.

"And you were her guardian and protector. Now she's dead, and you feel like you failed her once again. Because no matter what you ever did, you were always a failure. And no matter how much you tried to make her, she never loved you. And no matter how hard you tried to replace that love with women from ports scattered around the Middle Sea, it never filled that hole, it was never what you wanted, it was never what she so obviously, so spitefully, withheld from you every single day of your life."

He peered up at Diokles with bloodshot eyes. "First a considerate lover and now a philosopher. What's gotten into Delphi's most beloved blackguard?"

Diokles didn't answer. He stood and looked out the half-open window. A dazzling shaft of morning light split the room in two. The ground was covered in a light dusting of snow and Delphi, clothed in a mantle of white, seemed pure and holy. He closed the shutter. Nikos lay back on the bed, his face hidden in the crook of his arm.

"I remember the first time I saw you," Diokles said. "It was at the Kastalian Spring. It wasn't too long after the earthquake, after the rest of my family was killed when our house was flattened. I must have been six or seven, and I was living with my uncle." He chuckled. "You were so fat, with a big round belly like a puppy. Always at your mother's heels. But she never paid you any attention. You would call to her and she would ignore you. You would pluck at her hem and she would kick you away like you were a dog underfoot. So I picked you up and asked my uncle if I could keep you. Like a stray, I guess."

Nikos was still, and Diokles wondered if he'd gone back to sleep. "I always thought of you as the little brother I lost," Diokles said. "But maybe I wasn't such a good older brother." His voice was rough. He cleared his throat and walked to the door. "This thing with Charis. I don't know how she was playing you, but I know you and I know when a woman is involved, you're willing to be played. More than that, I don't want to know. That's over. She's dead and we can't do anything about it except figure out who moved her up to the theater and how to keep you out of trouble. As for your mother, I hated the sight of her, and I'm glad she's dead. But if you want me to help you find her killer, I'll do whatever you need."

"Zeus," was all Nikos could choke out. He didn't think he could take much more. Not only had he been tempted to cheat Diokles and Kleomon for a taste of Charis, he'd been double-crossed, threatened with blackmail, and he'd ended up with two dead bodies on his hands. Now not only was his mother dead but that conniving, grasping Kalliope couldn't wait to get her hooks in him and Diokles of Delphi stood before him professing a brotherly love that no one who knew him would imagine possible. He couldn't think straight.

On his way back to Delphi from the farmhouse, he had turned everything over in his mind a thousand times, but nothing made sense. What could anyone have to gain by stripping Charis naked and moving her body up to the theater? Why, if someone had seen him leave Charis on the steps of the temple, hadn't they accused him of murder, or at least, tried to blackmail him? Why would anyone want to kill his mother—or, the better question was, why would anyone want to kill her at this particular time? Did Phoibe really have the sight as she claimed? Had she been right all along? Were the priests trying to discredit and destroy Gaia's cult?

No, that didn't make sense. He agreed with what Eumelia, priestess of Argos, had said in the cave, that the powerful priests of Apollon had nothing to fear from a few scattered priestesses of Gaia. But there were only two things connecting Charis with Melanippe, the cult of Gaia and Nikos of Dodona. The only person who had anything to gain by hurting both was Kleomon. But would he have enlisted Diokles to help him? No! But who else had admitted over and over again that they couldn't wait to see Melanippe dead? Maybe Diokles was involved after all. The harder Nikos had dug his heels into his mount's flanks, the faster they had flown over the snowy road and the more convinced he was that Kleomon and Diokles were behind everything.

It didn't make any sense, but after seeing Kalliope leering at him over his mother's body, he desperately needed someone to blame. He had stormed into Diokles' room, yanked Aphro off him, and laid into him like, well, like a madman. And Diokles had taken it. He had never raised a hand to him. Then after Nikos had stormed around Diokles' room, he laid waste to his own and destroyed several of the most delicate pots Palamedes had ever created. Then he slid to the floor, refused to think about Althaia of Athens, and drank himself into oblivion.

Now Nikos knew Diokles was telling the truth. So he was back to square one with no idea who to blame. Except himself.

"About the wrecked rooms, the broken chairs, and the shattered pots...." Nikos said.

"Yes?"

"Put it on my tab."

"With pleasure," Diokles pulled the door shut.

# CHAPTER FORTY

"I am doing everything propriety demands," Phoibe fumed as Georgios and her mother, Rhea, listened helplessly. "Personal invitations to the funeral were sent to Philon and Kleomon. All the priestesses will have a part in the ceremony. Kalliope will sing the elegy for Melanippe while Nikos lights her pyre, but I will light Charis's pyre and sing her elegy. It's my right and I will not give it up." She glared at her lover and her mother. Ever since Georgios returned from his unsuccessful journey to find Charis's brother with her own mother instead, the two of them had been against her, questioning every decision she made. And she had no Charis to back her up, no Melanippe to bolster her confidence.

"No one is asking you to give it up. All we are asking is if it is too much for you." Georgios's voice was soft as his fingertips smoothed the damp tendrils plastered to Phoibe's fevered brow. He sat on her bed and held her still-trembling body against his.

"I am not an invalid. My visions are not so debilitating, my sanity not so compromised that I cannot fulfill my duties. I know how it looks, that this one was—"

"Daughter," Rhea said, "we do not question your sanity." Rhea raised a cup of wine to Phoibe's lips and nodded imperceptibly at Georgios. "We know you cannot control when the goddess seizes you, or what messages you receive during your epilēpsía. Your visions are beyond our understanding. But we fear for your safety. We fear that when the goddess takes you, you will hurt yourself. Your control is weakening. We see it. I believe even you must feel it, you must know it."

"What more do you want from me?" Phoibe pleaded. She was lost, blind, groping in the dark without her guides. Charis, murdered. Melanippe, murdered. She was next. She felt it. And yet, she knew Georgios and her mother were right, too. It was all true, everything they said. Her visions were coming unbidden and they were no longer sent by Gaia alone. Ever since the morning at the Sacred Grove, the morning Apollon stole into her mind and took possession of her body and soul, she had known she was defeated. But she had not thought the battle would be lost so quickly.

"All we ask is that you not overburden yourself," Georgios murmured.

"I must sing the elegy, it is my final farewell."

"We understand that, but—"

"And tossing a torch on a pyre is hardly a taxing feat," Phoibe continued, her voice heavy with exhaustion and tinged with bitterness.

"Drink, Phoibe. The wine will do you good." Rhea again raised the cup and Phoibe drank deeply.

"We fear the priests's presence will agitate you, perhaps even incite a vision as violent as the one you just had." Georgios's words were soft, like a lover's whispered endearments.

"We fear not only for your safety, but also for the dignity of the Pythia of Gaia," Rhea added. "And we fear that in your vision state you will do or say something you will regret. Something that will damage the Oracle of Gaia. Do you want Philon and Kleomon to think you are losing control? Do you want to give them an advantage over you?"

"I am not so far gone." Phoibe slapped the cup away. Wine splattered down the front of her gown as the cup clattered to the floor and shattered into blood-red shards. She struggled to stand and held to her bed for balance. "I am the only one protecting the Oracle of Gaia, and you don't even see it! You say, 'Apollon has always been greedy, has always wanted Delphi to himself.' But I tell you it is different now. Melanippe saw it in her visions. Charis saw it in the bright light of day. She understood Philon and his hatred, his constant manipulating and endless plotting, and Kleomon and his appetites, his all-consuming greed. And now you are plotting against me, you doubt me, have always doubted me."

"We are not plotting against you," Rhea reached out to soothe her daughter.

Phoibe slapped her mother's hand away. "You doubted I could become the Pythia. 'Never before in the long history of our line has this honor been bestowed,'" Phoibe mocked. "You said it as if I would be just one more in a long line of failures. Well now the honor has been bestowed—on me! I am the Pythia and yet you question my motives, you question my sanity. And you," she rounded on Georgios, pushing him back on the bed, "you never wanted me to be Pythia. You were always content with less. Always asking why I wanted it, why I needed it. Always wanting to take me away from Delphi even though Delphi is my destiny. You say you love me, but you don't even know me. I am the one with the power and you two stand before me chastising me as if I were a child."

"Phoibe—" Georgios started.

"I will do this tonight," she sobbed as her legs buckled beneath her. She struggled to stay on her feet. "I will see this ceremony through and I will honor them." She swayed and Georgios leapt up and caught her before she crumpled to the floor. "I swear … I will show you … show you both … I can do this—"

Like the shattered cup, Georgios's heart broke into a thousand bloody shards. The pain of seeing all his worst fears unfold before him was worse than any beating he ever suffered in the pankration. He cradled her in his arms as easily as if she had been a child. But she wasn't. He knew that. She was the flesh and blood woman he loved and she was slowly but surely leaving him. His broad back bent over the bed as Rhea pulled down the blankets. He laid Phoibe on her feather-filled pallet and brushed the hair out of her glazed eyes. He had seen those eyes blinded by unknowing oblivion as the goddess possessed her body and soul. And he had lost himself in them countless times as he clasped her body to his, joined as man and woman in ecstatic, rapturous death. That was his religion. Phoibe was his goddess. He would be a shade without her. He bent and brushed his lips across hers, breathing in the scent of sweat, wine, and poppy juice.

"How long will she sleep?"

"Only a few hours," Rhea replied. "Enough to clear her mind and restore her strength."

"This was her third vision in two days. I almost didn't get to her in time. She was thrashing, clawing at me, calling me names—"

"I came running as soon as her attendant found me."

"By the gods, Rhea, she thought I ... I don't even know if I can say it."

"Come, Georgios. We must both know what we are dealing with if we are to determine how to help her."

"She threw herself at me, tried to rip off my clothes," he said as he held out his arms to show the bloodied tracks her nails had furrowed into his skin. "She pushed herself onto me, grabbed me, and begged me to take her, to take her again—" He choked on the words, forcing himself to get them out. "She was down on her knees, pulling at me, pleading with me to get it over with, to allow her to fulfill her destiny."

"But the prophecy—"

"Gaia forgive me, but her mind is failing her. Somehow she believes she is fulfilling the prophecy, but it can't be! I don't understand." He sank on to the bed. "She said it was already over." He looked up at Phoibe's mother. "Rhea, she called me Apollon."

"Apollon! That's not possible. The prophecy says: 'She will see the Oracles of Apollon and Gaia united or she will see them destroyed and the Sacred Precinct claimed by yet another.'"

"Damn the prophecy and damn Sofia! It never made sense. Never! Even if he had a thousand years, Sokrates himself couldn't have parsed one iota of logic in it. It was just the mindless babbling of yet another delusional woman who thinks the gods speak through her. This has ruined her, Rhea. Your daughter is lost. This foolish prophecy is devouring her from the inside out. She was fevered, ranting, her speech garbled, but I swear on my grave, she believes Apollon cannot defeat the goddess without destroying himself. And she has pledged herself to his destruction—even if it means her own destruction. Somewhere deep inside, she sees this and her mind is bent by this one thought, that she is the instrument by which the prophecy will be fulfilled, that her time will mark the beginning of the end of both Oracles of Delphi and that she will be the last Pythia of Gaia."

"Can it really be true?" Rhea looked down at her sleeping daughter and began to weep. "She is the daughter in whom all our hopes have been fulfilled. If Phoibe is unable to do her duties, who will take her place? There are so few attendants and they are all so young. None have the sight like Phoibe has, like Sofia had. Is our time really past?"

Silent tears spilled down Georgios' broad cheeks. "She is fighting it, Rhea. She is fighting hard. But in her visions she has given up. She has already given herself to Apollon and by doing so she has sealed the fate of both the god and the goddess. She believes she is the end. That something new may come, but that Apollon and Gaia are finished."

"This cannot be what the prophecy meant. Who can imagine the Sacred Precinct without Gaia, Apollon, and Dionysos? There is no one god who is both healer like Apollon and resurrected like Dionysos, who is both son of Zeus and mother of all creation. This god does not exist. No one god can manifest all these attributes."

Georgios had heard enough. His gripped Rhea's shoulders and shook her hard. "I don't care about your gods or goddesses. I don't give a damn who claims the Sacred Precinct and for all I care, Mount Olympos can crumble into the sea. Phoibe is the only goddess I want. She is my only life, and I will do everything in my power to prevent anyone or anything from destroying her." He turned and stormed out of the room leaving Rhea stunned and a hallway full of eavesdropping attendants crying in his wake.

# CHAPTER FORTY-ONE

"I suppose we must travel up to the funeral together." Philon leaned against the doorway to Kleomon's apartment in the temple complex.

"I don't like it any more than you do, but, as you always say, we must do our duty." Kleomon didn't turn around. He was busy adjusting the laurel wreath on his brow and admiring himself in the looking glass. "The Pythia is going with us as well, I assume. You've made all the arrangements?"

"As usual."

"Always the efficient bureaucrat."

"Someone has to do it, and that someone always seems to be me."

"It took a while, but I learned that every time I make a suggestion or even try to get involved, I am slapped down like an unruly slave. So now I leave all the details to you and spend my time on happier pursuits. By the way, how are the arrangements going for the re-dedication of the theater? I hope Melanippe's funeral hasn't thrown a kink in your planning. It's only two days away, remember."

"Menandros, Heraklios, and I have the ceremony well in hand."

"Wonderful. That leaves me free to keep my hands occupied in more, shall we say, satisfying ways."

"I was thinking, Kleomon," Philon said, "perhaps we can put our little conversation from the other day behind us. It appears the mystery of the girl on the theater altar will remain just that, a mystery."

"When those damned priestesses are no longer causing trouble and when my groin is no longer black and blue from your knee, we can put it behind us."

"I guess the elderly heal more slowly. At least, at your age, you can be comforted by the fact that your manhood was not threatened. I imagine a good, satisfying fuck is nothing more than a distant memory for you."

"Imagine what you want, since that's all you have now that the worms are the only things delighting in your sweet Sofia."

Philon felt the bile in his throat. The number of stars in the sky did not compare to the number of times he had wished Kleomon dead. "At any rate," he said, "Theron has bigger fish to fry now that Melanippe has tumbled to her death."

"Melanippe was a witch and a harpy," Kleomon turned to face Philon, "but she no more tumbled to her death than I can fly up to the Korycian Cave."

"She was also a blind, sick old woman who could have easily slipped on an icy path and landed head first in a ravine full of rocks."

Kleomon turned to look at Philon. "No doubt that's what the murderer wants us all to think."

"Where were you yesterday morning?" Philon asked nonchalantly.

"Right here. Entertaining. You can ask Palamedes. I called him in to show off one of his latest works. It's a beautiful piece. Would fetch a small fortune if it weren't reserved for the temple treasury. And how about you? Were you tossing a bitter old woman in a ditch or off enjoying one of your mysterious meetings with your new nymph?"

"What are you talking about?"

"Oh, Philon," Kleomon laughed heartily. "You think I'm stupid, but I know all about your meetings with your new protégé. Sounds like she's a bit too young for your taste, though. And too skinny. A bit boyish. More to my liking, I think. Perhaps you would introduce us, to make amends for my ill-treatment. Oh!" Kleomon looked down at his lap and rubbed his hand over his crotch, "Looks like my manhood has recovered after all."

Philon prided himself on his ability to show no emotion. It was a skill and an art. To breathe normally and look straight at the object of your distress while imagining all the ways in which you could make him or her suffer. He had imagined plenty of ways to make Kleomon suffer. He could tic them off right now, one by one, to calm himself. First he would—no, it was too much bother. Kleomon was not worth it. He was simply a nuisance, nothing more. For now.

"By the way, I saw Heraklios leave your quarters earlier," Kleomon went on. "For my part, I haven't seen hide nor hair of him. Perhaps he didn't need to question me because I'm not at the top of the suspect list."

"We were discussing the re-dedication. And he was boasting about his contribution to the funeral tonight," Philon sneered. "Being a Makedonían with both family and official connections to Epirus, he is donating a white bull for sacrifice—on behalf of Philip, Olympias and Alexander, of course."

"Pray, what are we donating? The usual? A couple of fatted rams?"

"As a matter of fact, yes. A dozen of our best. It promises to be a big crowd and there must be plenty to eat for the feast. Perhaps tonight will mark the beginning of a new relationship with the priestesses of Gaia. I imagine the rams should be getting there soon."

"It's so good I can depend on you, Philon."

"Are you ready?" Philon asked, remembering to keep his breathing even. "If we do not leave soon, we will be late."

"I am always ready, my friend. You should know that by now."

# CHAPTER FORTY-TWO

The frigid mist and the dusting of snow Delphi received the night before were gone. After the previous day's bone-chilling weather, they had all hoped the day would break clearer. Now, Althaia wondered if there had ever been a day as bright and crisp. She stood at the edge of the outcrop and looked across the horizon, awestruck at the rugged beauty. Rock-studded hillsides tumbled down into small plateaus and then down again to the valley floor. Whitewashed Kirra gleamed like a pearl against the glittering lapis gulf beyond. Below her, Theron and Praxis poked around at the rocks looking for more fragments or splinters of wood. Behind her, Heraklios and his nephew, the lieutenant, who could barely meet Althaia's eyes, were busy doing the same. She, however, found it hard to keep her mind focused. She squinted and shaded her eyes with her hand. Her hat was at Menandros's and she knew she'd have a headache fit for a titan before the morning was over. But she didn't care, because even though the day was beautiful, she thought only of the night to come.

With messengers riding back and forth between Thea and Phoibe since first light, plans had been finalized for a funeral ceremony for both Charis and Melanippe. On the wide shelf below the Korycian Cave, pyres would be lit, paeans sung, and a funeral feast celebrated. Althaia could not stop wondering what a funeral for a priestess of Zeus and Gaia would be like. Would there be sacrifices to Dionysos, the god that bound Zeus and Gaia together? And if so, would there be drumming and dancing maenads? Satyrs? Would it evolve into a Dionysian bakkheia? She knew the wine would flow, but she wondered just how far the priestesses would go—how far she would go. Nikos would be there. He would carry the torch to light his mother's oil-soaked bier. And after that? Would she and Nikos meet? Or would he disappear like he had last night—after Kalliope reached across and laid her hand on his. If he didn't disappear, if he stayed, if....

Her heart pounded and a flush of heat rippled through her body. It had been too long since she felt a man's fingers on her skin. Even then the fingers had belonged to her tender but half-hearted husband, Lycon, who, while he was intent on upholding his obligations under the marriage contract, was more intent on hurrying back to his lover, the Olympic hopeful he worshipped. She had to give Lycon credit for at least trying to please her.

No, Lycon was not a terrible lover. But Althaia wanted more. She was not naïve. Living in close proximity with three grown men, she had overheard—and seen—plenty. Lysandros had money to burn and when he hosted a symposium, he went all out—hetaerae, pornai, acrobats, musicians. He made sure everyone left satisfied and sated. She knew that, despite what her stupid, sheltered cousins said, women could, and did, enjoy sex. She would never forget the time Lysandros's sister visited and Althaia found an olisbos among her aunt's belongings. It took all Althaia's resolve to not collapse into uncontrollable giggles as the distinguished Athenian matron tried to explain that the obvious marble phallus was a pestle and that she had simply forgotten to pack the mortar.

Lying with Lycon was an obligatory part of the marriage contract, one that had only one purpose—to produce an heir. He always performed with perfunctory politeness and then got up and left her alone with her thoughts. Now, the thought of Nikos's sparkling green eyes, the little crinkles that spilled down his cheeks when he smiled, his full lips tasting hers, his tongue teasing her breasts and his fingers probing her most private places made her lightheaded. Even the air seemed to be quivering with excitement.

* * * *

"They're not going to find anything. Not after that rain." Heraklios came up behind her.

Startled and disturbed from her pleasant thoughts, Althaia turned red as a pomegranate. "It doesn't hurt to look," she said, hoping her voice sounded normal.

"It's a waste of time."

"Still…."

There was an awkward silence. Heraklios didn't seem inclined to move and Althaia wasn't inclined to make small talk. "I wanted to apologize," he said finally. "For my men. For last night."

Althaia didn't look at him. She did not want to talk about last night. She didn't want to think about Half-an-ear's threats, his breath, his hand between her legs. She was safe, and she didn't ever want to think of it again. Ever.

"The young one. I shaved his head, personally. He'll be in irons for a few days. I thought you'd like to know."

She thought of the boy's long stringy curls, probably the most handsome thing he owned. Now gone. She wanted to hate him. She could see him standing near the ledge, a lookout, straining to watch, laughing. But he wasn't the one who touched her. She had wished the boy dead, but now she almost felt sorry for him. Humiliation among his fellow soldiers was punishment enough.

"I understand members of the Makedonían court are frequent visitors to Dodona," she said, changing the subject.

"Indeed. Alexander himself consulted with Melanippe before he joined his father's troops."

"Then there will be many powerful people glad to know you are going to great lengths to find the priestess's murderer," she offered.

"That's why I'm here," he smiled grimly.

"Althaia!" Theron called up to her as he and Praxis scrambled out of the ravine. Praxis reached the top first and held up a small piece of wood between his fingers.

"We'll be right up. Keep looking, maybe there's more up there on the ledge," he yelled.

Althaia looked up at Heraklios and smiled. "It doesn't hurt to look," she said and started walking along the ledge, examining the ground as she went.

"Okay," Heraklios looked at his nephew, "spread out and keep searching."

It didn't take long for Theron and Praxis to ride back up to the road and around to the outcrop on the other side of the ravine. Althaia ran up to Praxis as he dismounted.

"Let me see."

Praxis drew the fragment from his pouch and handed it to Althaia. She held it up between her fingers. The piece was not quite two inches long, slender, cylindrical, and carved in a distinctly elegant arc marked by delicate geometric grooves. Between the engraved marks, the wood was smooth, fragrant and burnished so it shone with a rich gold hue in the bright sun.

Heraklios came up behind her and grabbed it from her hand. "It's intricate. An overlaying design almost like a—"

"Serpent,"Theron said as he joined them. He drew out the pieces Althaia found the night before.

"Where'd you get those?" Heraklios asked.

"In Melanippe's cloak. Althaia found them last night during the ritual washing of the body."

He offered it to Heraklios who tried to fit the ruby-eyed piece to the new one. "It doesn't quite fit, but it is obviously the same wood. Same design."

"So it looks like we've found ourselves a murder weapon."

"This morning, when I showed the ruby-eyed fragment to Thea—"

"Who's Thea?" Heraklios interrupted.

Theron ignored the question and continued. "—she recognized it immediately. It was part of Melanippe's walking staff. But, and here's the important part, Thea said Nikos carved it for his mother years ago and that now Melanippe could barely get around without it. She also said Melanippe had it with her when she and Kalliope left the farmhouse after the message arrived."

"Who is Thea and what message arrived when?"

"Look, there's nothing on the ground here," the lieutenant said, joining the group at last. "The only thing up here," he held his mud-covered shoe up for everyone to see, "is plenty of mud from yesterday's sloppy weather."

Theron stopped and slapped his hand to his forehead. "We're looking for the wrong thing. We don't need any more pieces of the walking stick."

"What are you talking about?" Heraklios asked.

"Thea's note," he answered.

"Who the hell is Thea?"

Theron shielded his eyes and surveyed the ledge. The others watched, waiting. After a moment, he found what he was looking for and headed toward it. "According to Althaia's observations," Theron said as the others followed in his footsteps, "Melanippe was dead before she hit the rocks. And because the body was contorted by the way she lay in the ravine, she had to have died, or at least have been in the ravine, two or three hours earlier, enough time for the death rigor to begin to take hold. Now, in Thea's note, she said a message arrived for Melanippe and that she and Kalliope had immediately gone out. Because of her infirmities, she took her walking stick which was then, obviously, used to bludgeon her to death. Thea said it was midmorning when they left. The boy found the body in the mid-afternoon."

"Late afternoon," Heraklios corrected him. "Who is Thea?"

"Mid-afternoon. It was late afternoon by the time he and his father got to your office. They had to walk from here into Delphi."

"Go on," Praxis encouraged, as Althaia watched Theron put the pieces together.

"Melanippe was ill, nearly blind, and the weather was terrible. She couldn't have gotten very far from the farmhouse before she met her killer. Either she was killed near the farmhouse, brought here and dumped into the ravine or brought here, killed and then dumped in the ravine. Either way, she had to have been transported here. It is too far for her to have walked."

"And it's doubtful a murderer would just sling a dead body over his shoulder and walk down the road with it," Praxis added. "He could have draped the body on a horse or a donkey, but it still would've looked like a body. He must have put it in a cart or wagon so it was hidden from any passersby they might meet. Then he could have pulled the cart close to the edge and simply given her a nudge."

"Then, out she'd roll, right down onto the rocks below. All we have to do to find where she was killed, or at least to find where she was picked up and brought here, is to find cart tracks," Althaia said.

Without saying a word, Theron pointed at the ground, and the rest of them looked down to see Theron's muddy boots straddling the unmistakable impression of the narrow wheels of a small cart.

"Oh, and Heraklios," Theron said, "Thea is Theodora, the priestess of Gaia from Pytheion in Thessaly, my twin sister."

# CHAPTER FORTY-THREE

Nikos tied a bedroll to his horse's saddle cloth and surcingle and cinched it tight. The door to The Cove's stable slid open and he looked up to see Diokles' walk in with two bedrolls and a stuffed carryall bag. "Where are you going?" Nikos asked.

"Your mother's funeral."

"I didn't invite you."

"No, but Phoibe did. She's invited all the families with ties to Gaia's cult. I'm taking Aphro. To make up for being so rudely interrupted last night."

Nikos' heart skipped a beat. He was still nursing a headache and still embarrassed by his behavior last night.

"So if you happen to get in the mood tonight after the feast," Diokles went on, trying to keep the mood light, "you'll have to find someone else to fuck. Aphro's off limits."

"Can't imagine I'll be in the mood."

"Who knows, maybe your Athenian will be in attendance."

"Her shadows, Theron and Praxis, will be there too."

"A young soldier with a very bad haircut is sitting in irons out in the middle of Heraklios's courtyard today, and our names are on everyone's lips. We're apparently heroes, Nikos. Riding in on our thundering steeds and saving the helpless maid and her slave."

"She's not a maid. She's married."

"Doesn't matter. I bet she's spent the whole day dreaming of delicious ways to demonstrate her gratitude."

Nikos gripped his horse's reins and started for the door. He turned and looked back at Diokles. "Why are you really going?"

"I told you. Phoibe invited me." Diokles led his horse from its stall and began brushing it. "And, I figure your mother's murderer will be there celebrating his success. Two people keeping an eye out is better than one."

"Theron has his teeth in this as well."

"Good. You play that right and he can help us find your mother's killer while we keep him away from discovering your role in Charis's death."

"If Theron suspects I had anything to do with Charis, he'll see I pay—or worse. It won't matter what happened at that damned ravine."

"What's the worst punishment you could suffer? You didn't kill her, and all they can do is pin her desecration on you. It's not like they're going to stone you or give you a big draught of hemlock. There might be a hefty fine and maybe a period of banishment. But so what? You've got plenty of money, and it's not like you live here anyway. So what are you worried about? "

"Althaia will find out."

Diokles stopped brushing and took a long look at Nikos. "Aphrodite really has you by the balls with this one, doesn't she?"

Nikos's chest constricted and he felt he might choke with the pain of it, but he stroked his horse's muzzle and said nothing. What was there to say? It didn't matter if Eros's arrow pierced him straight through the heart. A married woman like Althaia of Athens could not take a lover and would never have a man like him anyway.

"You know Phoibe even made a big show of peace by inviting Kleomon and Philon," Diokles said, changing the subject.

"My mother served Zeus as well as Gaia. The priests of the Sacred Precinct of Apollon cannot be excluded from her funeral rites."

"Phoibe's crazy enough to do whatever she damn well pleases."

"Crazy, but not that crazy."

"It's just like you, Nikos. Always willing to give a woman the benefit of the doubt. Rumor has it she's been holed up sick since Charis turned up dead—visions, seizures, can't keep her food down—the works. I'll be surprised if she can hold herself together for the funeral."

"Georgios will keep Phoibe grounded. He is a simple but honest man—and he loves her."

"Okay, darling Sappho, your unshakeable faith in the power of love is astounding. It's foolhardy, and I don't understand it, but for mysterious reasons that completely baffle me, I'm beginning to admire it. Tell you what, let's bet on it. I'll wager all the proceeds from that Palamedes psykter we're saving for our favorite Etruscan collector that Phoibe gives us all a night we'll not soon forget."

Nikos thought of the broken pots he'd destroyed in his rage. He had swept them up and held the shattered fragments in his hand, turning the bigger pieces over and over in his fingers. Palamedes's talent was truly a gift from the gods and Nikos had destroyed some its most beautiful expression. Figures etched in the deepest blacks and ochre reds on backgrounds of snow white. So alive, he wondered they did not leap out of his hand and dance gaily across the room or charge ferociously into battle.

"I'll take the bet," Nikos said with his first smile of the day. "But if I win, we don't sell it. I keep the wine cooler."

# CHAPTER FORTY-FOUR

"Where did all these people come from?" Althaia gasped. She struggled to hold on to Praxis's hand as he barreled his way through the crowd.

"I think all Phokis is here," Praxis yelled.

"Look at the torches on the plain below," Nephthys gasped. "It's like hundreds of stars twinkling beneath our feet."

"Free food." Theron called out as he came up behind them. "Phoibe, Philon and Kleomon, and Heraklios are all trying to outdo each other. There's going to be enough food here to feed an army encampment. Alright everyone, stay together. I found my sister. We have a place right up front. With the priestesses."

"With the priestesses of Gaia?" Zenon could not believe his luck. Menandros told him that each priestess traveled with at least two attendants. Eight priestesses multiplied by two attendants equaled a good chance of finally losing his virginity.

"Let's get settled quickly. I must set up my writing desk before the ceremony starts." Menandros shuffled along behind, breathing heavily.

The shelf below the Korycian Cave was filled with dignitaries from Delphi, Krissa, Kirra, Arakhova, Amphissa and the other surrounding villages while the rest of mourners were camped out on the plain below the cave ready for the funeral feast.

Althaia saw Philon and Kleomon right up front—lying regally upon their couches, beds fit for kings, not servants of the gods. Immediately behind them, rested a curtained palanquin in which, rumor had it, the Pythia of the Oracle of Apollon sat. Kleomon fussed with his robe and openly fondled a clearly devoted attendant while Philon scanned the crowd with the look of someone already bored with the whole occasion. Theron guided their group toward Thea who, with her attendants, had saved an ample area for them. They settled in on blankets already cornered by lamps, cups and plates piled with dried fruits, bread, cheeses, and bladders of wine enough for a week of festivals.

"Sit with me, Althaia," Thea said. She patted a pillow and Althaia gladly dropped to the blanket to join her. Thea looked up at her brother and nodded as Theron turned on his heel and disappeared into the crowd. "Theron aims to move about the crowd. Watching, listening. He would have Praxis join him, but I understand he has instructed your slave to relax and leave all concerns about your safety to Theron." She turned and Althaia followed her eyes to the blanket behind them where Praxis was already stretched out, his head resting in Nephthys's lap.

Near Praxis and Nephthys, Menandros busied himself with opening wax tablets and sharpening styli in the hopes of recording the evening's events as an eyewitness to history—and as fodder for his plays. Beside him, Zenon sat on his knees surveying the line of priestesses and making mental notes of the attendants he intended to try his luck with first.

"Why are you not participating in the funerary rituals? Althaia asked.

"My duties tonight are to the living," Thea answered. She motioned for an attendant to pour a cup of wine for Althaia and thought about the conversation she'd just had with her brother.

"I don't know, Thea, according to the good people of Delphi, Nikos has quite a reputation," Theron had protested when she brought up the subject of Althaia and Nikos.

"She is not a child and he is not a fiend. In fact, from what I now know of your past, the two of you are not so different."

"By the gods, Thea, I would not wish a man like myself on Althaia in a thousand years. When I was Nikos's age, I made it my life's work to not care about anyone or anything. And then I met Lysandros who was, well, an extraordinary man. And there was Althaia. From the very first day, she reminded me of you." He stopped and looked into the distance. "Well, anyway, she is more than an employer, more than a student, she is—"

"I understand," she interrupted, her own voice thick with regret. "But remember, no matter what else she is to you, she is a woman first and foremost. I have seen, as have you, how the two of them look at each other. There is a connection there, a desire deeper than mere flesh and blood, deeper than lust and release. Come," she said, "do not try to tell me you have never looked at a woman the way Nikos looks at Althaia."

Despite himself, he could not suppress a smile. "I do not deny it," he sighed.

"So why do you seek to deny this joy to her?"

"I don't want to deny her joy; I want to protect her from pain."

"Brother, I am not blind. Nor am I deaf. I know Nikos is involved in things I do not approve of, that you surely will not approve of. But I am not his keeper. The mistakes he has made, he carries heavy in his heart—of that I am certain. Listen to me. He is a good man. His whole life he has been searching for one thing and I think, in your Althaia, he has found it."

"As much as I fear you are right, I swear to you that I am willing to renounce my impiety, fall prostrate before Olympos and pray to all the gods devised by man that you are wrong."

"That would mean going home, my dear brother, right to the very foot of Olympos," Thea said. "I would like that. Even if just for a short while. And even if you decide not to renounce your impiety." Theron said nothing and the quiet had stretched between then. Then he excused himself and disappeared into the crowd.

Coming back to the moment, Thea took a sip of her wine and said, "Theron said you made a discovery today regarding Melanippe's death, but he didn't have time to tell me what was found."

Althaia told her about the additional wood fragments and the discovery of the cart tracks. "We followed them from the ravine and they lead directly to an old, overgrown well near the farmhouse. Our theory is that whoever killed her did it there and then threw the rest of the walking stick into the well, bundled her in the cart, and then dumped her body in the ravine."

Thea looked off into the distance. "Melanippe had long been a troubled woman, but she did not deserve to die in such a way."

"No one deserves such an ignominious death," Althaia said.

"How far is the well? I don't think I know it."

"Maybe a fifteen-minute walk from the house, longer in the bad weather that day. The well looked like it hadn't been used in years. There were fresh marks—stone scraping against stone—on the well cover. In addition to the cart tracks, we found several sets of different-sized footprints clustered around the well and leading back and forth in the direction of the house. Praxis tracked them for a ways, but they were difficult to follow. We wanted to talk to Kalliope about what had happened, how she came to be injured, but you all had already left the farmhouse, and then, well, we needed to get ready to come here for the funeral."

"I'm glad you are here," Thea said. "It will give us a chance to get to know one another."

"Theron guessed that since Melanippe was such an important priestess, Phoibe would likely turn the funerary rites into a spectacle to demonstrate that the cult of Gaia is still strong, at least here in Delphi. He said"—Althaia mimicked Theron's voice—"such an event does not happen every day and we might as well enjoy it."

"And as I said, I'm glad of it." Thea squeezed Althaia's hand. "Tonight we will celebrate happier times in Melanippe's life. But first I want to ask if you are truly well. Theron also told me about what happened at the ravine."

Althaia tried to look unfazed, but could feel the heat color her cheeks. "Yes … I am unhurt. Nikos…."

"I thank the goddess Nikos and Diokles came along when they did." Thea paused and looked out over the crowd. "I've asked Nikos to join us after he lights the pyre," she said, watching Althaia's face out of the corner of her eye. "I've known Nikos his whole life, you know. I often spent time in Dodona, studying with Melanippe."

"What was he like, growing up, I mean?"

A smile tugged at Thea's mouth as she looked off into the distance. She could picture the Sacred Grove, see the priestesses busy at their work, hear Nikos running around, poking his wooden sword in bushes, challenging saplings to bloody duels, and generally ridding the place of all the invisible shades and daemons threatening the priestess's work. "He was all boy," she said fondly. "Unfortunately, he was surrounded by all women. He was built like a little Ajax with an appetite like a Titan, and once he learned to walk, he never slowed down. He was always running headlong into trouble, always too willing to take a dare, to ride faster, fight harder, always trying to prove himself a man, trying to be worthy." She turned to look at Althaia. "Melanippe never loved him as a mother should love her only child. Never forgave him for being his father's son—"

"Why? What do you mean?"

"It's a long story, best told by Nikos himself, if he can ever bear to share it. At any rate, it is not my tale to tell. At least not tonight. Suffice it to say, he never knew his father, and his mother despised the very thought of the man. The rest of us tried our best to fill the void in the boy's life. I spoiled him, the other priestesses spoiled him, and the men and women of the village spoiled him, but what he wanted most was his mother's love."

"Why did he stay to serve his mother so long if she treated him so poorly?"

"Duty, guilt, love, anger, who knows what motivates another person? I do know he is a good man—and he deserves a good woman."

Althaia swallowed the heart that threatened to leap out her throat. She looked straight at Thea. "I don't know why you are telling me this."

"I'm an observant woman. It's part of what makes me a good priestess. I saw the way he looked—or didn't look—at you the other night. And I saw your face when Kalliope touched him, and when he walked by you without a word."

"Thea, I cannot be that woman. I'm already married. I live in Athens. I can't—"

"Perhaps not," Thea said with a sigh of finality although Althaia was fully prepared to continue counting off the many reasons she and Nikos could not be together, even though in her mind she had thoroughly examined, scientifically dissected, and illogically rejected every one of those reasons to return over and over again to the one burning idea that inflamed her mind: Nikos.

Thea poured more wine and chewed thoughtfully on a fig. "You know I envy you, Althaia of Athens."

"Envy me, why?" Althaia was still chafing to justify herself.

"You have my brother's undying devotion. That is a gift I will never have."

"I don't know," Althaia stammered, thrown off by the sudden change of topic. "You seem to have picked up where you left off." She didn't know why she said that. She had no idea where Thea and Theron had left off—or why.

"It is better than I expected. Much better. This meeting. Besides the murders, of course."

Althaia took a deep drink. Dare she ask? Now that Thea had brought it up, she was dying to ask. Theron's past was the one topic that could keep her mind off Nikos.

"Has he ever told you how we were parted?" Thea continued.

"No. I mean, he promised to. After I met you. He said he would tell me everything. But with all the excitement, he hasn't had a chance."

"Would you like me to tell you? He has given me leave to tell you our story."

"Yes," Althaia found she was tearing up. "He is as dear to me as my own father."

"You do my brother great honor by comparing them thus. So, while we wait for the funeral to begin, let me tell you our tale in the hopes you will understand Theron, and, perhaps, give me leave to come back into his life without feeling the intruder."

"Intruder?" Althaia started to protest, but Thea held up her hand to silence her.

"Please, listen and do not think ill of me."

Althaia nodded, her mouth dry in anticipation.

"Theron and I, like most twins, were close. But when we were twelve, our lives changed. A little brother was born. While he was a baby, his care was entrusted to me and the wet nurse. But as he grew, toddling around, he came to dote on Theron who would do tricks for him. Stand on his head or produce a coin out of his ear, silly things like that. Our brother's name was Leonidas, our fat little lion-hearted boy, and he followed Theron everywhere.

"As we grew older, I was stuck inside, weaving and embroidering, reciting prayers and learning the rites and rituals necessary for a priestess of Gaia. Theron and Leo spent their days outside, together, seemingly without a care in the world.

"One day, Leo fell ill with fever. Theron stuck by his bedside day and night, holding his hand and telling him of the adventures they would have together once he got better. I sat with them until Mother ordered me back to my handiwork and recitations. Finally, after he had drifted in and out of consciousness for almost five days, I glanced over to the bed on which Leonidas lay just as his long lashes fluttered their last and fell still. It was early morning, and first light had not yet touched the eastern sky. Theron was wrapped in a blanket beside him, fast asleep. They wouldn't let me wake him. Mother said he needed to sleep in order to help in the fields. The time for mourning would not last forever and men's work waited.

"But after we had washed and wrapped Leo in his burial shroud, I woke Theron anyway. He was distraught. He wept like a woman and Father had to keep him away from the body. Our parents had already buried three children and they were well aware that Leonidas may not be the last.

"During the funeral, our mother went about her duties as priestess of Gaia Pytheion, shedding not a single tear while Theron sat on his knees by the mound of freshly dug dirt, rocking back and forth, crying. Never one to show a shred of emotion—or mercy—mother turned away from Theron even as he tore his clothes and pulled his hair in frenzied grief for his little acolyte. Friends and relatives averted their eyes first from Theron's grief and then from Mother's stoic resolve. I could do nothing but stand beside my mother and serve her or, later, suffer the lash.

"I longed to sit beside my twin, to hold and comfort him. After all, I had not died; I was still there to offer him love and admiration. But he suffered his grief alone, for I was not allowed to grieve with him. A priestess must rise above such petty human emotions to serve the larger purpose of the gods. That is what our mother believed.

"Mother tolerated Theron's cries for a time and then, before the whole gathering, said, 'The goddess has spoken and we cannot question her ways. It is time for you to be a man. Stand now and stop mourning the boy's death like an animal in the wild. It is not befitting the son of a priestess of Gaia and a warrior of Thessaly.'

"Theron looked up, his face streaked with dirt and the salty tracks of tears and spat at her—and, by the gods, I will never forget his words—he said, 'You didn't love him! You don't love anybody! I hate Gaia and I hate you!' Our mother looked across the grave at our father and spoke calmly. 'I have lost two sons this day, for this boy is no longer my own. He has rejected everything that I am. Take him to the stable. He can live there from now on, but he will not return to my house.'

"Althaia, I tell you my heart beat like the drums of war on a battlefield choked with armies. I longed to go to Theron, but fear of my mother held me in place as if I were a marble statue with my feet rooted in stone. I felt the swell of my twin's emotions in my own breast and thought I might vomit. Instead, I swallowed the bile and stood silently by our mother's side even as Father carried my other half, stunned and limp from exhaustion, toward the stable.

"Our father was a farmer and a warrior and he had seen many men come and go in his lifetime. He was a poor but honorable and brave man whose fortunes were tied to the priestess of Pytheion. It was her fathers' land his hand tilled and her fathers' silver that held them over when crops were poor. On his death bed, my father finally spoke to me of that day. Father saw that Theron's very soul had been wounded by Leonidas's death just as surely as if his heart had been pierced by a warrior's lance. As a man, he knew Theron was better off separated from the implacable cruelty of our mother. Even before that day, I believe he knew Theron would never stay to inherit the land. He had seen that his son was at once too tender for war and too inquisitive for a pastoral life tethered to the land. So he stroked his son's sweaty hair and felt the rise and fall of his ragged breathing against his chest as he kicked open the stable door and set him on the ground. Theron, already tall and lanky for his age, stood slump-shouldered, watching silently as our father prepared a pile of blankets in an empty stall. Father then walked toward the door and turned and looked into his son's eyes. Theron was no longer crying. 'Today,' our father said, 'you are a man.' Then he put his fist to his heart, turned and left the stable, pulling the door shut behind him. That was the last time our father ever saw his son.

"I watched the scene from a distance, my whole body burned in anger—not just at my mother, but at Leonidas and Theron as well. Although Leo had been with us just four winters, he had changed everything. I knew I would have eventually been separated from Theron—a brother and sister must always go their separate ways. Theron would be a great horseman and warrior, and I would be a priestess. But as I watched Father and Theron disappear into the darkness of the stable, I flushed with hatred—especially for the boy who lay entombed within Grandmother Earth. Leonidas had stolen Theron's love from me before it was time. And our mother had pushed him from me for all time.

"That night I lay awake, straining to hear some noise drifting on the cool air from the stable. Should I try to get up and sneak out toward the stable? How badly would mother beat me if I were caught? Finally, after hours of lying quietly, I slipped out from beneath my blanket and stole my way through the house and out across the wet grass. By the time I reached the stable, Theron was gone.

"Frantic, I tore down the path that led toward the edge of our property and then beyond, eventually leading to the pass at Thermopylae where the brave Leonidas, King of Sparta, led 300 warriors to their deaths defending all Greece from the Persian horde. Leonidas again! He's gone looking for Leonidas, I thought. I convinced myself he'd lost his senses.

"I dared not yell, but instead kept running, slipping, falling and then scrambling back up to keep running again. My nightgown was muddy and torn when I crested a small rise and saw him in the distance. That moment is emblazoned upon my mind. I stood, bent over, hands on my knees, panting. I could go no further. I focused my mind on his and willed him to turn and see me, to return to me. I saw his horse stop. I saw him turn. Don't leave me alone, I prayed. Not with her. Please come back home, I whispered, my breath ragged. My twin remained still, silhouetted against the glow from the silvered moon. Nothing was said. We were already too distant. We looked at each other, a gulf widening between us. After a moment, he raised his hand in farewell then turned and continued riding down the path away from Thessaly, away from me."

Althaia blew her nose into her cloak. She clutched Thea's hand and held it to her breast. She could not see through her tears and could no more speak than if her tongue had been cut out. Thea's eyes brimmed with unshed tears; her face mottled from holding her emotions in check. Althaia held Thea's hand to her lips and kissed it. "Thank you," she whispered. "Now I understand, finally. Now, I know."

* * * *

Thea looked up and saw Theron standing on the ledge watching them. He touched his hand to his heart. He had done many difficult things in his life, but he was glad he did not have to tell Althaia that tale. He, Lysandros, and Praxis had shared the basic outlines of their childhoods, but they were all content with the outlines. Men were able to take the measure of a man without needing to know every bump and curve in the road that took them to their destination. But he knew Althaia would want details. As a woman, she would want more. And he knew he was not prepared to give them. Even now.

# CHAPTER FORTY-FIVE

Nikos clenched his teeth, gripped the hilt of the ceremonial sword and swung it down hard on the bull's neck, nearly lifting his feet off the ground with the effort. The animal's knees buckled, its eyes rolled in the back of its head as it bellowed in pain and surprise. It was a clean cut, but still Nikos felt the spray of hot blood splatter across his face and arms. It was a priest's job, and he was no priest. He took no pleasure in the sacrifice and quickly stepped aside to let Heraklios have his turn at the altar. The bull Heraklios faced was snow white. Must have cost a fortune. Nikos's bull was black as pitch. Not exactly appropriate for the funeral of a priestess, but he was done caring about what was appropriate and what was not.

He reached for a cloth to wipe his face, and found Kalliope on the other end of it. Everywhere he turned, he found her staring up at him. She held out a pitcher of spring water, poured it over the cloth and started to dab at his face. Nikos pulled the cloth away, wiped his face and arms, made a feeble attempt at wiping the blood off his chiton, which only smeared it across the white fabric, then handed the cloth back to her, turned on his heel and walked back to where he had to wait for his next part in the macabre play.

The girl was driving him mad. He heard Kalliope hurriedly replace the pitcher and fall in behind him. He said nothing as they took their places and waited. Eumelia of Argos led the other priestesses through the funerary rituals, pouring libations and setting out offerings of honey cakes and wine.

He listened absently as they sang the prayers of the dead and wished it was Althaia standing next to him instead of Kalliope.

After a few moments, Kalliope could no longer keep her silence. She leaned in and whispered something about sharing the funeral feast and of their journey home to Dodona. She clutched at his sleeve and not-so-innocently rubbed her small breasts against his arm. She was nearly on top of him, sucking up all the air he needed to breathe. "By the gods—" he gasped.

She looked up sharply. "Are you alright? Can I get you something, anything? Wine? You look pale." She reached up and touched her hand to his face. He pushed it away and saw a look of hurt and surprise flash across her face only to be replaced by something so hard it made him shudder. Her need to be needed by him made him dizzy, and he mumbled some platitude in apology. Back home, she seemed to be always bumping into him, turning up randomly as though she knew his movements before he did. But tonight was even worse. She stuck closer to him than his shadow. He couldn't bear the way she stared at him—one minute all dewy-eyed with childish infatuation, the next eyes narrowed with cold determination. And always she seemed on the verge of revealing something, hinting at this and that like she knew his deepest secrets. Thea always thought there was something strange, too all-knowing and smug about her. But Melanippe never questioned Kalliope's actions or motives. Perhaps because the girl was a sycophant of the highest degree and his mother never knew she was being taken for a fool.

Melanippe. His mother. Her body rigid on the bier for all to see. Nikos knew that when he touched the torch to her oil-soaked pyre, hundreds of mourners in the valley below would watch the flames leap high and dance in the night sky. He gripped the unlit torch in his hand and imagined the fire blazing, already consuming the fetid flesh of his mother's decaying body. He just wanted it over with. He wanted it all over.

* * * *

Georgios watched as Phoibe climbed atop the podium set before the two pyres. After her terrifying vision and violent seizures that morning, the poppy juice had calmed her and she'd slept most of the afternoon. But now, surrounded by torchlight, she looked like a daughter of heaven and his whole being ached with love—and fear. He saw her steady herself, raise her arms to the sky and wait for the valley to quiet. Then, in rich, clear tones, as if the goddess herself possessed her voice, she began to sing the elegy for Charis. Georgios prayed she would not falter, that her feet would stay strong and firm beneath her.

* * * *

Rhea leaned against the rock face near the mouth of the sacred cave and listened to her daughter sing. Even as a child, Phoibe sang like one of the Mousai, her voice pure enough to inspire even the most frustrated poet. It usually filled her with joy, but now Rhea was exhausted, bone weary with worry and dread. Although Phoibe had wakened refreshed, she was wary. Whether of Rhea and Georgios or of her own daemons, Rhea could not say. While Phoibe slept, Rhea had prayed. She asked the goddess—and the gods—to show her how to help her daughter, how to protect her, but they were all were silent.

"Madam." Rhea jumped as a man emerged from the shadows. "I am told you are Rhea of Arachova, Phoibe's mother."

Rhea pushed away from the mountainside and squared her shoulders. "The Pythia of Gaia is my daughter. Why? Who is asking, sir?"

"My apologies. I am Theron of Thessaly, brother to Theodora, priestess of Gaia Pytheion."

"Ah! So you are the famous brother." Rhea examined Theron head to toe. "My daughter does not have a high opinion of you."

Theron smiled a smile that would warm the heart and soul of any weary widow. "Yes, I'm afraid you are right. Your daughter and I are, sadly, not destined to be the best of friends. But perhaps you and I might get off to a better start. In fact, I am hoping you can help me."

"I help you? How?" Rhea arched her brow in suspicion.

"It has come to my attention that a woman accompanying Phoibe's friend Georgios claimed to be Charis's relations and took possession of the body from the priests of the Sacred Precinct. Do you know who that woman might have been?"

"What business is it of yours?"

"Heraklios tasked me with investigating Charis's death. I had hoped to speak to her brother and was surprised he did not claim the body."

"Unfortunately, Charis's brother has gone missing."

"Missing? That is interesting."

"Not really. He was not, shall we say, a predictable sort of man."

"So, that brings me back to my question. Do you know who the silent woman in the wagon accompanying Georgios was? Who acted the part of Charis's mother?"

"I did."

"Indeed...."

"And why not? It was my daughter's prerogative to claim her handmaid and her duty to conduct the funeral rites. Charis's brother was once again nowhere to be found, so Georgios and I took matters into our own hands and delivered Charis back to Phoibe in the hopes that—" Rhea looked past the torches surrounding her and watched Phoibe silhouetted against the starry sky.

"In the hopes that...." Theron urged.

She shut her eyes to listen and to shut out the prying man.

Theron watched Rhea. "Phoibe is young to hold such an important position."

"What is it you want?" Rhea said. Her voice was ragged with exhaustion.

"I want to help you. And your daughter."

"I do not need your help," she said.

"Charis is dead. She was Phoibe's handmaid. Melanippe is dead. She was Phoibe's most trusted adviser amongst the priestesses."

"And?" Rhea took a step back and steadied herself against the rock face. "What are you saying?"

"I am saying I believe Phoibe's life is in danger."

Rhea stumbled back and Theron reached out to steady her. "So she is right, it is the end," she whispered.

"What is the end?" Theron took a step closer. "I know Phoibe believes the priests of Apollon are conspiring against her. You must tell me what you know so I can help prevent any harm from coming to her."

"It is said the gods work in mysterious ways, and we are but instruments in their plans, but still I did not believe her." Maybe it was just her exhaustion, but Rhea wanted to trust this man, tell him all her fears in the hopes he might be able to do something. But what could he, a mere mortal, do to change the course of history? If the gods have deemed something to be so, no man or woman can change it. We must accept it as best we can, even if….

Theron watched the emotions flash across Rhea's face. "Rhea, you must trust me. I want to help Phoibe, so I am counting on you. If you see anything, hear anything, find anything that does not seem 'right'—you know what I mean, a mother knows when things are not right—please contact me. I am staying with Menandros the playwright. If you do not feel comfortable contacting me directly, go through Theodora."

Rhea straightened up again. "I have borne two sons and a daughter, buried a husband, and managed a farm alone for some fifteen years. I do not fear being seen in the company of a man, alone."

Theron smiled again. "I thought not. Unfortunately, I cannot linger now. It seems Phoibe's elegy is over and I am intent on watching Kalliope's performance. Know, madam, that while some may call me a rogue, or worse, once I have signed on to a task, I am determined to see it done. On the funeral pyres are two women whose souls cry out for justice. Maybe you and I, Rhea of Arachova, can agree on that, even if your daughter and I cannot." In a bold move, he took her free hand in his, bent, and let his lips brush lightly against her knuckles. "Please let me help you," he whispered and then turned to walk away, to disappear back into the shadows from which he could watch Kalliope without being watched himself. But then Rhea spoke again.

"Phoibe is sick," she said, and before she could stop her tongue from forming the next sentence, it was already too late. "Her mind is broken by violent visions, by the lure and threat of fulfilling Sofia's prophecy."

"I know of the prophecy," Theron said, turning back to Rhea. "What form does her sickness take?" He was next to her, intent on hearing her every word as she continued.

"Her visions have always been troublesome, but lately … she has had three terrible episodes since last night, and this morning, we, Georgios and I, could barely keep her from doing herself harm. I had to lace her wine with poppy to calm her."

"Who has access to her? Is there anyone new attending to her? Anyone new in the household?"

"No. At least I don't think so. I am rarely here in Delphi. But Georgios keeps her well protected and everyone in her household is dedicated to Gaia and the oracle. No one would do her harm—no, this is the work of the gods. Apollon himself has appeared to her." She leaned back heavily on the rock face and resisted the urge to sink to the ground. Theron reached out to her, brought her close, and held her tight against the broad plane of his chest. She relented for but a moment and then pushed herself away from the comfort of his arms. She would not allow herself to be overcome with fear and grief. Not yet. Even if it was the end, she must remain strong for her daughter. Phoibe would need her.

* * * *

Like vapor from a steaming kettle, Kalliope's high, unearthly voice rose above the crowd. In contrast to the rich timbre of Phoibe's song, Kalliope's was ghostly, as thin and pale as the girl herself. The mourners were transfixed until, finally, the last note of Melanippe's elegy floated over the valley like the echo of a dream. Nikos and Phoibe stepped forward, lighted torches in hand, and, as one, set the two oil-soaked pyres ablaze.

Kalliope climbed down from the podium and hurried toward Nikos, but he had already tossed the torch into the inferno and headed in the opposite direction. She watched as he picked his way down the path to join Theodora and that woman from Athens. She saw him bend forward to kiss Theodora on the cheek and then take Althaia's hand in greeting. No wealthy matron from Athens was going to show up and stand in her way. She would make sure of that.

She searched the crowd for her attendant and found the silly girl gossiping and giggling like a child. Disgusting. Kalliope had no use for such ridiculous behavior. Tomorrow, she would have words with the girl. Tonight, there were more important things to attend to. She stepped back up on the podium, found the man she was looking for and signaled to him. At least she could count on him to do her bidding.

# CHAPTER FORTY-SIX

"I have never eaten so much in my life," Althaia said, handing her plate to Thea's attendant. "I heard someone say Heraklios and the priests arranged for one hundred rams to be sacrificed on the plain below." She searched her brain for interesting things to talk about, but kept coming up empty. They'd already covered the weather, the constellations, the vintage, and the best way to prepare squid. She was running out of things to say without saying the one thing she wanted most to express.

"One hundred rams would be a feast indeed," Nikos said. "More like ten if I know Philon and Kleomon. The amount of food doesn't matter. Like all Hellenes, the people of Phokis will seize any excuse to celebrate and my mother's funeral is as good as any." He waved his hand and Althaia turned. "It appears Praxis and your handmaid are going in search of some fresh, less crowded air," Nikos said.

Althaia turned to see Praxis pull Nephthys to her feet. He smiled, bent, tilted her face to his, and whispered something that made Nephthys gasp and pull back, eyes wide in delight. She dug her brown fingers into his golden curls and pulled his lips down to hers. Althaia was sitting no more than ten feet from them, and neither one even turned to look at her. But, she noted, she did not feel even a twinge of jealousy as Praxis took Nephthys's hand and guided her through the crowd, off to who knows where.

"Since Thea went to find Theron, it appears we are now alone," she said.

* * * *

"There's no need to fear, we are not yet alone. Thea left her attendants to see to our every need. And the playwright is still here, although his houseboy," Nikos motioned off into the distance, "has found an entertaining diversion." Nikos's heart was full to bursting, and he doubted he could ever thank Thea enough for this one fleeting moment of complete happiness after a week's worth of absolute hell. Althaia followed Nikos's line of sight to see Zenon surrounded by a gaggle of eager young girls.

"By the gods, I believe poor Zenon will be too weary to journey back to Delphi tomorrow," Althaia laughed. "And," she said, her voice so soft Nikos could barely hear it, "be assured I am not afraid."

Nikos did not speak, he did not trust his voice. He wanted to bury himself in that place where the curve of her neck met the plane of her shoulder. She was a wonder of geometry and it struck him that he wanted nothing more than to make a lifelong study of her. He took hold of her hand, and like when they rode side by side to the farmhouse, felt Althaia's fingers curl into his.

The warmth of her fingers slithered up his arms and his hair stood on end. He felt his pulse beat at his temple, at the base of his throat, and down to his center, thrumming in sync to the rhythm of the drums sounding on the plain below. Somewhere in the crowd, a flute and lyre played a duet while revelers clapped and sang along. The smell of hot coals, roasted meat, incense, kannabis, spilled wine, and sex saturated the air. The night was alive with desire and his skin burned as hot as the pyres themselves. His fingers traced the outline of Althaia's collarbone from the edge of her shoulder to the base of her throat. She held his gaze as he pressed his thumb into the small depression. "Perfect fit," he whispered.

She wanted to lean back and pull him down to her. But instead of losing herself completely in the middle of the crowd, she tried to maintain her dignity, keep her bearings. "Um, is this a normal funeral for a priestess of Gaia?" she murmured.

"Nothing about my mother was normal, so why should her funeral be?" His fingers set off on their journey again, skimming her skin until they reached the smooth roundness of her other shoulder.

"About your mother, I must speak to you."

Nikos spun around. Kalliope! By all that was holy, would the girl never leave him alone? He pulled back his hand and reluctantly looked up at the young priestess standing over them. The girl's expression was somber and she looked like she had been crying.

"Now?"

"Now. It is of the utmost importance."

Nikos made no move to get up. He was done with his mother. Done with the priestesses of Gaia—except for Thea, of course—and especially done with Kalliope. He had fulfilled his duty and now the new priestess could dig the bones out of the pyre and carry them home like the sacred icons the whole world believed they would be. "What is so important it cannot wait?"

Kalliope held up the small purse she had taken from Melanippe's body. "Your mother's most treasured possessions. I thought you would want to go through them with me. But if you don't want to, if you would rather I keep the tokens your father left…."

The fury that flashed across Nikos's face would have scared Althaia had she not felt the same rage in every atom of her being. She remembered how Kalliope had ripped the purse from between Melanippe's, pale legs. Kalliope had not seemed eager to share the contents with anyone then. Althaia clasped Nikos hand tight, willing him not to leave her, not to go with this scheming little girl.

"Give me the purse," he held his hand out. "I will go through it here. I'll take what's mine and you can have the rest."

"I couldn't," Kalliope said, clutching the purse to her heart and stepping back out of his reach. "It is too painful for me. I apologize, Madam," she said to Althaia, her voice thick with the pretense of mourning, "but these small trinkets are so dear to me. I would rather review the contents of the purse in private, with my beloved mentor's son."

"All right," he said through clenched teeth. "Stay here, Althaia. Do not move from this spot until I get back." He squeezed her hand and stood to go.

* * * *

Althaia watched as Nikos followed Kalliope up the path toward the cave and then disappeared over the ledge. She looked at the people around her, still drinking, eating, singing, kissing, fondling, still happy.

"Watch out for that one." A familiar voice brought her back to her senses.

"What?" Althaia said as she turned to look at Menandros, who was watching her intently.

"That girl. I would wager a whole talent, if I had that much silver, that she would boil up her babies and serve them for dinner if it would get her what she wanted."

"That's Melanippe's successor, the new priestess of Dodona."

"Then we should all get down on our knees and pray for Melanippe's immediate resurrection."

# CHAPTER FORTY-SEVEN

"Enough. I can't stay here any longer." Althaia pulled on her boots and stood up, hands on her hips in frustration.

"My dear," Menandros said, lowering himself back to the ground. "Just now, when I went to take a piss, I saw them, arguing, up by the mouth of the cave. Your Nikos did not look very happy."

"Zeus, I hate that cave," Althaia growled, stepping over empty baskets of food and half-empty bladders of wine.

"Take a torch," Menandros called. "And promise to tell me everything that happens as soon you get back."

Althaia yanked a torch out of its stand and climbed up toward the cave. She pushed her way through the crowd toward the dark mouth that cut into the mountainside like a stab wound. Neither Kalliope nor Nikos were anywhere to be seen. She marched over to a group of boys and girls sitting in a circle playing a version of knucklebones that obviously included removing articles of clothing. "Have you seen Kalliope or Nikomachos, son of Melanippe?"

"Which one you want?" a boy about Zenon's age slurred. "'Cause I just saw Kalliope run thataway and Nikos go thataway." He pointed in two directions at once and the whole group burst into giggles.

"Nikos. Which way did he go?"

"Into the dark."

"What?"

"Into the dark," he turned and pointed at the mouth of the cave.

That's just great, she thought. She took a deep breath, gripped the torch, dipped her head and entered the womb of Gaia. The flickering light from a dozen lamps danced on the dome and walls of the cave. Groups of two or three, or even more, lay together on blankets spread on the cold floor. Whispered moans and muffled laughter hung in the damp air.

She held the torch low, near the steep slope and carefully made her way to the bottom. She peered around the great hall, but there was no one sitting alone. She thought of the day she and Theron had attended the priestess' meeting. When Nikos—she was sure it had been him—had hidden in the shadows. He had probably been in the cave dozens of times and would know all its nooks and crannies. He could be hidden in the shadows now, or he could be, oh, please Gaia, no.

She turned toward the gaping, toothy maw of the inner chamber. Please don't let him be in there, she prayed. She looked longingly up toward where she knew the mouth of the cave waited to release her back to the celebration waiting beyond. Then, again, back to the jagged opening leading into the unknown. Stalactites hung like dripping fangs while their mates, serrated stalagmites, rose from the monster's misshapen jaw, ready to shred anyone who dared cross the lip into the yawning emptiness beyond. She shuddered. She thought of her dream. The man from the shadows who led her into the dark. The last place she wanted to go.

Perhaps Nikos wasn't even in there. The boy playing knucklebones had been half-drunk. Perhaps Nikos had gone back to the blanket, maybe he was even waiting for her there now. Wondering where she was. Maybe Menandros was wrong and Nikos and Kalliope weren't arguing. Maybe, maybe, maybe. Maybe she'd just go a little further and take a quick look. She didn't have to step over the threshold. She had a torch and if Nikos was in that eerie cavern, he'd surely see her.

She tucked her skirt in her belt with one hand and held the torch high in the other. The rocks were green with moss, and slick with age and she slipped more than once as she felt her way up toward the monster's mouth. Finally, she stood at the lip and peered in. In the distance, one lamp, wick low, fluttered its way toward oblivion.

"Nikos?"

"Althaia." His voice hung in the air, heavy, like the weight of the mountain surrounding them.

"I waited, but you never came back." Without thinking, she stepped over the mossy lip with a full body shudder. She lowered the torch to illuminate the uneven ground, and made her way toward the lamp.

"You shouldn't be here," he said even as he reached up to take her hand and pull her down to him.

"You look terrible," she knelt before him, ran her thumb across his cheek. The tension and awkwardness that had marked their conversation before dissolved like wisps of smoke from a candle flame, as if stepping into the dark had stripped away all the pretense of the outside world.

"I've ruined everything." The last glow of the lamp's wick faded to nothing more than a few scattered pinpricks of orange and yellow, like cat's eyes winking at them.

"What have you ruined?"

"Us. This. You should go now, before it's too late."

"It's already too late," she whispered as she lowered her lips to his. She dropped the torch and it rolled away, sizzling against the damp floor until it came to rest in a puddle and disappeared, like the world around them.

The hazy glow of lamplight, barely visible through the chamber's misshapen mouth, was their only connection to the people and places beyond. In the deep of Gaia's womb, there was nothing left but the two of them, folded into each other by the weight of desire and expectation. The envelope of black rendered them nearly blind, but it didn't matter.

Nikos traced the frame of her face and then her neck, his lips following the trail his fingers blazed. His heart pounded in his ears, a war drum driving the engine of his desire forward. His fingers fumbled in the dark as he unwrapped her himation, loosened her belt, and lifted her chiton over her head. He was afraid to touch her, afraid of what his need might unleash.

She knelt before him, naked, ready to give herself to him, to take him into her deepest recesses, body and soul. But he didn't touch her. Then she heard movement, the rustle of fabric, and reached out to find only Nikos. She ran her fingers across his chest, up over his shoulders, and pulled him to her.

"Wait," he groaned. "Your boots." She felt his fingers crawl their way down her legs until they found the lacings of her boots. One by one he untied the leather thongs and slipped the invisible boots from her invisible feet. Then, his fingers, followed closely by his warm, moist lips, twirled and danced back up, like maenads or nymphs or acrobats teasing their way up the inside of her thighs, toward her center. He trailed his fingertips across her, dipping ever so slighty into her wet heat as she arched toward him. Then he pushed her back gently, laying her down onto her cloak which he had spread out below them.

She felt him, all sinew and muscle, stretch out beside her. His mouth found hers and he kissed her deeply, their tongues wrestling like two hoplites in hand-to-hand combat. She wrapped her arms around him, pressed her hands into the muscles of his back. She kneaded his flesh and scraped her nails lightly down to the small of his back and across the hard mounds of his buttocks while he explored the wonders of her geography—the rounded hills of her hips, the sloping valley of her waist, the flat plain of her belly. His fingers flirted up her stomach until his hand flattened against her ribcage, fingertips brushing against the swell of her breasts.

Then he stopped. His hand was still, nothing moved. She could hear him breathing, feel his heart thudding against her chest. A slow, steady drip, the cave's pulse, echoed from somewhere deeper in the darkness. Althaia held her breath, waited. Then he slid up and gathered her breast in his hand as his tongue circled the point of her nipple. She shuddered as a bolt of desire, hot as lightning, ricocheted through her body. She moaned and pulled his head to her, eager to have him taste her more deeply. He answered her need with his own, pulling her nipple into his mouth, sucking, biting, torturing her with the urgency for even more. She clung to him, diving with him into the depths of longing even as he delivered her from the death of loneliness, a death she hadn't even known she dreaded so completely.

But then he pulled back. She felt him sit up, heard him move away. She waited, not breathing.

"Althaia, I can't do this, I—" His voice was ragged and he trailed off. The taste of her, all wine and desire, threatened to choke him. The smell of her, jasmine and campfire, threatened to suffocate him. He knew he could reach out and take her. That she was willing. It wouldn't be like Charis. But it was Charis he couldn't stop thinking about, her taunts, her threats, her boasts, her laughter when her brother's blade found his throat, her face as he, as she .... He couldn't get it out of his mind, what had happened, his anger and resentment, his need to prove himself, prove he was a man to that old crone who was now nothing more than a heap of ashes, how his weakness had ruined everything. How he was caught, now, like a fly in a poison web of deception, how he was here, cut off from the world, and how Althaia was here too, offering herself to him freely, lovingly. How his need for her would ruin her, too. The ache of it all tore at him, unmoored him, and he felt like a ship foundering against a hostile shore.

She propped herself up on an elbow and reached out to him, finding only nothingness.

"I can't ... you don't know ...." His voice sounded as if it were ripped from his throat. "We can't do this."

"This is not wrong, Nikos. I don't know what's happened, but I do know that whatever else is going on in our lives—your mother, Kalliope, my husband, whatever—I know this is right. This. Here. Now." She leaned into the black, reached farther, and this time her fingers found flesh. She crawled to her knees and pressed her palms against the broad warmth of his back. He flinched—would she feel the scars Charis's nails had left in his skin?—but did not move away. She eased her hands under his arms to embrace him, her palms framed the muscles of his chest, felt the rapid hammering of his heart. She buried her face in his neck, pressed herself into his back and held him against her. She could feel the catch in his breathing, a sob captured, swallowed, before it escaped. Then another. And another. She tightened her grip, clasped him to her as if she were the ship's mast and he Odysseus, bound to her for safety.

He wanted to turn to her, hold her, possess her just once before it was all over. So he would have that one memory to hold on to. But that wasn't fair. He should tell her everything. That would make it easier for both of them. Then she would turn around and leave, and he wouldn't have the chance to hurt her. Then he would accept his fate like a man and go back to Dodona with Kalliope. After that, only the gods knew.

In her blindness, she didn't know how long she held him, but gradually his breathing settled, and she loosened her grip and felt him lean back into her. In turn, she bent forward and breathed lightly into his ear. "I'm still here." A shudder racked his body and she could feel the chill bumps on his neck.

"I have to tell you everything."

"Not now."

"Listen, to me, Althaia. You need to know what's happened, now, before—"

She clasped him tight again and breathed into his ear. "There is only one thing I need now."

All his resolve disappeared into the black. "Are you sure?" he whispered, his voice barely audible.

In answer, she nipped at his lobe, ran her tongue along the inside of his ear and lightly rubbed his nipples. She slipped her hand down his chest, down the firmness of his belly, until she heard the sharp intake of breath. Teasing him the way he had teased her, she felt him grow hard beneath her touch. She trailed her fingers down his shaft and rounded the tip. He gripped her wrist and held it firm. "Answer, me. Are you sure? Because once we start, there's no stopping."

"Thank the gods," she rasped as she closed her hand around him.

# CHAPTER FORTY-EIGHT

"Anything interesting to report?" Diokles asked. He lifted the blankets and pulled Aphro under them.

"My source, a very drunk, half-naked young man playing games up near the mouth of the cave said Nikos and Kalliope argued, that they were fighting about a piece of jewelry—a necklace or something—and that they very nearly came to blows. He said Nikos had to be pulled off her and that she ran off into the crowd. After she left, Nikos disappeared into the cave."

"Hmm. A necklace. Did he describe it?"

"Only that it was silver. He also said another woman—as beautiful as Aphrodite herself, he claimed—asked about them both and then went in after Nikos."

"You think it was the Athenian?" Diokles asked.

"Who else? And I think she must have found him because we haven't seen him come back out."

"Okay, now the question is who did Kalliope run off to meet?"

"That's a very good question and I—hey, scoot over. I'm cold—"

"Here," he said rearranging the blankets and wrapping his arm around her shoulder. "Better?"

"Much."

"Alright, go on."

"After I talked to the boy, I went back into the scrub to pee and who do you think walked by?"

"Wait, let me guess. Kalliope?"

She moaned as her hand began to dance its way down his belly.

"And? Can you get on with it? I'm beginning to lose my focus."

"And I followed her. I had to keep my distance, but I saw her meet with a man. Unfortunately he had a hood drawn over his face. They looked intimate, though. They were standing close, heads together. So I waited. When they were done, I followed him."

"Did they see you?"

"Not at first. So, you want to know where he went?"

"No, I'm sleepy all the sudden." The point of Aphro's elbow dug into his rib cage. "Ouch! Okay, of course, I want to know. Where did he go?"

"To the priests' encampment."

Diokles sat up, pulling the blankets up with him.

"Hey!" Aphro hissed. She pulled him down and pulled the blankets back up over them.

"By the gods, what would Kalliope be doing with someone who works for Apollon's priests?"

"I don't know. He must be a temple slave or one of their personal attendants. He was talking to one of the bodyguards when I think they saw me watching them. They turned toward me and that's when I acted like I was drunk. I stumbled, pretended I was going to fall and then tripped my way back here."

"Who knew taking a piss could be so productive? You should be a spy, my dear."

"I'll spy day and night, if you pay me more."

"I pay you plenty, already," Diokles said. His hand closed over her breast and squeezed. "You know better than to mistake me for a soft touch like Nikos. I'm not the son of a wealthy priestess with silver to throw around like rain from heaven. I have to work for a living and you are part of my bottom line." He ran his hand down the contours of her side and clutched the fullnesss of her bottom in his hand. "A delicious part, but bottom line nonetheless."

She sighed the sigh of a woman with no options. Diokles gave her protection. He gave her the freedom to choose other lovers, as long as she was there when he wanted her. Besides, he trusted her—no, relied on her. Talk about bottom line. She was the one who ran the Dolphin's Cove while he attended to his other business interests. Diokles allowed her to work independently as few other women could ever dream of doing without being a heterai. Nikos was sweet, always an attentive lover, but it was Diokles who would be there at the end of the day. And, for a woman like Aphro, that had to be enough.

"So, should we try to stay awake and watch the mouth of that cave in case Nikos emerges?"

"Our friend can take care of himself. I imagine he's much better off down there in the dark with the Athenian than up here near Kalliope. The few times I've had a good look at that one, I didn't like what I saw."

"Poor Nikos. I hope the Athenian is good to him."

Diokles smiled in the darkness and pulled Aphro over on top of him. "Me, too. But now it's time for you to be good to me."

# CHAPTER FORTY-NINE

Althaia woke and sat upright, breathing heavy. Nikos sat up, wrapping his arms around her. "What's wrong?"

"A dream," she gasped, her skin beaded with sweat despite the cool damp of the cave.

Nikos drew his cloak back around them. "Do you want to talk about it?" he whispered.

"My dreams ... I've had them, crazy ones, nightmares, since I was a child. Since my mother died. They come and go, but before we left Athens, I started having them again. Someone's always in trouble, about to get hurt, and I try to help, but I can never get to them in time. Theron says I haven't forgiven myself for the day my mother died—it's a long story—and that's why I keep having the same sort of dream. Anyway, a few nights ago I had a bad one, and now I just had the same dream. The same, but different. Do you know what I mean?"

"You don't have to talk about if if you don't want to."

"No, I want to because," she turned to him in the dark, "you're in it."

"Me?"

"There's a man, leaning over something, doing something. In the first dream—the one I had before—I couldn't see what he was doing, but tonight I could see everything. There is a woman lying at his feet and he is undressing her. But not like a lover. And not like he is assaulting her. He's just undressing her. Like a little girl might undress a doll. It's very strange. He keeps looking over his shoulder, and I keep trying to get closer, to see what he's doing. I'm suddenly very afraid, and I turn to run, but I can't move. He grabs me, and I see the glint of a knife. I know he's going to hurt me. Then something changes, and I'm not afraid anymore. I'm not afraid because it's not that man anymore. It's someone else." She held her hand against his face. "It's you, Nikos. I remember. The feel of you. The smell of you. Your breath in my hair, against my neck. It's like my daimon knew I would meet you. That you would save me, like you did at the ravine."

"What night did you say you had the first dream?"

"Our first night here. The night before I discovered Charis's body in the theater."

"Oh, god," he groaned. "What else did you see? The other man. Can you remember anything else about him?"

"No, that's it. I'm surprised I remember that much. Sometimes bits and pieces of the dreams stay with me, but usually they fade, if not by morning, then within a few days. But I know it was you." She smiled in the dark and let her fingers trail from his face, along his jaw line and down his neck, "This afternoon I had another dream. You were most definitely in that one. And it was not a nightmare." She pushed him back against the floor, and lay on top of him, her breasts pressing into him.

"Althaia, please." He rolled her off him and sat up. "I would stay here, blind with need, and love you until the end of time, but we both know that is impossible. Especially now, with this dream. As much as I fear and dread this, it's time to face what comes next. You deserve to know what will happen when we leave our cocoon."

"I was afraid to come in here. That monster's mouth is a fearsome thing. But now I treasure that gash, for if others were as afraid to enter as I, no one will dare invade our privacy. Nikos, this is our sanctuary. Why must we bring the outside world into our safe harbor so soon?"

"Here," he said, groping around the floor and then handing her chiton and boots to her. "I think it must be nearly morning. We need to get dressed. I'll be right back."

Panic seized her. "Don't leave me here."

"I'm going to find someone to relight the lamp. So I can see you." He pulled on his clothes and felt for her hand, felt his way up to her face and then kissed her. "I would never leave you here. I promise. Now get dressed or you'll get chilled."

She heard his bare feet pad across the floor. Blindly she pulled on her clothes and waited. Time stood still as she sat, frozen, eyes shut tight against the darkness. Soon she heard him approach and dared open one eye. She let out a long breath, opened both eyes wide and took in the full length of him. He walked toward her, lamp in hand, a halo of light framing his face like a god.

He sat down, cross-legged, in front of her. "You need to trust me because now I am going to tell you the truth. I'm going to tell you things that you do not want to hear." He clutched her hand and held it tight as if the physical connection would continue to bind them together no matter what.

"Nothing you can tell me will change how I feel."

"That is a lovely and foolish sentiment, and it cleaves my heart in two."

"But, it's true. I—"

He put a finger to her lips. "Hush, please, and listen."

# CHAPTER FIFTY

Althaia's fingers hurt from Nikos's grip, yet she knew she gripped him harder. In silence, she had listened to every agonizing word as he told her about his relationship with his mother, how Kalliope had followed him since she first arrived in Dodona, how he had sold stolen treasures from the Sacred Precinct with Diokles and Kleomon that Charis and her brother had supplied them. She did not want to believe him, but his green eyes, shadowed in pain, were windows to the truth. The cave's pulse, that reassuring drip, drip, drip, went on, oblivious to the tribulations of mere mortals.

"The marks on your back. I could feel them in the dark," she whispered. "It was your skin, your blood, I found under Charis's fingernails."

"Yes," he admitted. "And now Kalliope says she will see me punished or see me married before the next moonrise. She says nothing now can stand in her way. Althaia, she means for us to leave Delphi, to return to Dodona today—as man and wife."

"But what did she mean 'nothing now can stand in her way?' Is she talking about your mother? And how did she find out that it was you who left the body on the temple steps? I don't understand how Kalliope can blackmail you and accuse you of murder when I am certain Charis's death was an accident."

"There is always Charis's brother. Sooner or later his body will be found. But Kalliope has proof that ties me directly to Charis's death."

"What proof can she possibly have?"

"You examined Charis in the adyton, right?"

"Yes, but—"

"Someone was watching you."

Althaia shuddered and her heart skipped a beat. "In the hallway, as we left the adyton, we felt a wash of fresh air as if a door had opened or closed. But we saw nothing, heard nothing. Why, if someone in the temple knew we were there, why did they not alert the guards?"

"Because someone saw a man leave a body on the temple steps, but could not identify the man in the darkness. That same person discovered it was Charis and decided to use her body to send a message to the priestesses. When he learned you were going to examine her body, he decided to watch and see if you would discover something that would lead him back to the man who left her on the steps, back to Charis's murderer. And you did. You found something."

"Yes." Althaia's voice was barely audible.

"That next morning at Menandros's … you were going to tell me what you found before Theron interrupted."

Althaia nodded. She was unsure where he was leading her, what he was trying to tell her.

Nikos pulled his hand from hers and reached over to pick up one of his boots. He reached into the shaft and pulled out a small leather purse. Fingers shaking, he loosened the tie. "You found this," he said as he pulled out a silver necklace with a single polished orb dangling from its chain, lamplight flickering across its surface.

Althaia almost choked on her surprise. "Where did you get that? It was hidden at Menandros's."

"I took it from Kalliope this evening."

"But how did she find it? Did she order someone to break into Menandros's house?"

"She didn't have to. This is not the necklace you found stuck in Charis's throat. My father took two of three silver balls from the torc he wore around his neck and threaded them on silver chains. He left one for his lover and one for his son. It's all I ever had of him. My necklace is what killed Charis. This was my mother's. She never wore it anymore, and I thought she kept it in Dodona, but Kalliope said she always wore it in a little pouch tied around her waist, hidden in case she was ever robbed."

Althaia clutched at Nikos's hand. "I saw Kalliope take the pouch from your mother. It was the first thing she did after you left the farmhouse, before the ritual cleansing began. By all that is holy, Nikos, she took it because she knew what I had found in the adyton. She took it because she meant to blackmail you with it."

"As soon as she learned what it was you had found, she knew I was responsible for Charis's death."

"Stop saying that. Your necklace may have killed Charis, but you did not. It was an accident. You didn't mean for her to die."

"It may have been an accident, but she would not be dead had I not been there in the first place, had I not been willing to … to betray my partners so I could—"

"Nikos," Althaia interrupted. "She aspirated the ball, choked on it. You didn't stick it down her throat. You didn't kill her!"

"Look at me," he took Althaia's face in his hands. "Since the end of the last Sacred War, I have been profiting from treasures stolen from the Sacred Precinct by people like Charis and her brother. I was the conduit for getting those treasures into the hands of collectors around the Middle Sea. I was willing to cheat my best friend just to make love to Charis. I killed her brother and abandoned his body to the wolves. Althaia, I am no innocent no matter how much you might wish it so. The truth is Charis would not be dead if it were not for me."

They were both quiet as the silver ball swayed, a pendulum silently marking the moments they had left together. How long they sat without a sound, neither of them could say. Finally, Nikos broke the silence. "What I want to know is who watched you and told Kalliope what you found? Who amongst the temple workers knew the body was in the adyton? Who knew about your plans to examine it, and, more importantly, how is that person connected to Kalliope?"

"We were told Philon's personal guards moved the body from the storehouse."

"Who told you?"

"Palamedes. Well, he told Praxis. He was the one who helped us get into the adyton."

"Palamedes, the temple artisan?"

"Yes. He and Praxis are both Syrians, and my father arranged for them to meet years ago on my first trip to Delphi. Palamedes said he saw Philon's guards moving the body through the tunnels below the temple. He was the one who led us through the tunnel from outside the Sacred Precinct walls into the subterranean temple complex while you created the diversion with the mob. It was Palamedes who laid the thread, like Theseus in the labyrinth, from his quarters to the adyton, and—"

"Althaia, we traffic in his work."

"What do you mean you traffic in his work?"

"Diokles, Kleomon, and I. We takes pieces of Palamedes's work from the temple treasury and sell them abroad. The artisan doesn't even know it, but his work is sought by collectors from Massalia to Phoenicia. Even Egypt."

"Or perhaps he does know and doesn't much like the idea that the three of you profit from his talent while he remains a temple slave. Does he know you? I mean, have you met him personally? Would he recognize your necklace?"

"Of course, I've met him often in Kleomon's apartment in the temple complex. He knows I'm the son of Melanippe and that I have money to spend. He knows I admire his work. But what connection can he have to Kalliope? He must be near sixty and has been a temple slave since he was a boy. Kalliope is not yet sixteen and has rarely set foot in Delphi."

"That is what we must discover. If Kalliope is so obsessed with you, she may have had the means to pay someone to keep track of your activities while you are in Delphi. Perhaps Palamedes is no more to her than a spy, getting paid for keeping an eye on you, and by spying on you he also learned of your activities with Kleomon and Diokles. If you are stealing and selling his works abroad, he has reason to hate you. Kalliope and Palamedes may each have their own motivations, but the one thing they have in common is you."

"But there's another piece to the puzzle, Althaia. Kalliope is now priestess of Dodona. Perhaps once she learned about my connection to Charis's death, she decided to kill my mother and blackmail me. She would, in one stroke, possess the two things she desires above all else—Melanippe's position and Melanippe's son."

"It makes perfect sense— "

"But wait … why wouldn't Kalliope have removed my mother's purse as soon as she killed her? Why wait until the ritual cleansing?"

"I don't know. Maybe a traveler was approaching. Maybe they had to hurry to bundle up the body and dispose of it. Think, Nikos. It wouldn't really matter to Kalliope. She knew the body would be discovered, and she knew she would take part in the ritual cleansing. All we have to do is prove it."

"Althaia, you're forgetting one thing: the body rotting under the haystack. However much you want to rationalize my role in Charis's death, I killed her brother with a blade to the heart, and I do not regret it."

"Can I ask you something?"

"All that I am is bare to you."

"All those years, why didn't you just leave Dodona, leave your mother's service?"

"I don't know. Even now I can't explain it to myself."

"Try. Explain it to me."

"A boy with no father yearns for the love of his only parent, I suppose. And even though I was the bastard child of an unmarried woman, I was also the son of a powerful priestess. There was a legitimacy in that position that had a power I chose not to renounce. Being the son of Melanippe of Dodona meant that I had the means to travel freely, meet powerful people. Once she fell ill and no longer traveled farther than Delphi or Pella, I continued to travel on her behalf—taking messages back and forth to other priests and priestesses, to others who honored the Sacred Oak. I was her conduit for knowledge and contacts beyond Dodona, Epirus, Hellas. I was useful to her and she was useful to me. And, most of the time, it was not such a bad life. I have seen much of the world in my travels. I guess I came to believe that her dependence on me was her way of showing she did love me. I know it is beyond pathetic. A grown man pining for his mother's love like a babe in arms, especially after she got sick, after her mind began to go."

"Listen to me, Nikos. Perhaps your mother did love you, perhaps she died protecting you." Althaia reached for the purse. "I was there when Kalliope took this from your mother's body. There was a ruthlessness about her. Yet, during the ritual cleansing, her actions were tender … I can't explain it. As much as I am loathe to admit it, I do believe Kalliope had some affection for your mother. Perhaps she didn't set out to kill her. What if Kalliope intended to confront your mother with the evidence you were involved in Charis's death and force her to arrange a marriage between the two of you. What if your mother refused? Maybe that's when Kalliope decided to kill her—or had someone else wield her walking stick against her."

"Her walking stick?"

"Yes, we know that's how she died. We found pieces of it in the ravine and stuck in her cloak, fragments of a serpent with ruby eyes. At first we didn't know what the broken piece came from, but we showed it to Thea and she knew at once it was from your mother's walking stick."

"I carved that for her," Nikos whispered. "When I was just a boy. I must have made five or six of them before I got it right."

"Oh, Nikos, I'm so sorry. Theron has the fragments."

"I don't think I want to see them."

"Those pieces represent one beautiful thing you and your mother shared. Someone took all that away from you when they used it to end her life. I think that someone was Kalliope. Kalliope and Palamedes."

Nikos eyes misted over. "It's a nice story, but even now I can't pretend to hope my mother would ever have done such a thing as take my side against Kalliope."

"Think! Think of the look in Kalliope's eyes. You know she is capable of anything. Even if your mother didn't protect you, she would not have wanted such a woman to be her successor if she knew she intended to blackmail you. She would have realized her mistake, the moment Kalliope opened her mouth and demanded you."

The possibility began to sink in and, like flotsam saving a drowning man, Althaia saw that Nikos wanted to grab onto it. "You did not hear the words we exchanged the last time I saw her—just yesterday morning," he said. "They were not the words of a mother who loved her son."

"Perhaps not, but some people are not able to give voice to their emotions. And some do not recognize what is valuable until it is lost. It is true you may never know what your mother was thinking in her last moments. But there are several things we do know. Someone moved Charis's body and someone watched me examine her in the adyton. Someone killed your mother with her own walking stick. Kalliope took the purse from your mother's waist. I saw her take it. She insisted on keeping it even though Thea said it should be yours. At your mother's funeral, Kalliope pulled out your mother's necklace and threatened to go to Heraklios and tell him you murdered Charis unless you married her. If your mother was in favor of you marrying Kalliope, Kalliope would not have had to blackmail you. And if your mother was not dead, Kalliope would not be a priestess."

"Do I dare hope that Melanippe of Dodona stood up for me, that she took my part at the very end?"

"I think there can be no other explanation."

"By the gods, this is making my head spin. But, Althaia, I would, for all the world, not have you involved in all this."

"If you thought that by telling me all this, I would turn on my heel and walk away, you were mistaken. In the night, you said you loved me, but you do not yet know my reputation for stubbornness. Nikos, you have been a fool. You have made terrible mistakes, but the fact is that there is no innocent victim in your tale."

"You're innocent."

"I'm not a victim."

"But I have drawn you into this and the last thing I would have is you suffering for my mistakes."

"I do not intend to suffer for them. I intend to help you rectify them."

# CHAPTER FIFTY-ONE

Georgios held Phoibe's hair away from her face as she retched again. Her skin was the color of smoke. Since they returned from the funeral, her condition had rapidly deteriorated. Rhea picked up the basin, opened the door and handed it to an attendant.

"Bring it back quickly," she urged. "And more wine. Hurry."

"I'm better," Phoibe whispered. She sank back into the bed. "I think I will be better for a while. I need to sleep so I can reserve my strength for the re-sanctification ceremony."

"You do not still intend to go to the theater tomorrow?" Georgios asked.

"The invitation came directly from Philon, and I no longer have the strength to defy a priest of Apollon."

"You are not well enough to travel even the short distance to the Sacred Precinct," Rhea objected.

"My hero will carry me." She stretched out her arm and laid her hand on Georgios's arm. Her fingers were icy and he held them tight to warm them.

He smiled wanly. "I would carry you to the ends of the earth. But perhaps it's smarter to take a litter."

"Then I shall travel in style—like the Pythia of Apollon in her curtained palanquin."

A rap at the door signaled the attendant's return. Rhea hurried to the door and retrieved a new pitcher of wine and the emptied basin. "Is she going to die?" the girl asked as she peeked into the room. "Is she going to die just like Sofia?"

"My daughter is not going to die," Rhea said and shut the door in the girl's face.

# CHAPTER FIFTY-TWO

"Tomorrow, we end this," Theron said, slamming his cup down on the table so hard Menandros's dogs began to bark. He turned to Diokles who stood to leave. "Everything depends on you. Are you certain you can be prepared?"

"We have much to do in the next few hours, but with Althaia's funds to back us up, I'm certain Aphro and I will have the ready cooperation of every shopkeeper in Delphi."

Earlier that morning, as dawn broke over the Korycian Cave and mourners nursed their headaches and packed their belongings to return home, Nikos and Althaia had emerged into the daylight to find Diokles and Aphro waiting just outside the mouth of the cave. After Aphro reported on Kalliope's activities the night before, the foursome hurried to track down Theron, Praxis, and the rest of their group to tell them everything that had transpired. Theron immediately related what he had learned from Rhea, Phoibe's mother, and wondered if Kalliope might also have something to do with Phoibe's sickness. If the girl was willing to blackmail Nikos and murder one priestess, he suggested, might she be willing to murder another? But what would she gain from Phoibe's death, Praxis asked, and how could she accomplish such a feat? Did she have accomplices in both the temple complex and in Phoibe's household? Someone who would be willing to poison the Pythia of Gaia?

Both Theron and Praxis wanted to set off immediately to find Heraklios so he could arrest Kalliope and interrogate her before it was too late. Diokles, too, argued for interrogating her, but he wasn't interested in going through proper channels. Why not grab her, hold her feet to the fire—literally—and force her to confess? Thea wanted to assemble all the priestesses and confront Kalliope on sacred ground while they were still at the cave. And Nikos said he didn't care how she was held accountable, as long as he found out who had moved Charis's body and why, and as long as he could be certain that everyone in Delphi—and across all Hellas—discovered who had murdered his mother and why.

As Althaia listened to everyone argue, she noticed Menandros scratching notes on his wax tablet and heard him muttering under his breath: "Oh, what Euripides could have done with such material!"

"That's it!" she had clapped her hands and exclaimed.

"That's what?" Theron asked as everyone turned toward her.

"Menandros just gave me the most brilliant idea."

At the sound of his name, Menandros looked up, blinking. "I did? What? What did I say?"

"You said, 'Oh, what Euripides could have done with such material.' So what would he have done? Murder, intrigue, betrayal, revenge … this is the stuff of tragedy. Aeschylus, Sophokles, Euripides, the greatest tragedians turned stories like this into plays to reveal and explore the dark side of human nature, and, with Menandros's help, we can do the same."

"What are you saying?" Nikos asked.

"Tomorrow Menandros is putting on a play for the re-sanctification celebration for the theater. He told me he's been working on a new type of play, but why not stage something revolutionary, something that's never been done before? Like the great playwrights, we can transform Kalliope's story into a tragedy that exposes her for what she really is. Together we can write a play that will portray her as a murderer and blackmailer, and we can force her to name her accomplices—all in front of Heraklios, the priests of Apollon, and her sister priestesses." No one had said a word. "Don't you see," she continued, trying to convince them all, "we can use the play to trick her, to catch her out in front of everyone without giving her or her accomplices a chance to leave Delphi and escape justice."

At first, Theron, Praxis, Thea, and Nikos thought it crazy, but with Menandros, and even Nephthys, on her side, she gradually won them over, and after converging on Menandros's house once they left the funeral site, they had spent the rest of the day composing their tragedy.

As Diokles took his leave to prepare and set the trap, Theron glanced over at Praxis who shook his head. "Take heart, Praxis," Theron said, "Althaia's plan is sheer madness, but if everyone does their part, it just might—*might!*—work."

"Where in Zeus's name is Zenon?" Menandros blurted suddenly. "I still can't believe Palamedes is Kalliope's accomplice, but if it's true, perhaps Zenon is in danger. The boy went to see him at the temple and now ... well he's been gone most of the day. Perhaps something has happened to him."

"No one wants to believe Palamedes is involved," Althaia said, "but who else—"

"It doesn't sit right in my gut," Praxis interrupted. "Would having his work stolen and sold around the Middle Sea drive him to conspire with Kalliope in murder and blackmail?"

"You know as well as I do that men have done far worse for less significant reasons," Theron said.

"I know, but...." Praxis began pacing again, glancing occasionally at Nephthys who had kept the gathering supplied with food and drink while they conspired.

"Would anyone like anything more?" Nephthys asked.

"More wine," Menandros grunted and held out his cup. Nephthys reached for it just as Zenon walked into the andron. Menandros jumped up so quickly he dropped the cup, shattering it on the tile floor as he grabbed the boy by the shoulders. "Where have you been, boy?"

"I, uh"—Zenon blushed and looked at the floor—"stopped by the, um, Cove for, um—"

"Oh, Zenon," Menandros shook his head. "Your wick isn't even dry and you have to go dip it in the font again. You better get used to oiling up your palm or you'll go broke faster than Koroibos of Elis ran the first stadion. You don't want to be the Olympic champion of whore-mongering."

Zenon turned red as a radish and took an eager interest in the kitchen door.

"Help clean up this mess you caused," Menandros ordered, trying not to show how relieved he was that the boy was safe.

"Did you tell Palamedes about your conquests at the funeral feast?" Praxis asked.

"I couldn't find him. He wasn't in his quarters or his workshop."

"Perhaps he was preparing for tomorrow's festivities," Theron suggested.

Zenon shook his head as he bent to gather the shards of broken pottery. "No one's seen him since yesterday."

"Interesting," Theron said, casting a glance toward Praxis.

"Why is that interesting?" Zenon asked.

Theron scrambled for an answer. "I thought I'd buy a pot of his, a gift to Menandros for his generosity as our host."

"Oh, Theron, my friend," Menandros clapped in delight. "You don't have to—"

"Of course I don't have to." Theron rolled his eyes.

"I thought I would go see him tomorrow before the ceremony," Zenon said. "You can come with me if you want."

"Excellent idea. I think I'll do just that."

# CHAPTER FIFTY-THREE

"Starting early, I see. Good," Theron said as he and Zenon met Diokles and Aphro at a long table set up at the entrance to the theater.

"Better early than late, I always say." Diokles watched as Aphro directed servants from The Cove like a general on the battlefield.

"How profound," Theron said. "Innkeeping and petty crime are evidently not your only talents, Diokles. You should have been a poet."

"Oh, but I am. Ask Aphro. Just last night I was extolling the virtues of her—"

Aphro stomped on his foot and smiled. "Master Theron, young Zenon, please forgive him. He is a brute."

"But today, Madam, he is an indispensable brute," Theron replied with a grim smile.

"By the way," Aphro winked at Zenon, "it's good to see you again so soon."

Zenon blushed as Theron squeezed the back of his neck. "Just see to it he does not become a regular at The Cove. A boy his age could go broke in a week if someone didn't stop him."

"It's a good thing your Athenian is wealthy," Diokles said, as he watched the slaves unload amphorae from the back of a wagon. "Aphro and I had a wonderful time spending her money yesterday. I'll have ten full kraters of wine and back-up amphorae at the ready in case it's a bigger crowd than expected."

"You were able to find enough white wine, I presume," Theron said.

"Delphinians are a thirsty bunch. I had to buy out every one of my competitors."

"See you don't pad the bill. Althaia may be wealthy, and in this case willing to spend as much as it takes, but it's Praxis who oversees the accounts."

"Don't worry. I make it my life's work to know who I can cheat and who I can't." He slapped Theron on the back and moved off to supervise the unloading of the amphorae.

"Let's see those goblets, Aphro," Theron said as she finished setting out ten beautifully painted, narrow rimmed drinking goblets on a richly embroidered cloth.

Theron held one up, turned it around and then peered into the mouth.

"They were the best we could find on such short notice," she said. "The opening isn't as small as we'd have liked, but I think they'll do."

"They'll have to do. That they're painted black on the interior helps," he said. He placed the goblet back on the table. "And the fact that the rest of us will be drinking from plain cups will only emphasize their beauty. Now, which one is for Kalliope?"

"Can you not see the difference?"

"No." He stepped back and studied each goblet. Aphro waited.

"Can you see a difference, Zenon?"

"They all look the same to me."

"Ah!" Theron exclaimed after a moment. "This one." He pointed. "The maid is carrying a sword, not a thyrsus."

"Very good," Aphro clapped. "At first glance it's difficult to see the difference between a walking staff tipped with a pinecone and a sword with a fancy hilt. I thought it was appropriate."

"Indeed. And did you have any problems with the recipe?"

"I mixed it a dozen times and tried it out on several of the boys. Now I know who's been stealing barley cakes from the storeroom. I thought it was rats."

"So it worked."

"Like a charm."

"Good. I haven't had occasion to use it in many years. What about the coloring? The thickening agent?"

"I've already added it to the bottom of her cup. She'll see that the wine poured in will be a lovely golden hue, but as the wine sits in the cup, that will change. I had to work out the right consistency. At first it was too thick. Like a paste. The key was to add a little water to let it dissolve and not to use too much garum. It still tasted like day-old fish guts, so then I added honey. But you'll see," she smiled and held up the goblet reserved for Kalliope.

"Kalliope's tiny. There's barely any meat on her bones so it shouldn't take much to do the trick. Besides the fact that her serving won't be diluted with much water, the garum and beetroot will thicken and stain her white wine blood red and the belladonna will induce a euphoric delirium that will transform the new priestess into a truth-telling font of information."

"At least that's the plan," Theron mumbled as he turned to Zenon. "All right," he put his hand on Zenon's shoulder. "Let's find Palamedes."

"Follow me," the boy said as he led Theron down the steps toward the temple. "Everybody down here knows me." He turned to Theron, "Don't tell anyone," he lowered his voice, "but I've even been into the Pythia's private chamber. Palamedes took me in. Introduced me. She was veiled the whole time, but she was nice. She gave me sweets."

"That's quite an honor, Zenon. I promise I won't tell a soul."

Zenon chattered on as Theron followed him down the torch-lit subterranean corridor under the temple. This is the same hallway Althaia and Nephthys walked following Palamedes's thread, he thought. He was nearly sick with fury at the idea of such a man playing them for fools, having the two women so close to him, alone, down here in the dark. Theron trusted Praxis completely and knew him to be an excellent judge of character. If Palamedes had fooled Praxis, he could likely fool anyone. But the prospect of the old artisan being a murderer still didn't feel right. Now Kleomon, on the other hand. Or even Philon. But Palamedes? The truth was only the gods knew what secrets were locked in the hearts of men—and since Theron didn't believe in the gods, it was up to men like him to pry the secrets out. One by one, if necessary.

"Here it is." Zenon stopped in front of a closed door and knocked.

They waited a moment and Zenon knocked again.

"Perhaps the priests have him helping with the re-sanctification ceremony," Theron said.

"But he hardly ever does any work like that," Zenon said. "He should be here."

"Maybe he is at his workshop or at the theater. Maybe he's going to watch Menandros's play." Or maybe he has fled and is on his way to who-knows-where, Theron thought.

"But what if he's sick? He's awfully old and no one saw him yesterday. Someone should check on him."

"What are you doing down here?" They turned to find Basileios, Philon's personal bodyguard, behind them. He had the same disdainful look on his face that he'd worn the night Theron and Althaia had dined at Philons. "Ah, Theron of Thessaly, where is your beautiful employer?" He looked around as if Althaia might be standing in the shadows. "You are usually always at her side. Has she gone missing?"

"My employer's whereabouts are none of your concern," Theron said, uneasy at the guard's boldness.

"Come now, you cannot fault a man for appreciating a beautiful woman, can you?" Basileios laughed as if he were joking with an old friend.

Theron ignored that and said, "Zenon came to visit Palamedes yesterday, but couldn't find him anywhere. And he's not here today, either."

"Have you seen him?" Zenon asked.

The guard mussed Zenon's hair as if he were a child, not a young man of sixteen. "He's probably up at the temple workshop. You know how he gets when he's working on a special piece. Why aren't you helping Menandros get ready for the ceremony? And when's he finally going to let you have a part in one of his plays?"

Zenon beamed. "Today. Of course, I don't have any lines—I play the shade of someone already dead—but still."

"You've got to start somewhere. Now, you better go get ready." The guard moved to escort them out when Theron spoke up.

"I don't imagine you have a key. Zenon's awfully worried about his friend, and we wouldn't want him preoccupied for his theatrical debut, would we?"

"I don't know if Philon and Kleomon would want me unlocking doors to anyone's private chambers."

"But if it will allay Zenon's worries...."

Basileios stared hard at Theron.

"I'm sure you know how close Zenon and Palamedes are, and if it would ease the boy's mind…."

"Alright," Basileios relented. "For you, Zenon." He took a key off an iron ring, slipped it into the lock, and opened the door.

The room was neat and simple. A sleeping pallet lay snug against the far wall and shelves lined the rest of the space. The shelves were full of vases and lekythoi, plain cups, kylixes and kraters, and an assortment of jars, pots and other vessels of all shapes and sizes in various stages of completion. A small potter's wheel and stool sat in the corner surrounded by buckets of slick, wet clay and dirty water. Next to it, on a high table, a pitcher, a basin of water, and a stack of drying cloths were arranged. Theron walked over to the table and felt the wick on the lamp. Cold. Papers were spread on the table, sketches for works in progress or future works. Palamedes was not here, that much was obvious. But it was also obvious he hadn't packed his things for a long trip. If he's gone, Theron thought, he must have left in a hurry.

"Don't worry, Zenon. You know Palamedes isn't one for crowds. He's probably laying low until this whole ceremony is over. I'm sure someone will find him sooner or later." The guard adjusted the sword at his hip and rested his hand on its hilt.

Theron paused as Basileios ushered Zenon back out to the hallway. Something is not right, he thought. He sniffed the air—the musty scent of cold stone, wet clay, packed earth, and something else, almost like…. Someone has been in the tunnel. But where is the opening? He could've kicked himself. He never asked Althaia or Nephthys about the tunnel. He knew exactly where it began, where the stone opening was in the Sacred Precinct wall, and he knew where it ended. Here. In this room. *But where?* There were shelves lining every wall. *Damn! Where is the tunnel?*

"Satisfied?"

"Smells like Palamedes's got a dead rat in here," Theron said.

"We get 'em down here all the time. Usually the snakes take care of them," Basileios said. "Time to go. Menandros wouldn't want his new star actor to go missing."

"No, he wouldn't," Theron said. Something about Basileios made Theron's hackles stand on end, but the man was right. They had no more time to waste.

# CHAPTER FIFTY-FOUR

Althaia scooted Praxis and Nephthys over so Theron could take his seat beside her. They sat on the far right side of the theater, near the entrance. From their vantage point, she could see across the stage to the center front rows of the audience. In the very center seat of the front row sat a woman clothed in the purest white. She was completely veiled, although a laurel wreath sat on her brow. The Pythia of Apollon. She looks lonely, Althaia thought.

On either side of her, Philon and Kleomon sat, attended by their personal guards and surrounded by Delphi's most prominent citizens. Directly behind them, the priestesses of Gaia sat on brand new feather pillows adorned with silk tassels and gold and silver embroidery. As it promised to be a chilly day, Althaia had asked Diokles to purchase woolen throws to keep the priestesses warm and comfortable. She hoped Praxis was keeping an accurate record of everything Diokles and Aphro put on her account.

Thea had ushered the priestesses in. It was her job to ensure they sat in the right places, or the plan might fail. Phoibe sat directly behind the Pythia of Apollon and behind her sat Georgios and her mother, Rhea. They seemed to be propping Phoibe up. Maybe Theron's suspicions were true. Perhaps Kalliope—or someone—was poisoning Phoibe. She looked more than sick. She looked as if Hades himself sat at her elbow, not Georgios.

To Phoibe's right, closest to Althaia, the priestesses of Athens, Sparta,

Elis, Corinth, and Tegea sat while positioned to her left were Thea, Kalliope and Eumelia of Argos—and, of course, Nikos. Thea had been right. Kalliope insisted Nikos sit beside her, amongst the priestesses. He must feel a fool, Althaia thought. But it was too late to worry about it. The die was cast.

* * *

"Ladies and gentlemen," Philon began, "distinguished citizens and leaders of Delphi, General Heraklios, Pythia, and our honored guests, the priestesses of Gaia, please allow us to welcome you to the re-dedication of the sacred theater of Delphi."

The theater wasn't full, but the crowd, which was bigger than Theron had anticipated, roared in approval. The locals usually had to wait for the beginning of the season for a new play. And rarely did a play come with free wine before, during, and after the production. Diokles had seen to it that rumors about the play spread like wildfire. Menandros was a popular character in town, and news that his play was to be a totally new kind of production brought out a bigger crowd than usual. Several members of the chorus had been buzzing about it since they left their secret rehearsal late the night before and, now, the whole theater was humming with anticipation. First a body on the sacred altar of Dionysos, next a murder and the funeral feast for the priestess of Dodona, and now this. Seldom had Delphi seen such excitement—at least not since the war was over.

Philon quieted the crowd and continued, "It is unfortunate that we must gather here today to cleanse and purify the sacred altar, but it is our duty and our honor to share this ceremony with the great people of Delphi to whom Apollon—and Gaia—" he bowed graciously toward the priestesses—"have entrusted their oracles." Again he had to quiet the crowd as they clapped and cheered even louder. How is it, he wondered, that such an ignorant bunch could think so highly of themselves? "Our illustrious playwright has written a new play for the occasion. A play in which we are all to have a part in pouring the libations, drinking in honor of Dionysos, and re-sanctifying his sacred altar. Now, let us all raise our cups in honor of Menandros." He raised his goblet and drank deeply. The crowd followed his example and did the same.

The audience fell silent and Althaia watched as Menandros, wearing the mask of Dionysos, walked onto the stage.

"Lo! I am Dionysos, god of theater, of wine and fertility, the son of Zeus and his beloved Semele, brother of Apollon, the god of light and sun, of truth and prophecy, and I am come to the land of the Phokians, to Delphi's Sacred Precinct, to rededicate my sacred thymeli, the altar upon which sacrifices are made. In one hand I brandish my thyrsus, in the other my wine cup, that I may lead you, my worthy attendants, in the rites and rituals of re-sanctification."

The small chorus entered from the parodoi on either side of the stage. They stood in the center, like a curtain hiding Menandro's exit, and began to sing.

"People of Delphi! Why must the god himself come here today to re-sanctify our sacred altar? Do you know? Have you heard the tale? Today all will be revealed and the culprit caught, the villains vilified and the righteous sought. The play you witness will be for naught unless, together, we untie this Gordian knot. Now, raise your cup and take a sip for the time will come when the truth will slip, drip by drip, from the villain's lip. Now, behold"—the leader of the chorus, the coryphaios, held up a cup and took a drink—"let us together, Dionysos's attendants all, drink to a happy ending to a sad story of sin and sacrilege."

Like ripples across a pond, one by one audience members looked at each other and then followed the coryphaios's example and tipped their cups to drink as the chorus split into two groups and took their places on either side of the stage. An actor entered from the right. He was wearing the mask of a young man, unbearded. Nikos. He carried a body, Zenon wrapped in a cloak, and lifted it high as if in offering.

"Dionysos forgive me for I carry in my arms the truth of my own unbridled nature, base with unshaken lust and rapacious greed. Unhappy wretch that I am, my need was not sated with pleasure and my desires were not were gratified. I, like Pentheus, am misfortune's mate, a fool who would not listen to wisdom, but who sought to take what was not mine and slew what would not yield. I leave my unfortunate friend on the temple's sacred steps and pray that Apollon's grace will ensure her peace."

Nikos had blanched and Althaia and Thea had both argued against the dialogue being so graphic, but Menandros threw a tantrum and claimed the whole scheme depended upon the opening scene. "I am the playwright and, believe me, when I say we must have a dramatic hook. Otherwise, the audience will lose interest and our plan will be for naught," he had said. Now Althaia wrapped her arms about her, holding her elbows tight in her palms. She imagined Nikos carrying Charis thus, leaving the girl's body to the mercy of the priests, his heart filled with anger, shame, remorse—and the worst, fear. The actor bent and placed Zenon on the steps to the skene behind the stage. He turned toward the audience, looked around furtively and ran back through the parodos.

The chorus lifted their voices again and Althaia held her cup at the ready.

"The first offense was thus commissioned. We drink, we drink to its remission."

Along with the leader of the chorus, Althaia and the rest of the audience drank again and then watched as Menandros, now wearing a satyr's mask and outlandish phallus, entered from the far parodos and approached the body.

"Who was that shadowed man? Who left this gift upon the temple steps?" The satyr lifted the cloak and gasped. "Now I see! My goals are nearly met and this, a gift from Olympos, will see me home." Menandros lifted Zenon, heaving a bit which made Althaia and her company smile at his efforts, and carried him to the thymeli. He pulled back the cloak just enough to reveal a woman's mask. Althaia nearly jumped out of her seat as the crowd gasped.

The satyr turned to the audience and declared, "The gift is given and received. Now I wait and plan and spy and scheme to discover the giver's identity. Then I will take the news to my patroness and receive my reward in silver and gold—or perhaps with favors—" the satyr pumped his hips forward, his long stiff phallus swaying before him—"more manifold!"

The crowd whooped and cheered and Althaia felt she might be sick. Still, she raised her glass with the rest of the crowd as the chorus sang: "Dare our villain wait and observe the revelation he deserves? We drink, we drink to steel our nerves."

The fact that she was about to see her part in the tragedy played out before all Delphi began to sink in. This whole production may have been her idea, but that didn't mean she was enjoying it. She looked over at Nephthys, who returned her gaze. Praxis held Nephthys's hand tight, and Althaia grabbed Theron's arm. She needed to be grounded for what came next.

Two actors, both wearing female masks and holding a string between them, tiptoed in from the right and approached the thymeli, the altar where Zenon still lay. "Aha! Here we are! In the holy of holies. Among the riches of righteousness, the crucible of discovery where we reveal just what kind of death befell our maid."

From behind the altar, the satyr stuck his head out and waved to the audience. "I am hid and hidden bid these brave, foolish souls to reveal what I, too frightened, seek."

Althaia's fingers dug into Theron's arm as the first woman bent over Zenon. After a moment of complete silence, the actor turned to face the crowd. "Behold! What have we here?" He held up Nikos's necklace, the very one she'd extracted from Charis's throat, and let it swing slowly from his fingertips. Time stopped as a collective gasp rose from the audience. Tears clouded Althaia's eyes and she turned toward Nikos. His face was white as death. He sat unmoving, still as an image carved on a funeral stele. Beside him, an obviously confused Kalliope fidgeted in her seat. How much longer must this go on? Althaia wondered. But she knew the answer. The play was exactly as long as it needed to be. Exactly as long as it took for the drug in Kalliope's wine to work its magic.

The second actor clasped his hands over his heart and cried. "O! The very instrument of her demise!"

Just then, the satyr poked his head out from behind the altar again and addressed the crowd. "Thank you. Thank you, a thousand times. These unwitting servants of my ambition provide me now the ammunition to see my campaign through."

Kalliope, her voice already thick from unwatered wine and belladonna, stood up and looked down at Nikos. "Wait!" She said loud enough for everyone to hear. "How did they—what's going on here? I don't like this play."

Nikos and Thea were supposed to have encouraged Kalliope to drink enough for the effects of the drugged wine to be evident to everyone. Apparently they'd done that part of their job well. Althaia watched as Nikos reached up to pull Kalliope down next to him and bent down to whisper in her ear. She wanted to look away, but couldn't. She knew his lines as well as he did; after all, she'd helped write them.

"By the gods, Kalliope, I don't know," he was to whisper in her ear, letting his warm lips linger on her lobe while his hand slipped around her waist and pulled her toward him. "Someone is out to ruin me, shame me into admitting my guilt. If my part in Charis's death is revealed, I won't be able to marry you and return with you to Dodona. Our future will be ruined. But we can still escape! If only we knew who moved Charis's body from the steps of the Temple to the altar in the theater. We could blame him for Charis's death and be free to leave Delphi together."

Kalliope leaned into Nikos. She lifted her face toward him and went to drape her arms around his neck as Thea's arm shot across Kalliope's shoulder to rescue the young priestess's goblet. The goblet's part in the play had not yet come and everything would be ruined if it missed its cue. Kalliope planted a drunken kiss square on Nikos's lips and whispered something in his ear that made his face flush red.

Across the stage, Althaia couldn't drag her eyes away from them. Theron followed her line of sight and gently turned her face back toward the stage. "Don't watch. Like any actor, he has to play his part."

Althaia turned back to see the chorus change positions again. Behind their movement, Zenon had jumped down from the altar and disappeared. Now, one of Menandros's actors hobbled out wearing the mask of an old woman. The actor leaned heavily on a tall walking staff, on the top of which sat, secured by a leather thong, the ruby-eyed serpent from Melanippe's staff.

Kalliope's voice cut through the quiet. "Where'd they get that?" And then Nikos and Thea could be heard shushing her. It was not quite time yet. A little more wine … a little more time….

From the other parodos, Menandros, still wearing his satyr mask and giant phallus, entered and danced around, entertaining the crowd with his lewd antics. Behind him, an actor wearing the mask of a girl strode out, nearly knocking him over. The old woman looked up: "Hail and well met my dearest friend. What news to share today?"

The actor playing the young girl twirled around like a child in a new chiton and said: "Only this; I am to be wed!"

The old woman replied: "This is unexpected news. Who is to be your handsome groom?"

The young girl answered: "Why don't you guess? You know him best!"

The old woman straightened up and started to hobble off the stage, waving her hand in dismissal. "No! That cannot be true. He will not be wedded, will not be bedded, especially to you!"

The young woman continued her twirling and prancing. "Poor old, befuddled thing. He will be wedded, he will be bedded and you will bless us both." Althaia couldn't tear her eyes away as the satyr thrust himself up against the young woman's behind.

The old woman held up her walking stick as if to reprimand the young girl. "Your words astound me, silly girl. You must think my son a stupid oaf. Nothing could lure him to your bed. On that I swear my sacred oath."

The girl addressed the audience. "Her son will gladly take me to bed—if he wants to keep his head." The actor pulled the necklace out and dangled the silver ball and chain again before the audience. "A wedding gift for my groom. Here, take a closer look. Plucked straight from the throat—yes, the handmaid's throat—to ensure my love leaves Delphi with me or that he hangs from the nearest tree."

"Hey!" Kalliope jumped up and pointed at the actors. She steadied herself using Nikos's shoulder. "That's not how it happened."

Althaia could only guess what Nikos was feeling, but she knew she wanted to throttle the girl. But she watched as Nikos reached up and, once again, pulled Kalliope down to him. She couldn't remember what he was supposed to say next.

On stage, the old woman cried out: "It cannot be!"

"It is, I'm afraid, and the lure is this—your son will be wed or he will be dead with a murderer's conviction." The actor playing the young woman danced around, teasing the old woman.

The old woman held her cane high above her head and shook it ominously. "Hades will unchain Cerberus, throw open the gates, and let the shades run free before you ever gain consent from me."

The young woman laughed. "You will rue the day, you ancient crone, if you say no to me. You will be dead and I'll be wed and this"—she held up the necklace—"is my key."

Althaia squeezed her eyes shut. But she knew what was happening on the stage. The young woman grabbed the cane and pretended to beat the old lady who then fell to the ground. A collective gasp echoed up toward the stadion and while everyone in the crowd began chattering, the chorus changed places, once again providing the curtain behind which the actors left the stage. As they moved, they sang: "Good citizens of Delphi! You have seen through the veil and heard the sad tale, and the noose is growing taut. Now, raise your cup and drink deep and full as we unravel our Gordian knot."

As if in a trance, everyone—including Kalliope—raised their cups to drink. From amongst the chorus, Menandros entered again, this time as Dionysos. He hung his head in sorrow and stumbled a bit as he made his way to lean against the sacred altar.

"My friends, devotees, bacchinates, the sorrow overwhelms. My heart is heavy when it should be light, my soul is mourning when it should be filled with delight, my cup empty when it should be—wait, a revelation! Am I not the god of wine and wine cups? *En oino álétheia*, I declare. In wine, there is truth."

Dionysos lifted his cup to his face and peered into it—like Menandros had done the night before when he sought to retrieve a bug drowned in the sweetness within and came up with the idea to use the libations to out Kalliope. He looked up at the audience and pointed into his cup. "It is in my power to transform water into wine—and wine into blood. And, now, at this moment, one cup in our midst holds the answers I seek, one person amongst us the truth she will speak. For I have transformed the golden wine of goodness into the deepest red of the victim's blood. Look now to your left, look now to your right. *En oino álétheia*. In wine, there is truth."

The chorus took up the cry: "Look now to your left, look now to your right. One cup holds the answers he seeks, one amongst us the truth she will speak."

Althaia turned in her seat and watched the crowd. Audience members looked around, murmuring, unsure what to do. Theron bent down and whispered, "Menandros definitely deserves a laurel wreath for this, and if everything goes as planned, I'll weave it and place it on his brow myself."

The chorus continued to sing: *En oino álétheia*. In wine, there is truth. Look to your left, look to your right...." Menandros's Dionysos went along the front row, stealing glances left and right and peering into audience members' cups as people up and down the rows turned to their neighbors, confused about what exactly was going on.

Althaia couldn't help but watch to see what Kalliope would do next. She couldn't hear her over the buzz of voices filling the theater, but she saw Kalliope grab her wine cup back from Thea and peer into it. She watched as Thea nudged Kalliope's elbow just enough to tip the cup over and then saw her rear back and scream as thick, blood-red wine trickled down the front of Kalliope's cloak and dripped into her lap.

The chorus stopped singing. Menandros waited. Kalliope stood, pulled at the fabric and stared at the stain. "Why's mine red?"

# Chapter Fifty-Five

Menandros held his cup high and spoke, his voice booming as if he truly was a god. "And now we have our proof. The net was cast, the quarry caught, my altar purified. But wait, where is her accomplice? Has he fled? Will she take the blame, bear the shame, her partner unidentified?

Kalliope looked around as if still confused as the chorus began chanting again: "*En oino álétheia. En oino álétheia. En oino álétheia.*" Althaia saw that everyone in the theater was staring at the girl. The Pythia of Apollon was turned around completely in her chair and, on either side of her, Philon and Kleomon looked on with shock. Heraklios's guards appeared as if by magic and took positions around the theater.

Menandros walked toward the front of the stage and the chorus quieted. "You stand alone, Kalliope, accused by the gods of blackmailing Nikomachos of Dodona and murdering his mother, the famous priestess of Zeus and Gaia." A loud gasp and clamor rose up amongst the audience members, but Menandros held up his hand the the whole theater fell silent. "Will you take the blame and bear the shame alone? Will you accept the guilt, pay the price and sacrifice alone? Or will you name your partner? Now! Kalliope, this is your chance to tell the truth. The gods demand it."

"I can't tell!" Kalliope steadied herself against Nikos and whispered loud enough for the whole theater to hear. "It's a secret."

Menandros stepped aside as Theron stood, took his wine cup up to the center of the stage and leaned against the altar. Casual, and appearing without a mask, Theron's demeanor caused the whole crowd to hold its breath.

"And now we come to the final act," he said, his voice filling the theater. "In order to complete the re-sanctification, we must know all the actors in this murderous tragedy. So, tell us Kalliope, what is supposed to be a secret?"

"Which secret?" Kalliope swayed on her feet and Nikos actually had to reach out to steady her. "There are so many. Sometimes I get confused."

"The newest priestess of Dodona will have to do better than that. Why don't you start with your decision to blackmail Nikomachos and how you know what happened in the adyton."

The audience began murmuring and leaning forward as one, pushing, shoving, some even climbing over seats to get a better view.

"I'm not supposed to tell. As long as he marries me, I promised I wouldn't say what happened. Otherwise, Nikos might get into trouble."

"He can't get into any more trouble. We already know he was there when Charis died. But we also know her death was an accident. An unfortunate accident, Kalliope. He did not murder her, and you cannot blackmail him into marrying you."

Pale and breathing fast, her eyes bloodshot and dilated wide, Phoibe tried to stand and reach out toward Nikos—and then she closed her eyes and fainted. Georgios pulled her to him, Rhea fanned her face and lifted a cup of wine to her lips.

"But Nikos has to marry me." Kalliope leaned over Nikos and looked drunkenly into his eyes. "I'm the priestess of Dodona now, and you have to do what I say."

Kleomon pivoted in his seat, turning back and forth between Kalliope, Phoibe, Nikos, and Theron, while Philon stared at Theron, his face the color of ash.

On the stage, Theron continued, "Kalliope, who was in the adyton—or rather, who was on the other side of the curtain when Althaia performed the examination of Charis's body? And who killed the priestess of Dodona?"

"Wait, how do you know where he hid? And why are you asking me all these questions? He was the one who hit the old woman, not me." Kalliope, clutching her wine cup, plopped back down in her seat like a little girl who had just been reprimanded by an angry parent.

"Who hit her, Kalliope? Who killed Melannipe?"

"Why should I tell you? I don't even like you." Kalliope took another drink of wine, and Theron signaled for Thea to take her cup from her. She's had enough, he thought. But when Thea reached for it, Kalliope slapped her hand away. "You have your own cup, Theodora of Thessaly," she sneered. "Why don't you go up there with your brother? I don't like you, either."

"*En oino álétheia*," Theron said. He signaled to Heraklios who, with his nephew the lieutenant in command, marched more guards into the theater. They took positions on the stage and up the stairs, facing down the audience rows. He hoped Aphro's potion was strong enough to make Kalliope name her accomplice before things got out of hand.

"We have seen the power of the gods as today Dionysos has turned wine into blood before our eyes," Theron announced to the crowd, pacing before them. "If Kalliope's accomplice is here today, perhaps the god has transformed his wine as well. The soldiers will watch as each one of us tips our cup and pours wine so all can see. If your heart is innocent of this crime, your wine will serve as a sanctifying libation to the god. If not, it will serve as your indictment. Now, pour!" Theron tipped his cup and poured a healthy draught onto the theater paving stones as Menandros watched. There was, of course, no way to color the wine of an unknown accomplice, so they could only hope, if the man was in the theater, Kalliope would point him out when she saw his wine pour out clear. Hopefully, as long as she was not too far under the influence of the belladonna, she would realize that she alone would be held accountable for Melanippe's murder if she did not name him.

Philon remained immobilized, while Kleomon could hardly sit still, swiveling this way and that as everyone began pouring and talking at once. The Pythia lifted her veil to watch, her eyes wide in fascination. Theron strode over to them, towered over them. "Deepest apologies Pythia, but everyone must pour. Now." The Pythia of Apollon, her face pale and somber, looked up at Theron and handed her cup to him. He tipped it over and poured out a thin line of wine, then handed it back with a respectful bow.

"I don't know what you're about, Theron, but this is the most entertaining day I've had in a long time," Kleomon said as he tipped his wine cup over and dripped a clear golden stream onto the ground.

Next to him, Philon huffed and started to rise. "Where are my guards?

I demand an end to this ridiculous performance." Behind Theron, two of Heraklios's soldiers stepped forward and Philon sank back into his seat.

"I'm afraid I must ask you to pour, Philon," Theron said.

"Whose idea was this?" Philon practically spat the words. "You think by intimidating a poor, lovesick girl into confessing to murder you have proven yourself some sort of servant of the gods? I know what you really are. I know—"

"Pour!" Theron demanded.

Philon turned his cup upside down and dumped the contents onto the ground.

Heraklios's voice rang out. "Libations or indictments?" he called to his guards.

"Libations, sir," the lieutenant announced. "There is no other guilty party in the theater. Kalliope alone is guilty of desecrating the altar of Dionysos, blackmailing Nikomachos of Dodona, and murdering Melanippe of Dodona, priestess of Zeus and Gaia. It is up to the Amphiktyonic League to sentence her for desecration of the Sacred Precinct and for Niomachos to demand retribution and receive the blood price for his mother's murderer."

"Wait!" Kalliope frowned. She clutched her goblet as if it were a child's favored toy from which she could not bear to be parted and clamored over her seat, stepped on some Delphinian dignitary's lap, and teetered over Philon's chair. Philon reared back into his seat, putting as much distance between himself and Kalliope as humanly possible. "Heraklios! Restrain this poor girl."

Kalliope grabbed the cup from Philon's hands and peered into it. "This magic doesn't work right." She tipped the cup over and dribbled out the last few drops of his wine onto the paving stones.

Philon planted both hands on Kalliope's shoulders and shoved her backwards. "This is madness! The poor girl's been drugged!"

Theron put his arm around Kalliope's waist and pulled her back against him, away from Philon. He glanced at Kleomon and growled, "Get the Pythia out of here." Kleomon grabbed the Pythia's hand, and they walked warily behind the altar until they were safely behind Heraklios and as far away from the deranged girl as possible. But Kleomon had no intention of going any farther; he couldn't wait to see exactly what was going to happen next. And neither could most of the people in the audience, many of who were crowding forward, stepping over rows of seats and into the aisles to get a better look at what was going on down front.

Theron picked up Kalliope by the waist and placed her on the altar; her legs dangled as if she were a child sitting on a high stool. "Why did you say the magic doesn't work right? What did you expect to see in Philon's cup?"

"Why should I tell you? You can't punish me."

"I can't, but Heraklios can. And he will. What did you expect to see in Philon's cup?"

"Stay away from me." She reached out with her leg to push Theron away from her. He dodged her foot and stepped back. He glanced over at Heraklios who then stepped forward.

"Kalliope, you must talk to us. Let's start with the priestess of Dodona. How did she come to die at the bottom of a ravine?"

"I'm the priestess of Dodona."

"How did Melanippe die? Who hit her?"

"I don't know why anyone cares. She was a disgusting old woman." She looked out at Nikos. "I'm sorry, my love, but you know it's true."

"Kalliope. You are trying my patience. Who took Melanippe's walking stick and bludgeoned her to death with it? Who dumped her body in the ravine? You didn't do those things, did you?"

"Of course not, you stupid man. Papa did it."

"You must say your Papa's name."

Kalliope shuddered. "I'm not supposed to ever say it. Ever."

"If your papa murdered the priestess, you must name him or you will be punished for his crime," Theron said. "That's not fair, is it?"

"Nothing he does is fair," she said, her voice low, trembling. Just name your accomplice, Theron pleaded silently, and let's get this over with. They'd come this far and must now see it through, but by the gods, it might have been better to handle this Diokles's way.

"If you don't want to say his name, if you're forbidden from telling, just point. If he's in the theater, point to him," Thereon urged.

She suddenly whirled and pointed to Heraklios. Everyone in the audience gasped. "If I don't point him out, you'll make me pay for his crime?" There was a collective sigh of relief as Heraklios nodded. "If you were there when the deed took place and will not name the man who wielded the walking stick against her, I will have to hold you accountable for her death."

She dropped her cup with a clatter and buried her face in her hands. No one moved, no one made a sound. No birds trilled in the trees, no leaves rustled. It seemed as if the wind had even stopped to listen. "You won't let him hurt me, will you?" Her voice was muffled, barely audible.

"On my honor as a soldier, I swear it," Heraklios answered.

Then she raised her face, wiped her eyes with her sleeve, and pointed straight at Philon. "That's him. There."

Philon leapt to his feet. "This is outrageous! Kleomon, you've known me for years. You know I have no offspring."

With his arms folded across his chest and a wide smile across his fleshy face, Kleomon met Philon's gaze and said nothing.

Philon turned to the audience behind him and pointed at Theron. "Theron of Thessaly is a known assassin. He arrived here the night of Charis's murder, he killed the priestess of Dodona, and now he's blaming it on this poor deluded girl. Heraklios, you can't let him get away with this."

Kalliope edged closer to Heraklios, as if standing in the general's shadow offered her the protection she needed. "Theron?" she laughed. "Theron wasn't the one who found Charis on the temple steps. Theron wasn't the one who made Basileios strip her and carry her up here. Right here. On this altar." She patted the cold stone with the palm of her hand, and a soft smacking sound rang through the theater. "He wasn't the one who claimed it would drive Phoibe mad, help push her over the edge." She turned to Nikos. "I didn't know about it until later. I swear."

The hair stood up on Theron's neck and he scanned the theater for Basileios. Where is he? Kalliope started toward Philon again, but the drugs were making her legs wobbly and she fell at his feet, knocking him back in his chair. She clutched at his knee and pulled herself up to lay her head in his lap. "Tell them I didn't know. I didn't do anything wrong."

"Get away from me," Philon kicked her in the stomach and sent her sprawling. Then he stood and began barking orders at his body guards. "Take her to my quarters at the temple. She needs a physician's attention immediately. Heraklios, I'm ashamed of you. Once again, I must clean up the mess. Once again, I must take charge—"

"Do you dare disown me now, Papa?" Kalliope clutched at the hem of his robe. "After all I've done for you? After you made me leave home and go live with that nasty witch in Dodona?

"Philon," Theron said, "this girl has made serious accusations against you. Do you deny them?"

"I don't answer to you," he spat. "She's so drugged, she can barely stand."

Kalliope scrambled to her feet and marched at Theron as if she was going to ram him with her head. She stopped short and teetered back on her heels. "Did you poison me? Am I going to die like Sofia and Phoibe?"

*Ah, so that's why Phoibe is sick and that's why Sofia died so suddenly.* Theron looked up at Thea who, like the other priestesses, was at once riveted by Kalliope and trying to care for Phoibe who was, although now conscious, pale as death. The audience also appeared to be of two minds—the ones sitting farther up wanted to move down to get as close to the action as possible while the ones sitting down front tried to draw back from the tragedy.

"Did your Papa poison Sofia?" Heraklios asked as he signaled more guards to approach.

"Sofia?" Kalliope said, looking up at Philon. "No, Papa fucked her, he didn't poison her. Charis did. He said Charis was a snake and whoever killed her did the whole world a favor."

"Stop this now!" Philon tried again to gain control of the situation. "Heraklios, restrain her. This has gone on long enough. She's mad, insane!"

"Heraklios, she is mad, insane," Kalliope mocked, trying to stand again.

"Why is your Papa poisoning Phoibe?" Theron asked.

"To kill her. By the gods, you are a stupid man. My papa is not stupid. He speaks a dozen languages. Did you know that?" Kalliope poked her finger in the middle of Theron's chest. "How many languages do you speak?"

"By all that is holy, make her stop!" Philon demanded.

"By all that is holy … You know, Phoibe is holy." The crowds turned almost as if their heads were on a pivot, clamoring for a chance to see Phoibe, to see what role she played in these tragic events. Kalliope continued, "She has the sight, and she knew the priests were plotting. Or at least one was. I can't speak for the old fat one," she waved her arm toward Kleomon. "But Papa? Plotting, plotting, plotting. Always wanting more, more power, more money, just more. He sent me to Dodona where I was to charm Melanippe and become her successor. Then he went to work on Sofia—hard to picture them as lovers isn't it?" She shuddered. "Then when Charis poisoned Sofia, he got mad. I'm sleepy. Why am I so sleepy?" Her knees buckled and she tipped forward. Theron caught her, sat her back up on the altar where she leaned into him like a child being carried off to bed.

"'Daughter, you must do your duty and both Delphi and Dodona will be within our grasp,'" she mimicked and pointed at Philon. "Duty and power. That's all you ever talk about. But I didn't want to do my duty. I didn't want to go to Dodona. Melanippe was mean and sick and she smelled like sour flesh and piss. But it turned out all right because Nikos is strong and handsome—and he's going to be my husband."

"Kalliope, why did your papa want to kill Phoibe?" Heraklios asked.

"Why, why, why? Why always why?" Kalliope started to climb off the altar. Theron, afraid she might fall, grabbed at her waist then doubled over in pain as she planted her foot in his groin. Heraklios started toward them, but she glared at him and he stepped back, ready, for the moment, to let her have her say. "I'll tell you why." She yawned, grabbed at Theron's cloak and whispered. "Because my papa is the smartest man in all Greece. Smarter than Aristotle. Smarter than Platon. Smarter than you." She reached out to poke at Theron's shoulder again and instead fell forward into his arms.

* * * *

At the entrance to the theater, Aphro turned to Diokles. "Perhaps I put used too much belladonna."

"You think?"

"Or maybe it was the mandragora. Or the pinch of herba apollinaros."

Diokles' eyes widened. "Zeus's beard, woman! You could have killed her."

Aphro shrugged. "When you've got only one chance to catch a rat...."

* * * *

"I've had enough of this farce." Philon stood to march toward the exit when the soldiers took a step forward. "I'm not going to let to this deluded girl accuse me of crimes I could not possibly have committed." The soldiers drew their swords. He stepped back and slumped down in his chair.

Theron propped Kalliope upright against the altar. "Go on." He knelt beside her. Whatever Aphro had put in her drink—and he was pretty sure it was more than his truth-telling concoction—he knew there was little time left before the girl would be out for a very long time.

"I was telling you a story, wasn't I?"

"Yes, about your Papa, about Philon."

"Shh! You can't say his name."

"About your papa, then."

Kalliope's face blanched. She swayed, leaned forward and retched. "I don't feel good. You didn't poison me, did you? Am I going to die like Sofia?"

"No, you are not going to die."

"I think I'm going to die. Nikos!" She tried to scramble to her feet. "Don't let me die on our wedding day!"

Theron grabbed her arm and pulled her up short. "You're not going to die."

"You're trying to kill me!" she screamed, wrenched free, and threw herself at Philon's feet. "Papa, help me!"

Althaia groaned and Praxis put his arm around her. She tried to see Nikos, but soldiers blocked her view. They were trying to keep the audience from surging forward, but their job was proving as difficult as trying to talk the tide out of coming ashore.

"Get this madwoman out of here," Philon screeched, shaking her loose as if scorpions had crawled up his legs.

Kalliope looked up at Philon, helpless, like the young girl she was. "I may only be the daughter of a slave, but you said you loved me." Tears ran down her confused face and she had trouble keeping her eyes open and keeping her head from bobbling about on her neck as if it had come loose.

By now Heraklios, the lieutenant, and two soldiers flanked Theron, ready to clap Philon in chains and haul him away. Theron wanted nothing more than to scoop Kalliope into his arms and get her away from Philon, away from the theater, away from the crowds. They may have achieved their goals, but this was a disaster. Kalliope's shoulders were shaking, racked with sobs as Philon looked down at her with utter hatred etched on his face. What causes men to use daughters like political tools, marrying them off or sending them away as if they were nothing more than goods to be bought or sold? A wave of revulsion washed over him as he remembered all the women he'd known who'd been pawned off to uncaring husbands who treated them like one more piece of property. He thought of Althaia, and of his own twin. Are they not my equals?

"I have no daughter, and I have committed no crime," Philon growled at her.

Wiping her tears, Kalliope looked up at Theron and Heraklios. This time there was a cold calculation in her eyes. "If he won't own to being my father, ask him if he'll own to Palamedes."

Theron stomach lurched. "What about Palamedes?" He knelt and grabbed her wrist, his sympathy vanishing like so much smoke.

"If you'd like to find him, try his tunnel. Though I imagine you'll need to hold your nose. He probably doesn't smell too good anymore."

*I knew something was not right in his room.* Theron cursed his stupidity, and turned to see Praxis leap from his seat and run out of the theater with Nephthys and several of Heraklios's soldiers in his wake. Nephthys would know how to access the tunnel. By the gods, I should've trusted my gut, he swore to himself. He should've have trusted Praxis's intuition. He slid the dagger from his belt. The need to plunge it into something was nearly overwhelming. Kalliope made an easy target, but Philon was the one he wanted.

He let go of Kalliope and she fell back in a heap at his feet. The lieutenant rushed up and knelt beside her. Her head lolled backward and she started to cry again. Then she lay her head on the lieutenant's lap and fell fast asleep.

Theron loomed over Philon's chair and pressed his blade into the side of his neck, poised just so against the artery pulsing below Philon's pale skin. "What did you do with Palamedes?" One flick of the wrist and Philon the priest would be history. "Why kill him?"

Theron felt Heraklios at his side. "Be careful, Theron. Philip will want the bastard to go to Pella for a show trial."

Theron ignored him and pushed his blade into Philon's flesh until a tiny bead of blood trickled down the priest's neck. "Why kill Palamedes?"

"A slave shouldn't ask so many questions," Philon said. His eyes flicked up at Theron and then across the altar toward Kleomon. He smiled sanctimoniously, reached up, clasped Theron's wrist and pulled the knife hard into his own neck. Theron jerked his hand back unleashing a great spray of blood that splattered across his chest and face. Philon's eyes glazed. He reached up, slowly, clamped his hand over his neck as if he wanted to feel the warm stickiness of life one last time. Blood gushed through his fingers, painted them red, and pulsed down his arm. Then Philon of Patra, senior priest of the Temple and Guardian of the Oracle of Apollon, slumped back into his chair one last time, eyes staring, a sardonic smile frozen on his lips.

# CHAPTER FIFTY-SIX

At once the crowd erupted and people streamed down the steps and into the aisles. Some wanted to get as far away as possible, but most wanted a good look at the pompous priest who acted as though he was better than everyone as he bled out over the theater paving stones. Soldiers tried to usher them toward the door as quickly as possible, but it was useless.

Thea shuddered and then turned back to Phoibe who still lay in Georgios's arms. Her skin was white, her breathing shallow, and Rhea mopped her brow with the edge of a blanket dipped in wine. The other priestesses watched and prayed that Philon had not, at the end, accomplished his goal.

Next to her, Nikos stood on his seat and tried to spot Althaia through the stream of people. He saw her turn, searching for him even as she was swept up in the crowd rushing toward Philon. She waved at him, then her eyes widened and someone moved in front of her.

"Nikos!"

How he heard her voice over the noise, he would never know. He jumped up a row higher. Someone knocked into him and he grabbed Rhea's shoulder to steady himself. Over the heads and shoulders of the audience members and soldiers, he finally spotted her, flailing frantically, kicking mercilessly.

Basileios. A full head and shoulders taller than Althaia, Philon's body-guard banded his forearm tight around her neck, and walked her in front of him, pushing inexorably through the crowd, toward the exit. With

Theron standing over Philon's body, Praxis and Nephthys gone in search of Palamedes, Nikos knew immediately that Basileios would try to use Althaia to get away, to user her as a hostage to try to bribe his way out of getting punished for his part in Philon's plans.

Nikos launched himself into the crowd. "Move!" he yelled even as spectators pushed forward. "Out of the way!" By the gods, what was wrong with these people? He pushed and shoved, just as violently, just as desperately as the man holding Althaia by the neck.

* * * *

Althaia knew Nikos heard her. He would get to her, just like he had at the ravine. But this time, she meant to fight. If the man who held her thought he could escape using her as a human shield, he was sorely mistaken. That morning, she had remembered her father's advice and stowed her little dagger in her boot. She hopped on one foot, buoyed by the crowd, and pulled the knife out. Basileios looked down just in time to see the steel blade gleam as it plunged into his thigh. He roared in pain, reached down and ripped the knife from his flesh. He gripped the hilt in his fist and plowed his fist into Althaia's jaw.

Nikos was close, almost there. He saw Althaia's head snap back. Then he saw Diokles push through the crowd toward her. Diokles was pointing up at the sky, yelling something. At first he couldn't tell what it was, but then he heard Aphro's voice, high and piercing over the droning of the crowd: Clear shot! Clear shot! Diokles was running interference.

Nikos pushed an old man out of the way and shoved into a young couple still chattering excitedly about the spectacle. He leapt over the rows of seats, climbing two at a time, until he reached the top. He leaned over the edge. Almost directly below him, Basileios struggled to break through the crowd, to gain the path and escape from the theater and the Makedonían guards at his heels.

Diokles was relentless, cutting through the crowd of unsuspecting Delphinians like a trireme plowing through rough seas. He reached them, grabbed Althaia and wrenched her away just as Nikos bellowed. "Basileios!" Surprised by the voice from above, the guard looked up. *Please Gaia*, Nikos prayed, *I need just one clear shot.* As soon as his dagger left his hand, he smiled. Nobody bested him with a blade. It was a pure release, a pure flight, a pure hit. It landed right at the base of Basileios's neck, right at that soft place lovers like to kiss, right at that place in Althaia's neck where Nikos's thumb had been a perfect fit.

# CHAPTER FIFTY-SEVEN

Althaia leaned into Nikos as Basileios's body was laid out next to Philon's. Theron, Heraklios, Kleomon, and Menandros, with his arm around Zenon's shoulders, huddled around Praxis and Nephthys. Heraklios's guards had already cleared all the spectators from the theater.

"It was a good thing Zenon followed us," Praxis said. "Otherwise we wouldn't have had any idea where we were going. It's a maze down there. When we got to Palamedes's apartment, the door was locked and of course no one had a key so we had to break it down. It took three of us and I think one of the men nearly broke his shoulder. Once we were in, Nephthys took over." He turned to her. "Tell them."

"After Althaia and I entered the room the night she examined Charis in the adyton—"

"*The adyton?* This is too much to take in," Kleomon interrupted.

"We'll explain later," Theron said. "Go on."

"That night Palamedes showed us how the entrance to the tunnel worked. There was a secret door—a panel in his wall that slid open behind one of his shelves."

"Zenon wanted to go in first," Praxis picked up the story again, "but I wouldn't let him. Nephthys held him back while I headed into the tunnel with a torch." He took a deep breath. "From the tracks in the dirt, it looked like Palamedes had been dragged in to the passageway as far as Philon's guard could go. Once the tunnel got too low, he simply left Palamedes there. The knife wound didn't kill him right away. He'd tried to crawl back toward his room and, beside him, in the packed dirt of the tunnel floor, he had used a stone to try to scratch out Philon's name. He never finished."

"I could smell it, the stench of death," Theron muttered.

"Yes, but it was faint and the passage was cold. You couldn't have known."

"I feel terrible," Althaia said.

"Don't even start," Praxis interrupted. "He didn't know we thought"—he looked over at Zenon, not wanting the boy to know they ever suspected his friend—"he didn't know. He was dead before the funeral ceremony even began."

"Still," Althaia whispered.

"All these years, Philon had a daughter. How could I not have known?" Kleomon wondered aloud. "He always said I had lousy spies. By the way, what did you put in Kalliope's wine?"

"A secret recipe I learned at the court of the Great King of Persia. A recipe that was obviously not followed as closely as I instructed," Theron said. "I think Diokles and Aphro added a few ingredients of their own."

"Speaking of ingredients being added to wine, I sent two riders up to Phoibe's house," Heraklios said. "It won't take them long to find out who has been poisoning Phoibe and with what. Then we'll know if there's any hope."

"Theron," Thea called out, waving her arm urgently. "Hurry."

The Pythia of Apollon, with her veil pulled back over the laurel wreath on her head, sat with Thea and the other priestesses as they ministered to Phoibe. The Pythia of Gaia's head lay in her mother's lap as Georgios bent over her, his face changing moment to moment from utter rage to sheer desperation.

As one, the group moved toward the Pythia of Gaia.

"Stibi." Phoibe said. She reached for Georgios's hand. "That's what Charis used. That's what she put in Sofia's wine. She said Sofia was weak, that her time was past. That the priests were intent on destroying the Oracle of Gaia. She poisoned Sofia with stibi so I would become Pythia. And that's what Philon used on me. I know it. I feel it. How did I not see it?" She gripped Georgios's hand and pushed herself up, trying to stand.

"Phoibe, don't. You're not strong enough," Georgios begged.

"No, I need this," she said. "I have to do this, now—just in case." She reached out to grasp the hand of the Pythia of Apollon and together they stood facing the others.

The Pythia of Apollon's face was lined with age and grave as a funeral stele as she helped steady Phoibe. Unlike Phoibe, she was well past her prime, a middle-aged woman who had already seen much of life. She was a daughter, a mother, a grandmother, a priestess. She was a child of Delphi, a servant of Apollon and a sister to the priestesses of Gaia. And she had been Sofia's friend.

"I need to say this so you will hear," Phoibe rasped, her voice faint. "So you all will hear." She cleared her throat. "The prophecy Sofia had on the morning of my naming ceremony shaped my life. I came to believe in it as if every word were the literal truth. But we know," she squeezed the Pythia of Apollon's hand, "those with the sight know, that it is not the words that count, it is the interpretation. And sometimes, the things we see do not make sense. They are fragments, whispers of the gods that mere mortals cannot hope to understand. And yet, people depend upon us to see, to predict, to know."

"Phoibe, please, say no more." Georgios pleaded. "Not now. Not like this."

Phoibe smiled down on him, but continued. "'This child shall be called Phoibe, like the Titan of old, Apollon's own grandmother. She will see the Oracles of Apollon and Gaia united or she will see them destroyed and the Sacred Precinct claimed by yet another.' Sofia's prophecy. My prophecy. Today it is fulfilled."

"What?" The priestesses gasped, and Georgios looked up, confused. "How can that be?"

"The Oracles are united. I am the last Pythia of Gaia. There will be no more. The sight has tortured me these many months and now it has left me and there are no others of our sisterhood to take my place. As I lay here today—my head resting in my mother's lap, my hand clasped by the man I love, my forehead cooled by Eumelia, the preiestess of Argos, my chilled body warmed by the blankets Thea of Thessaly drew over me, and my life lifted in prayer by each of the other priestesses here—I heard the voice of Gaia. There was no vision. No sight. Just her voice. And yet it was the clearest, most beautiful, most heartrending music I have ever heard. It was as pure as the cool, cleansing water of the Kastalian Spring and as warm and comforting as a lover's embrace. And once I utter the words Gaia bade me speak, I am done. I will retire from the priesthood. I will marry Georgios—if he will have me—and I will become a wife, and someday, hopefully, a mother. I will be, simply, Phoibe of Arachova."

Behind her, Rhea's gasped and began to weep. But Phoibe didn't turn. Instead, she held the Pythia of Apollon's hand to her breast, closed her eyes and, in a clear voice, said:

*"Tell the People:*
*Mother Earth has spoken*
*Gaia's oracle is broken*
*Apollon's hundred arrows*
*Silenced her sacred servant*
*Now, in one or one thousand years,*
*His fair wrought house will fall*
*And a god reborn shall reign."*

She looked at the other priestesses. "Until this new god, a resurrected god like our own beloved Dionysos, comes to Hellas and lays claim to Delphi, Apollon's Pythia will speak for Gaia, for Apollon, for all the gods. I am through. It is done." She lowered herself back down to her seat and let Eumelia pull the blankets up over her shoulders.

# CHAPTER FIFTY-EIGHT

"I am tired of mysteries," Althaia groused. She stopped, hands on her hips, and stood looking up toward the next turn in the Sacred Way. "Theron, I want to know now, before I set another foot on this path, why we must go back to the Temple of Apollon today. I am in no mood for this."

In point of fact, Althaia was in a perfectly foul mood. Already the ache of missing Nikos tore at her as if her arms had lost their reason for being and her heart had lost the purpose for its beating. The day before, Nikos and Diokles had gone up to the little shed where Nikos, Charis, and her brother had had their ill-fated meeting. It took awhile, but they were able to find what was left of Charis's brother's body and bury it. Althaia wanted to tell Theron and Praxis about the brother—she wondered if they didn't already suspect Nikos had something to do with his disappearance—and she didn't like keeping secrets from them, but she had decided it would do no good to bring up the dead man's fate.

Diokles had been insistent that if it hadn't been Nikos who ushered the bastard down to Hades, it would have been someone else he'd cheated and it would have been sooner rather than later. "Nikos did us all a favor," he'd said, and Althaia had let herself be convinced. After they returned, they'd all shared one last dinner together and then she and Nikos had spent the night together in her cozy guestroom in Menandros' house and she had known, once again, what it was like to be well and truly loved.

But now that Nikos had said his goodbyes and had set out to take his mother's bones back to Dodona for burial, Althaia was in no mood to be cheerful about anything. All she could see stretching endlessly before her was Lycon and weeks of unendurable loneliness and predictability as a wealthy, secluded matron of Athenian society. At least until Nikos arrived in Athens. But no matter how soon it was, it would not be soon enough. And in the meantime, she had to figure out how to deal with her husband.

"I'm with Althaia," Praxis, walking side by side with Nephthys, agreed. "The Temple of Apollon is the last place I want to be after ...."

"Come, you two. This is the end of a mystery. Do you not remember, just a few short days ago when all you cared to discover was why Lysandros bid us make the journey to Delphi in the first place?"

"That was a long time ago," Althaia said, as if those days were a thousand years past.

"Well, put one foot in front of the other, my dear, and you will come to know, at long last, your father's final wishes."

Grudgingly, but with a renewed sense of curiosity, Althaia picked up her skirt and once again began trudging up the slick paving stones toward the temple. She turned the corner and began the final ascent. Ahead towered the menacing serpent tripod commemorating the Battle of Plataea and beside it stood the gilded chariot of Helios gleaming against the mighty Phaedriades. The shining ones. Their bulk rose up behind the Sacred Precinct as if they were the imagined backdrop, the painted skene of a titan's theater. Despite the years of Sacred Wars that had taken their toll, this place, this whole rugged place, was still imbued with a mystical aura that took Althaia's breath away. Even if Phoibe was right, even if in a thousand years, another god took Apollon's place here, even if other temples were raised on the bones of Apollon's mighty foundations, it wouldn't matter. Delphi, for all eternity, would remain a place of awe and magic. Gods or no gods, Gaia, Apollon, or someone totally new from a strange land, Althaia didn't care. She knew the land, the smells, the light, even the air itself was sacred, alive. Gaia, Grandmother Earth, made sure of that.

And then, they were at the top. The Sacred Way flattened out and she rounded the corner of the Altar of Chios to see Kleomon and the Pythia of Gaia standing atop the temple ramp. Lining the ramp on either side stood

Nikos and Thea, Menandros and Zenon, and Heraklios and his nephew.

Stunned to see Nikos, Althaia looked back and forth between him and Theron. "You're still here! What is this? What is happening?"

"Your father's last wish, with a little dramatic flourish of my own."

"Theron, will you finally explain what is going on?" Praxis pleaded.

"Kleomon, you may begin," Theron ordered.

"Don't get the wrong idea, Madam," Kleomon said. "I have been wrangled into presiding over this event by forces beyond my control. It appears that for some time our Pythia and our potter Palamedes had some sort of an understanding with your father. This whole affair has apparently been in the works since before your father's death and today's ceremony was arranged by Lysandros and the Pythia, and, of course, Theron. I am here in my capacity as senior priest of Apollon—and as a reluctant participant."

The Pythia of Apollon smiled. Instead of a veil, a simple wreath of laurel adorned her silvered hair. Beside her, an attendant clutched the tether of a handsome ram. "Althaia of Athens and Praxis of Syria stand before us. Yes. Come on up, like that," she said.

Althaia and Praxis looked at each other and proceeded up the ramp. Praxis glanced back at Nephthys to see Theron wrap his arm around her shoulders and give her a gentle squeeze.

Kleomon held a scroll in his hand, and he unrolled it with great ceremony, glowered at the Pythia, and began.

> "This, the last request and testament made by me, Lysandros of Athens, is hereby recorded by Theron of Thessaly, my companion, trusted confidant, and executor in recognition of the fact that he has agreed that as executor he will ensure that my final wish is fulfilled and that after a period of approximately one year, my daughter and my slave, Praxis of Syria, now like a son to me, who was ripped from his family's hearth, sold to a Theban tyrant and found by me, wounded on the battlefield, nursed to health and welcomed into my household, shall travel to Delphi and there, before the Temple of Apollon, Praxis shall be granted his freedom along with the sum of one mina upon return to Athens and one mina per annum for as long as he remains overseer of the holdings transferred upon my death to my daughter and that Lycon, her kyrios and husband, is

named his legal patron. Further, Theron has agreed to advise Lycon, by showing him this legal document, attested to by the Pythia of Apollon, that he is as bound to his duties as Praxis's patron as he is to his duties to his wife, my beloved daughter, the true inheritor of all that I am and all that I own."

"What a windbag," Theron mumbled with a satisfied smile. Nephthys' knees wobbled and she clung to Theron' cloak.

Kleomon drew in a long breath and proceeded:

"And further, that because I was compelled in my heart to plan for the performance of this manumission after visiting the Pythia of Apollon and receiving abundant wisdom from her regarding the true worth of a man, I have paid to have a ram sacrificed to Apollon on this day at this hour and to have Praxis's name inscribed upon the temple's foundation wall as having been fully manumitted and freed according to the natural rights of man as laid down by the gods of Olympos, the legal rights of freedmen as constituted by the Athenian assembly, and, most importantly, the common sense and good judgment of sensible men who know Praxis to be a man of the most noble character."

Kleomon looked up. "It appears, Praxis of Syria, that you are a rich man. A free metic of Athens."

Praxis said nothing. He turned and stared at Theron who beamed back at him as if it was all his idea. Althaia sobbed, clutched Praxis' himation and pressed her face into his chest. "Praxis—" It was all she could choke out.

"I want to see it," Praxis whispered. "See where it is written."

"Of course you do," the Pythia of Apollon said, and she stepped down and took Praxis's hand. Althaia clung to his arm and the rest of the gathering followed as the Pythia led Praxis back around the Altar of Chios, down the Sacred Way and onto the flat, grassy platform from which the great stone polygonal wall supporting the Temple of Apollon rose from deep in the ground. There, for all to see, were the freshly engraved marks:

*Witnessed and attested to by the Pythia of Apollon,*
*Praxis, born a son of Syria, found on the battlefield by Lysandros of Athens,*
*free from this day forward.*

"Palamedes," the Pythia said quietly. "It was the last thing he did. It had been many years since he had engraved something on this wall. But he insisted, for you. His fellow countryman."

Praxis's eyes blurred as he traced his fingers along the cold stone, following the indentations of each line and curve. "I had allowed myself to hope, when Lysandros died, but then there was nothing in his will. So I resigned myself that it was not to be."

"Forgive me," Althaia could barely talk, "I was not brave enough to do it myself. I thought I would lose you."

Praxis pulled Althaia to his chest and whispered, "Enslavement is not a good way to bind to your breast those who love you most." After a moment, he cupped her chin in his hand and tilted her face toward his. "I will not leave, Althaia. For where would I go? I have no more family. You and Theron, master secret keeper, you are my family. And Nephthys." He looked up and held his hand out to Nephthys who came forward and folded herself into him. "Theron, Pythia, do you both attest that this is indeed the last testament of Lysandros? That a mina of silver awaits me upon our return to Athens?"

"I'm afraid it is too true, Praxis," Theron said somberly. "I am but a poor man who must now be content to bask in the reflected shadow of your newfound wealth."

"Althaia," Praxis looked down at her, at the two women he held in his arms. "I have but one request."

"Anything."

"I need a loan."

"A loan? For what?"

"I want to buy Nephthys and make her my wife. I will pay you back when we return home."

Praxis caught Nephthys as the blood drained from her face and her knees gave way. She clung to his waist and struggled to stay upright.

"No loan is necessary, Praxis," Althaia said, wiping the tears from her face. She took Nephthys's hands in hers and looked into her handmaid's ashen face and confused, gold-flecked eyes. "Praxis bought you as a gift for me," she said. "He thought a woman's companionship would do me good—although I think, in truth, he saw in you from the very beginning what I have been so slow to recognize. He saw you as a woman, as a lover, as a wife. Now,

I see you as a sister. An equal." She placed Nephthys's hands in Praxis's, stood on her tiptoes and kissed his cheek. "Your wife is my wedding gift to you. You, now a free man, can grant your bride her freedom."

Nephthys leaned into Praxis as he enveloped her in his arms and buried his face in her hair. Althaia reached out for Nikos who was suddenly at her side.

Theron cleared his throat and announced in a serious tone, "In the midst of all this merriment, I find myself in the unusual position of wanting to make a speech."

Althaia and Praxis looked at each other. "Unusual?" The emotion of the moment diffused in a sobbing burst of laughter.

"Indeed. I hear the bellowing of the sacrificial ram and believe our dinner is getting impatient for the slaughter. My stomach is rumbling and my throat is dry. The sun is marching high into the sky and my brow longs for the shade. This day has been a long time coming. In fact, I have kept this secret for over two years and that was not always an easy task.

"When we left Delphi, I was eager to see Praxis finally taste the liberating draught of freedom, but I was also eager, after so many years, to see my sister again. I never imagined the course of events we would face upon our arrival. This visit has been marked by tragedy and grief. Yet it has also been marked by new beginnings. Whether or not we have all come to terms with those new beginnings and the many challenges they pose for the future"—he eyed Althaia and Nikos—"they have changed our lives forever."

He threw his arms out dramatically and continued. "New friendships made, old relationships renewed, timeless traditions passed into history. There is much to celebrate, much to lament, and much to ponder. I am not yet ready to say goodbye to Delphi although we must soon turn our mounts toward Athens and return home. In the meantime, in an act of extreme generosity and kindness, I have decided to volunteer my friend Menandros's house as the site of a long-awaited, much deserved celebration. For tonight, I wish to drink myself silly with my friend, Praxis. A free man who, too soon, goes willingly into the bonds of slavery again as husband to his beautiful Nephthys."

"Such a generous offer," Menandros chided. "I suppose you're paying."

"I am. And even as we speak, Diokles and Aphro are readying the board and mixing the wine."

"Aphro!" Kleomon balked. "Beware she does not add any tinctures or powders to your cups."

"*En oino álétheia*, Kleomon," Nikos said, his arm circling Althaia's waist. "You must know there are no more secrets among our company."

"That's what I'm afraid of," the old man growled. "I have done my part and will leave you to your festivities. You will, I daresay, be happier celebrating without me. And I without you." He turned to walk back up the hill and then stopped. "I will see to it that the ram is sacrificed, skewered and sent to you for roasting. I bid you good wishes—even to you and your sister, Theron of Thessaly. Nikos, I am sorry that our profitable relationship has come to an end. Fortunately, I still have Diokles."

"You and Diokles are welcome to your profits. I," Nikos said, pulling Althaia to him, "have the greater treasure."

# CHAPTER FIFTY-NINE

Theron and Nikos were mounted, their horses snorting and stamping the ground, anxious to get under way. Praxis made one final check to see that the oxen were yoked tight to the loaded wagon, and Menandros shuttled around busily, ordering Zenon to check this or that, and trying to act as though he would not miss his guests.

"Of course I am planning on coming to the Dionysia and I hope to find a welcome place to stay in Athens. Can you recommend something, Theron?"

"By the gods, Menandros, since when have you been so coy? Of course you will stay at Althaia's."

"Menandros," Althaia asked sweetly as she climbed into the wagon and took her place beside Nephthys, "do you need a formal invitation or will you believe me when I say my home is open to you whenever you set foot in Athens?"

"Oh, I believe you!" He clapped. "But a formal invitation would be nice. Something to show about, you know. Your father's reputation for supporting the playwrights of the Dionysia is well-known and an invitation to stay with you would be quite the thing...."

"You need not hint around the edges anymore, Menandros," Althaia laughed. "Praxis handles all my accounts. He will see to it that you have the support you need to come to Athens so you can enter your plays in the greater Dionysian competition. And if your play isn't selected, you can stay with us for the festival."

Zenon's eyes grew wide and Menandros's face turned red, whether from embarrassment or exciement, Althaia didn't know. "Do you have enough food, wine, blankets?" Menandros began chattering. "Can I send Zenon in for anything else?"

"No please," Praxis exlaimed. "The only thing we need is to get on the road. We've said our goodbyes a thousand times already. Diokles and Aphro fed us until we could barely breathe. Heraklios and his nephew gave us enough wine to float an Athenian armada, Georgios and Rhea showed up with tokens of thanks from Phoibe, and Theron bid a fond, or,"—he shot an amused glance at Theron—"I suspect, more than fond, farewell to Rhea, and Thea and her attendants are probably halfway back to Thessaly by now. Nikos has a long road before him on his way to Dodona but he, at least, is traveling on horseback and will find the mountain roads easier going. We, on the other hand, must plod along with these fat oxen and make the most of the daylight.

"Oh, I know, I know. It's just that …." Menandros sniffed.

"My old friend, you're a sentimental fool," Theron said. "If you want something to cry about, go inside and unwrap your parting gift."

"A gift? Really, for me?" Menandros eyed the door with sudden longing. "You shouldn't have!"

"I didn't. It's from Nikos."

"From Nikos? I don't understand."

"It's just a small token of my gratitude for your help in writing, directing and playing the part of Dionysos in the play that salvaged my future," Nikos said.

"Just a small token?" Menandros's shoulders sagged. "Nikos, I'm sure a gift wasn't necessary."

"Never fear," Althaia laughed, "it's not that small."

Menandros brightened and glanced back again at his front door.

"Ah, now he can't wait to be rid of us," Theron said. He dug his heels into his mount's flanks and started down the path. Praxis leapt onto the wagon, took the reins in his hand and flicked them against the oxen's backs. The wagon lurched forward as Althaia and Nephthys arranged their pillows and blankets so that they could talk on the journey while Nephthys faced forward and could easily admire the broad expanse of Praxis's back and Althaia faced backward so she could watch as Nikos followed them until he branched off on the road from Delphi to Dodona. Once in Dodona, Nikos would lay his mother's bones in their final resting place near Zeus's Sacred Oak and then say his goodbyes to the other priestesses and villagers who had helped raise him. He would pack a wagon with his belongings, close the door to his house, and then turn his back on his birthplace and head to Athens. Neither Althaia nor Nikos knew what the future held in store for them, but they were both eager—and nervous—to find out.

Theron glanced over his shoulder and saw that Menandros had already disappeared into the house. He shook his head as he pictured his old friend's reaction when he uncovered the krater. Theron had to admit Nikos had a fine eye for craftsmanship.

"It's one of Palamedes's most beautiful works," Nikos had assured them when he brought it to Menandros's early that morning. "You rarely see a krater this size in the white background. See how the figures leap out at you? There's so much depth, so much color. You can count the hairs in Dionysos's beard."

Althaia had hesitated to touch it. She walked around it, peering closely at each figure. She had grown up surrounded by the finest art money could buy and yet she had never seen anything like the krater before her. Finally, she whispered, "The maenads are so *alive*. The detail, the drape of the fabric, the expressions on their faces ... the desire ... every line is so delicately drawn, so vibrant and yet so raw, so real."

"Certainly the satyr's desire is realistically depicted. I don't think I've seen anything quite that, um, impressive," Praxis joked and Nephthys flushed and looked away.

"It is the perfect gift for the playwright whose dramatic use of a well-placed phallus saved your skin, Nikos," Theron laughed.

"Given that we're former partners, you'd think Diokles and Kleomon would have let me have it on favorable terms," Nikos said. "But they didn't. If only Palamedes knew. This krater is the most expensive piece we've ever sold. Unfortunately, I'm the buyer."

"More expensive than that damned gold foil tiara you told me about?" Althaia asked.

"By far," Nikos said. "But it's nothing compared to the value of the second chance at life I have now—or to the price Palamedes paid for knowing the truth."

"The truth." Theron sighed. "I'm not sure anyone can ever know the full truth."

Althaia had clapsed Nephthys's hand in hers and looked across the krater toward Nikos, Theron and Praxis. "Perhaps. But in honor of Palamades, and for everyone who seeks it—whether they can truly find the truth or not—we should at least try."

# AUTHOR'S NOTES

This work of fiction draws from historical elements relating to the Oracle of Apollon in Delphi, Greece and the challenges that might have faced a wealthy, educated young Athenian woman finding her way in the world after the death of her father. The story takes place in 340 BCE, a time when the religious, philosophic, and political landscape of Ancient Greece was changing dramatically.

First a word about oracles: In the ancient world, there were many oracles. Although the oracle in Delphi, dating to around 1400 BCE, was the most famous and most popular of the ancient oracles, the oracles of Siwa, located in modern Libya, and Dodona, located in Epirus in Northern Greece, were considered to be much older.

According to myth, the first oracle at Delphi was founded by the Earth Goddess Gaia who, according to Hesiod, was the foundation of the everlasting gods of Mt. Olympos. Gaia was mother of Uranus, the starry sky, Pontus, the fruitless depths of the sea, Oceanus, the world ocean, and all the Titans including Kronos, Zeus' father.

Gaia set a drakon, a serpent, to guard her oracle and Apollon, who was a son of Zeus, slew the drakon and claimed the oracle for himself. Many scholars have written about a transitional period wherein people stopped worshipping mother goddesses and turned toward a male-dominated belief system. *Oracles of Delphi* imagines that conflict played out among the priestesses who believe the sacred site should still belong to Gaia and the powerful priests who control the prominent Oracle of Apollon and the Sacred Precinct that arose around it.

Today we think of an oracle as a person who dispenses wisdom. In ancient times, an oracle was often associated with a specific place or god rather than a particular person. At the site of the oracle, a priest or priestess would embody the prophetic wisdom of the god. At the oracle of Apollon in Delphi, the wisdom of the god Apollon was conveyed through a woman known as the Pythia. Over the years there were many Pythias and, in fact, for a time the oracle of Apollon was so popular that there were as many as three Pythias working in shifts.

With the rise of Christianity, and, some scientists speculate, with the reduced flow or elimination of the narcotic, trance-inducing gas issuing from a fault in the bedrock, the oracle of Delphi fell out of favor. The historian Plutarch (c. 46-120 AD), who served as the senior of the two priests of Apollon in Delphi, described the smell of the sacred pneuma as sweet and speculated that the weakening influence of the oracle in his time was caused by the pneuma's sporadic and weak emissions. (For more on the geology of Delphi, visit http://www.biblicalarchaeology.org/daily/ancient-cultures/daily-life-and-practice/the-oracle-of-delphi%E2%80%94was-she-really-stoned/ or read *The Oracle: Ancient Delphi and the Science Behind Its Lost Secrets* by William J. Broad.) In 393 AD, when Roman emperor Julian the Apostate tried to revive elements of classical Greek culture, he consulted Delphi's famed oracle and in response, the last Pythia issued this statement.

*Tell the King:*
*The fair wrought house has fallen.*
*No shelter has Apollon,*
*nor sacred laurel leaves;*
*The fountains are now silent;*
*the voice is stilled.*
*It is finished.*

Although the Pythia of Gaia is a main character in the book, the Pythia of Apollon is a minor actor. Other than the conduit of the oracular prophecy, scholars are unsure about the role the Pythia of Apollon played in the day-to-day life of the temple and the Sacred Precinct in Delphi. Thanks to Plutarch and the historian Pausanias, they know a bit more about the role of the priests and, therefore, to highlight the tension between the female/male religious traditions, I have focused on the priests of Apollon rather than the Pythia.

Second, a word about society, politics and culture: In 340 BCE, the philosophical, religious and political landscape of Greece was in the process of seismic change. The foundations of modern scientific thought were being laid, new philosophical ideas were gaining prominence and the power of the old gods of Mt. Olympos was fading. Additionally, wars for control of the Sacred Precinct of Delphi had been repeatedly waged and many of the treasuries had been stripped bare of their offerings. Gold and silver had been melted down and turned into coinage to pay for mercenaries. Beautiful trinkets were passed around to soldier's wives and lovers and many in Greece were outraged by the sacrilege. It was at this point that Philip II of Makedonía, who had set his sights on conquering Athens and controlling its powerful navy, stepped into the role of protector of Delphi, which was considered the navel, or *omphalos*, and center of the earth and was the most important religious site outside of Olympia. With Philip gaining power, Athens' days as an independent democracy were numbered, and her leading politicians spent much of their time arguing amongst themselves about how to confront Philip's armies.

Women in Ancient Greece, especially Athens, where Althaia is from, had very few rights. Although we are taught about the rise of democracy in Athens, democracy was only for citizens and citizenship was only for men. Women were often married at 13 or 14 years old and their husbands were always chosen by their closest male relative. In fact, in order to keep wealth in the *oikos*, or family unit, their husbands were often close male relatives. If a girl was the only surviving child of an Athenian citizen, she could inherit both money and property, but it was controlled by her *kyrios*, her legal guardian who was, if she was married, also her husband. In the case of divorce, that inheritance reverted back to her and went back with her to her *oikos* where it was under the legal control of her nearest male relative. In other words, the money or property was "hers" but she could not legally control it.

Slaves played a prominent part in the life of the Ancient Greek family, especially in Athens and slaves and free metics (non citizens) made up the bulk of the population in the city itself. Most citizens had at least one slave and in many cases, slaves were treated much like members of the family while in other cases, they were sent to toil away and die horrible deaths in the silver mines. It was not unheard of for slaves to run businesses on their own or on behalf of their masters. Often, beloved slaves were manumitted, or granted their freedom, or were allowed to save money in order to buy their freedom. Delphi was a popular place for dedicating newly manumitted slaves to Apollon. Today, visitors can still see the names of freed slaves inscribed in stone.

A note about setting: Anyone who has been to Delphi and sought out the Korycian Cave will know I fictionalized the setting around the cave itself. The amount of ground before the cave's entrance and just below it are not large enough for the sort of funeral event described in the book and the plateau below is too far away for any mourners to have seen or heard what was going on above them. The setting for the funeral was truly a flight of fancy. For photos of Delphi and the cave itself, visit kristinamakansi.com.

Finally, a word about spelling and other things Greek: Instead of using the more familiar Latin spellings, most Greek words are spelled the way they would have been spelled or pronounced in Ancient Greece. For instance, the god Apollo is Apollon. The philosopher Socrates is Sokrates and Plato is Platon and the word stadium is stadion. I say, when in Greece....